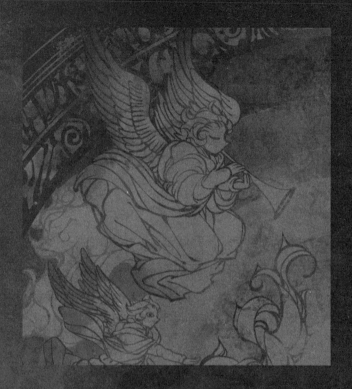

Seraph of the End
─VAMPIRE REIGN─

7

STORY BY **Takaya Kagami**
ART BY **Yamato Yamamoto**
STORYBOARDS BY **Daisuke Furuya**

CHARACTERS

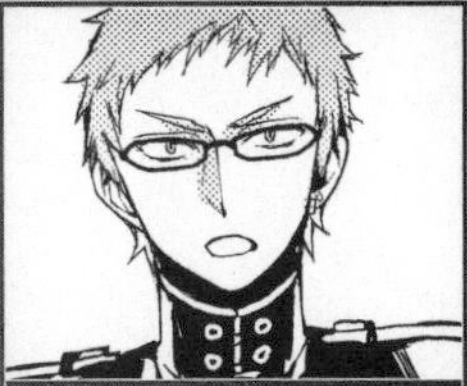

SHIHO KIMIZUKI

Yuichiro's friend. Smart but abrasive. His Cursed Gear is Kiseki-o, twin blades.

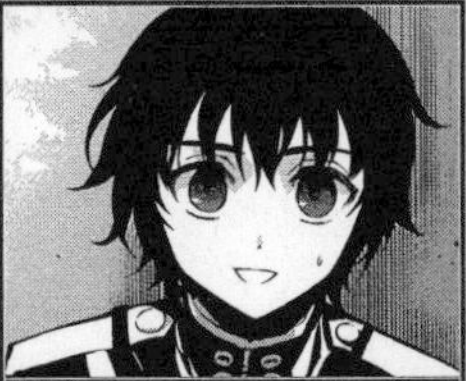

YOICHI SAOTOME

Yuichiro's friend. His sister was killed by a vampire. His Cursed Gear is Gekkouin, a bow.

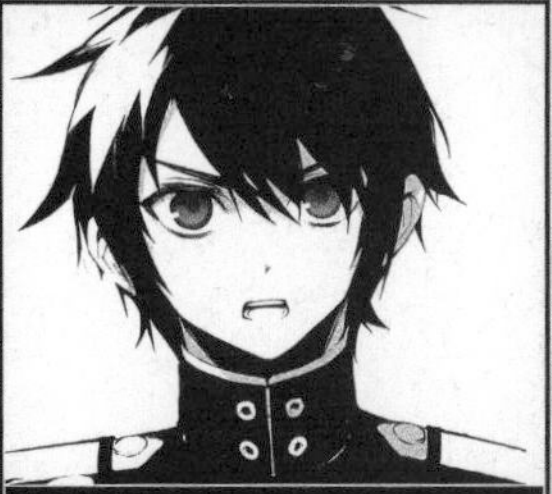

YUICHIRO HYAKUYA

A boy who escaped from the vampire capital, he has both great kindness and a great desire for revenge. Lone wolf. His Cursed Gear is Asuramaru, a katana.

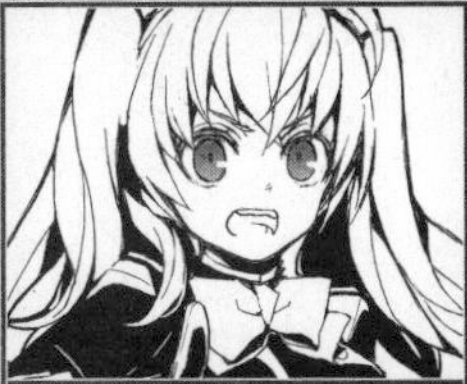

MITSUBA SANGU

An elite soldier who has been part of the Moon Demon Company since age 13. Bossy. Her Cursed Gear is Tenjiryu, a giant axe.

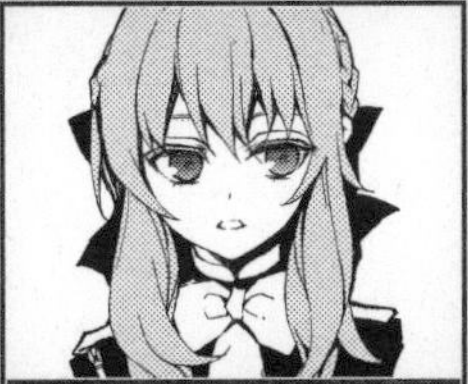

SHINOA HIRAGI

Guren's subordinate and Yuichiro's surveillance officer. Member of the illustrious Hiragi family. Her Cursed Gear is Shikama Doji, a scythe.

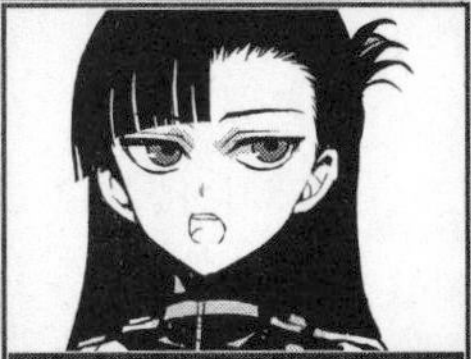

SHIGURE YUKIMI

A 2nd Lieutenant and Guren's subordinate along with Sayuri. Very calm and collected.

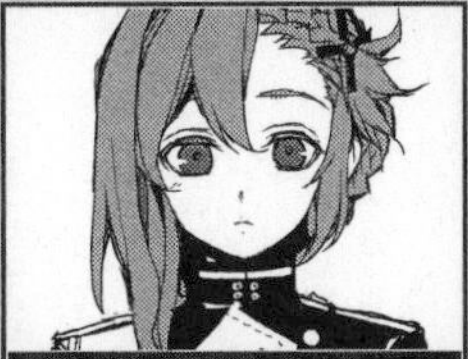

SAYURI HANAYORI

A 2nd Lieutenant and Guren's subordinate. She's devoted to Guren.

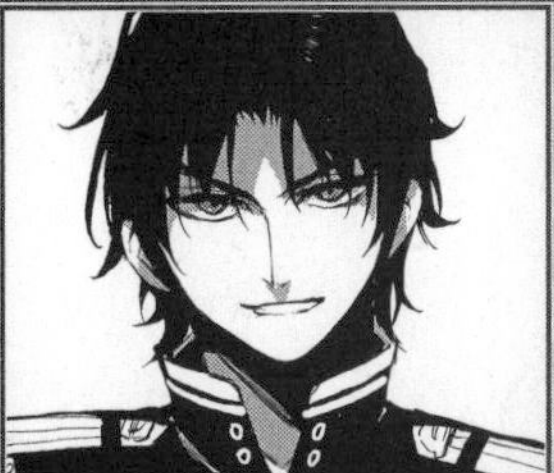

GUREN ICHINOSE

Lieutenant Colonel of the Moon Demon Company, a Vampire Extermination Unit. He recruited Yuichiro into the Japanese Imperial Demon Army. His Cursed Gear is Mahiru-no-yo, a katana.

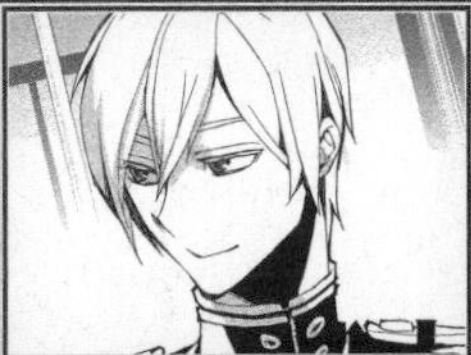

SHINYA HIRAGI

A Major General and an adopted member of the Hiragi Family. He was Mahiru Hiragi's fiancé.

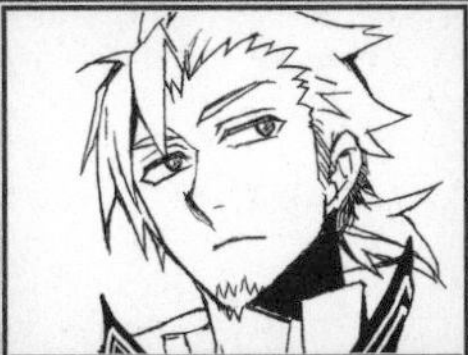

NORITO GOSHI

A Colonel and a member of the illustrious Goshi family. He has been friends with Guren since high school.

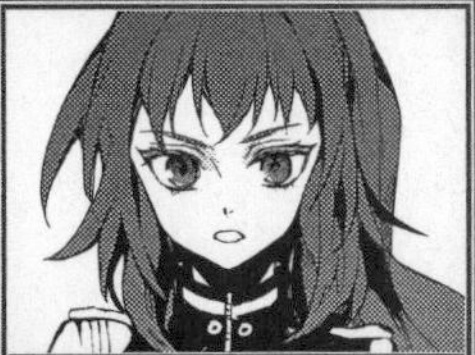

MITO JUJO

A Colonel and a member of the illustrious Jujo family. She has been friends with Guren since high school.

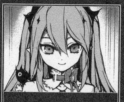

KRUL TEPES

Queen of the Vampires and a Third Progenitor.

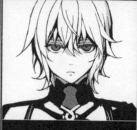

MIKAELA HYAKUYA

Yuichiro's best friend. He was supposedly killed but has come back to life as a vampire.

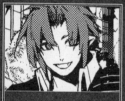

CROWLEY EUSFORD

A Thirteenth Progenitor vampire.

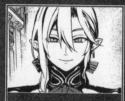

FERID BATHORY

A Seventh Progenitor vampire, he killed Mikaela.

STORY

A mysterious virus decimates the human population, and vampires claim dominion over the world. Yuichiro and his adopted family of orphans are kept as vampire fodder in an underground city until the day Mikaela, Yuichiro's best friend, plots an ill-fated escape for the orphans. Only Yuichiro survives and reaches the surface.

Four years later, Yuichiro enters into the Moon Demon Company, a Vampire Extermination Unit in the Japanese Imperial Demon Army, to enact his revenge. There he gains Asuramaru, a demon-possessed weapon capable of killing vampires. Along with his squad mates Yoichi, Shinoa, Kimizuki and Mitsuba, Yuichiro deploys to Shinjuku with orders to thwart a vampire attack. But in the midst of a fierce skirmish, he sees Mikaela—and he's with the enemy vampires! Confused and lost, Yuichiro is overtaken by a mysterious power within and goes berserk.

Yuichiro undergoes further training with his Cursed Gear. He not only grows stronger as a fighter, but also becomes much closer to his teammates. Meanwhile, the war between vampires and humans grows ever closer. Yuichiro and his friends head to Nagoya to rendezvous with Guren while Vampire Queen Krul Tepes gives Mikaela a top secret mission...

Seraph of the End
—VAMPIRE REIGN—

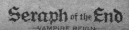

Seraph of the End
—VAMPIRE REIGN—

CONTENTS

7

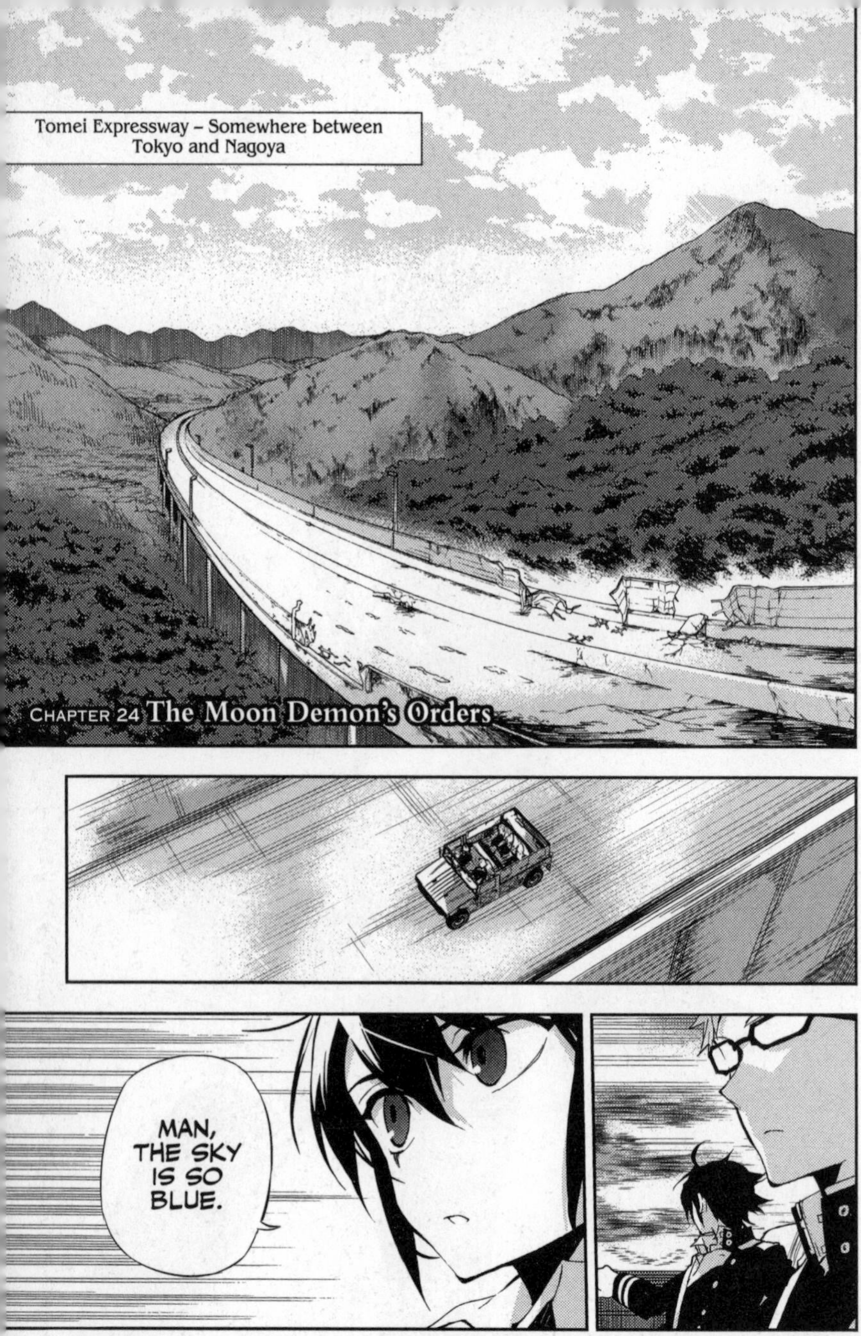
Tomei Expressway – Somewhere between Tokyo and Nagoya
CHAPTER 24 The Moon Demon's Orders
MAN, THE SKY IS SO BLUE.

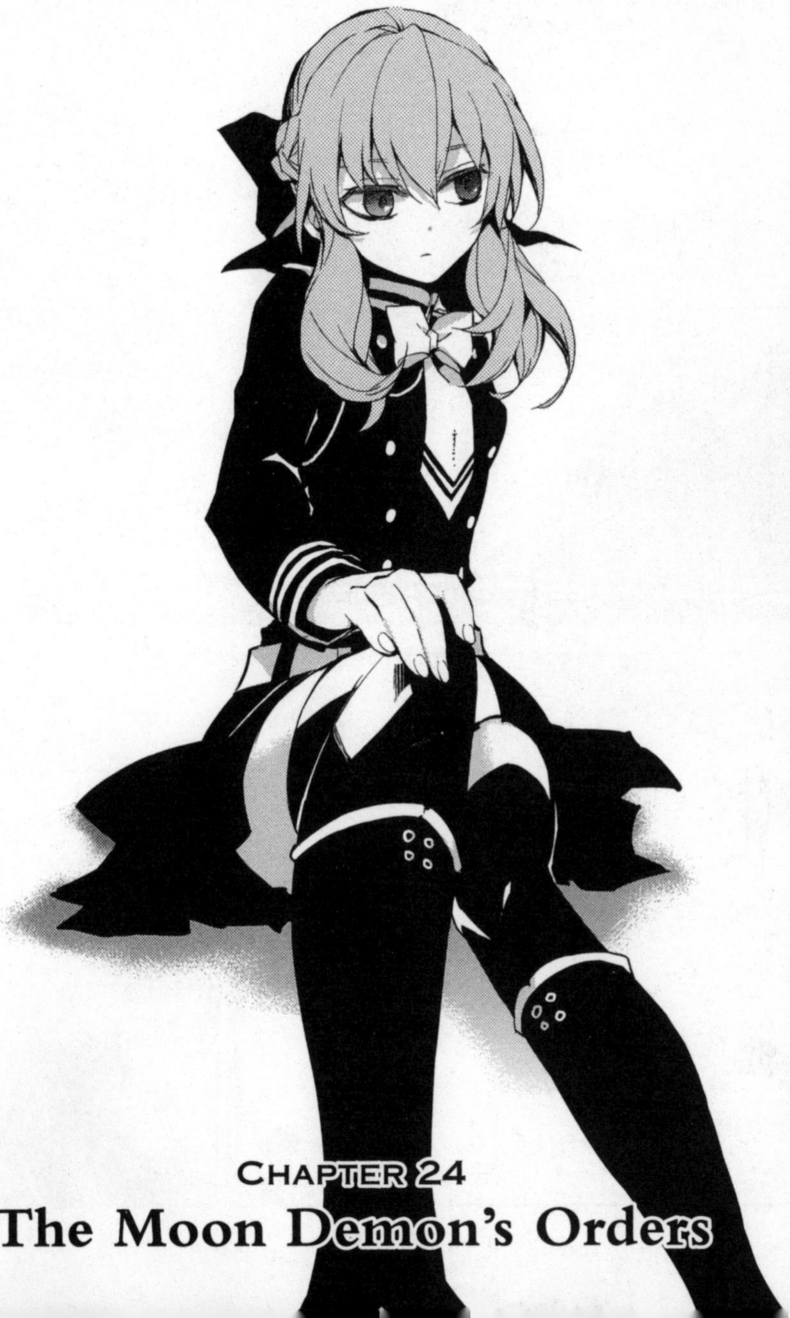

CHAPTER 24

The Moon Demon's Orders

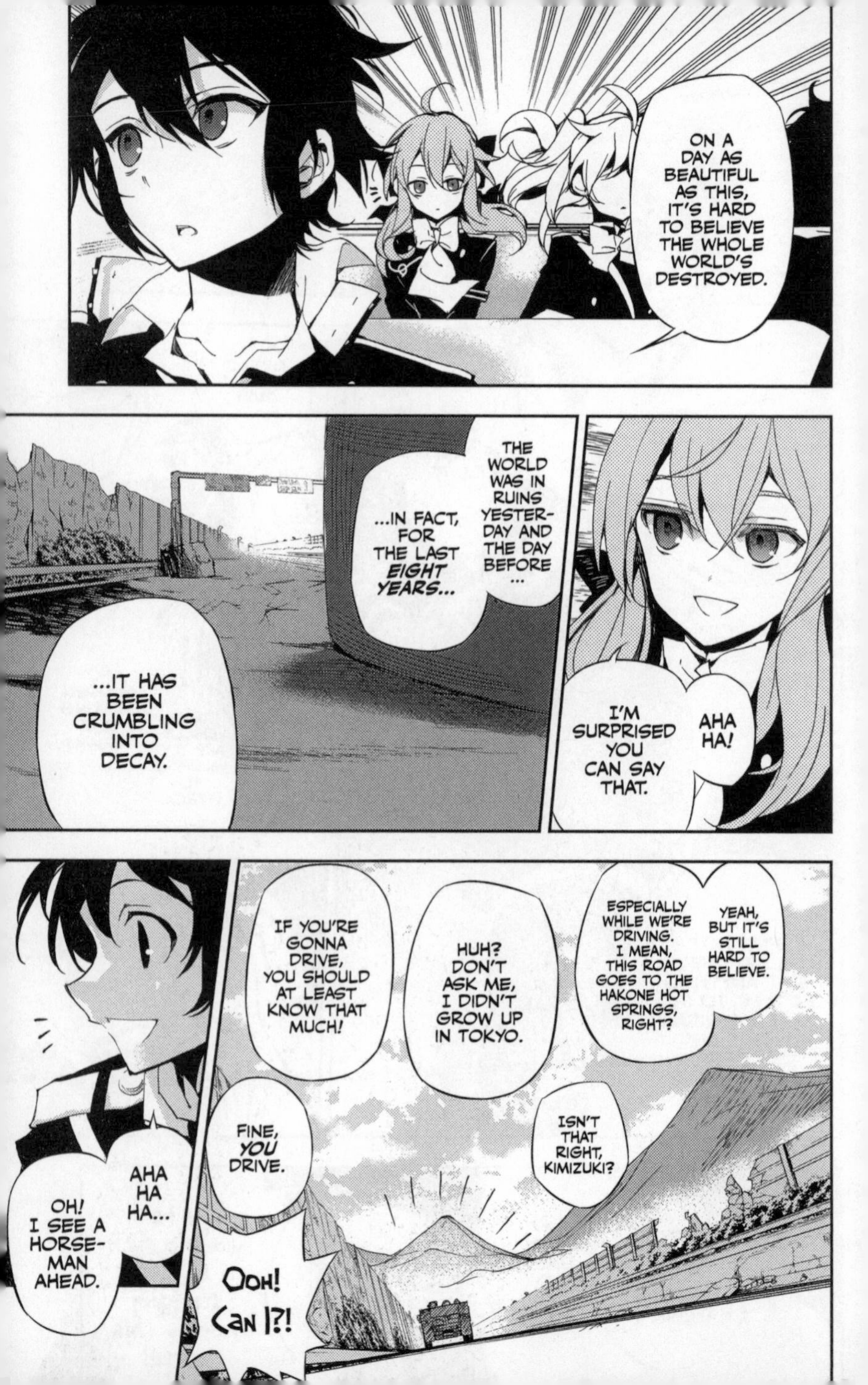
ON A DAY AS BEAUTIFUL AS THIS, IT'S HARD TO BELIEVE THE WHOLE WORLD'S DESTROYED.
AHA HA!
I'M SURPRISED YOU CAN SAY THAT.
THE WORLD WAS IN RUINS YESTERDAY AND THE DAY BEFORE...
...IN FACT, FOR THE LAST *EIGHT YEARS...*
...IT HAS BEEN CRUMBLING INTO DECAY.
YEAH, BUT IT'S STILL HARD TO BELIEVE.
ESPECIALLY WHILE WE'RE DRIVING. I MEAN, THIS ROAD GOES TO THE HAKONE HOT SPRINGS, RIGHT?
ISN'T THAT RIGHT, KIMIZUKI?
HUH? DON'T ASK ME, I DIDN'T GROW UP IN TOKYO.
IF YOU'RE GONNA DRIVE, YOU SHOULD AT LEAST KNOW THAT MUCH!
FINE, *YOU* DRIVE.
OOH! CAN I?!
AHA HA HA...
OH! I SEE A HORSEMAN AHEAD.

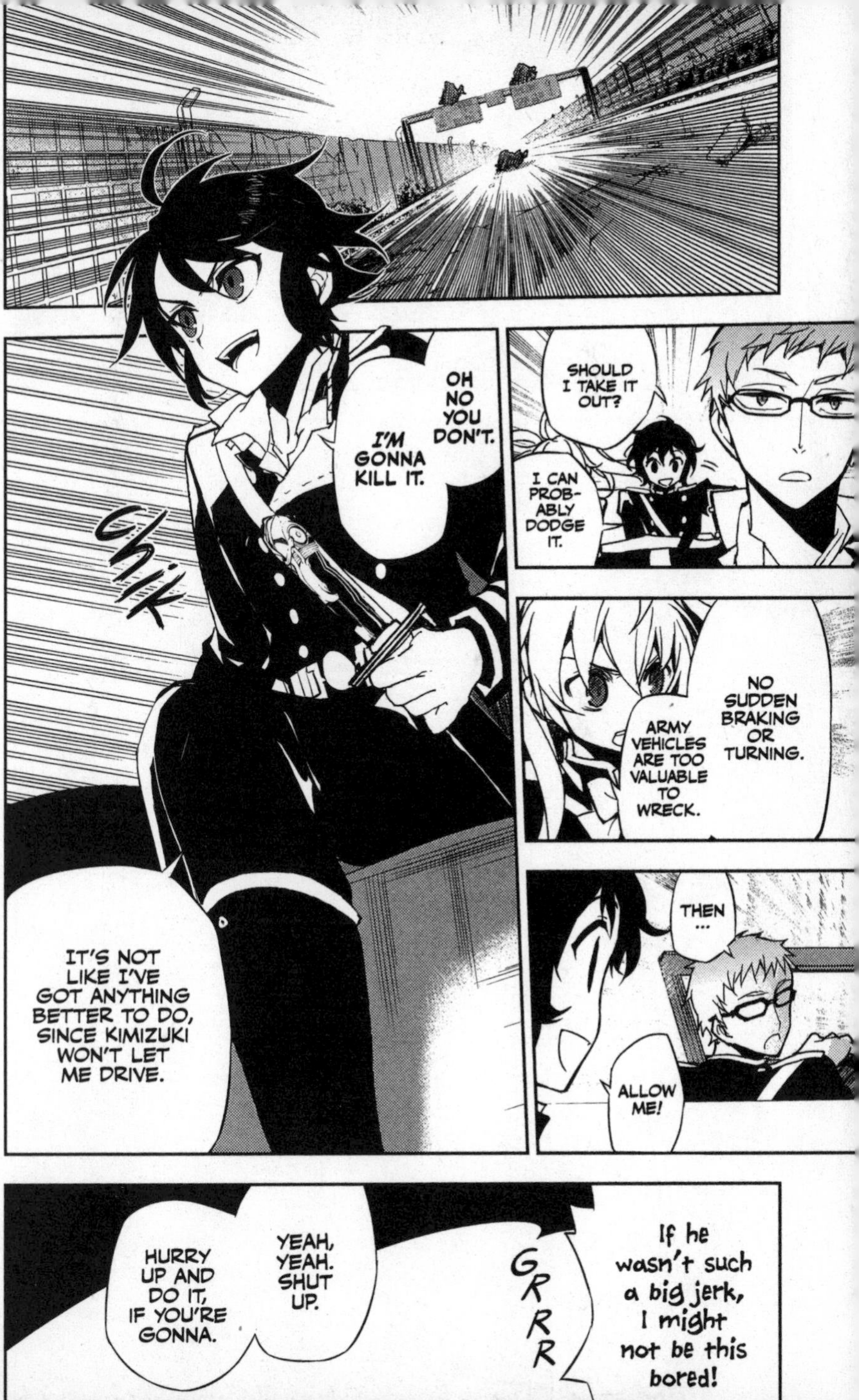
SHOULD I TAKE IT OUT?
I CAN PROB-ABLY DODGE IT.
NO SUDDEN BRAKING OR TURNING.
ARMY VEHICLES ARE TOO VALUABLE TO WRECK.
THEN...
ALLOW ME!
OH NO YOU DON'T.
I'M GONNA KILL IT.
CHIK
IT'S NOT LIKE I'VE GOT ANYTHING BETTER TO DO, SINCE KIMIZUKI WON'T LET ME DRIVE.
If he wasn't such a big jerk, I might not be this bored!
GRRR
YEAH, YEAH. SHUT UP.
HURRY UP AND DO IT, IF YOU'RE GONNA.

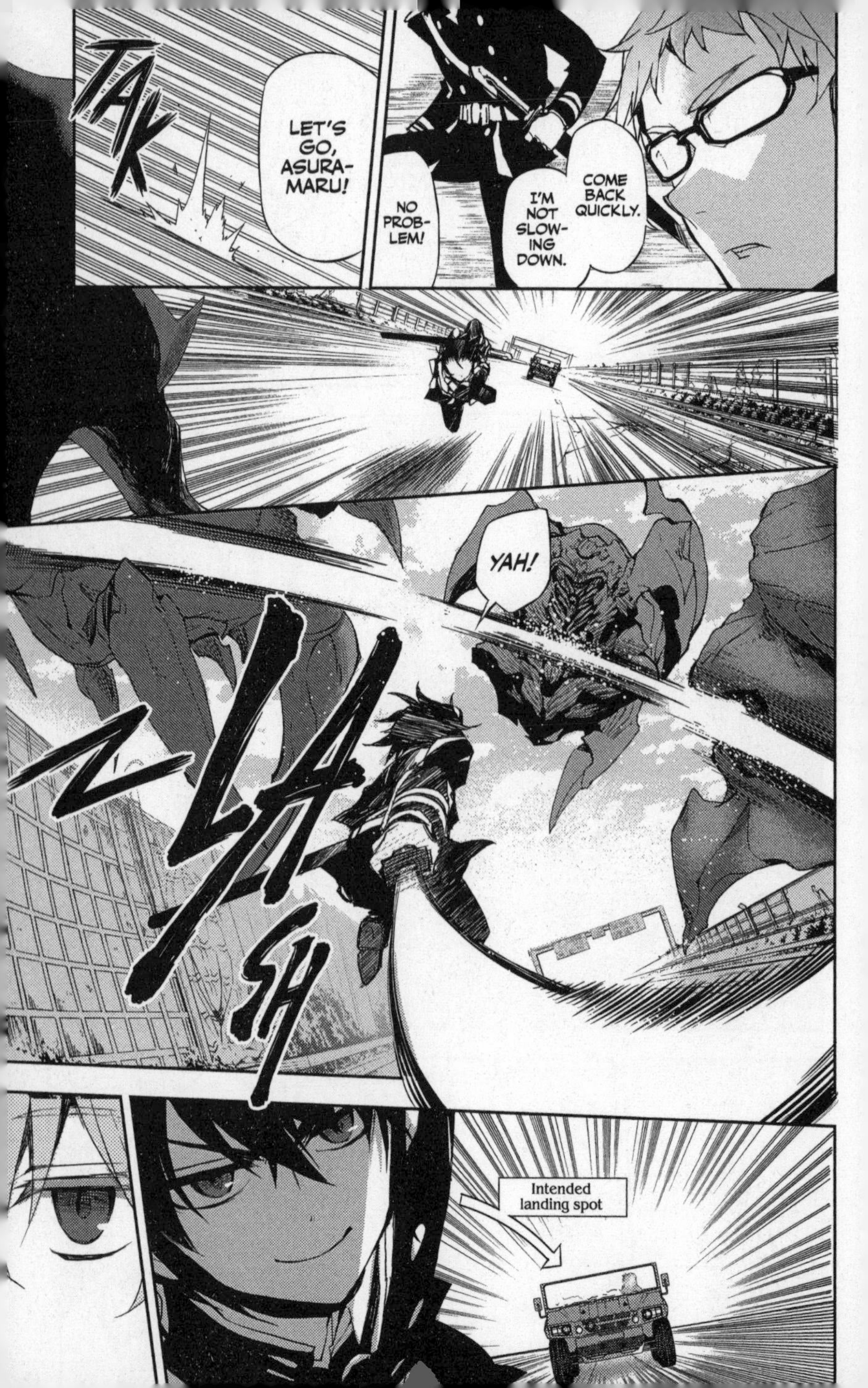
COME BACK QUICKLY.
I'M NOT SLOWING-DOWN.
NO PROBLEM!
LET'S GO, ASURA-MARU!
TAK
YAH!
ZLASH
Intended landing spot

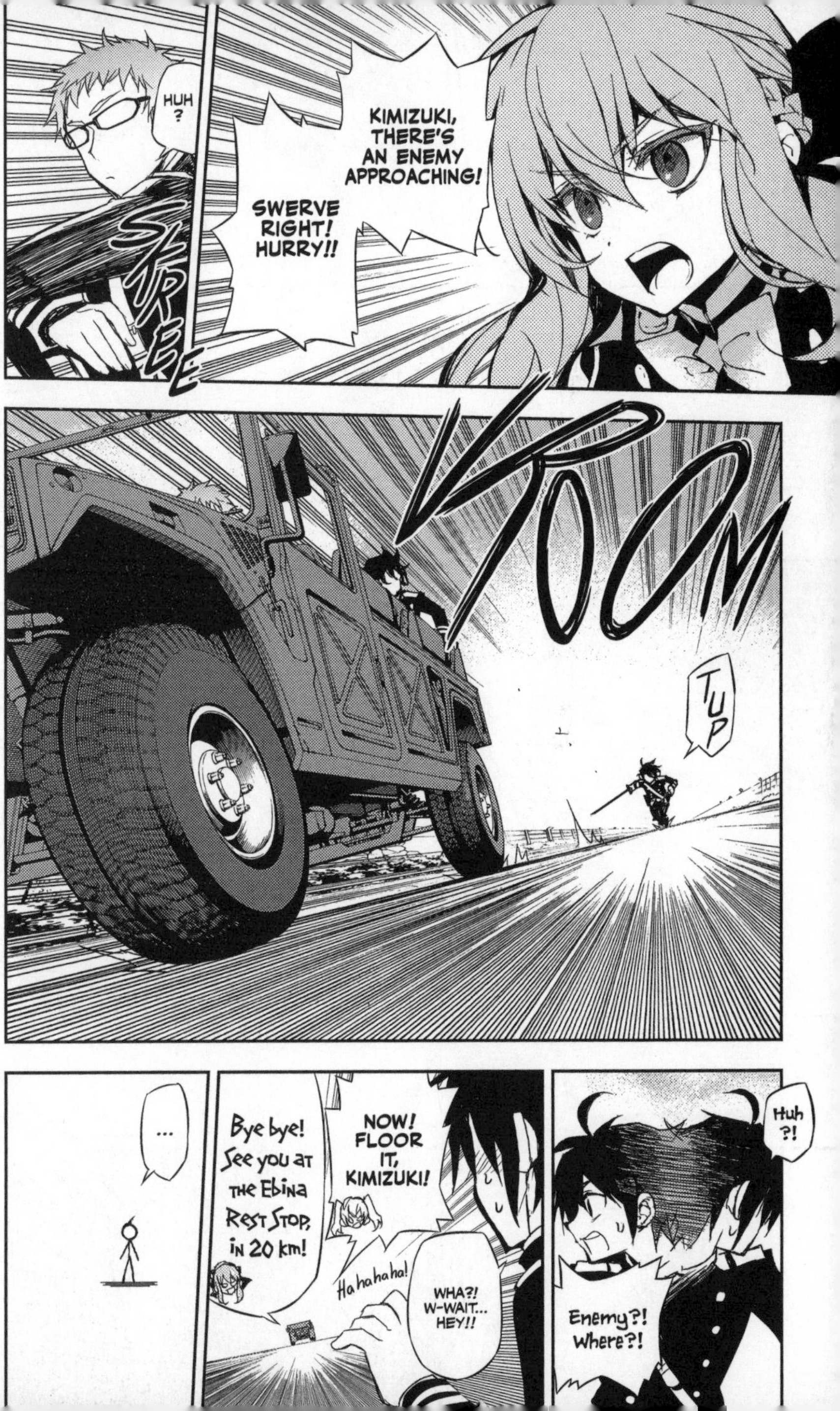
KIMIZUKI, THERE'S AN ENEMY APPROACHING!
SWERVE RIGHT! HURRY!!
HUH?
SKREE
VROOM
TUP
Huh?!
Enemy?! Where?!
NOW! FLOOR IT, KIMIZUKI!
WHA?! W-WAIT... HEY!!
Bye bye! See you at the Ebina Rest Stop, in 20 km!
Ha ha ha ha ha!
...

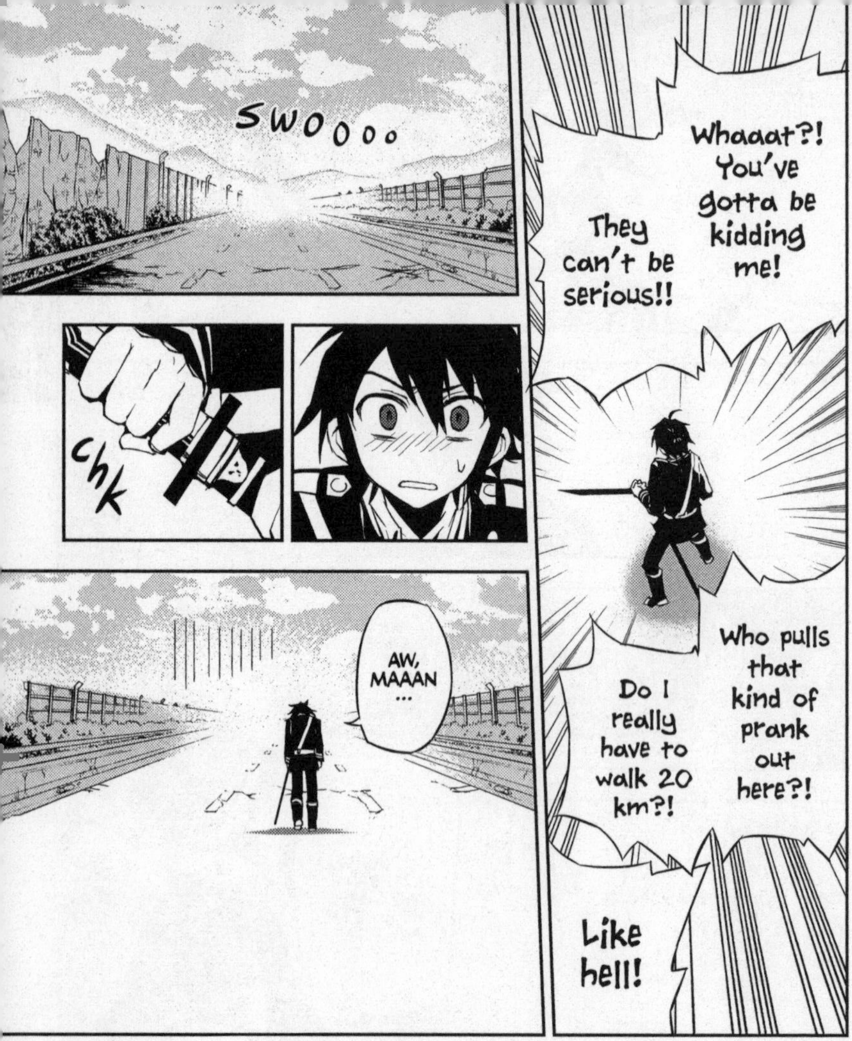
Whaaat?! You've gotta be kidding me!
They can't be serious!!
Who pulls that kind of prank out here?!
Do I really have to walk 20 km?!
Like hell!
SWOOooo
chk
AW, MAAAN...

Ten Minutes Later

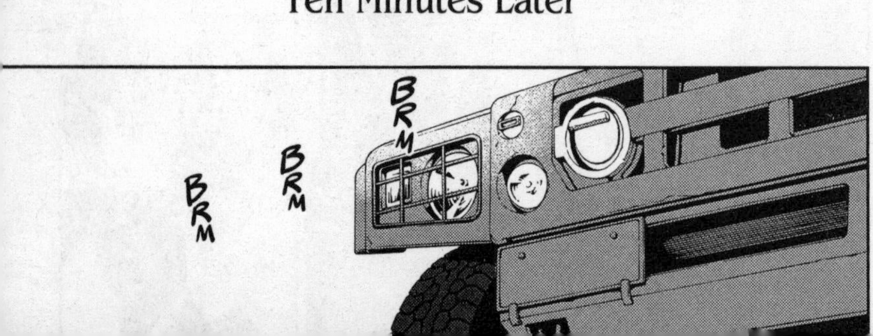
BRM
BRM
BRM

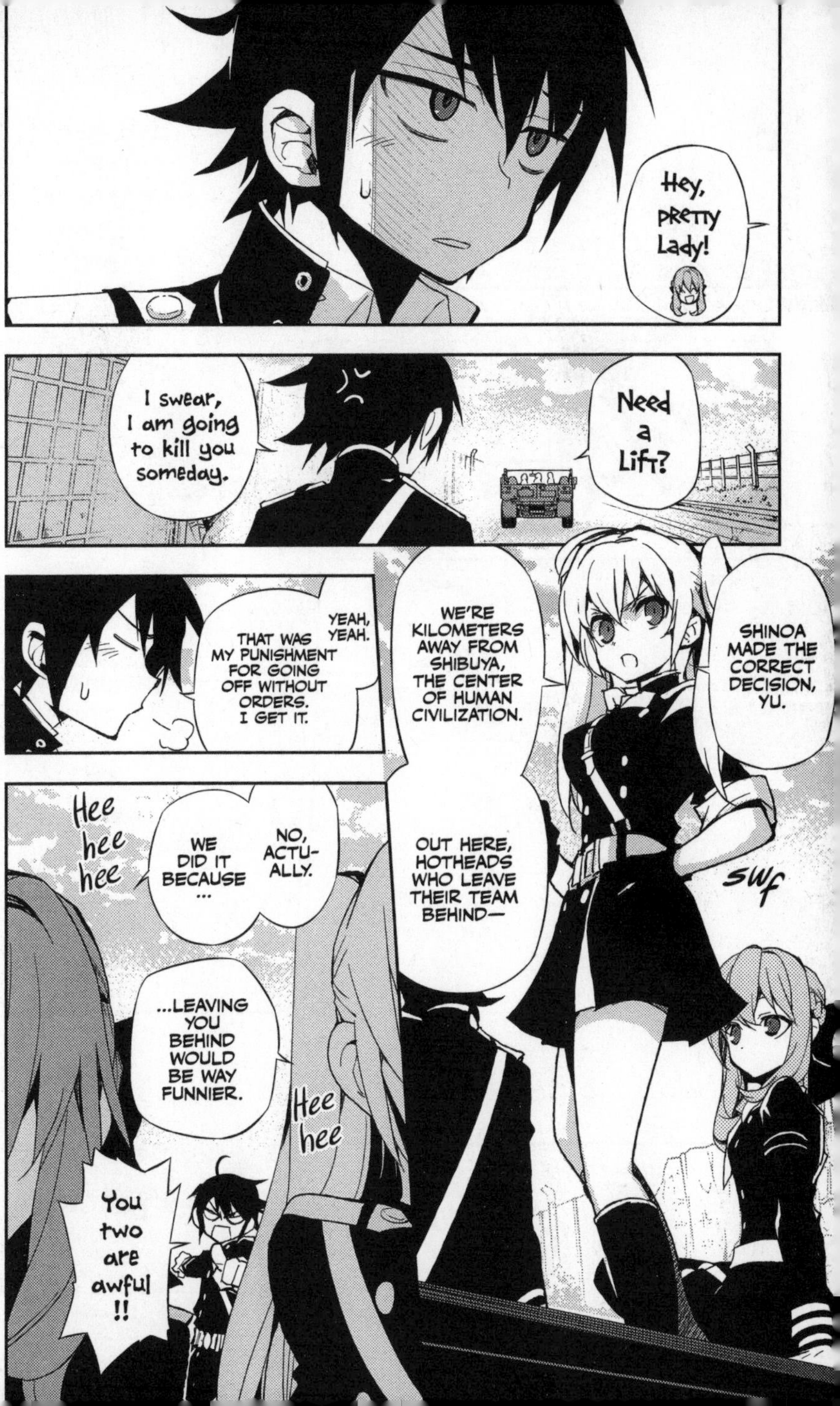
Hey, pretty Lady!
Need a Lift?
I swear, I am going to kill you someday.
SHINOA MADE THE CORRECT DECISION, YU.
WE'RE KILOMETERS AWAY FROM SHIBUYA, THE CENTER OF HUMAN CIVILIZATION.
OUT HERE, HOTHEADS WHO LEAVE THEIR TEAM BEHIND—
SWF
YEAH, YEAH.
THAT WAS MY PUNISHMENT FOR GOING OFF WITHOUT ORDERS. I GET IT.
NO, ACTU-ALLY.
WE DID IT BECAUSE ...
Hee hee hee
...LEAVING YOU BEHIND WOULD BE WAY FUNNIER.
Hee hee
You two are awful !!

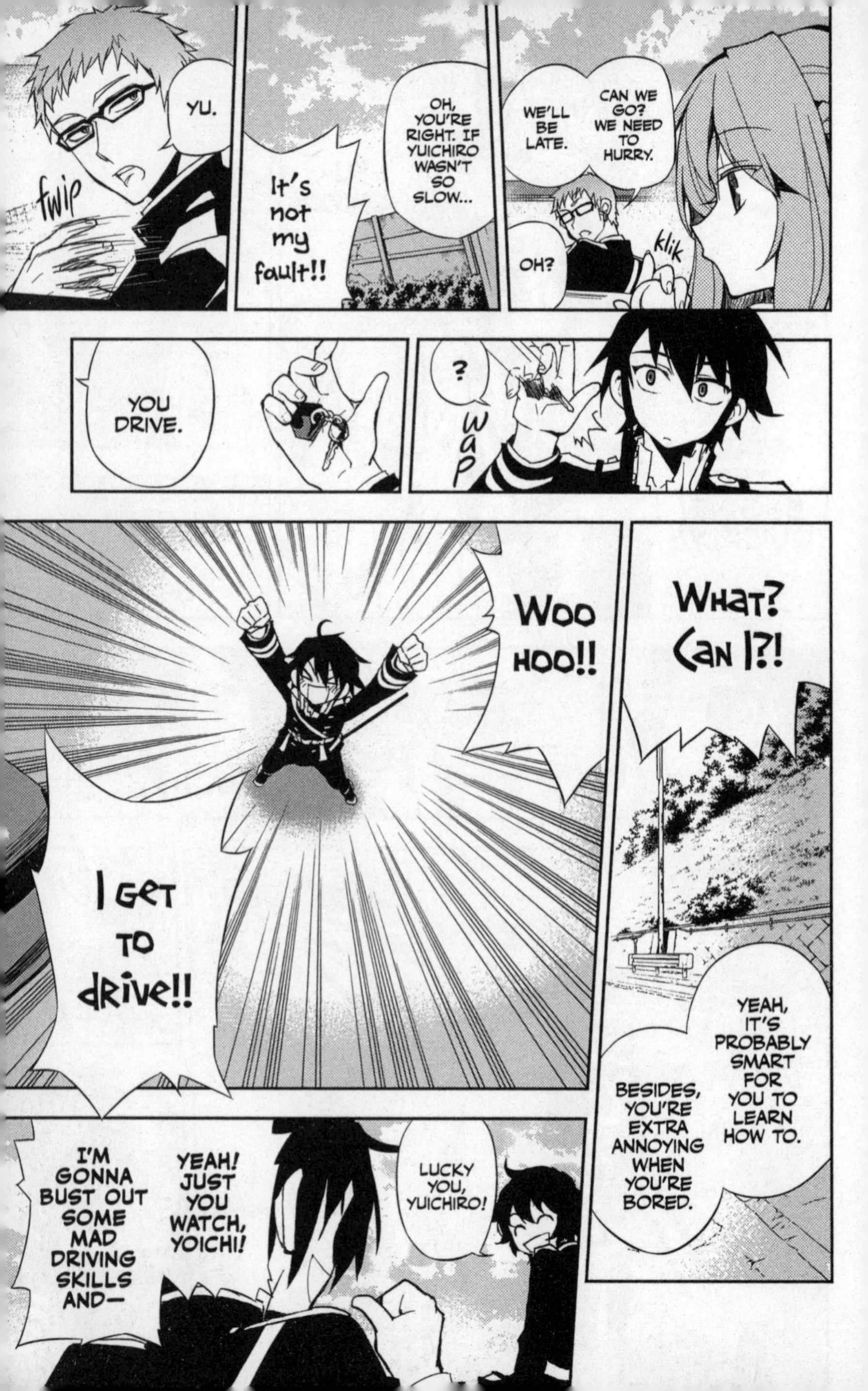
CAN WE GO? WE NEED TO HURRY.
WE'LL BE LATE.
klik
OH?
OH, YOU'RE RIGHT. IF YUICHIRO WASN'T SO SLOW...
It's not my fault!!
YU.
fwip
?
wap
YOU DRIVE.
WHAT? Can I?!
YEAH, IT'S PROBABLY SMART FOR YOU TO LEARN HOW TO.
BESIDES, YOU'RE EXTRA ANNOYING WHEN YOU'RE BORED.
Woo hoo!!
I get to drive!!
LUCKY YOU, YUICHIRO!
YEAH! JUST YOU WATCH, YOICHI!
I'M GONNA BUST OUT SOME MAD DRIVING SKILLS AND—

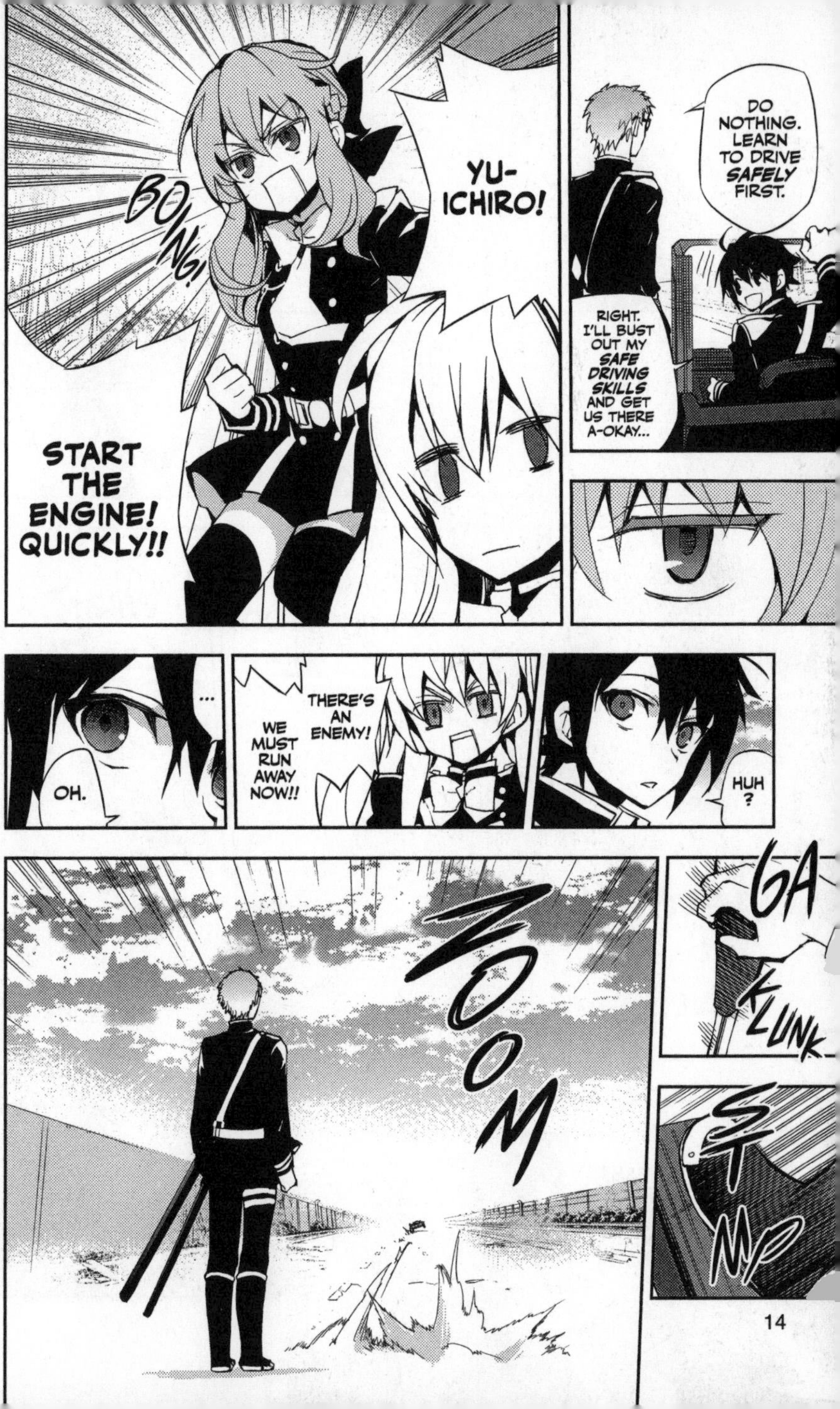

DO NOTHING. LEARN TO DRIVE SAFELY FIRST.
RIGHT. I'LL BUST OUT MY SAFE DRIVING SKILLS AND GET US THERE A-OKAY...
YU-ICHIRO!
BOING!
START THE ENGINE! QUICKLY!!
HUH?
THERE'S AN ENEMY!
WE MUST RUN AWAY NOW!!
...
OH.
GA
KLUNK
STOMP
VOOM

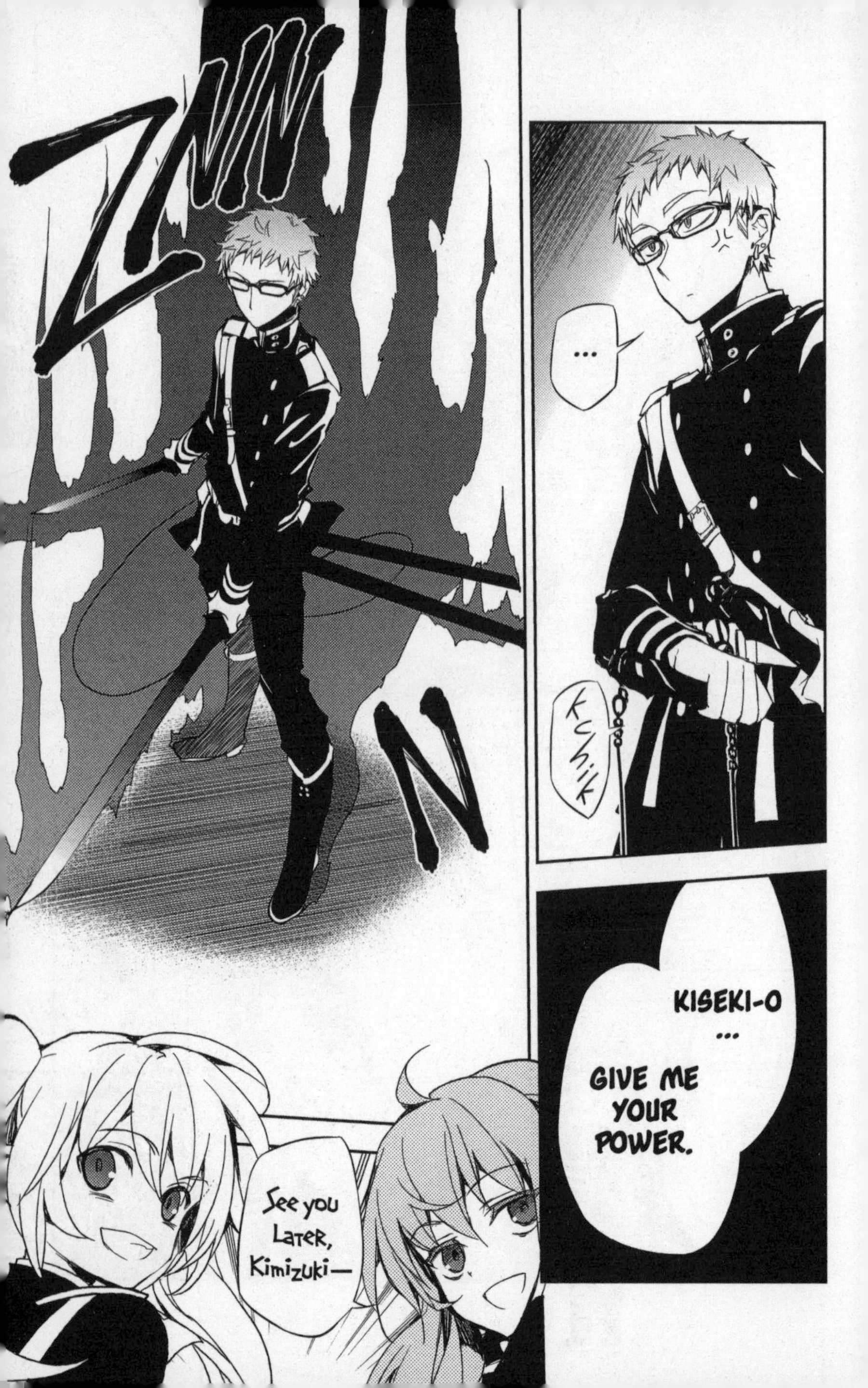
...
KChik
KISEKI-O ...
GIVE ME YOUR POWER.
ZNN
N
See you Later, Kimizuki—

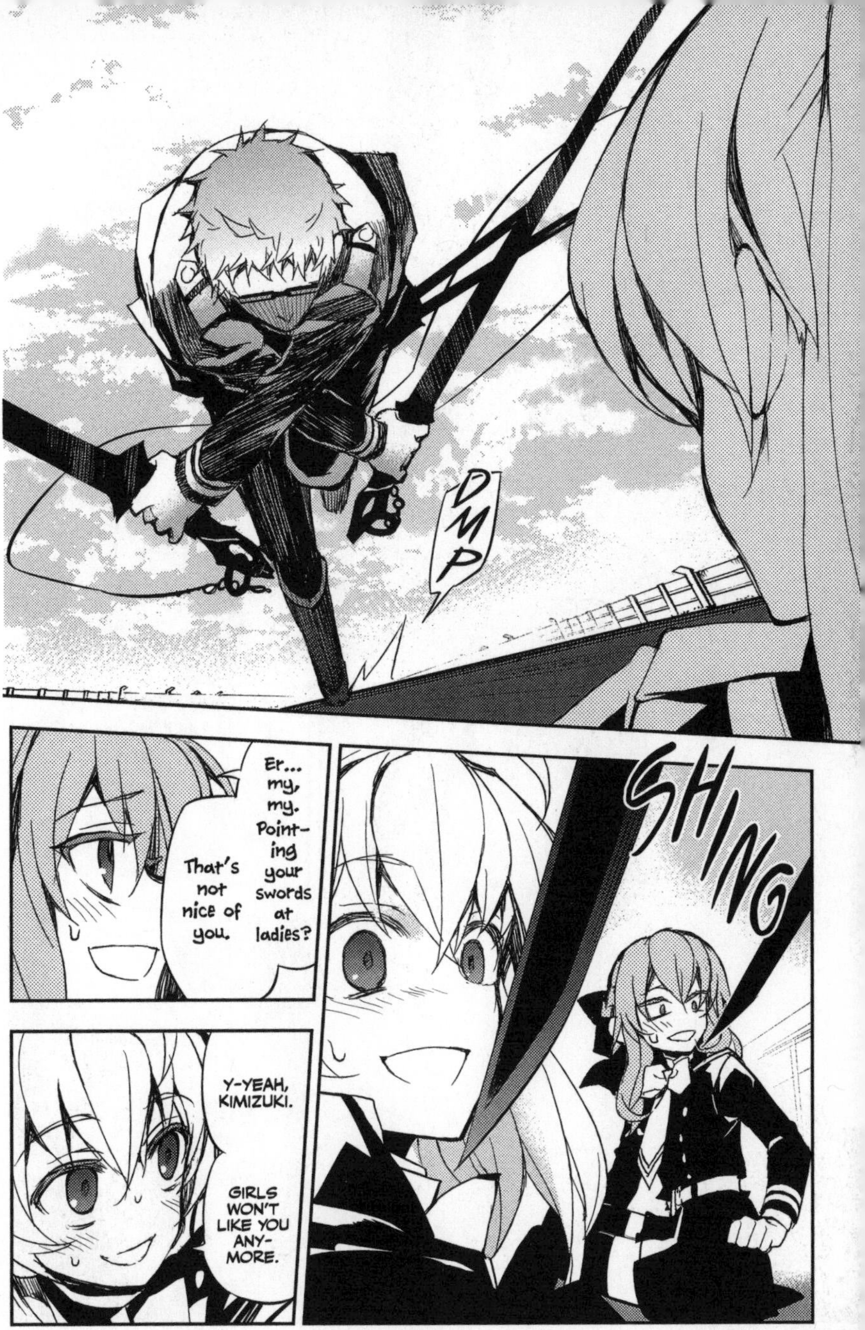
DMP
SHING
Er... my, my. Pointing your swords at ladies?
That's not nice of you.
Y-YEAH, KIMIZUKI.
GIRLS WON'T LIKE YOU ANYMORE.

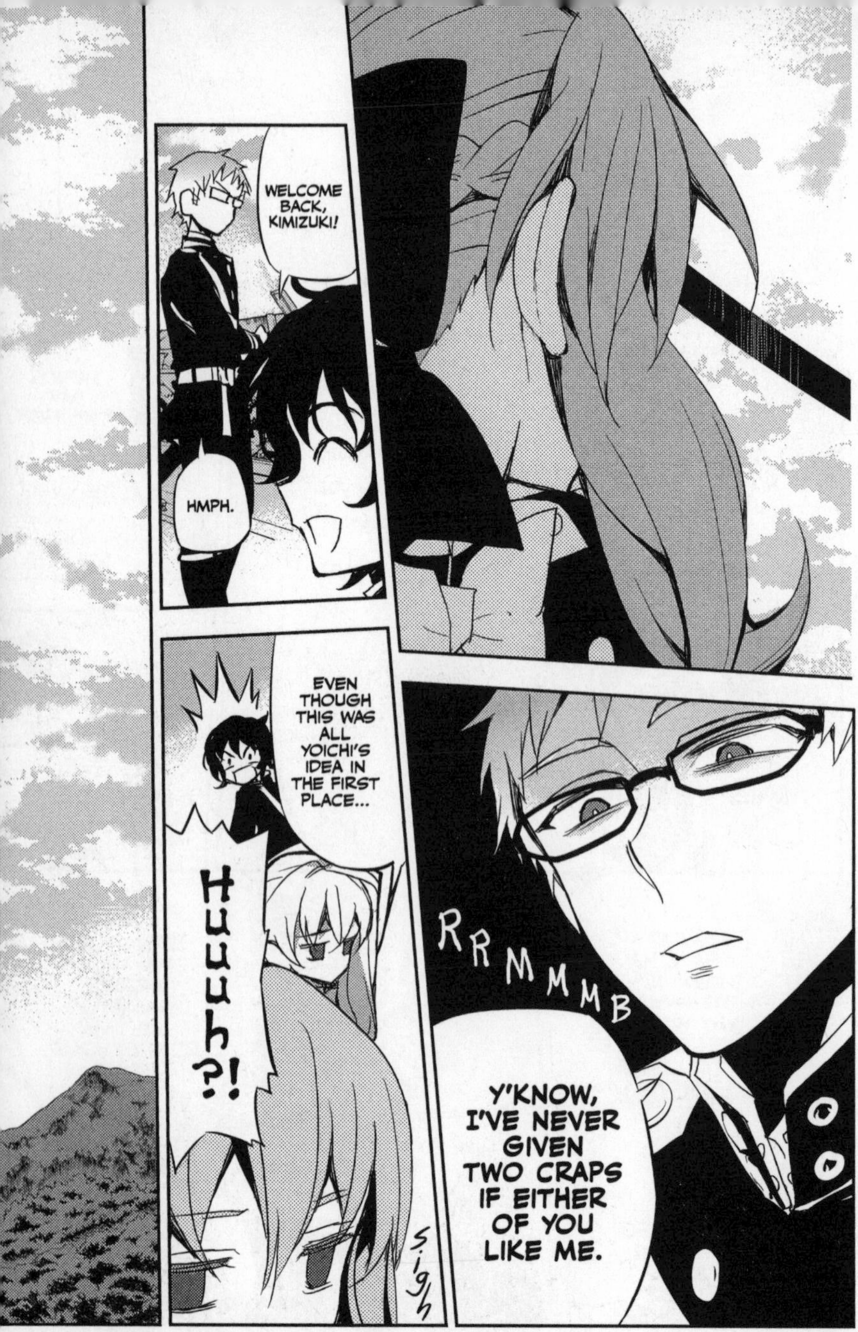
WELCOME BACK, KIMIZUKI!
HMPH.
RRMMMB
Y'KNOW, I'VE NEVER GIVEN TWO CRAPS IF EITHER OF YOU LIKE ME.
EVEN THOUGH THIS WAS ALL YOICHI'S IDEA IN THE FIRST PLACE...
Huuuh?!
sigh

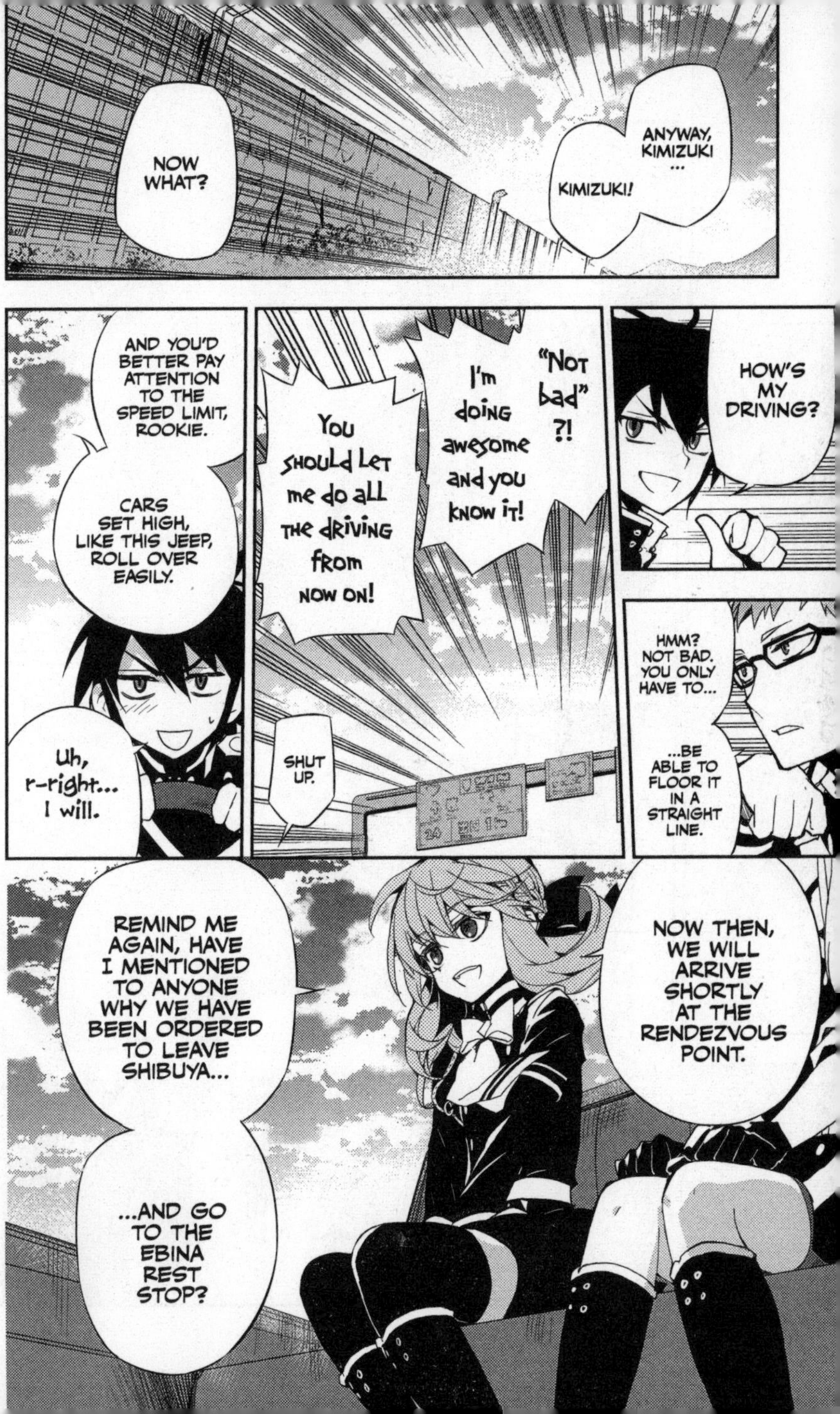
ANYWAY, KIMIZUKI ...
KIMIZUKI!
NOW WHAT?
HOW'S MY DRIVING?
HMM? NOT BAD. YOU ONLY HAVE TO...
...BE ABLE TO FLOOR IT IN A STRAIGHT LINE.
"Not bad" ?!
I'm doing awesome and you know it!
You should let me do all the driving from now on!
SHUT UP.
AND YOU'D BETTER PAY ATTENTION TO THE SPEED LIMIT, ROOKIE.
CARS SET HIGH, LIKE THIS JEEP, ROLL OVER EASILY.
Uh, r-right... I will.
NOW THEN, WE WILL ARRIVE SHORTLY AT THE RENDEZVOUS POINT.
REMIND ME AGAIN, HAVE I MENTIONED TO ANYONE WHY WE HAVE BEEN ORDERED TO LEAVE SHIBUYA...
...AND GO TO THE EBINA REST STOP?

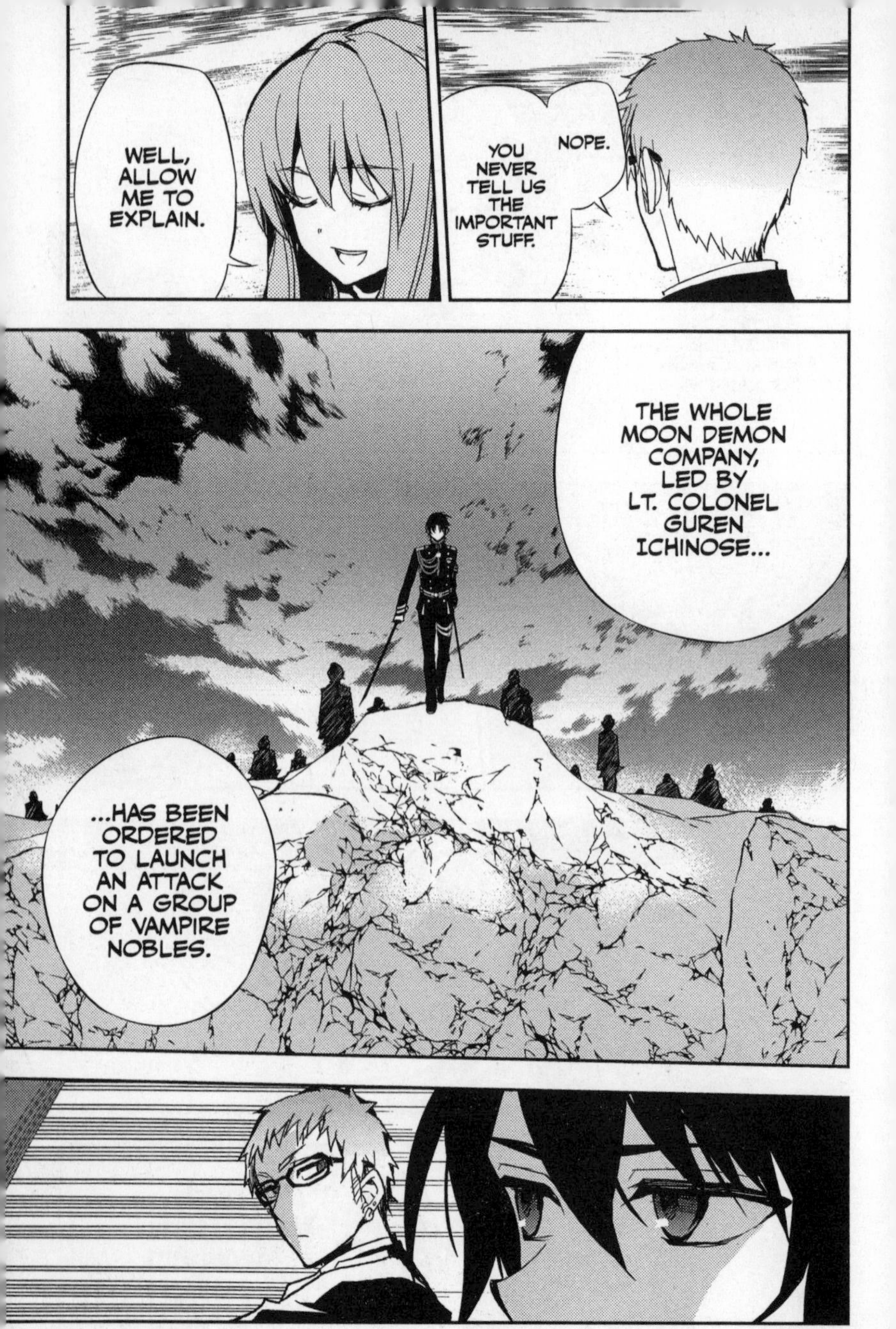
NOPE.
YOU NEVER TELL US THE IMPORTANT STUFF.
WELL, ALLOW ME TO EXPLAIN.
THE WHOLE MOON DEMON COMPANY, LED BY LT. COLONEL GUREN ICHINOSE...
...HAS BEEN ORDERED TO LAUNCH AN ATTACK ON A GROUP OF VAMPIRE NOBLES.

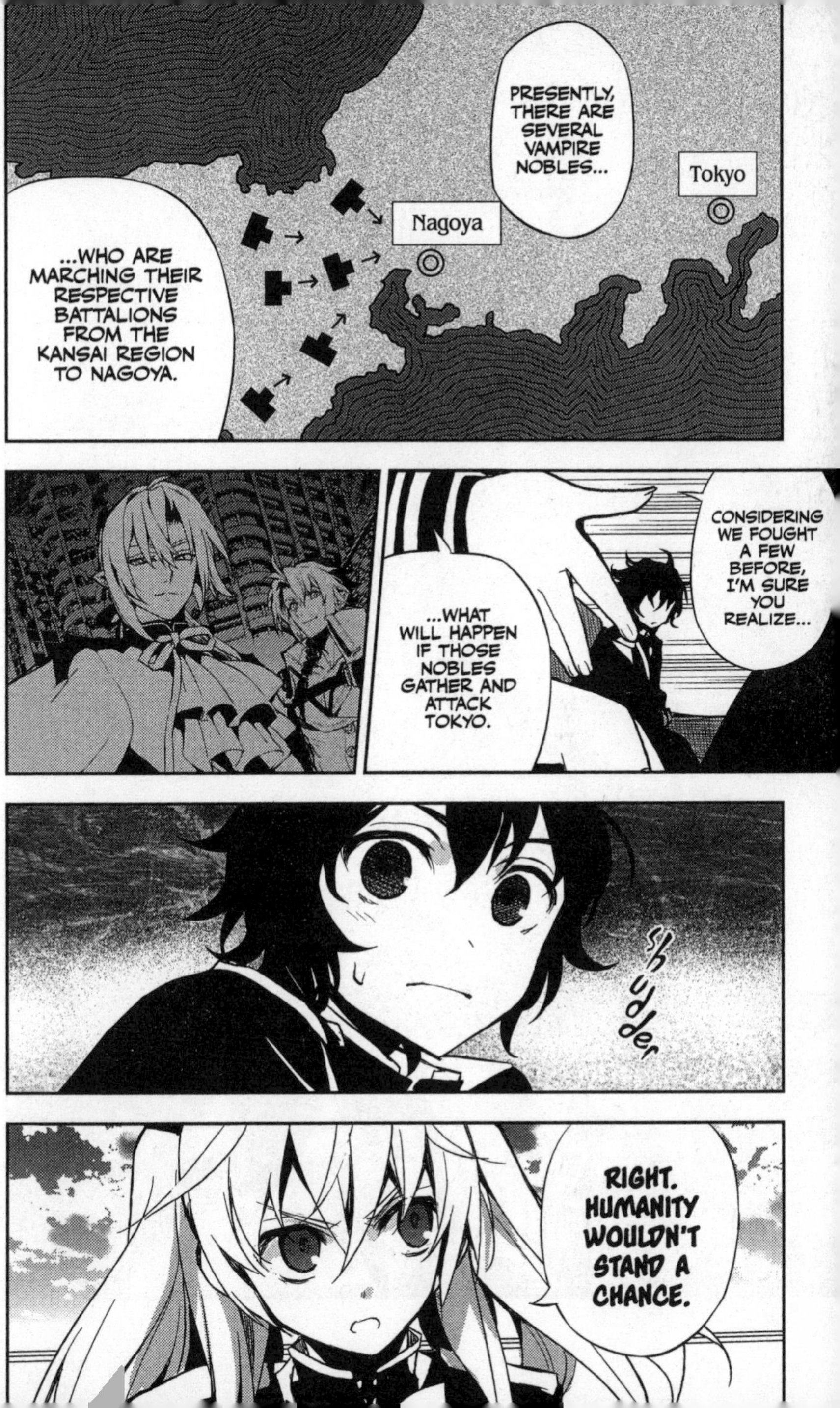
PRESENTLY, THERE ARE SEVERAL VAMPIRE NOBLES...
Tokyo
Nagoya
...WHO ARE MARCHING THEIR RESPECTIVE BATTALIONS FROM THE KANSAI REGION TO NAGOYA.
CONSIDERING WE FOUGHT A FEW BEFORE, I'M SURE YOU REALIZE...
...WHAT WILL HAPPEN IF THOSE NOBLES GATHER AND ATTACK TOKYO.
shudder
RIGHT. HUMANITY WOULDN'T STAND A CHANCE.

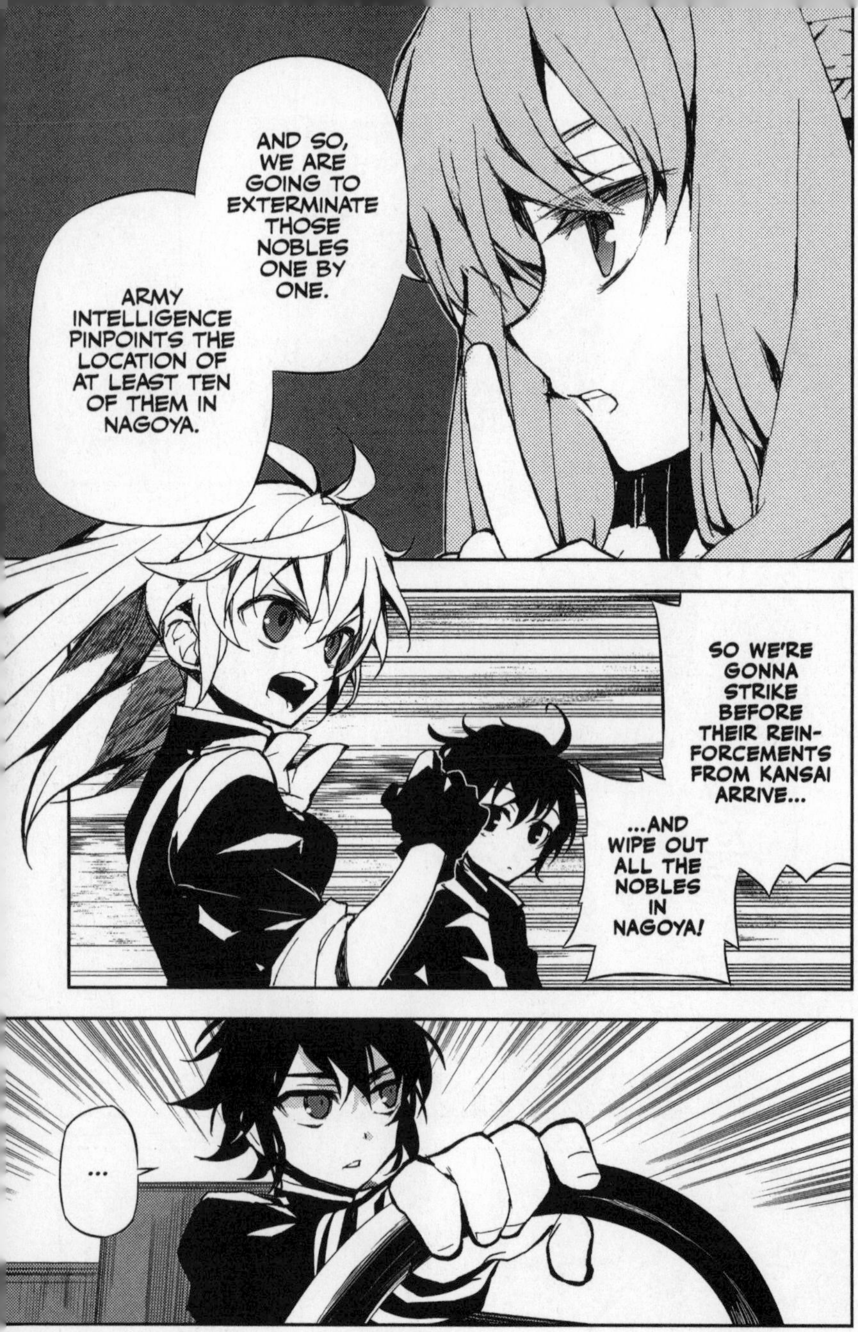
AND SO, WE ARE GOING TO EXTERMINATE THOSE NOBLES ONE BY ONE.
ARMY INTELLIGENCE PINPOINTS THE LOCATION OF AT LEAST TEN OF THEM IN NAGOYA.
SO WE'RE GONNA STRIKE BEFORE THEIR REIN-FORCEMENTS FROM KANSAI ARRIVE...
...AND WIPE OUT ALL THE NOBLES IN NAGOYA!
...

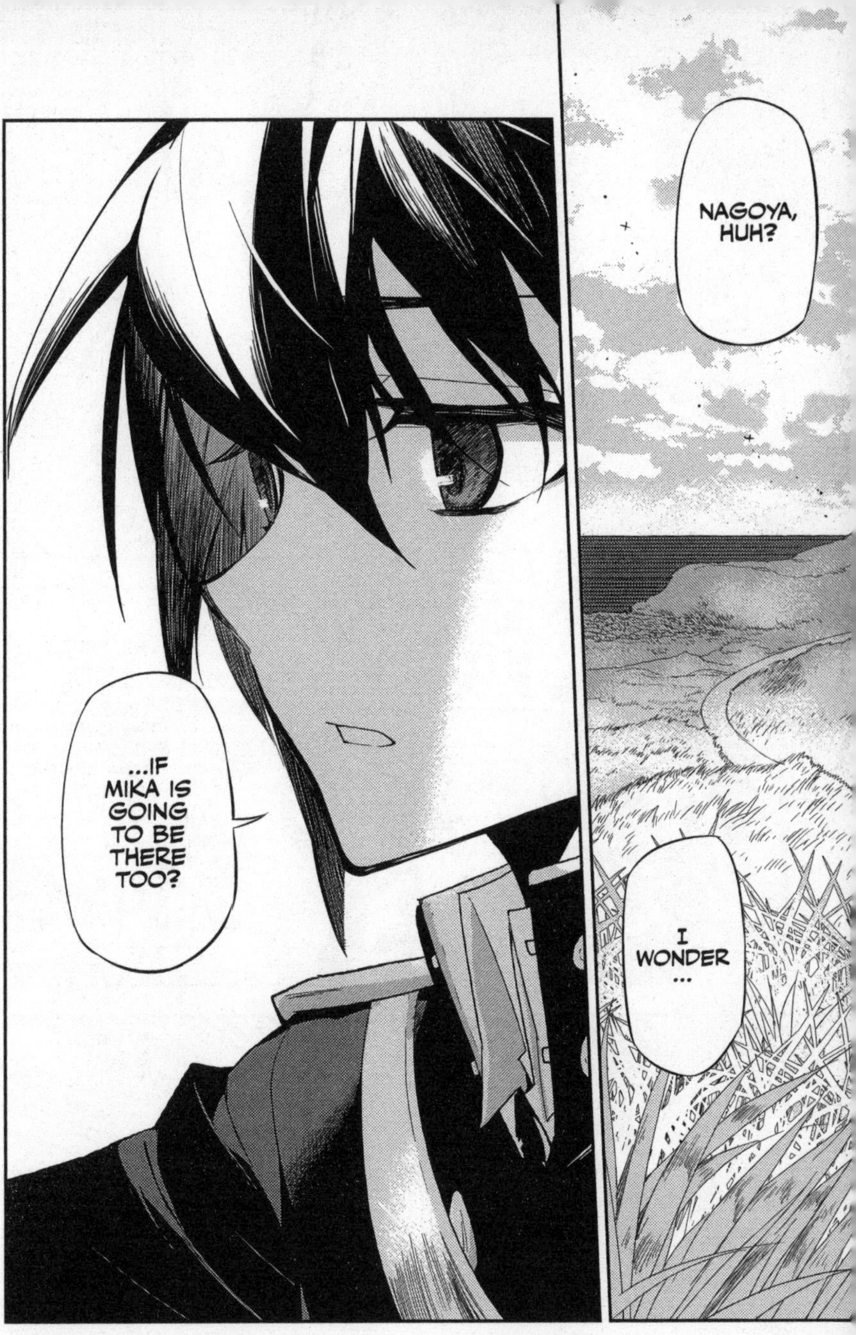
NAGOYA, HUH?
I WONDER...
...IF MIKA IS GOING TO BE THERE TOO?

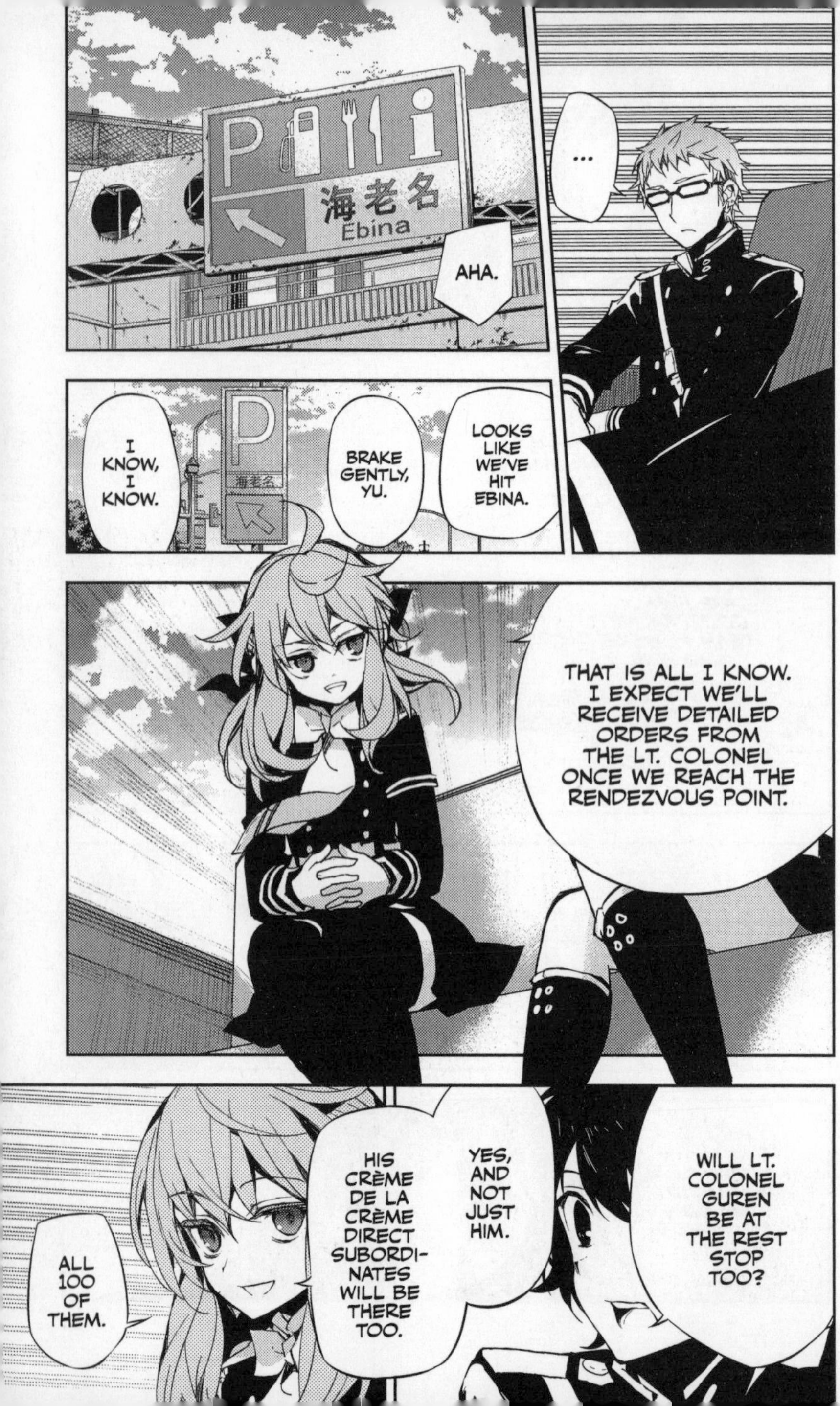
...
海老名
Ebina
AHA.
LOOKS LIKE WE'VE HIT EBINA.
BRAKE GENTLY, YU.
海老名
I KNOW, I KNOW.
THAT IS ALL I KNOW. I EXPECT WE'LL RECEIVE DETAILED ORDERS FROM THE LT. COLONEL ONCE WE REACH THE RENDEZVOUS POINT.
WILL LT. COLONEL GUREN BE AT THE REST STOP TOO?
YES, AND NOT JUST HIM.
HIS CRÈME DE LA CRÈME DIRECT SUBORDINATES WILL BE THERE TOO.
ALL 100 OF THEM.

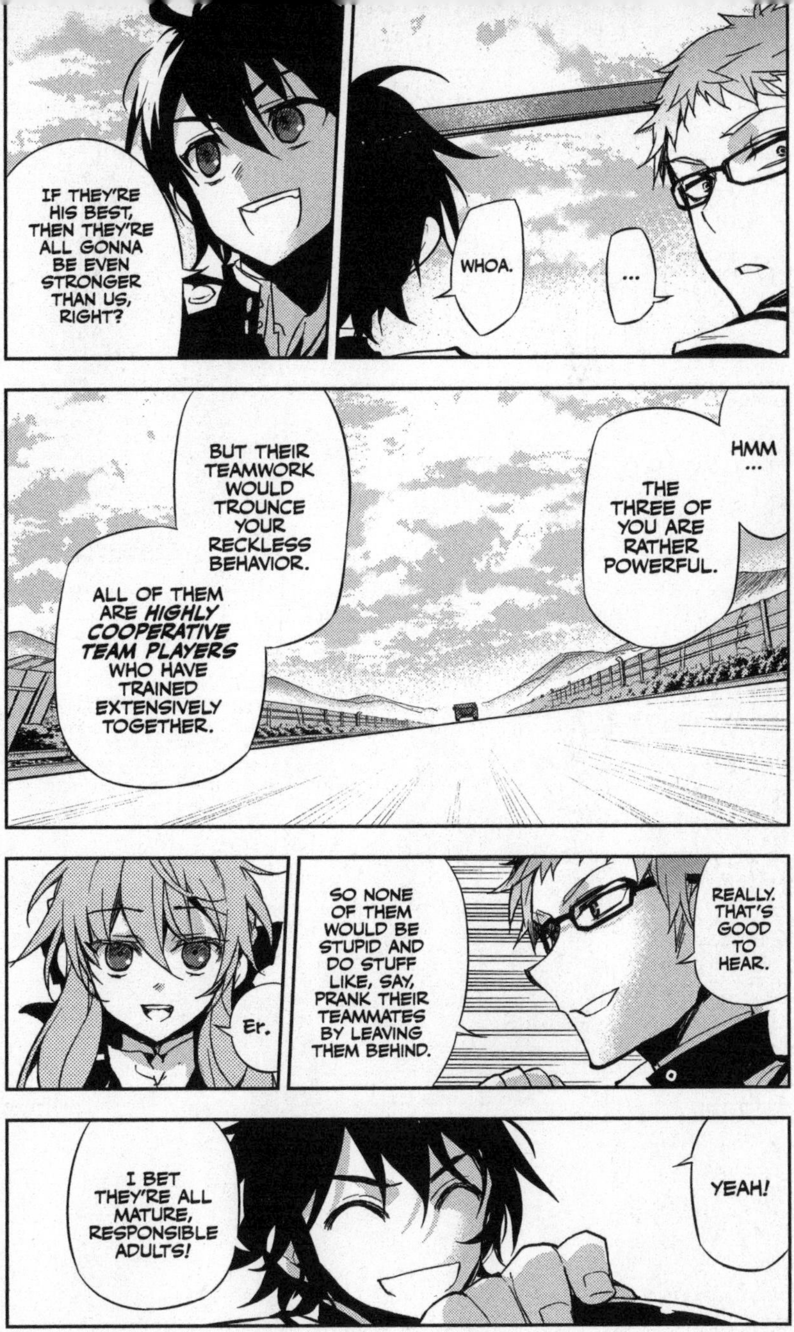
...
WHOA.
IF THEY'RE HIS BEST, THEN THEY'RE ALL GONNA BE EVEN STRONGER THAN US, RIGHT?
HMM... THE THREE OF YOU ARE RATHER POWERFUL.
BUT THEIR TEAMWORK WOULD TROUNCE YOUR RECKLESS BEHAVIOR.
ALL OF THEM ARE *HIGHLY COOPERATIVE TEAM PLAYERS* WHO HAVE TRAINED EXTENSIVELY TOGETHER.
REALLY. THAT'S GOOD TO HEAR.
SO NONE OF THEM WOULD BE STUPID AND DO STUFF LIKE, SAY, PRANK THEIR TEAMMATES BY LEAVING THEM BEHIND.
Er.
YEAH!
I BET THEY'RE ALL MATURE, RESPONSIBLE ADULTS!

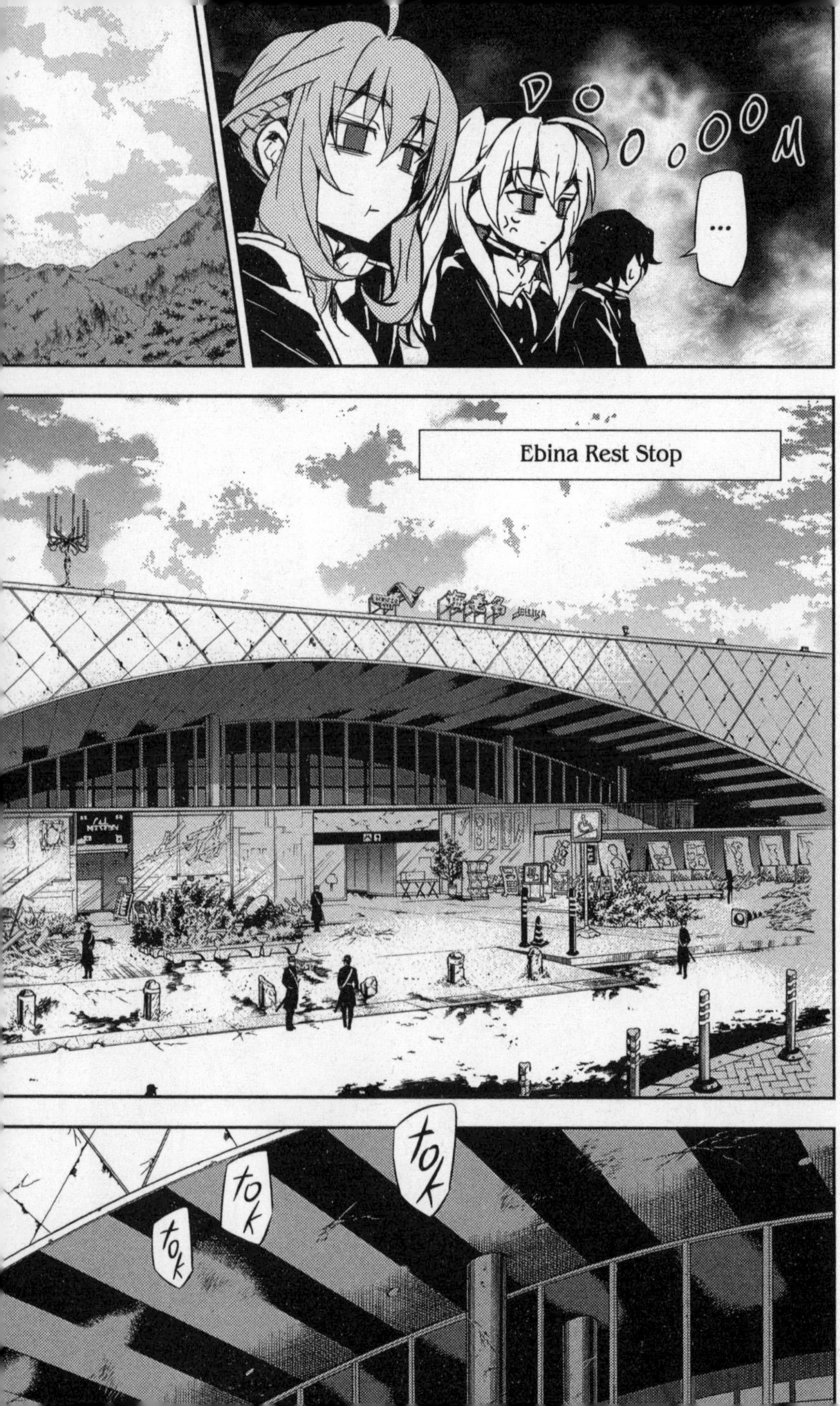
DOOOOOOM
...
Ebina Rest Stop
TOK
TOK
TOK

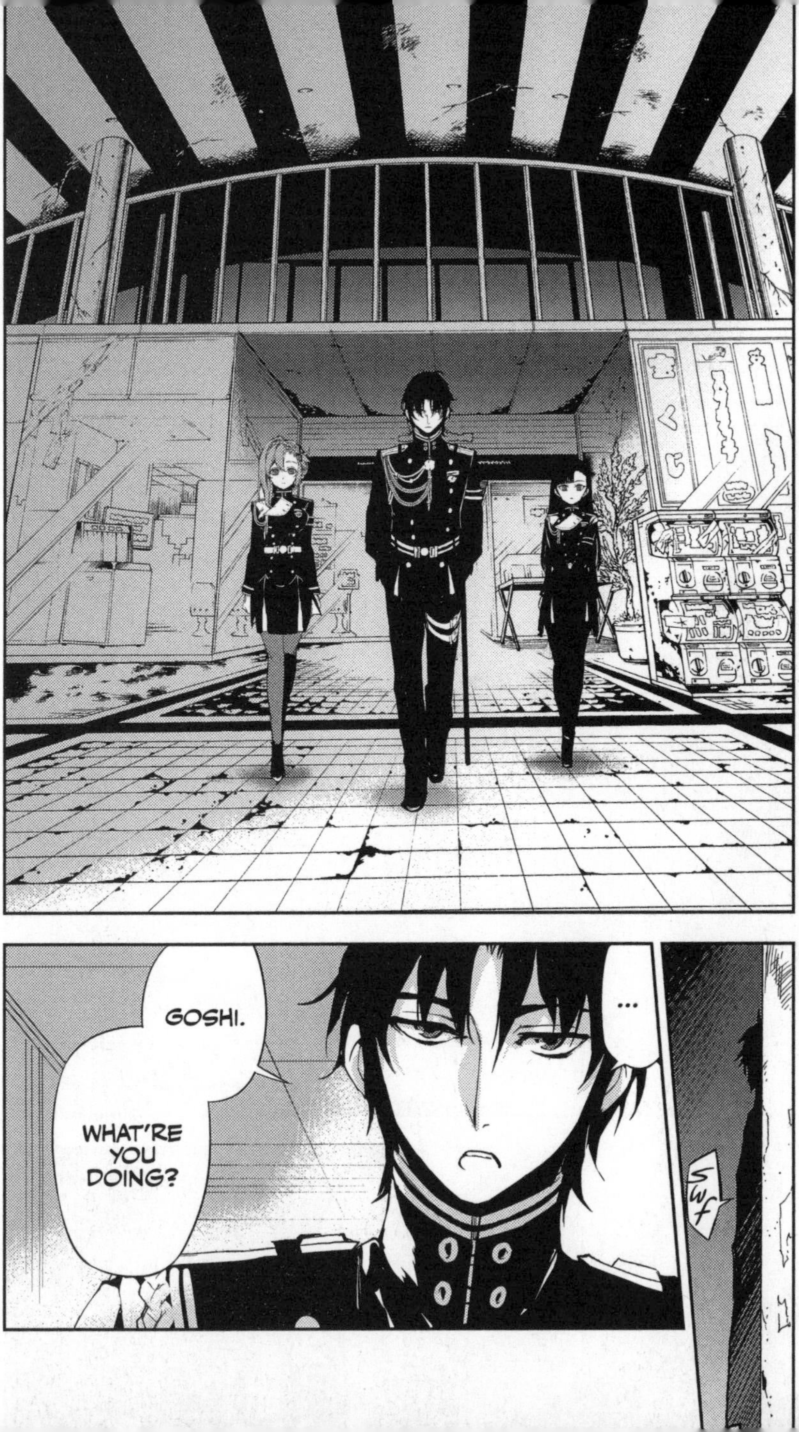
...
GOSHI.
WHAT'RE YOU DOING?
SWF

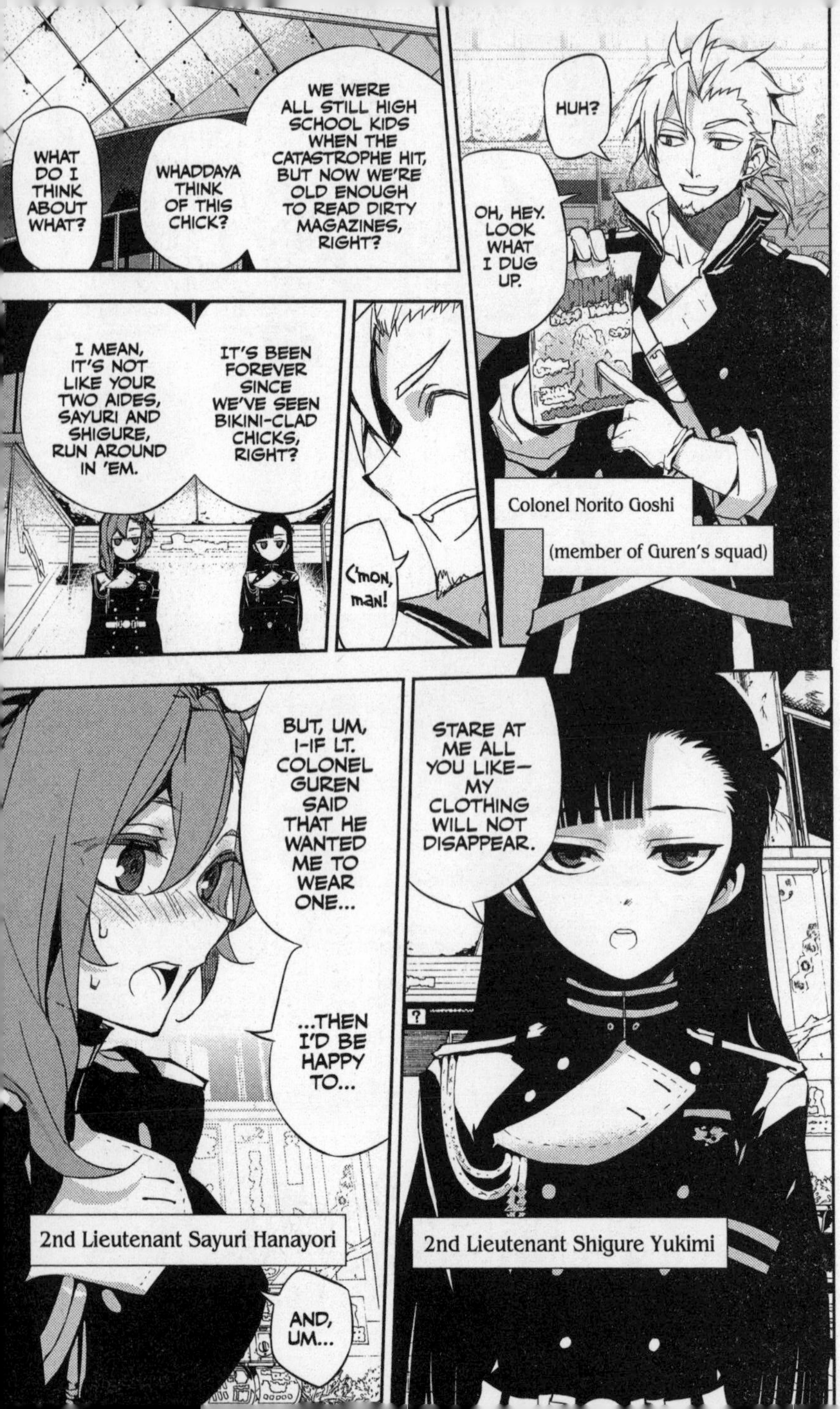
HUH?
OH, HEY. LOOK WHAT I DUG UP.
Colonel Norito Goshi
(member of Guren's squad)
WE WERE ALL STILL HIGH SCHOOL KIDS WHEN THE CATASTROPHE HIT, BUT NOW WE'RE OLD ENOUGH TO READ DIRTY MAGAZINES, RIGHT?
WHADDAYA THINK OF THIS CHICK?
WHAT DO I THINK ABOUT WHAT?
C'mon, man!
IT'S BEEN FOREVER SINCE WE'VE SEEN BIKINI-CLAD CHICKS, RIGHT?
I MEAN, IT'S NOT LIKE YOUR TWO AIDES, SAYURI AND SHIGURE, RUN AROUND IN 'EM.
STARE AT ME ALL YOU LIKE— MY CLOTHING WILL NOT DISAPPEAR.
2nd Lieutenant Shigure Yukimi
BUT, UM, I-IF LT. COLONEL GUREN SAID THAT HE WANTED ME TO WEAR ONE...
...THEN I'D BE HAPPY TO...
2nd Lieutenant Sayuri Hanayori
AND, UM...

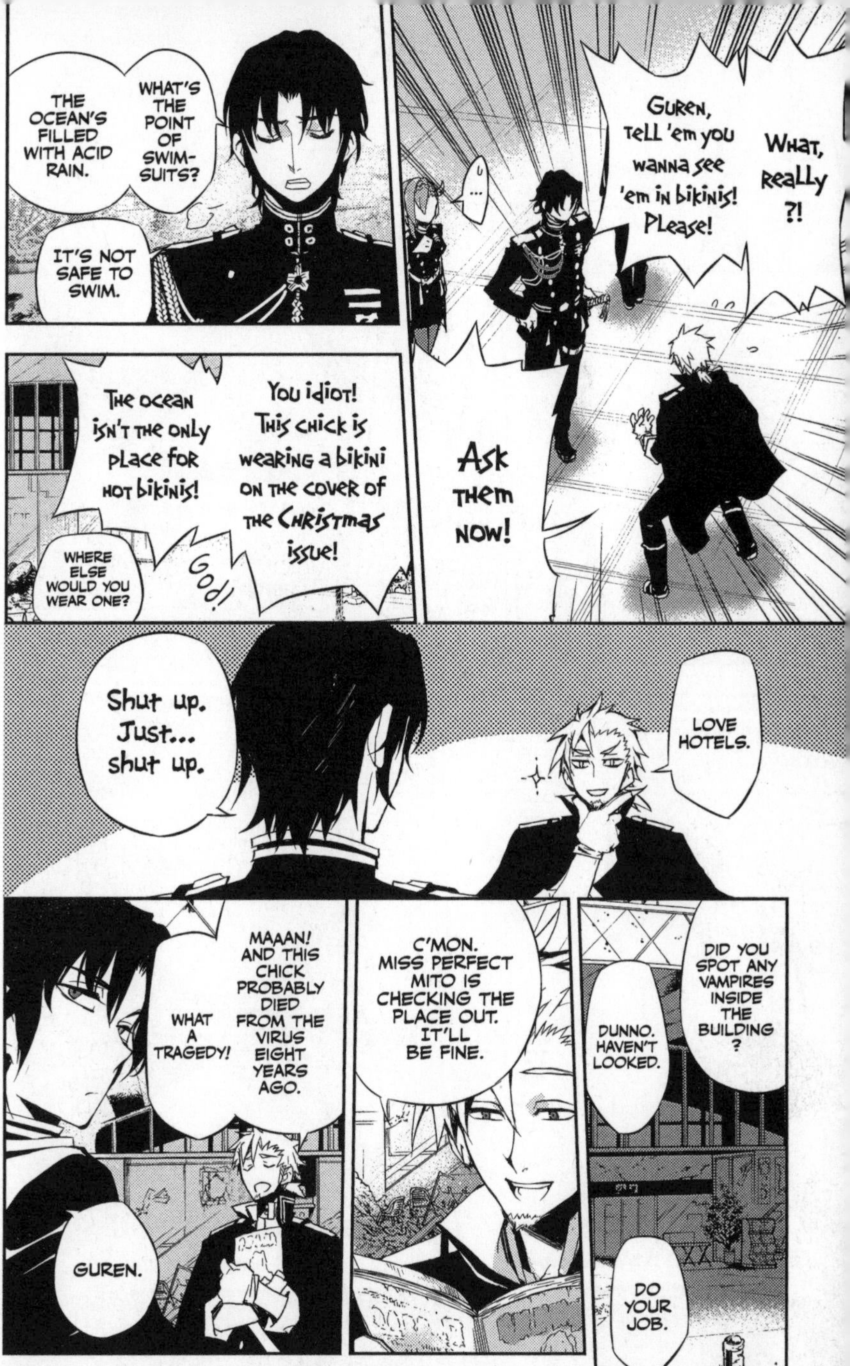

Guren, tell 'em you wanna see 'em in bikinis! Please!
What, really ?!
...
Ask them now!
WHAT'S THE POINT OF SWIM-SUITS?
THE OCEAN'S FILLED WITH ACID RAIN.
IT'S NOT SAFE TO SWIM.
You idiot! This chick is wearing a bikini on the cover of the Christmas issue!
The ocean isn't the only place for hot bikinis!
God!
WHERE ELSE WOULD YOU WEAR ONE?
LOVE HOTELS.
Shut up. Just... shut up.
DID YOU SPOT ANY VAMPIRES INSIDE THE BUILDING ?
DUNNO. HAVEN'T LOOKED.
DO YOUR JOB.
C'MON. MISS PERFECT MITO IS CHECKING THE PLACE OUT. IT'LL BE FINE.
MAAAN! AND THIS CHICK PROBABLY DIED FROM THE VIRUS EIGHT YEARS AGO.
WHAT A TRAGEDY!
GUREN.

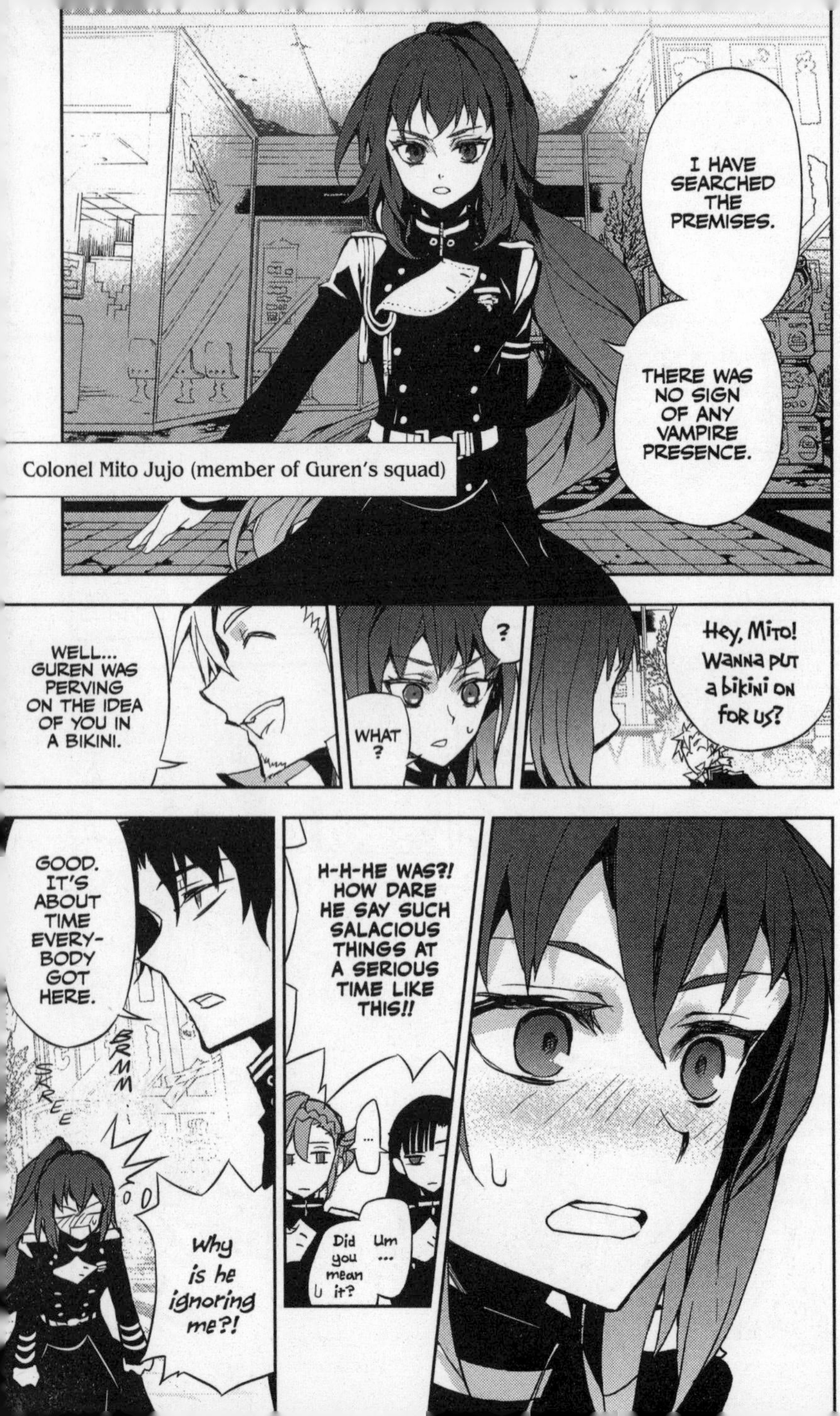
I HAVE SEARCHED THE PREMISES.
THERE WAS NO SIGN OF ANY VAMPIRE PRESENCE.
Colonel Mito Jujo (member of Guren's squad)
Hey, Mito! Wanna put a bikini on for us?
?
WHAT?
WELL... GUREN WAS PERVING ON THE IDEA OF YOU IN A BIKINI.
H-H-HE WAS?! HOW DARE HE SAY SUCH SALACIOUS THINGS AT A SERIOUS TIME LIKE THIS!!
...
Um...
Did you mean it?
GOOD. IT'S ABOUT TIME EVERY-BODY GOT HERE.
BRMM
SKREE
Why is he ignoring me?!

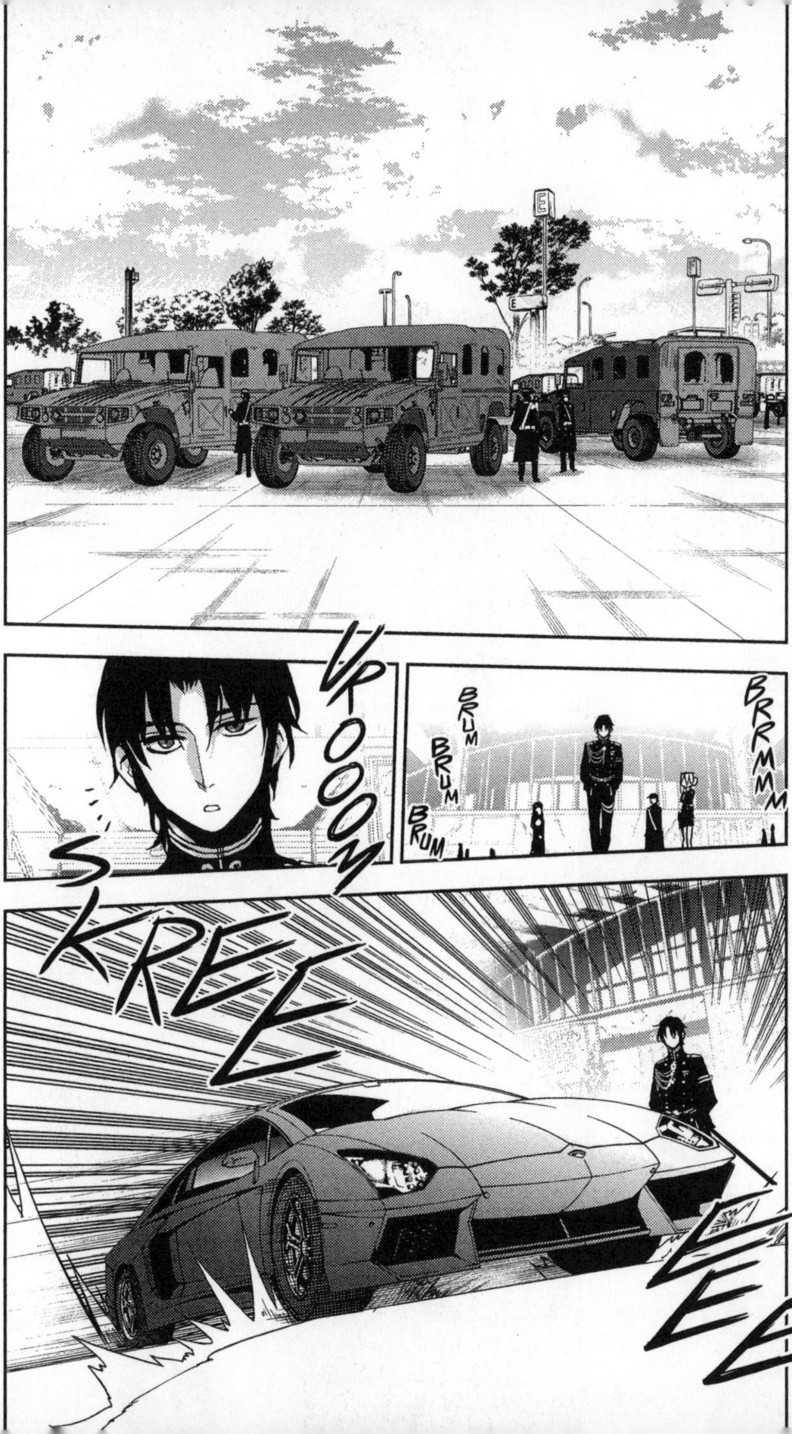
BRRMMM
BRUM
BRUM
BRUM
BRUM
VROOOOM
SKREEEEE

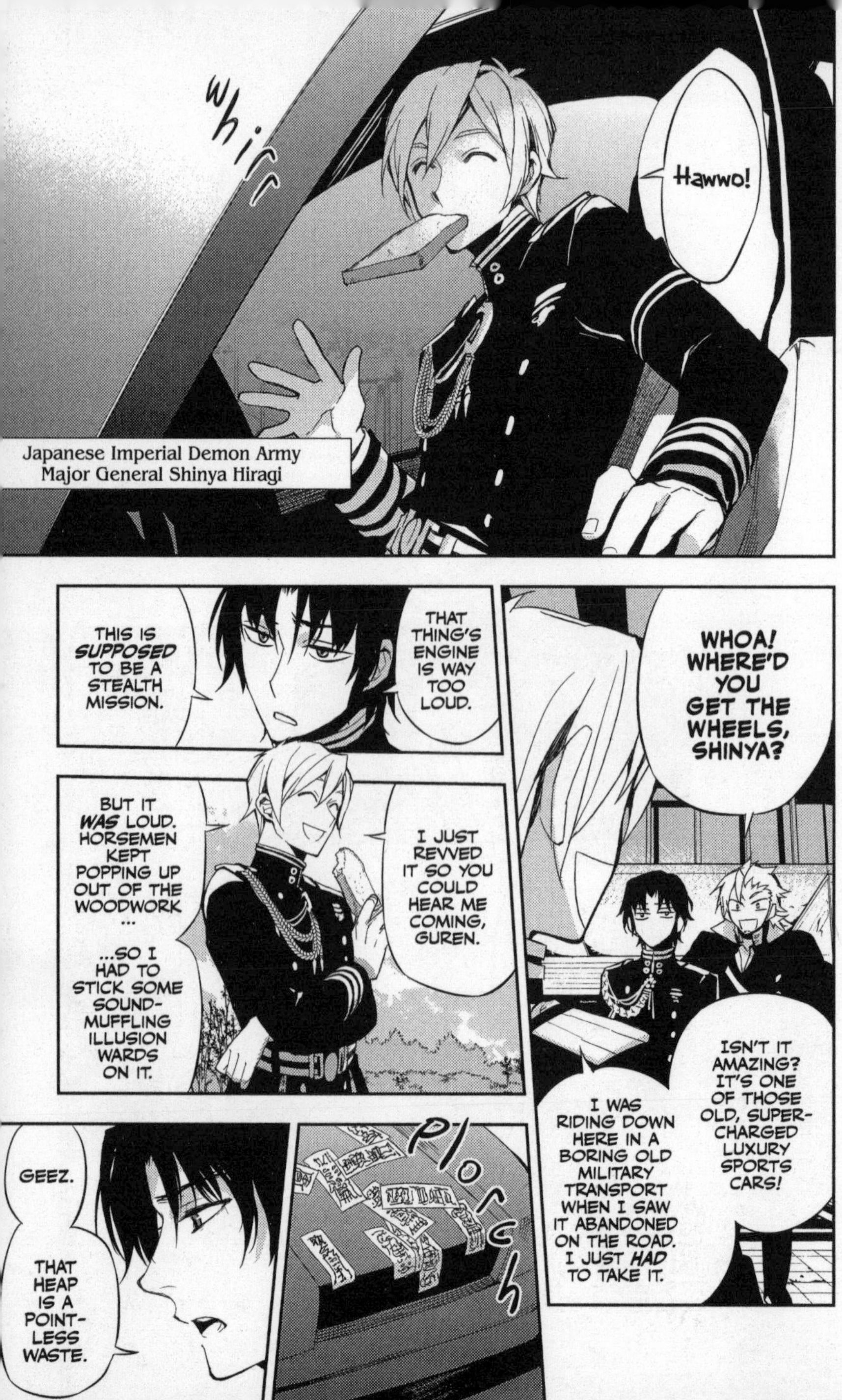
Hawwo!
whirr
Japanese Imperial Demon Army
Major General Shinya Hiragi
WHOA! WHERE'D YOU GET THE WHEELS, SHINYA?
ISN'T IT AMAZING? IT'S ONE OF THOSE OLD, SUPER-CHARGED LUXURY SPORTS CARS!
I WAS RIDING DOWN HERE IN A BORING OLD MILITARY TRANSPORT WHEN I SAW IT ABANDONED ON THE ROAD. I JUST *HAD* TO TAKE IT.
THAT THING'S ENGINE IS WAY TOO LOUD.
THIS IS *SUPPOSED* TO BE A STEALTH MISSION.
I JUST REVVED IT SO YOU COULD HEAR ME COMING, GUREN.
BUT IT *WAS* LOUD. HORSEMEN KEPT POPPING UP OUT OF THE WOODWORK...
...SO I HAD TO STICK SOME SOUND-MUFFLING ILLUSION WARDS ON IT.
plorch
GEEZ.
THAT HEAP IS A POINTLESS WASTE.

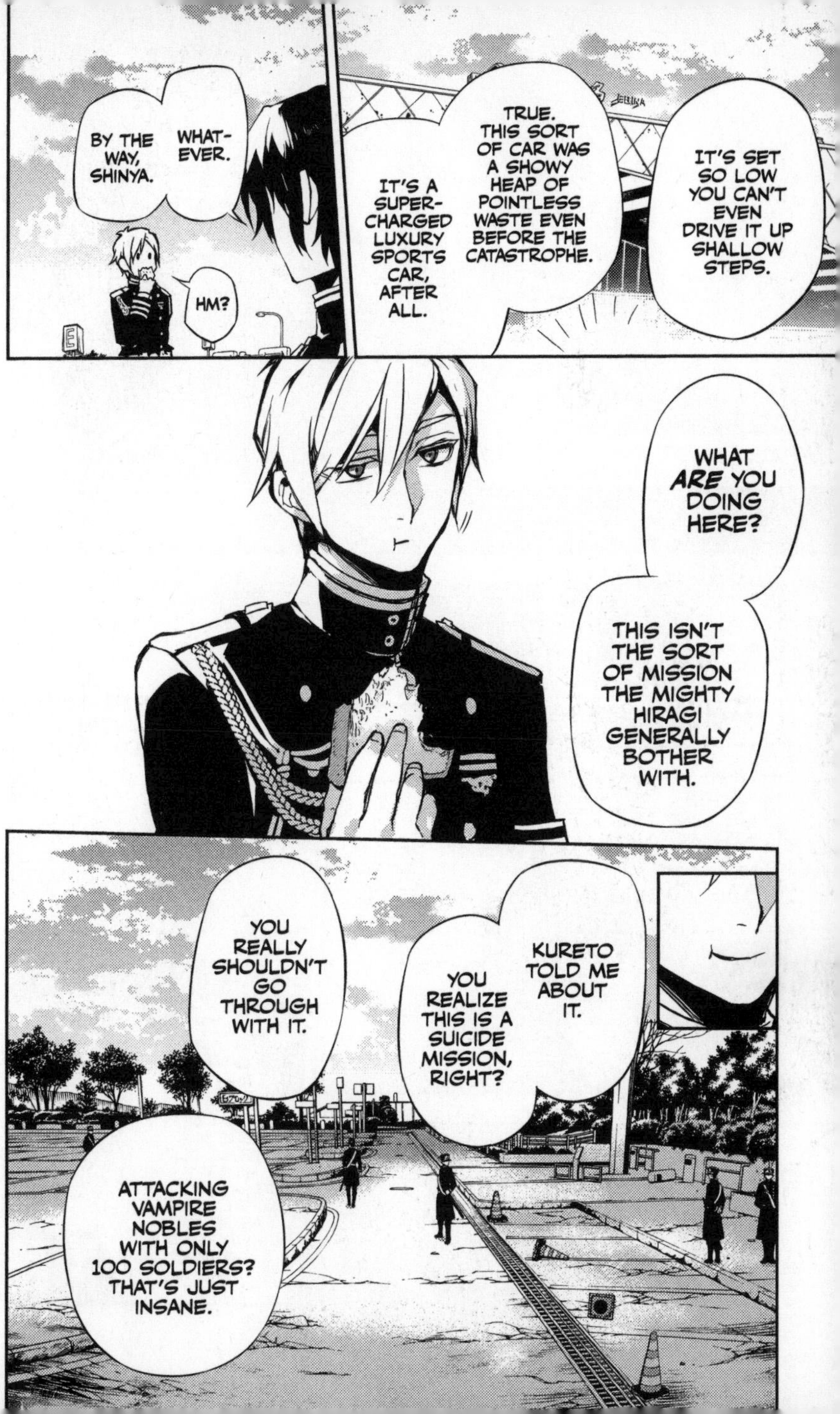
IT'S SET SO LOW YOU CAN'T EVEN DRIVE IT UP SHALLOW STEPS.
TRUE. THIS SORT OF CAR WAS A SHOWY HEAP OF POINTLESS WASTE EVEN BEFORE THE CATASTROPHE.
IT'S A SUPER-CHARGED LUXURY SPORTS CAR, AFTER ALL.
WHAT-EVER.
BY THE WAY, SHINYA.
HM?
WHAT *ARE* YOU DOING HERE?
THIS ISN'T THE SORT OF MISSION THE MIGHTY HIRAGI GENERALLY BOTHER WITH.
KURETO TOLD ME ABOUT IT.
YOU REALIZE THIS IS A SUICIDE MISSION, RIGHT?
YOU REALLY SHOULDN'T GO THROUGH WITH IT.
ATTACKING VAMPIRE NOBLES WITH ONLY 100 SOLDIERS? THAT'S JUST INSANE.

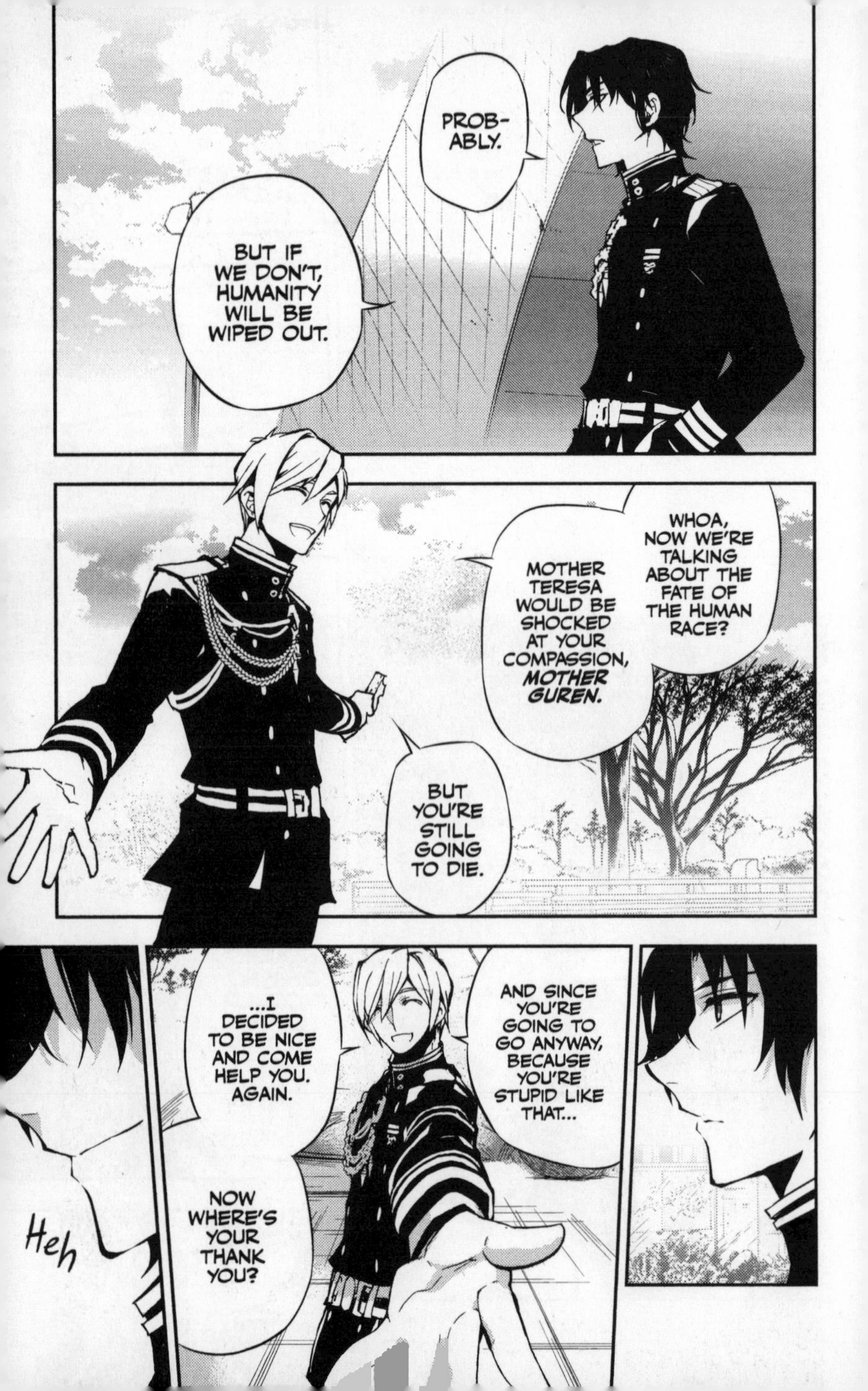
PROB- ABLY.
BUT IF WE DON'T, HUMANITY WILL BE WIPED OUT.
WHOA, NOW WE'RE TALKING ABOUT THE FATE OF THE HUMAN RACE?
MOTHER TERESA WOULD BE SHOCKED AT YOUR COMPASSION, ***MOTHER GUREN.***
BUT YOU'RE STILL GOING TO DIE.
AND SINCE YOU'RE GOING TO GO ANYWAY, BECAUSE YOU'RE STUPID LIKE THAT...
...I DECIDED TO BE NICE AND COME HELP YOU. AGAIN.
NOW WHERE'S YOUR THANK YOU?
Heh

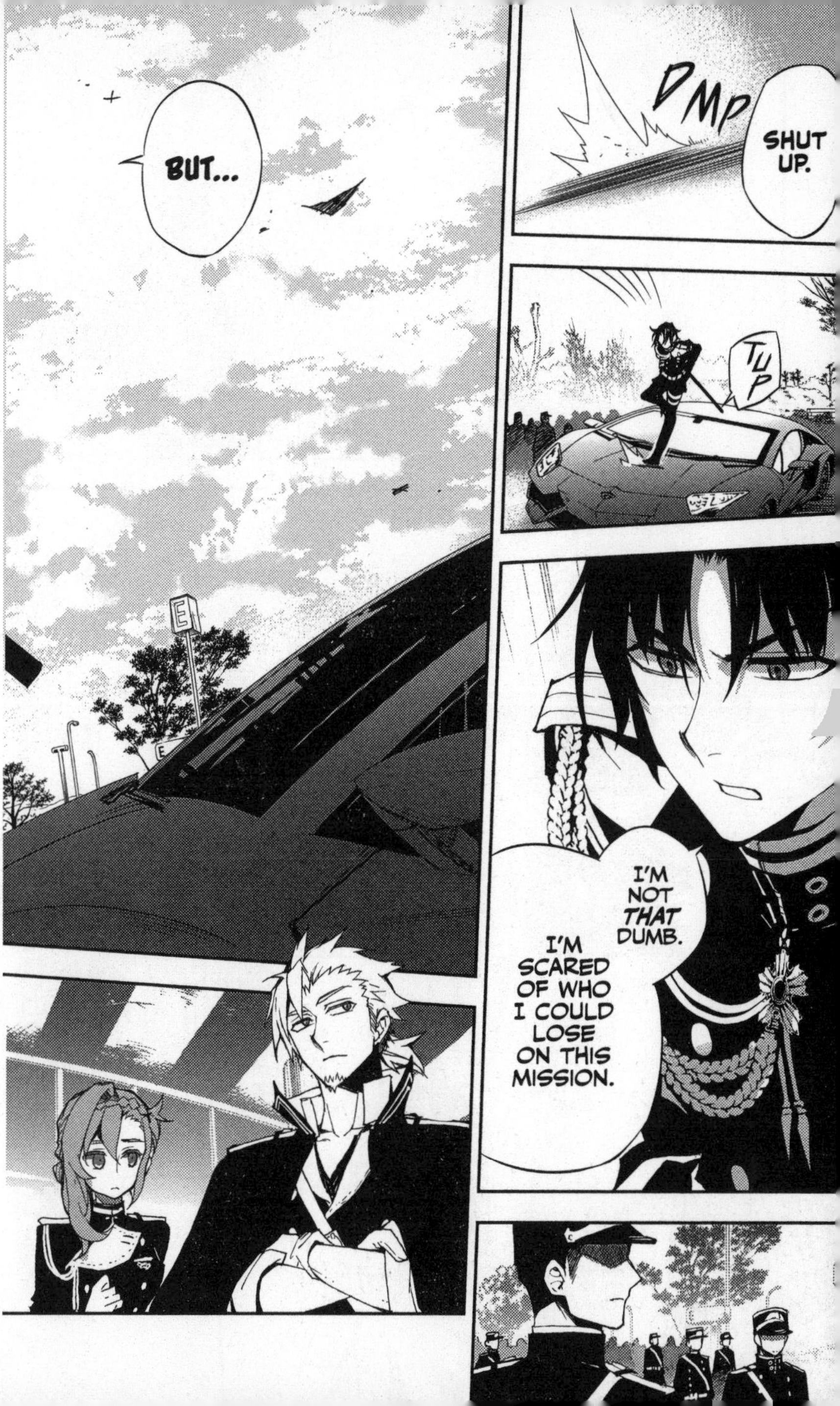
SHUT UP.
DMP
TUP
I'M NOT *THAT* DUMB.
I'M SCARED OF WHO I COULD LOSE ON THIS MISSION.
BUT...

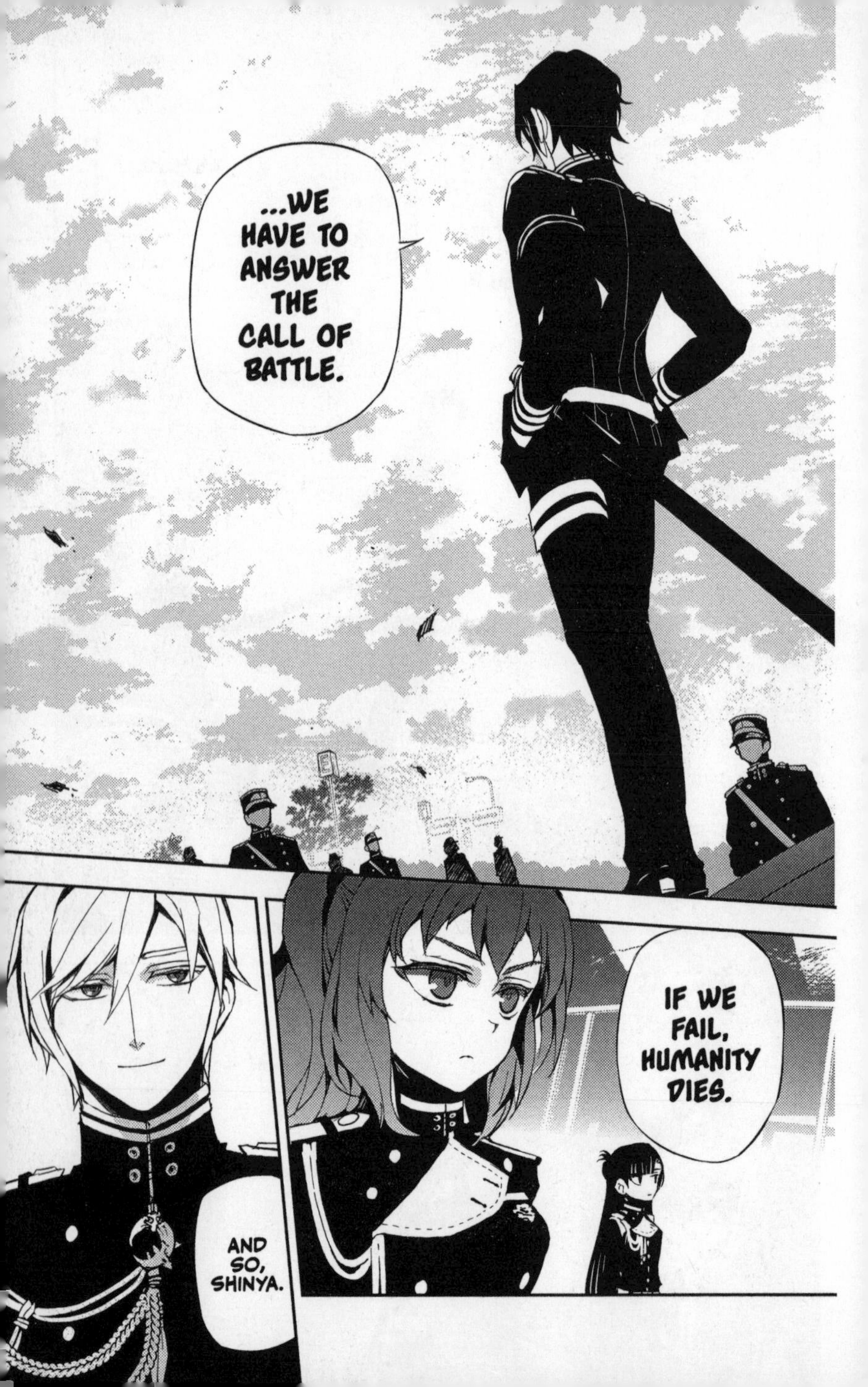
...WE HAVE TO ANSWER THE CALL OF BATTLE.
IF WE FAIL, HUMANITY DIES.
AND SO, SHINYA.

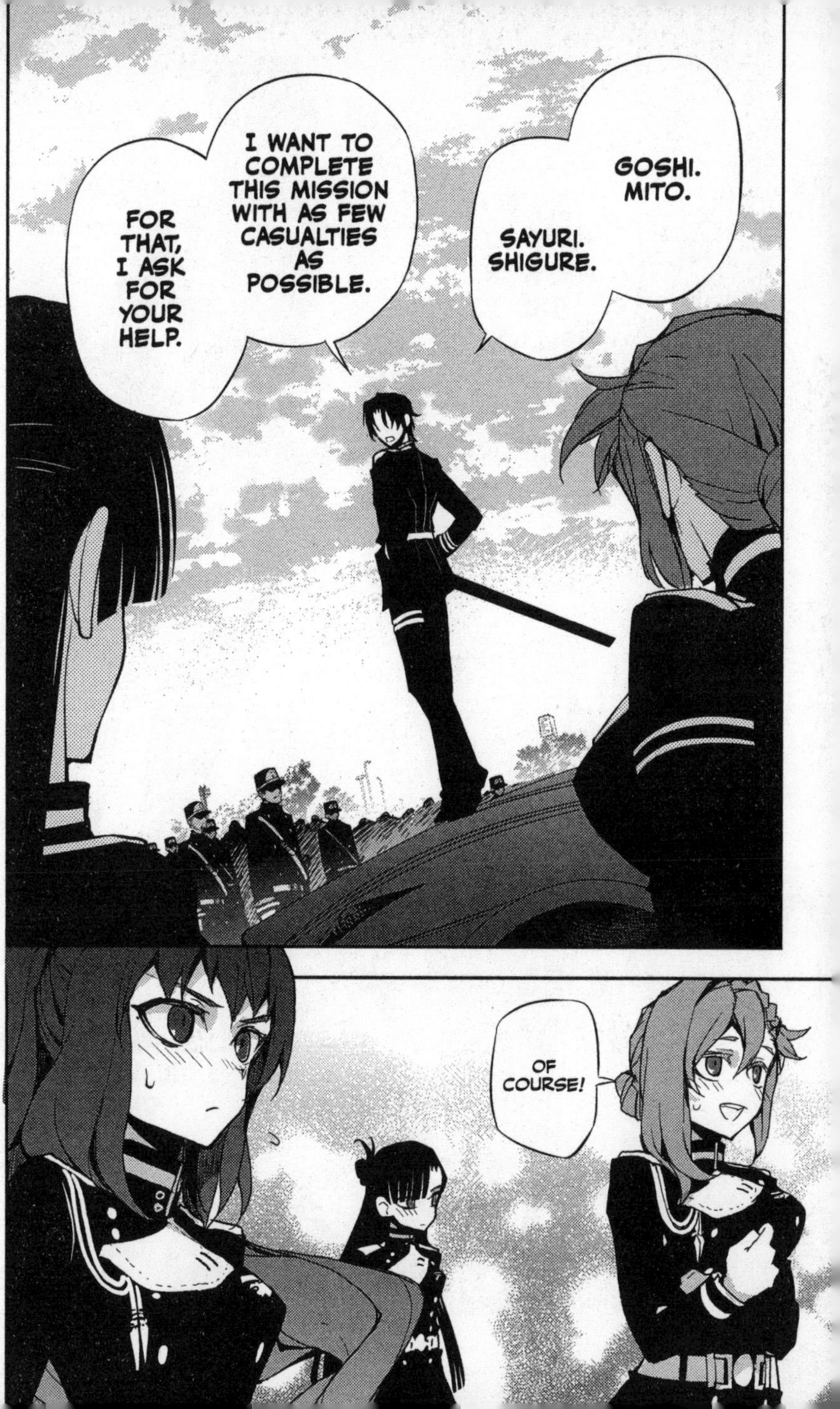
GOSHI. MITO.
SAYURI. SHIGURE.
I WANT TO COMPLETE THIS MISSION WITH AS FEW CASUALTIES AS POSSIBLE.
FOR THAT, I ASK FOR YOUR HELP.
OF COURSE!

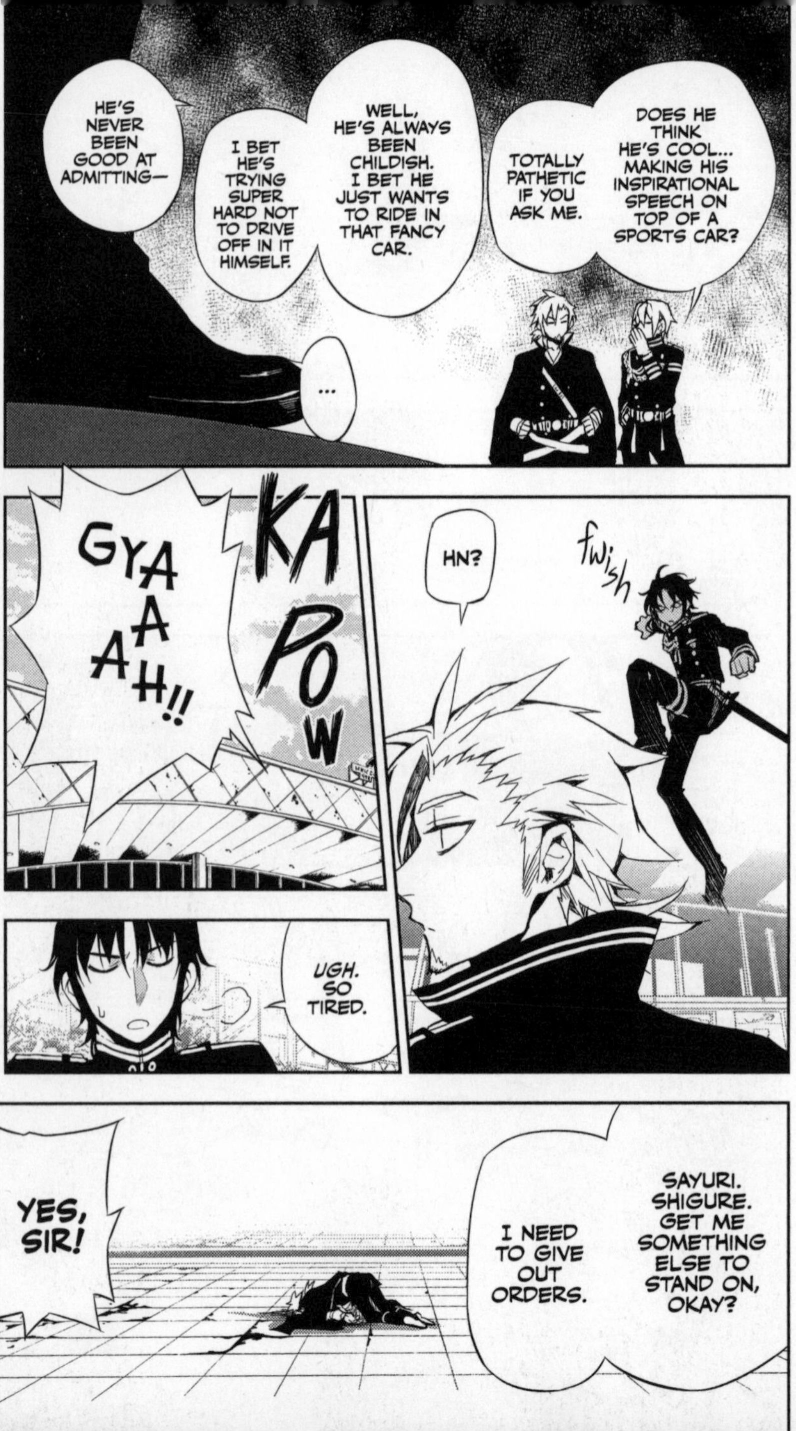
DOES HE THINK HE'S COOL... MAKING HIS INSPIRATIONAL SPEECH ON TOP OF A SPORTS CAR?
TOTALLY PATHETIC IF YOU ASK ME.
WELL, HE'S ALWAYS BEEN CHILDISH. I BET HE JUST WANTS TO RIDE IN THAT FANCY CAR.
I BET HE'S TRYING SUPER HARD NOT TO DRIVE OFF IN IT HIMSELF.
HE'S NEVER BEEN GOOD AT ADMITTING—
...
fwish
HN?
KAPOW
GYAAAAH!!
UGH. SO TIRED.
SAYURI. SHIGURE. GET ME SOMETHING ELSE TO STAND ON, OKAY?
I NEED TO GIVE OUT ORDERS.
YES, SIR!

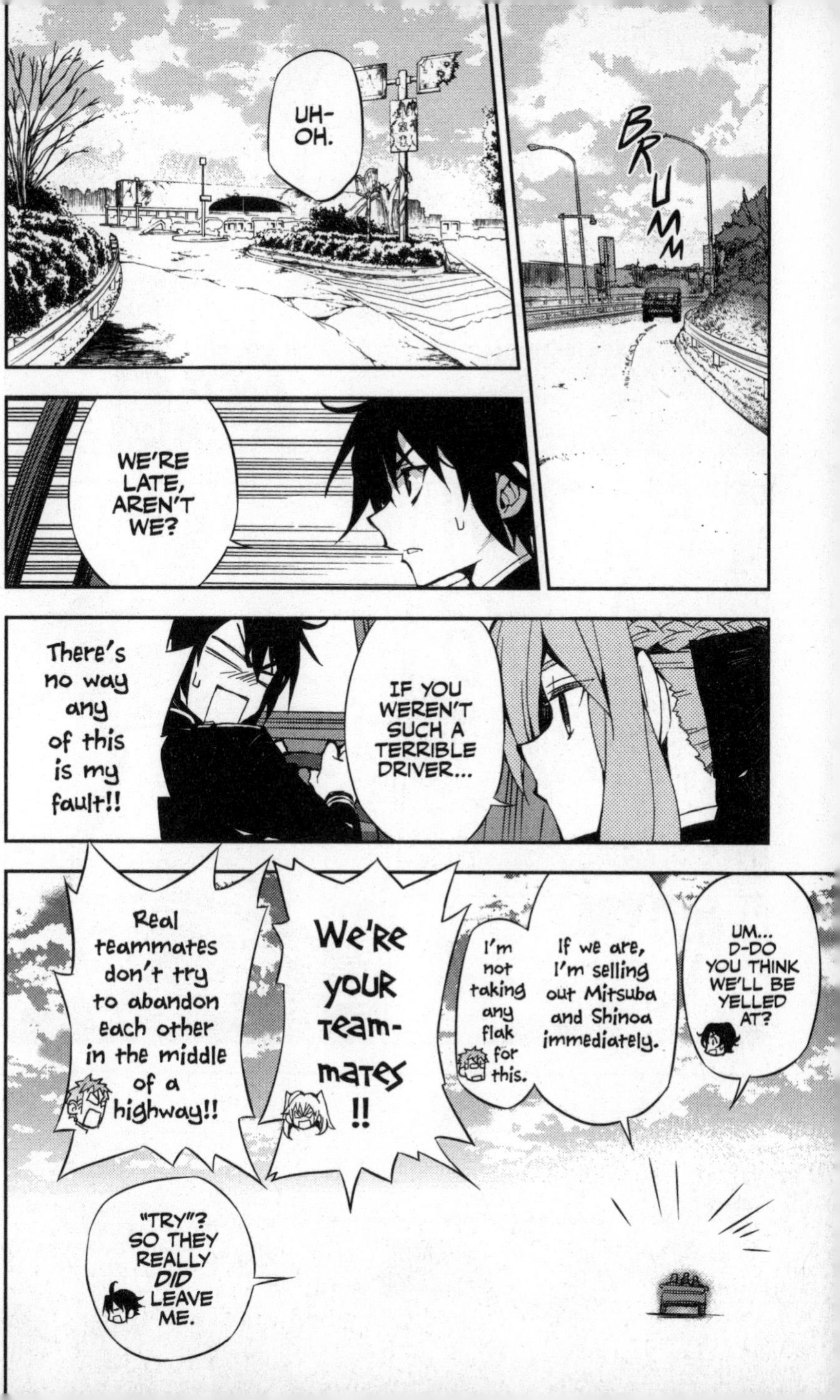
BRUMM
UH-OH.
WE'RE LATE, AREN'T WE?
IF YOU WEREN'T SUCH A TERRIBLE DRIVER...
There's no way any of this is my fault!!
UM... D-DO YOU THINK WE'LL BE YELLED AT?
If we are, I'm selling out Mitsuba and Shinoa immediately.
I'm not taking any flak for this.
We're your team-mates!!
Real teammates don't try to abandon each other in the middle of a highway!!
"TRY"? SO THEY REALLY DID LEAVE ME.

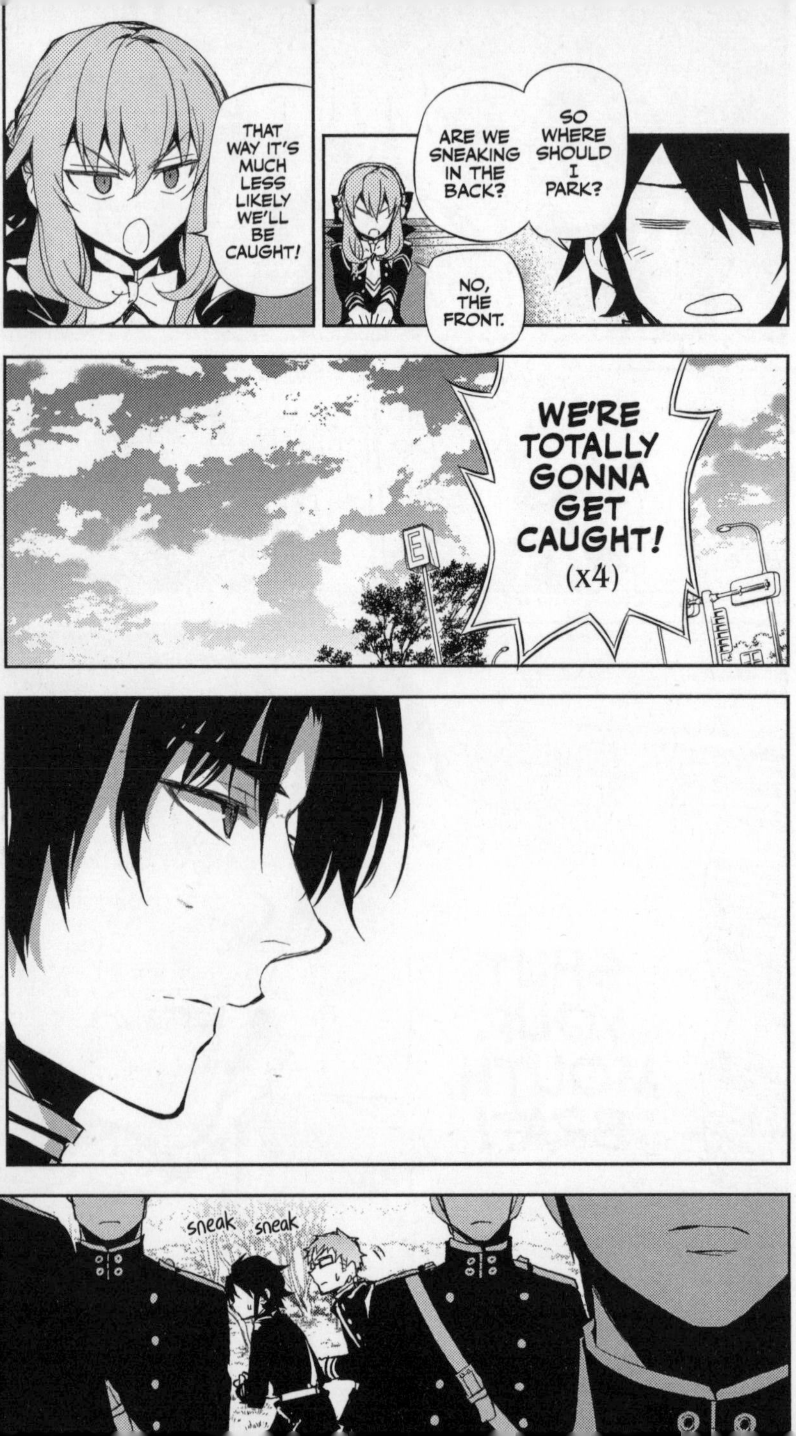
SO WHERE SHOULD I PARK?
ARE WE SNEAKING IN THE BACK?
NO, THE FRONT.
THAT WAY IT'S MUCH LESS LIKELY WE'LL BE CAUGHT!
WE'RE TOTALLY GONNA GET CAUGHT! (x4)
sneak sneak

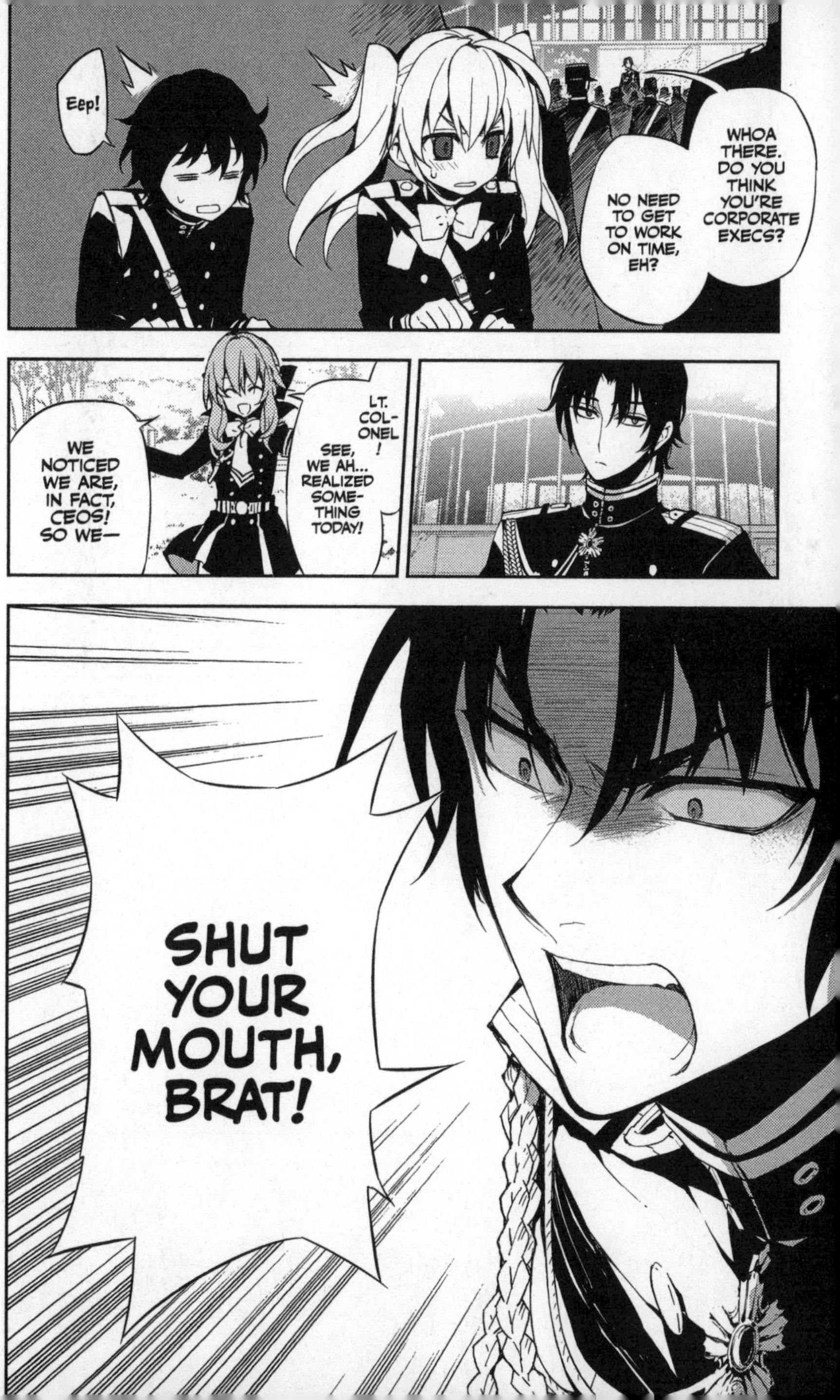
WHOA THERE. DO YOU THINK YOU'RE CORPORATE EXECS?
NO NEED TO GET TO WORK ON TIME, EH?
Eep!
LT. COLONEL!
SEE, WE AH... REALIZED SOMETHING TODAY!
WE NOTICED WE ARE, IN FACT, CEOS! SO WE—
SHUT YOUR MOUTH, BRAT!

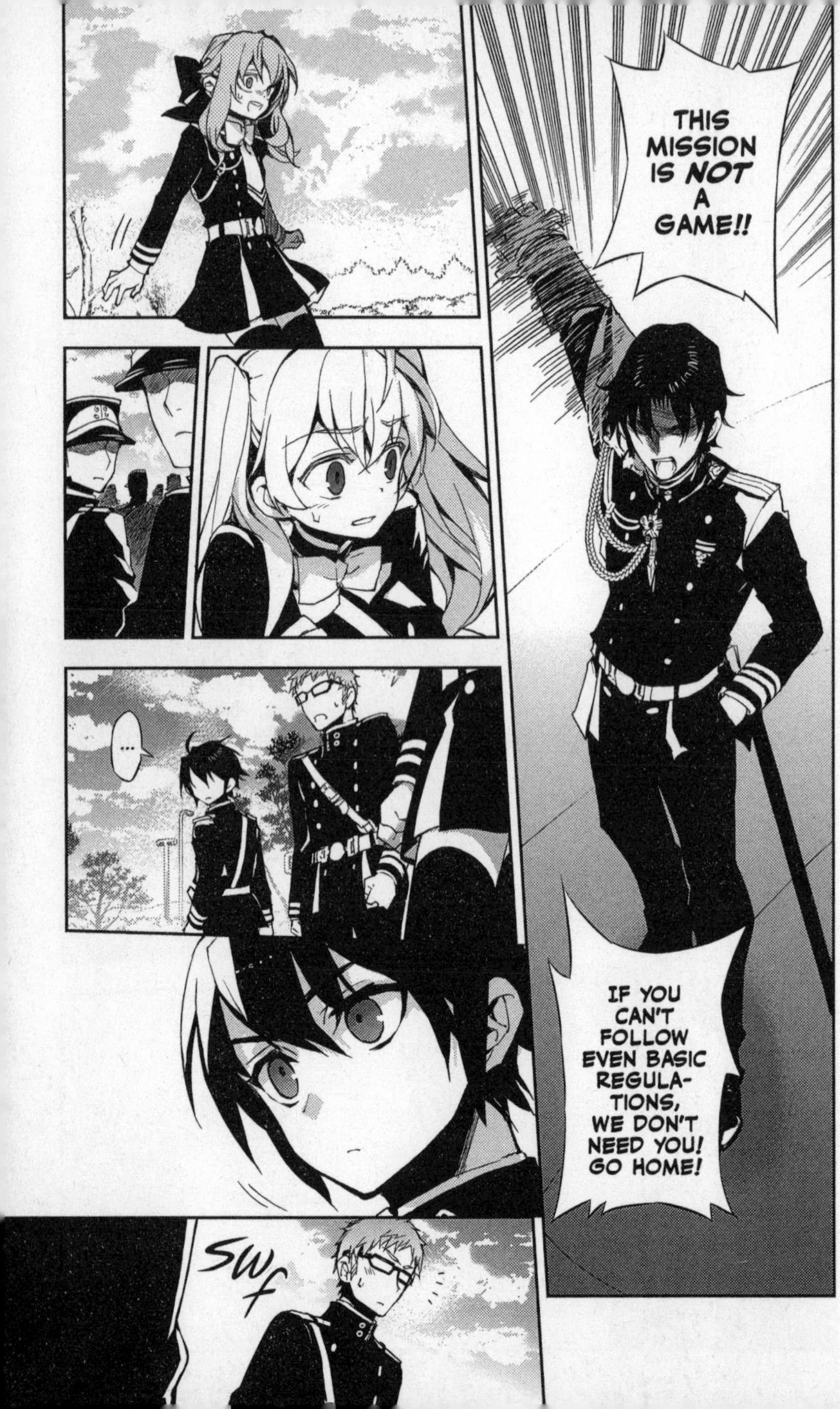
THIS MISSION IS NOT A GAME!!
IF YOU CAN'T FOLLOW EVEN BASIC REGULATIONS, WE DON'T NEED YOU! GO HOME!
...
SWF

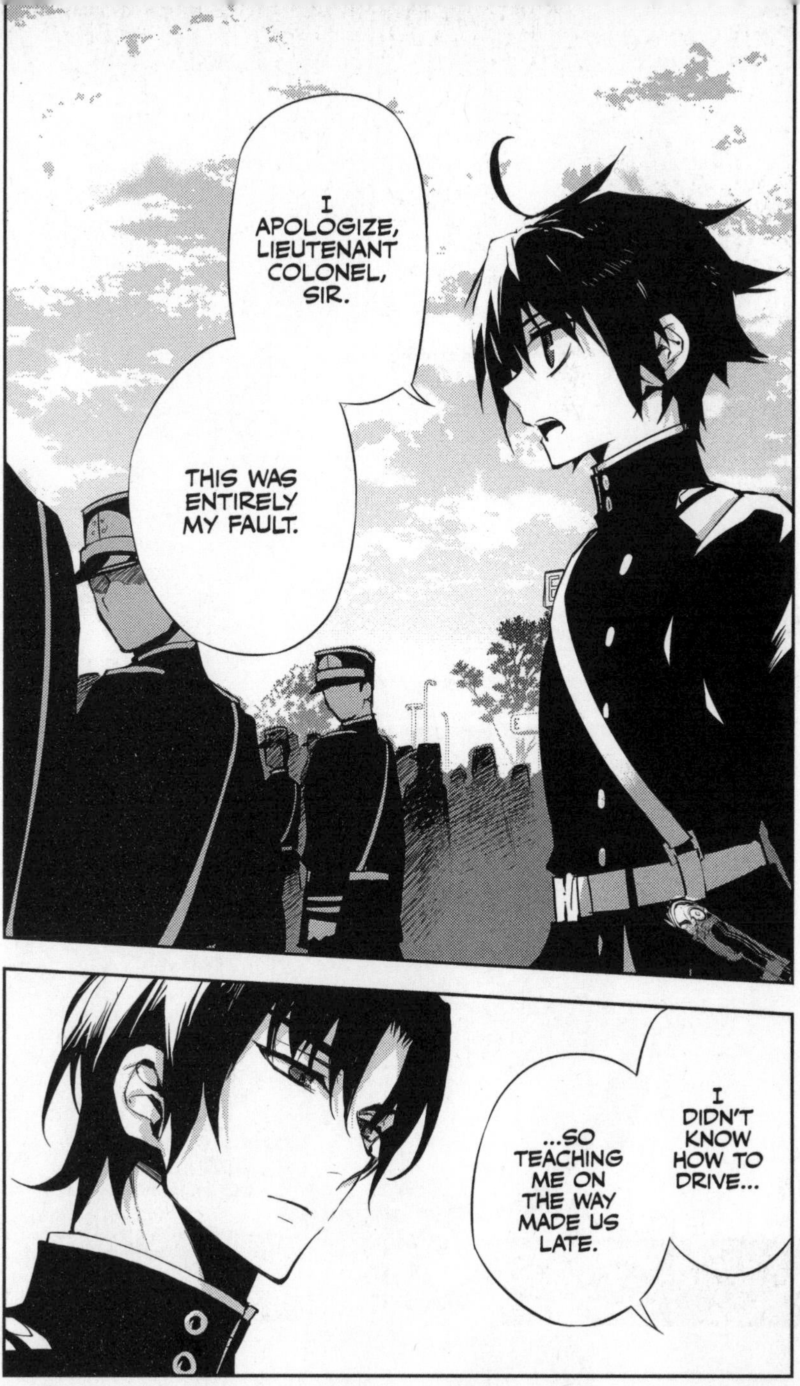
I APOLOGIZE, LIEUTENANT COLONEL, SIR.
THIS WAS ENTIRELY MY FAULT.
I DIDN'T KNOW HOW TO DRIVE...
...SO TEACHING ME ON THE WAY MADE US LATE.

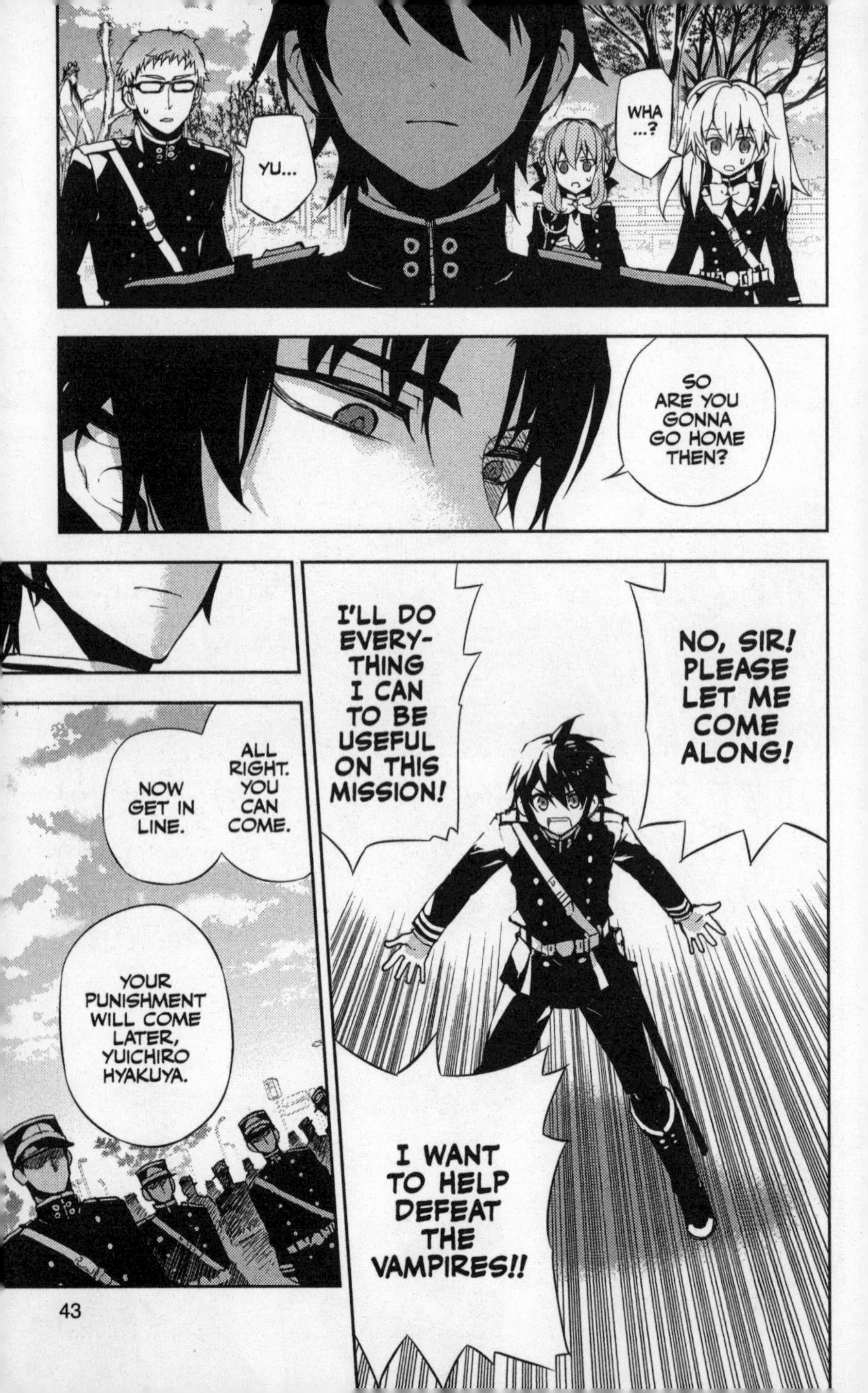
WHA ...?
YU...
SO ARE YOU GONNA GO HOME THEN?
NO, SIR! PLEASE LET ME COME ALONG!
I'LL DO EVERY-THING I CAN TO BE USEFUL ON THIS MISSION!
I WANT TO HELP DEFEAT THE VAMPIRES!!
ALL RIGHT. YOU CAN COME.
NOW GET IN LINE.
YOUR PUNISHMENT WILL COME LATER, YUICHIRO HYAKUYA.

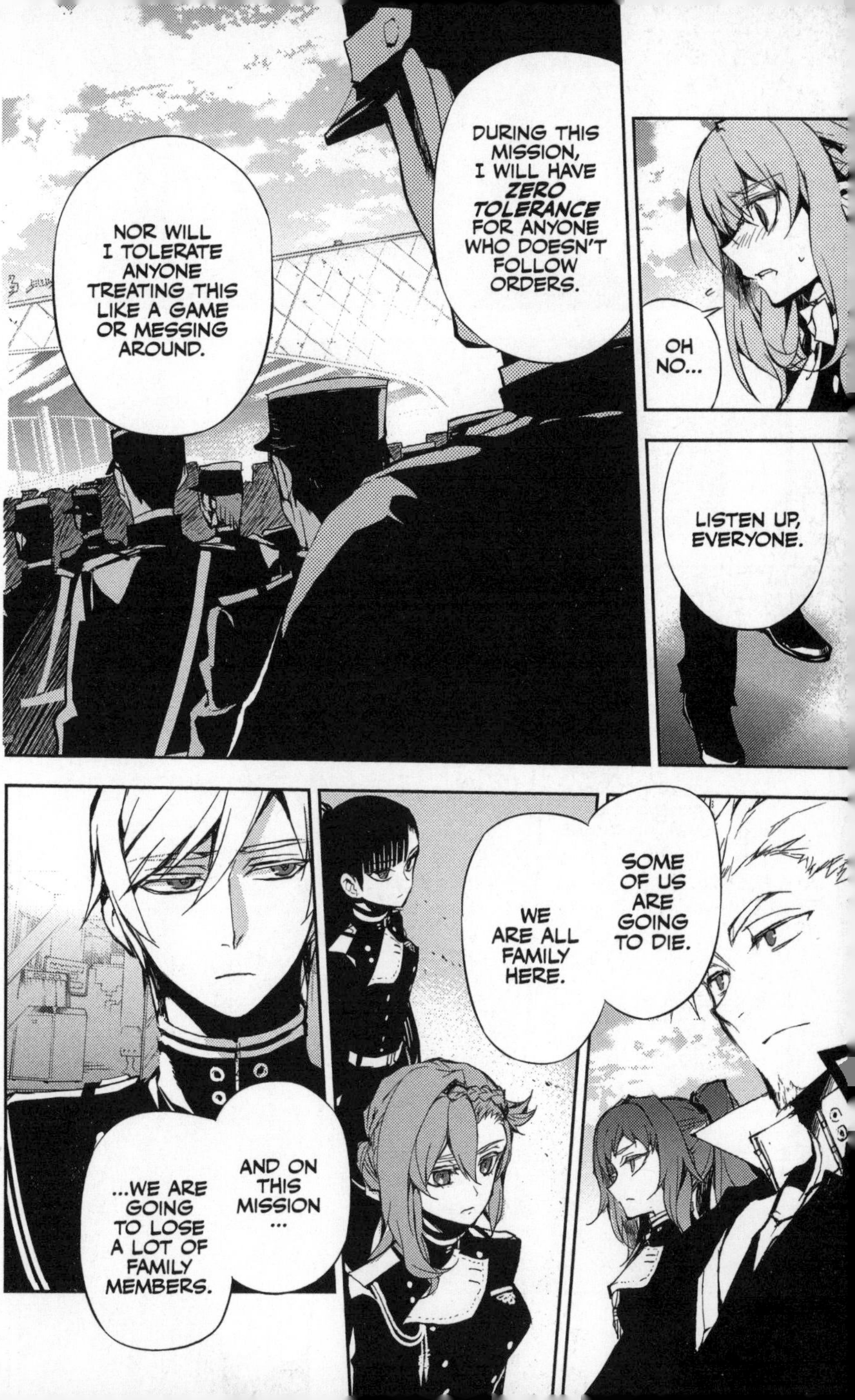
OH NO...
LISTEN UP, EVERYONE.
DURING THIS MISSION, I WILL HAVE ***ZERO TOLERANCE*** FOR ANYONE WHO DOESN'T FOLLOW ORDERS.
NOR WILL I TOLERATE ANYONE TREATING THIS LIKE A GAME OR MESSING AROUND.
SOME OF US ARE GOING TO DIE.
WE ARE ALL FAMILY HERE.
AND ON THIS MISSION ...
...WE ARE GOING TO LOSE A LOT OF FAMILY MEMBERS.

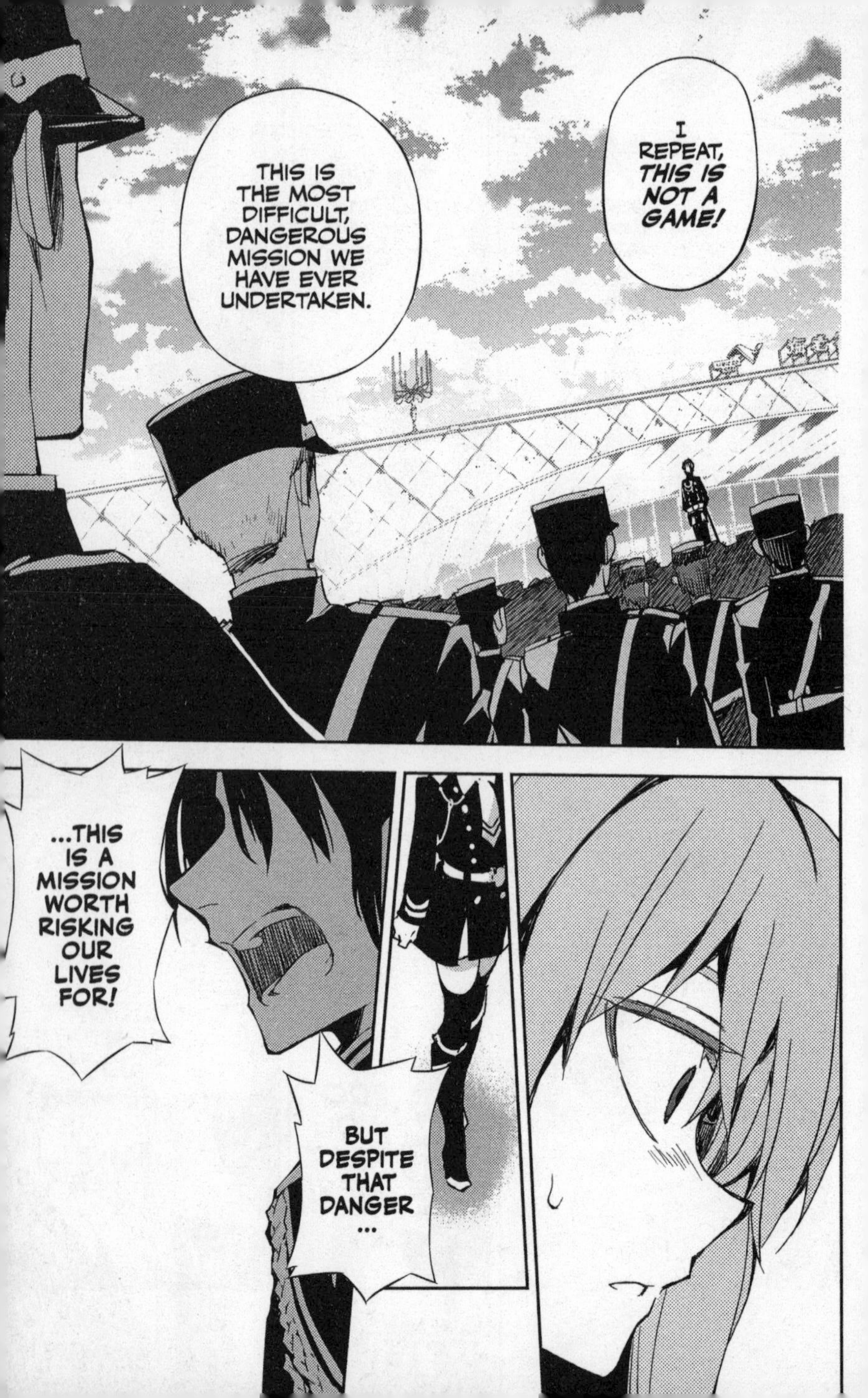
I REPEAT, *THIS IS NOT A GAME!*
THIS IS THE MOST DIFFICULT, DANGEROUS MISSION WE HAVE EVER UNDERTAKEN.
BUT DESPITE THAT DANGER...
...THIS IS A MISSION WORTH RISKING OUR LIVES FOR!

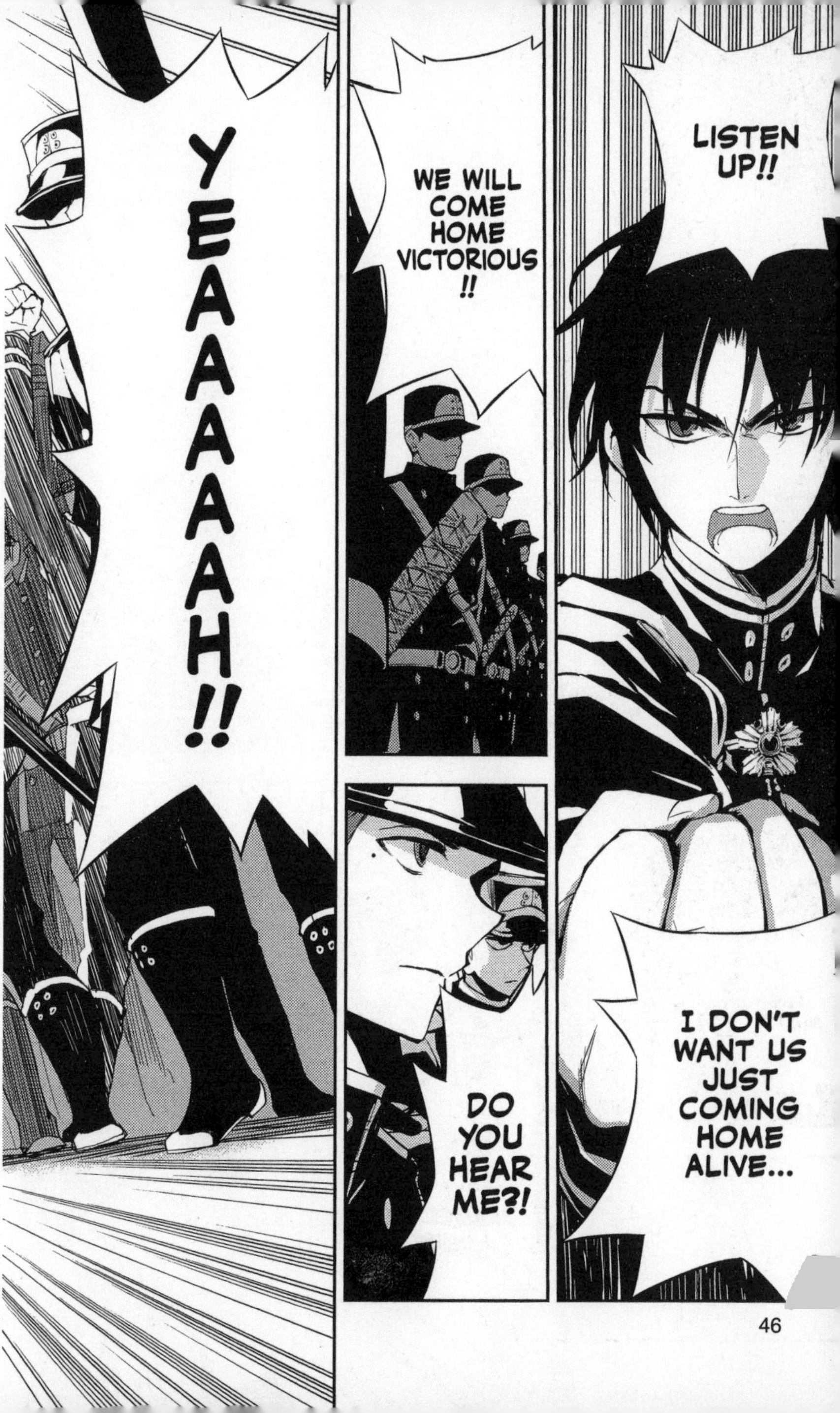
LISTEN UP!!
I DON'T WANT US JUST COMING HOME ALIVE...
WE WILL COME HOME VICTORIOUS!!
DO YOU HEAR ME?!
YEAAAAAH!!

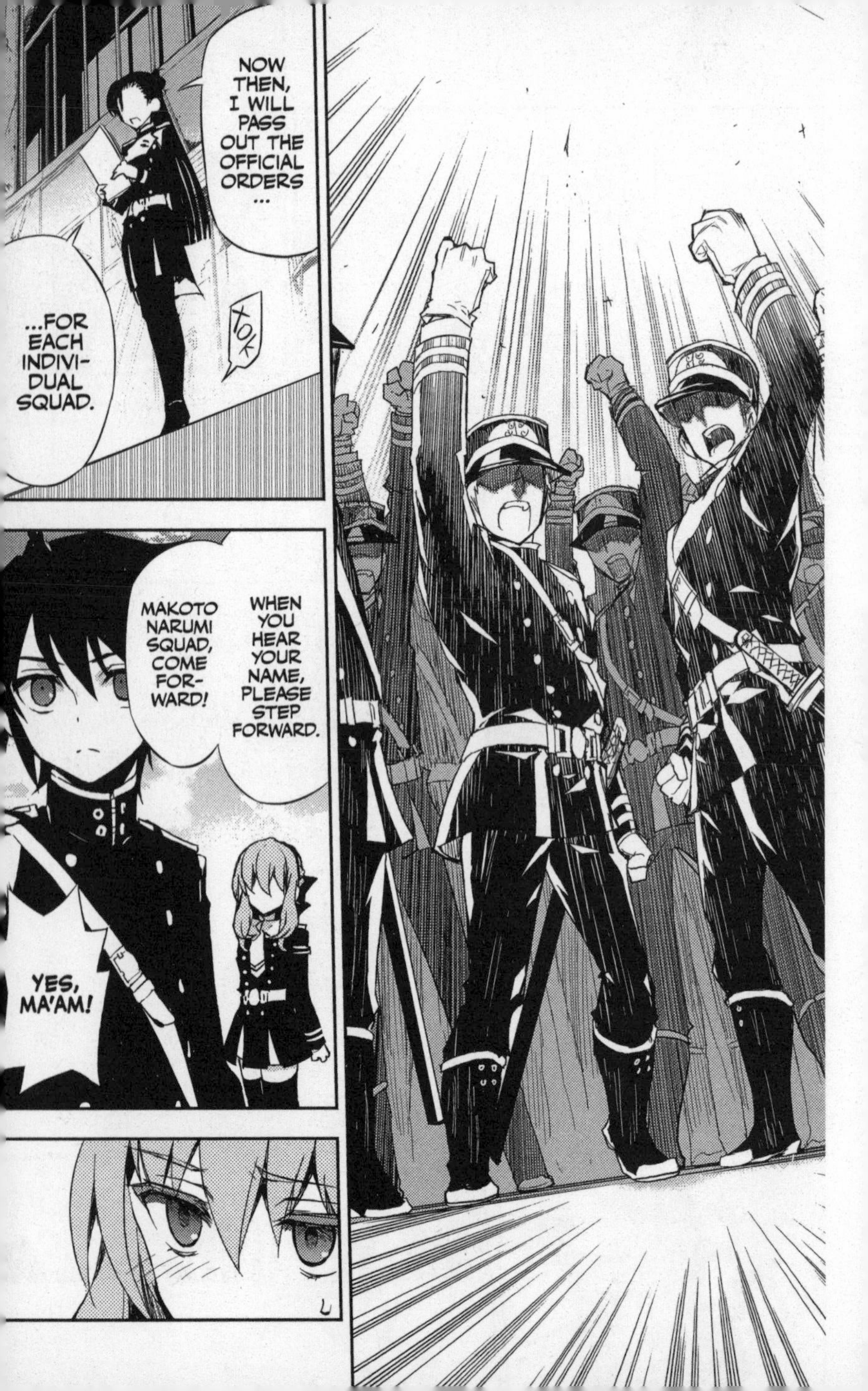
NOW THEN, I WILL PASS OUT THE OFFICIAL ORDERS...
tok
...FOR EACH INDIVIDUAL SQUAD.
WHEN YOU HEAR YOUR NAME, PLEASE STEP FORWARD.
MAKOTO NARUMI SQUAD, COME FORWARD!
YES, MA'AM!

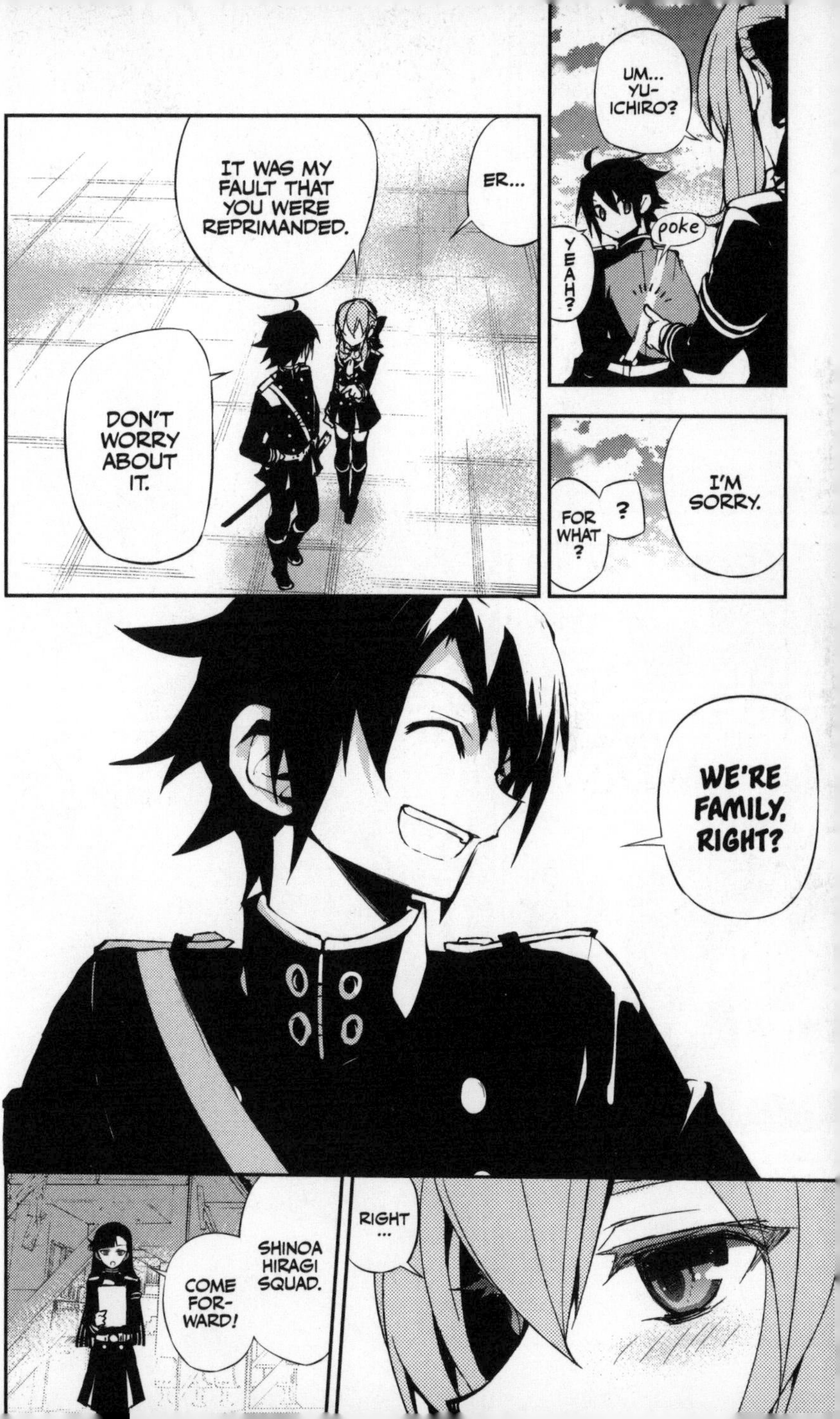
UM... YU-ICHIRO?
poke
YEAH?
I'M SORRY.
FOR WHAT?
?
ER...
IT WAS MY FAULT THAT YOU WERE REPRIMANDED.
DON'T WORRY ABOUT IT.
WE'RE FAMILY, RIGHT?
RIGHT...
SHINOA HIRAGI SQUAD.
COME FOR-WARD!

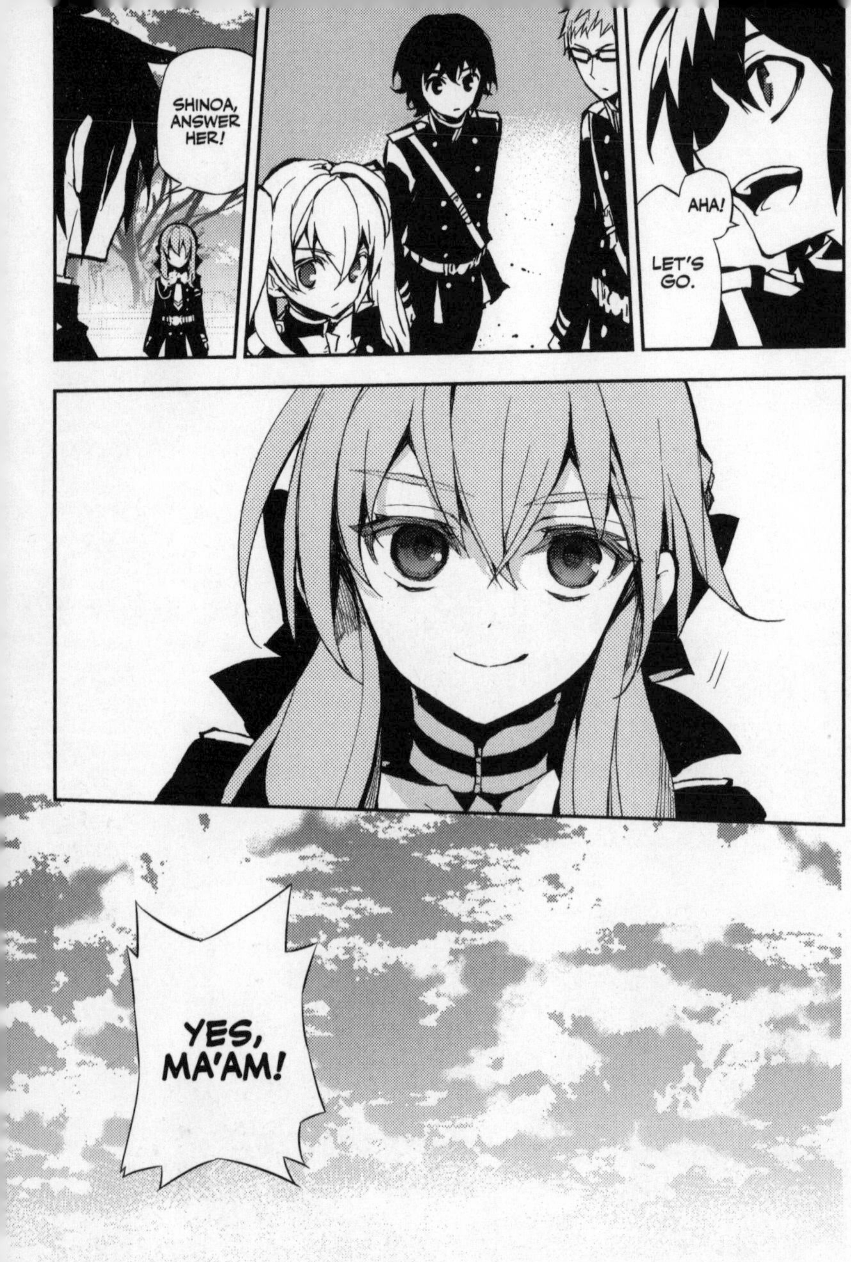
AHA!
LET'S GO.
SHINOA, ANSWER HER!
YES, MA'AM!

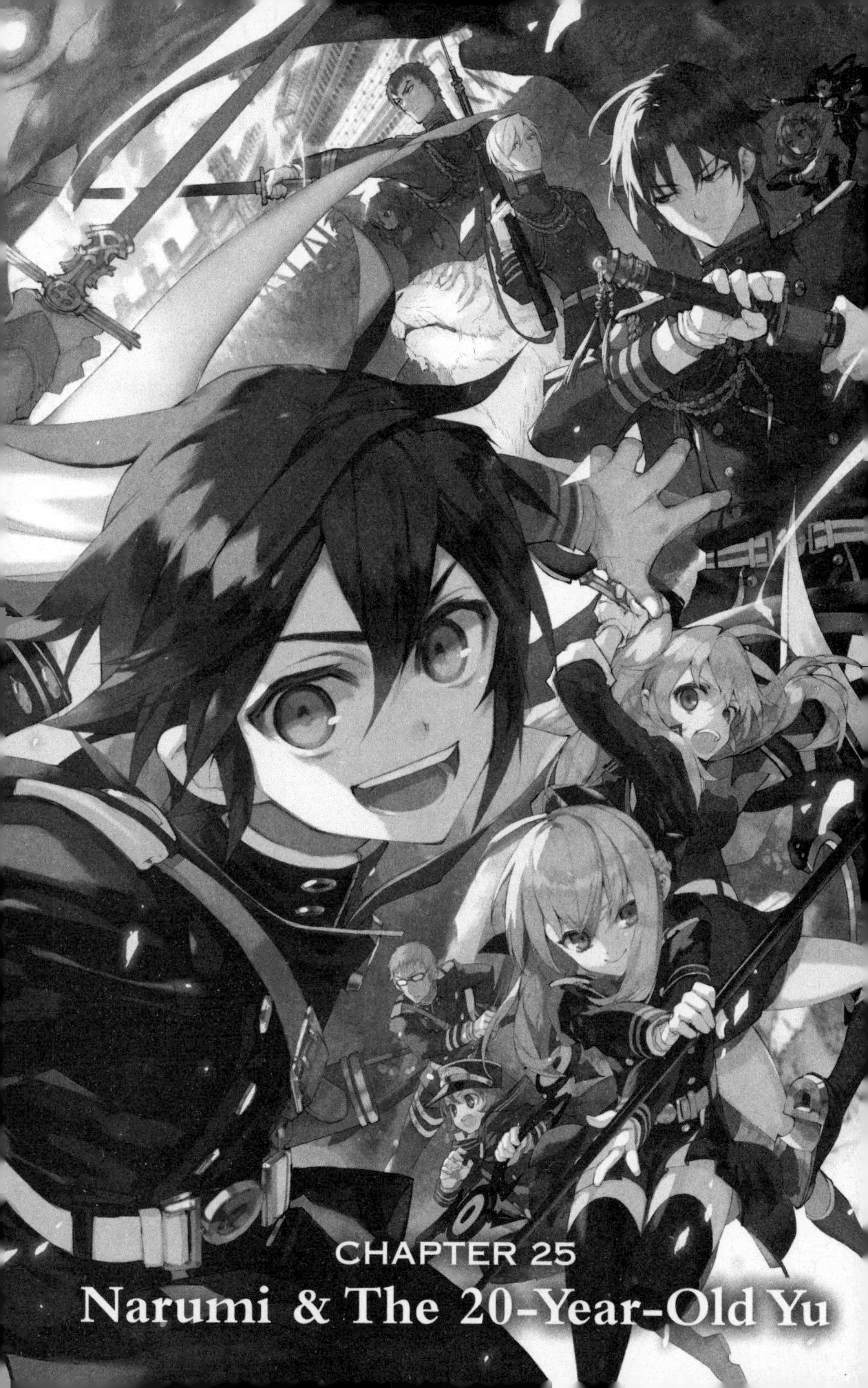

CHAPTER 25

Narumi & The 20-Year-Old Yu

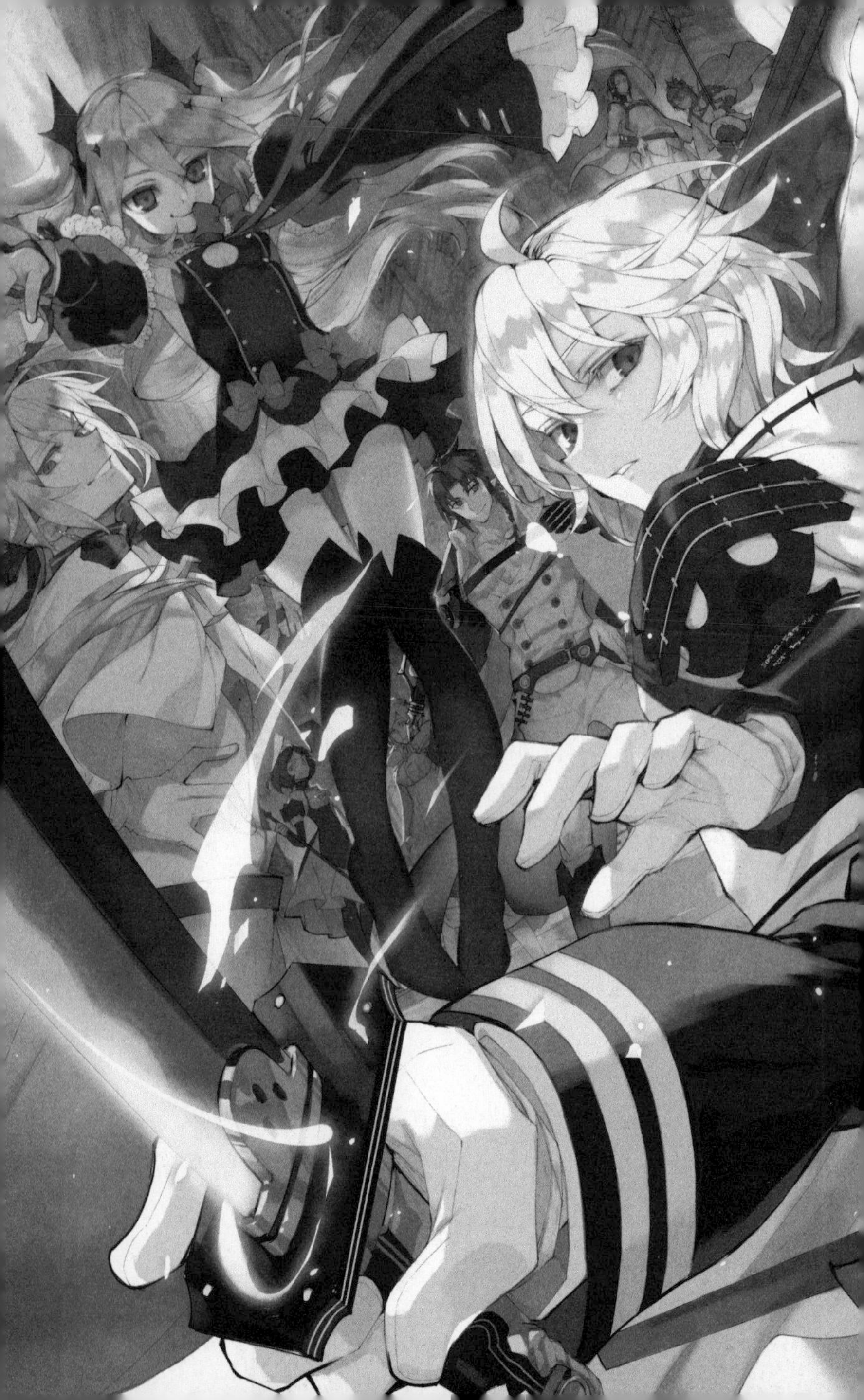

Seraph of the End
VAMPIRE REIGN

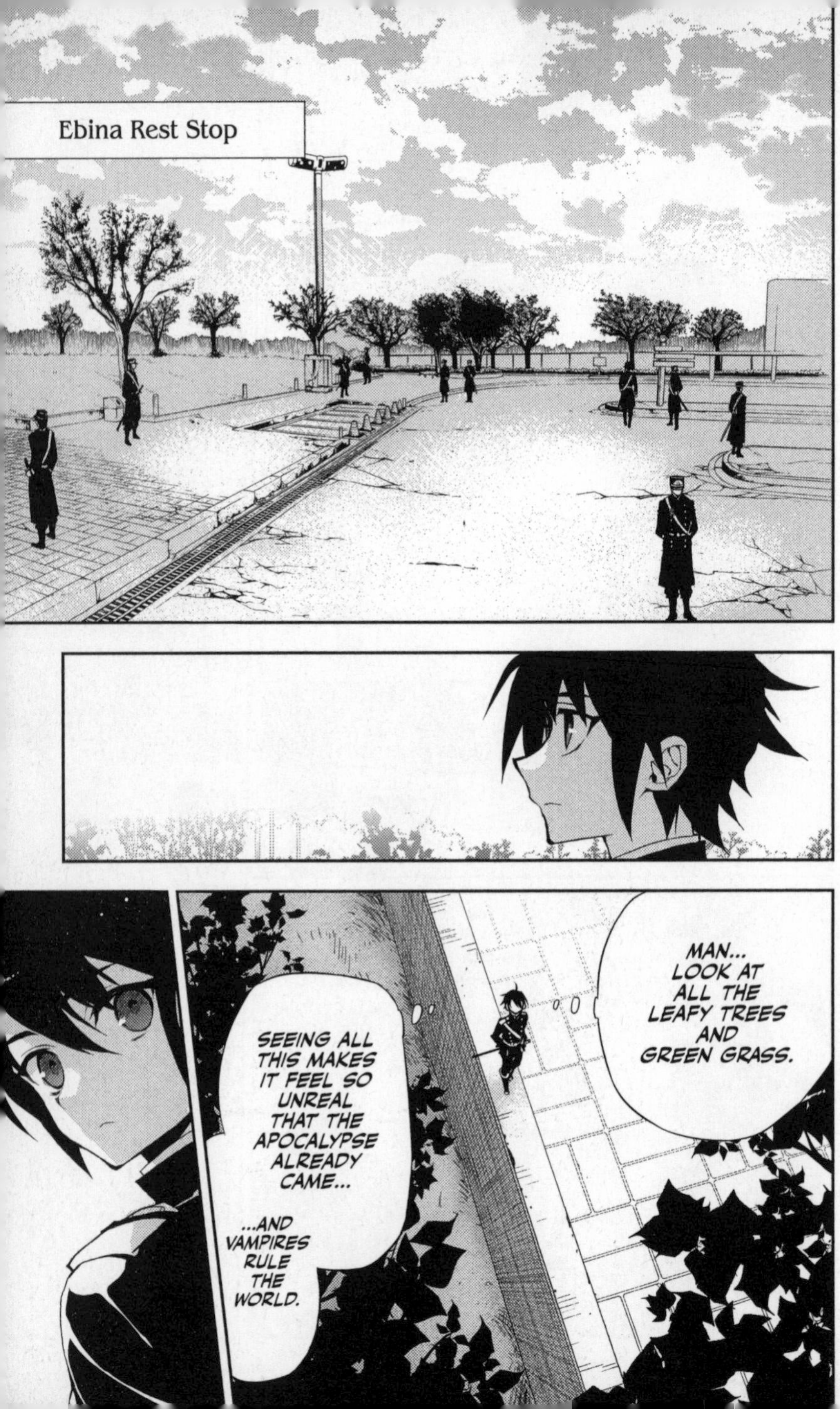
Ebina Rest Stop
MAN... LOOK AT ALL THE LEAFY TREES AND GREEN GRASS.
SEEING ALL THIS MAKES IT FEEL SO UNREAL THAT THE APOCALYPSE ALREADY CAME...
...AND VAMPIRES RULE THE WORLD.

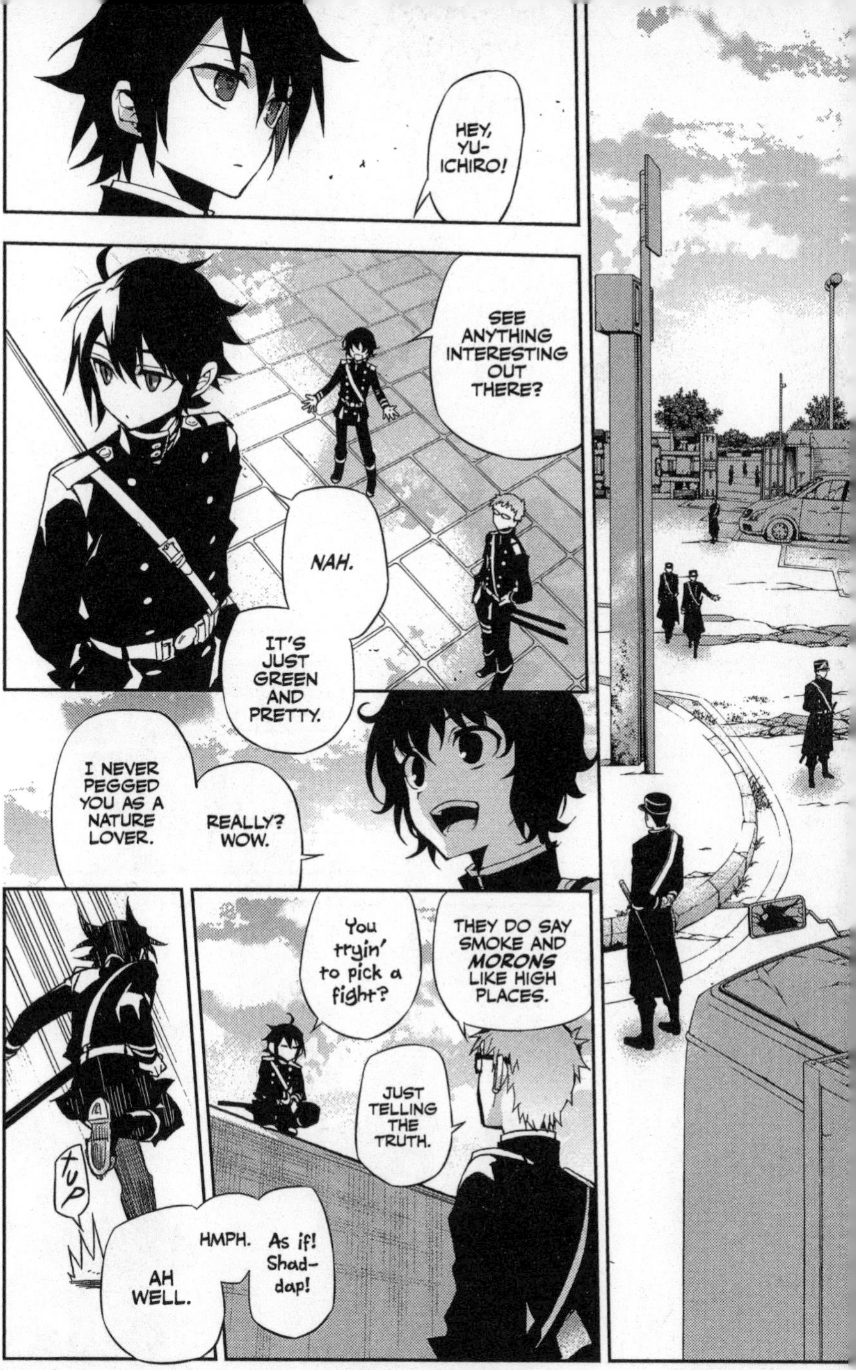
HEY, YU-ICHIRO!
SEE ANYTHING INTERESTING OUT THERE?
NAH.
IT'S JUST GREEN AND PRETTY.
REALLY? WOW.
I NEVER PEGGED YOU AS A NATURE LOVER.
THEY DO SAY SMOKE AND MORONS LIKE HIGH PLACES.
You tryin' to pick a fight?
JUST TELLING THE TRUTH.
As if! Shad-dap!
HMPH.
AH WELL.
TUP

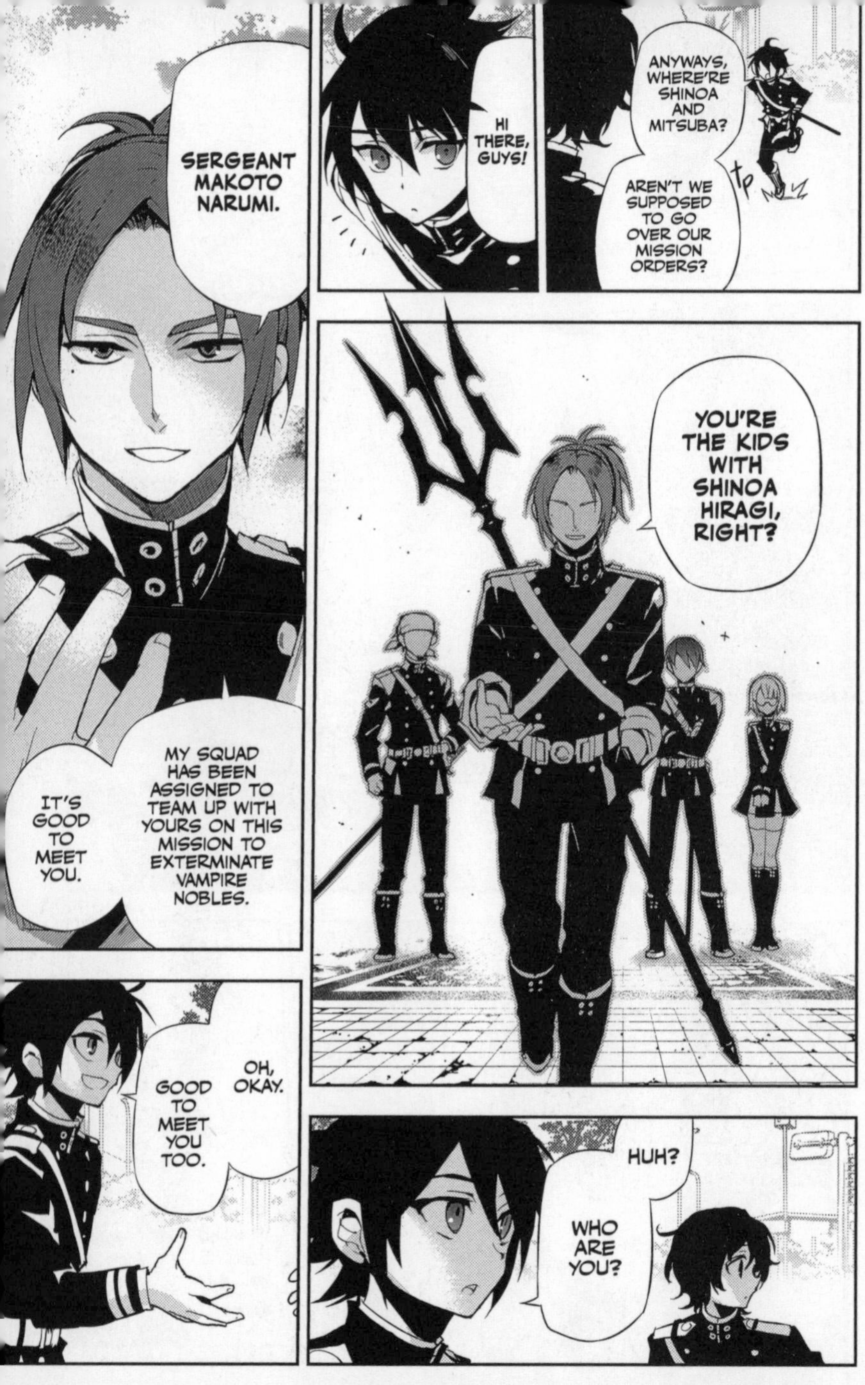
ANYWAYS, WHERE'RE SHINOA AND MITSUBA?
AREN'T WE SUPPOSED TO GO OVER OUR MISSION ORDERS?
TP
HI THERE, GUYS!
YOU'RE THE KIDS WITH SHINOA HIRAGI, RIGHT?
SERGEANT MAKOTO NARUMI.
MY SQUAD HAS BEEN ASSIGNED TO TEAM UP WITH YOURS ON THIS MISSION TO EXTERMINATE VAMPIRE NOBLES.
IT'S GOOD TO MEET YOU.
HUH?
WHO ARE YOU?
OH, OKAY.
GOOD TO MEET YOU TOO.

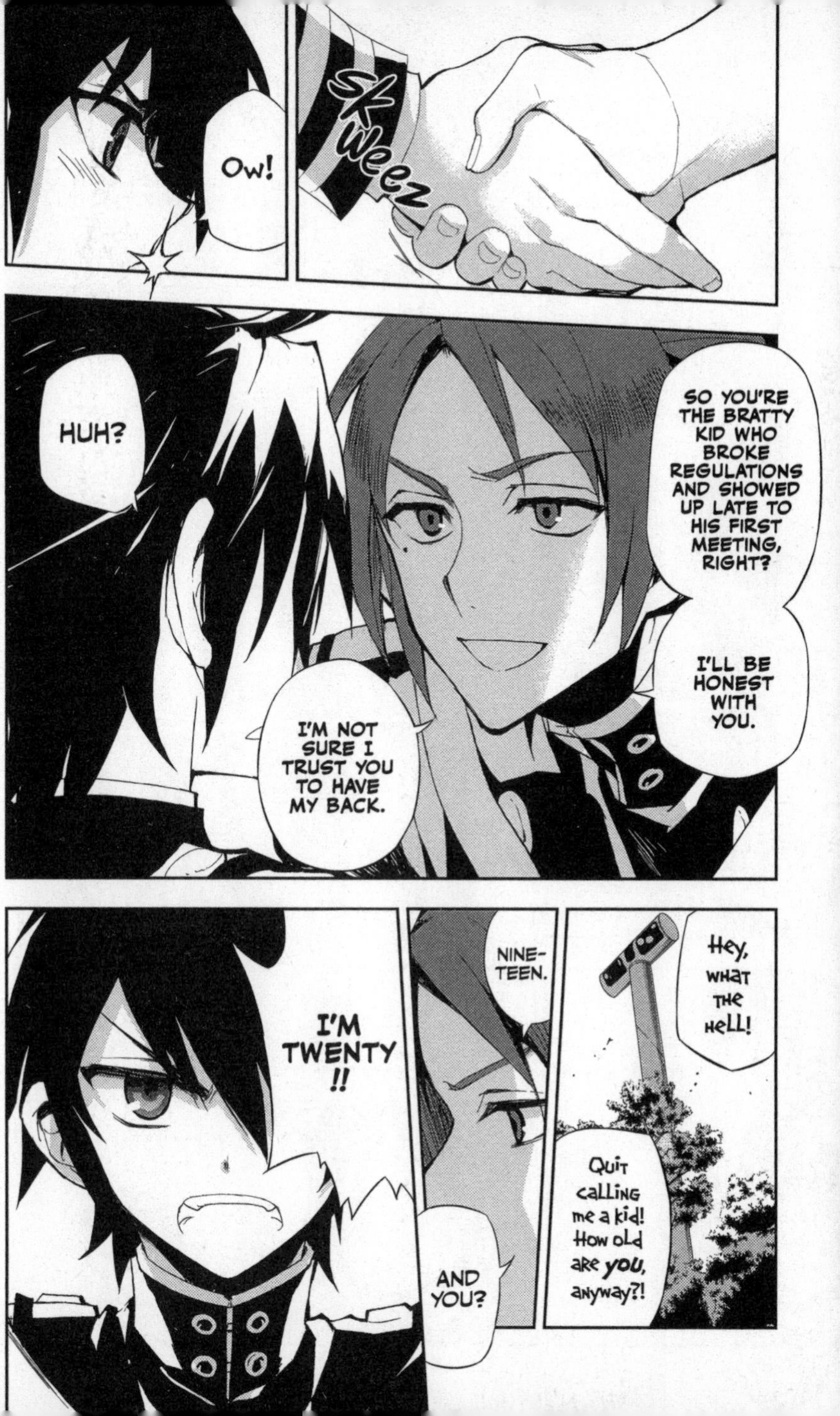
SKWEEZ
Ow!
SO YOU'RE THE BRATTY KID WHO BROKE REGULATIONS AND SHOWED UP LATE TO HIS FIRST MEETING, RIGHT?
I'LL BE HONEST WITH YOU.
I'M NOT SURE I TRUST YOU TO HAVE MY BACK.
HUH?
Hey, what the hell!
Quit calling me a kid! How old are YOU, anyway?!
NINE-TEEN.
AND YOU?
I'M TWENTY!!

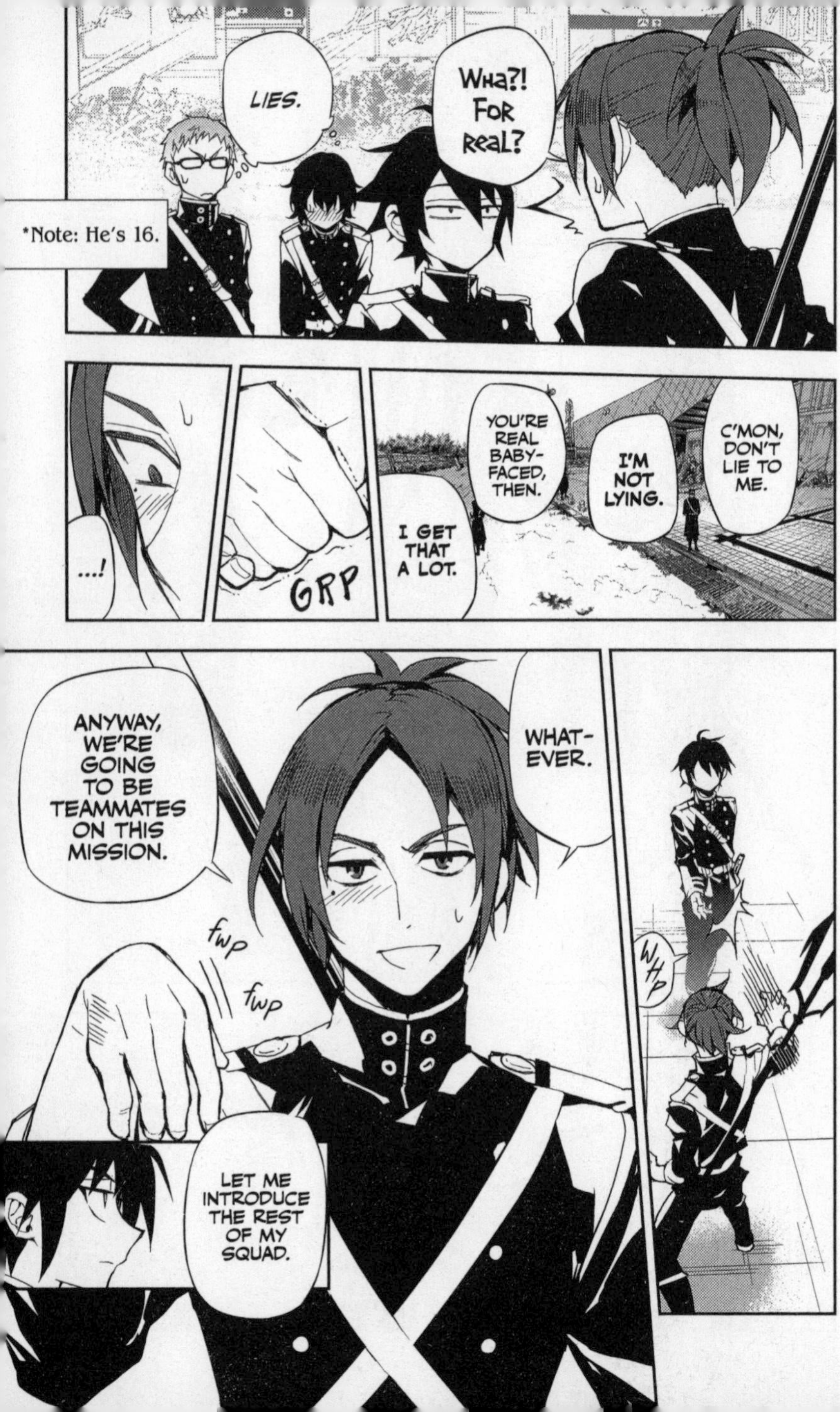
WHA?! FOR REAL?
LIES.
*Note: He's 16.
C'MON, DON'T LIE TO ME.
I'M NOT LYING.
YOU'RE REAL BABY-FACED, THEN.
I GET THAT A LOT.
GRP
...!
WHP
WHAT-EVER.
ANYWAY, WE'RE GOING TO BE TEAMMATES ON THIS MISSION.
fwp
fwp
LET ME INTRODUCE THE REST OF MY SQUAD.

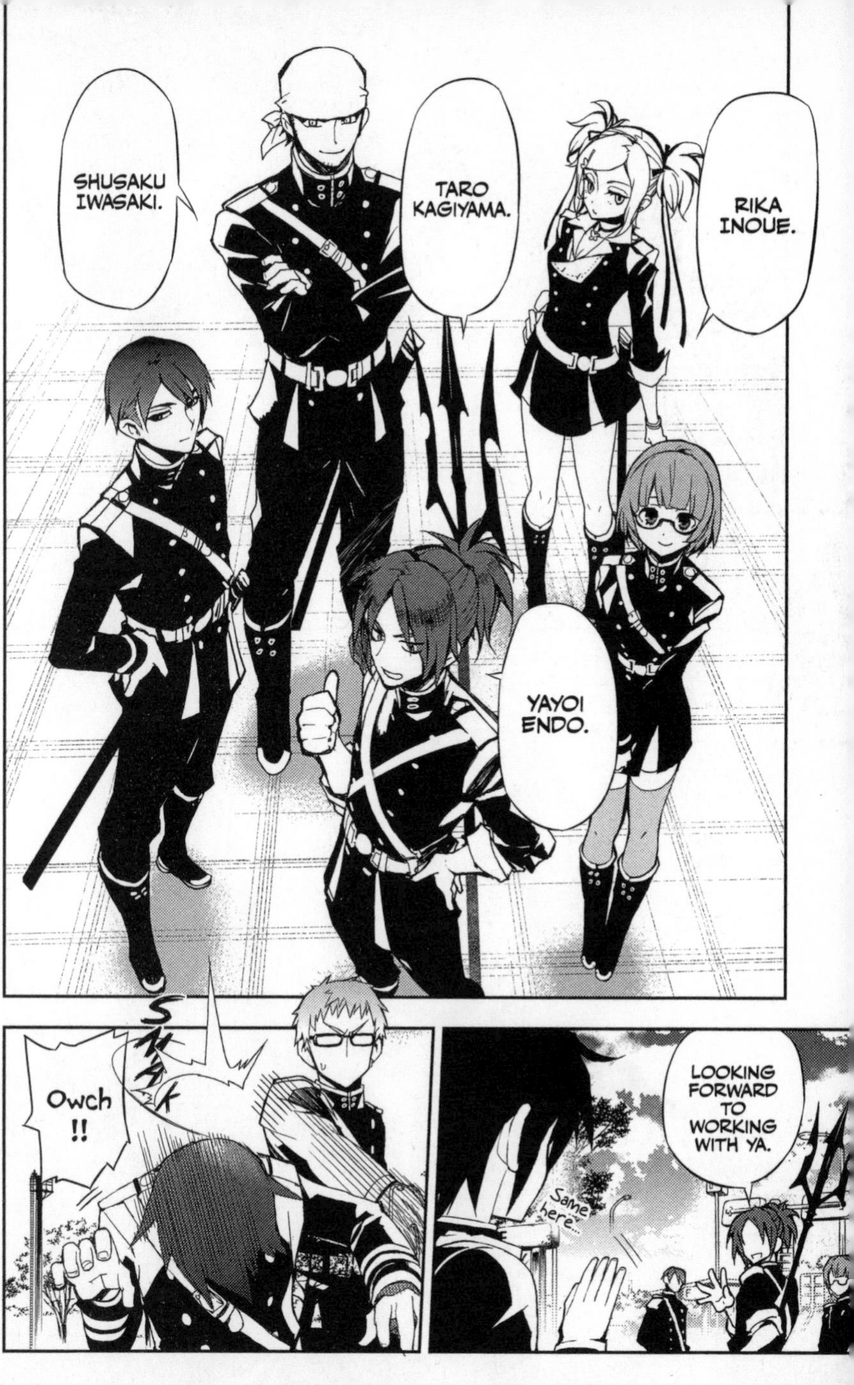
RIKA INOUE.
TARO KAGIYAMA.
SHUSAKU IWASAKI.
YAYOI ENDO.
LOOKING FORWARD TO WORKING WITH YA.
Same here...
SMAK
Owch !!

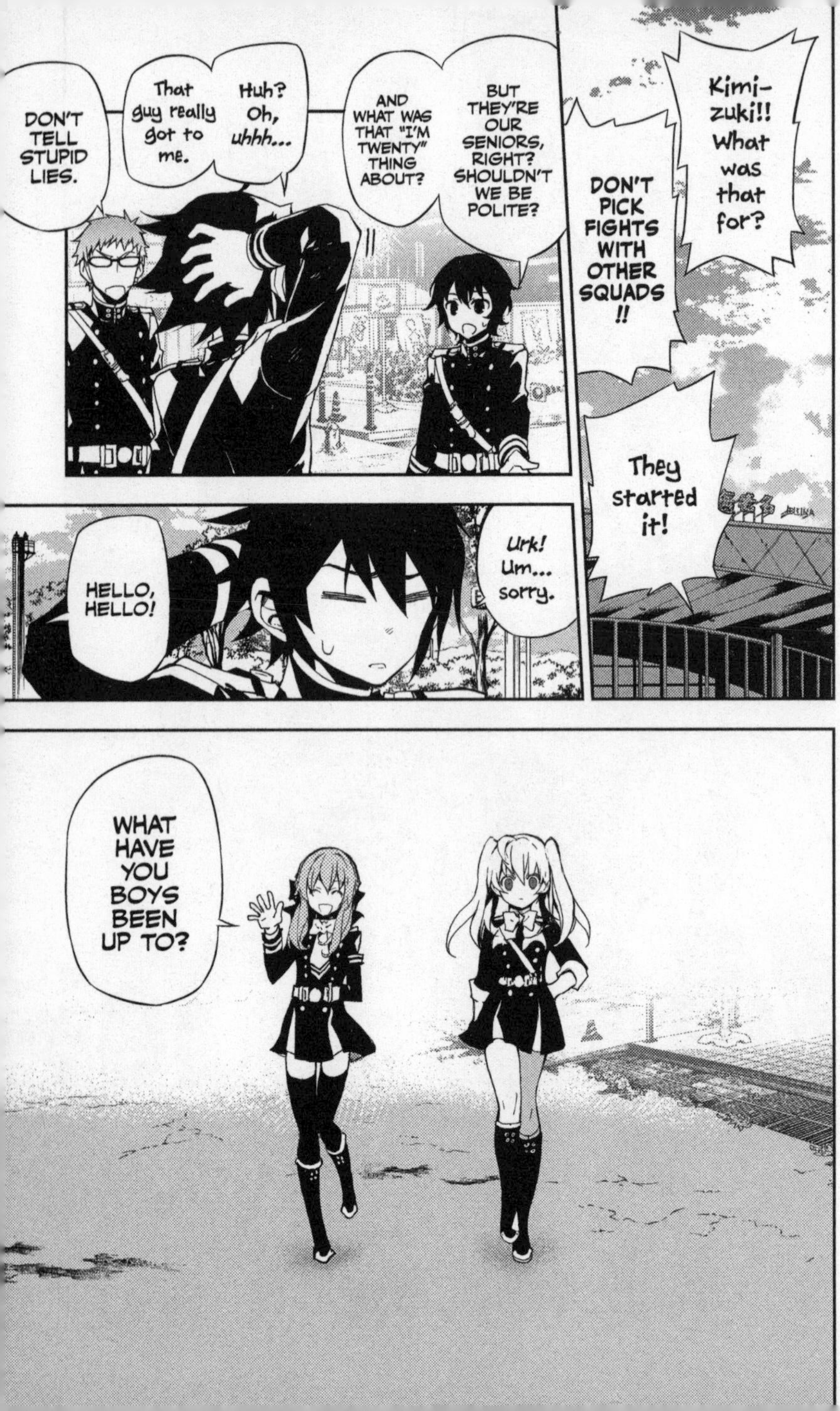

Kimi-zuki!! What was that for?
DON'T PICK FIGHTS WITH OTHER SQUADS!!
They started it!
BUT THEY'RE OUR SENIORS, RIGHT? SHOULDN'T WE BE POLITE?
AND WHAT WAS THAT "I'M TWENTY" THING ABOUT?
Huh? Oh, uhhh...
That guy really got to me.
DON'T TELL STUPID LIES.
Urk! Um... sorry.
HELLO, HELLO!
WHAT HAVE YOU BOYS BEEN UP TO?

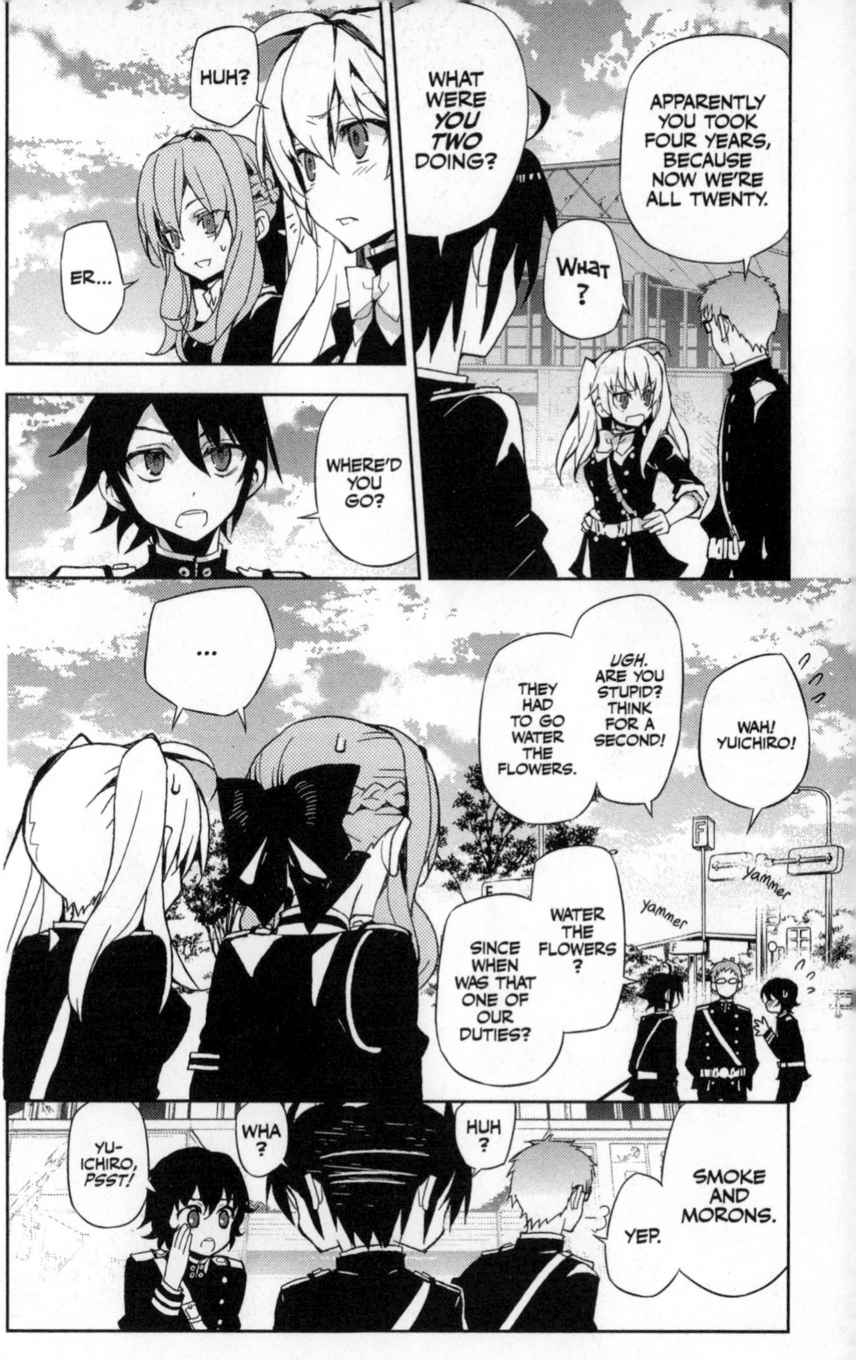

APPARENTLY YOU TOOK FOUR YEARS, BECAUSE NOW WE'RE ALL TWENTY.
WHAT WERE *YOU TWO* DOING?
WHAT?
HUH?
ER...
WHERE'D YOU GO?
WAH! YUICHIRO!
UGH. ARE YOU STUPID? THINK FOR A SECOND!
THEY HAD TO GO WATER THE FLOWERS.
...
yammer
yammer
WATER THE FLOWERS?
SINCE WHEN WAS THAT ONE OF OUR DUTIES?
SMOKE AND MORONS.
YEP.
HUH?
WHA?
YU-ICHIRO, *PSST!*

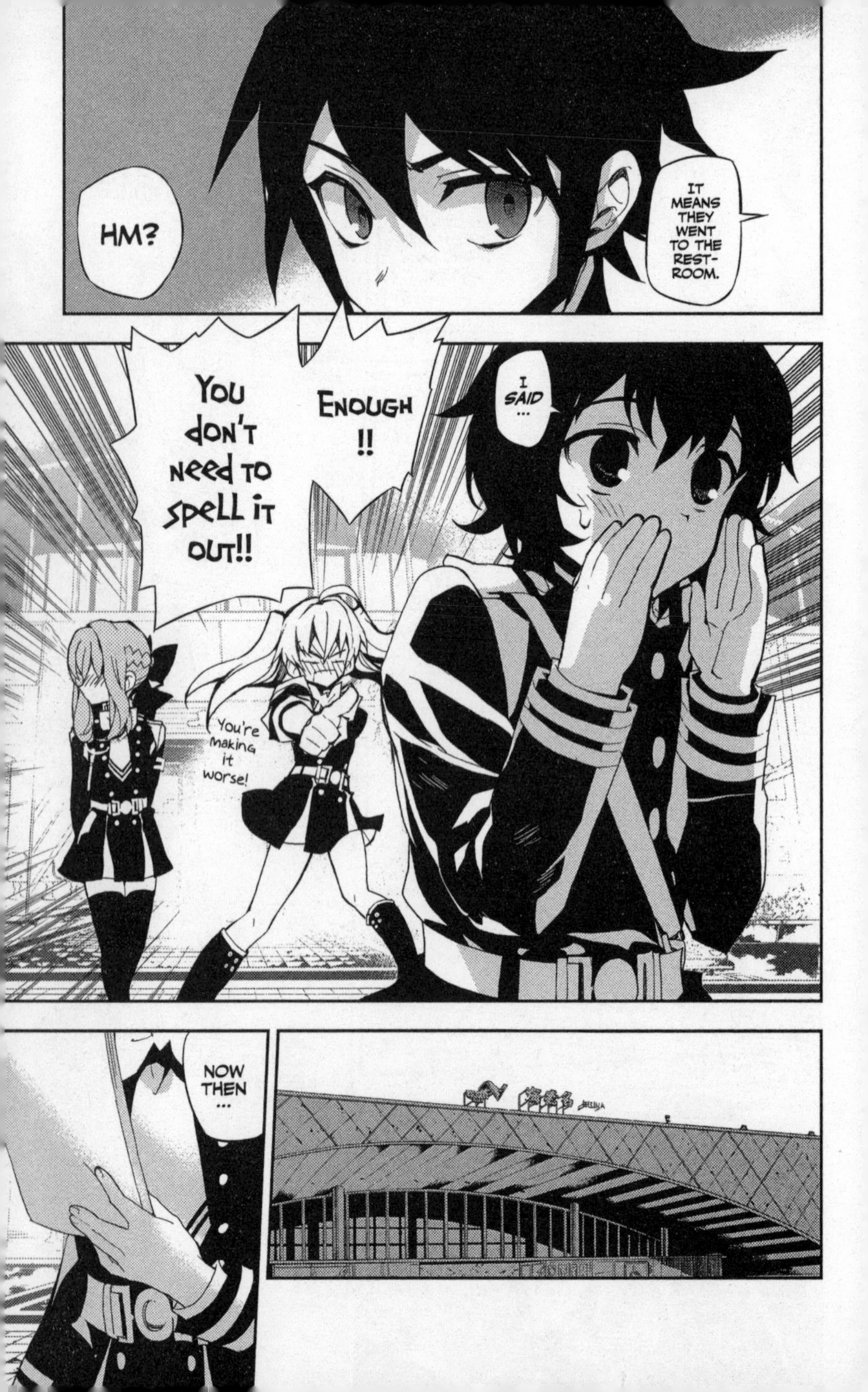
IT MEANS THEY WENT TO THE REST-ROOM.
HM?
I SAID...
ENOUGH!!
You don't need to spell it out!!
You're making it worse!
NOW THEN...

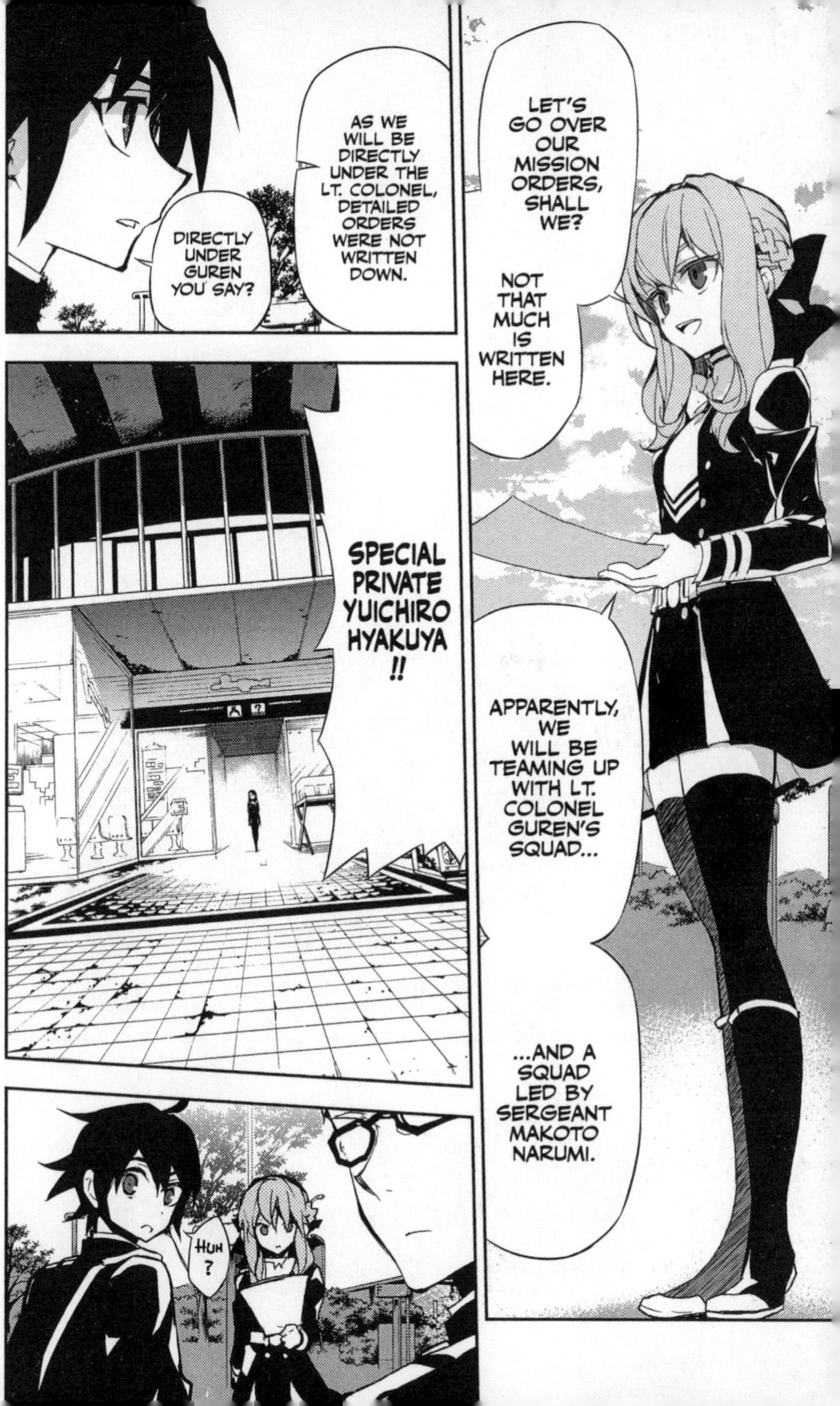
LET'S GO OVER OUR MISSION ORDERS, SHALL WE?
NOT THAT MUCH IS WRITTEN HERE.
APPARENTLY, WE WILL BE TEAMING UP WITH LT. COLONEL GUREN'S SQUAD...
...AND A SQUAD LED BY SERGEANT MAKOTO NARUMI.
AS WE WILL BE DIRECTLY UNDER THE LT. COLONEL, DETAILED ORDERS WERE NOT WRITTEN DOWN.
DIRECTLY UNDER GUREN YOU SAY?
SPECIAL PRIVATE YUICHIRO HYAKUYA !!
HUH ?

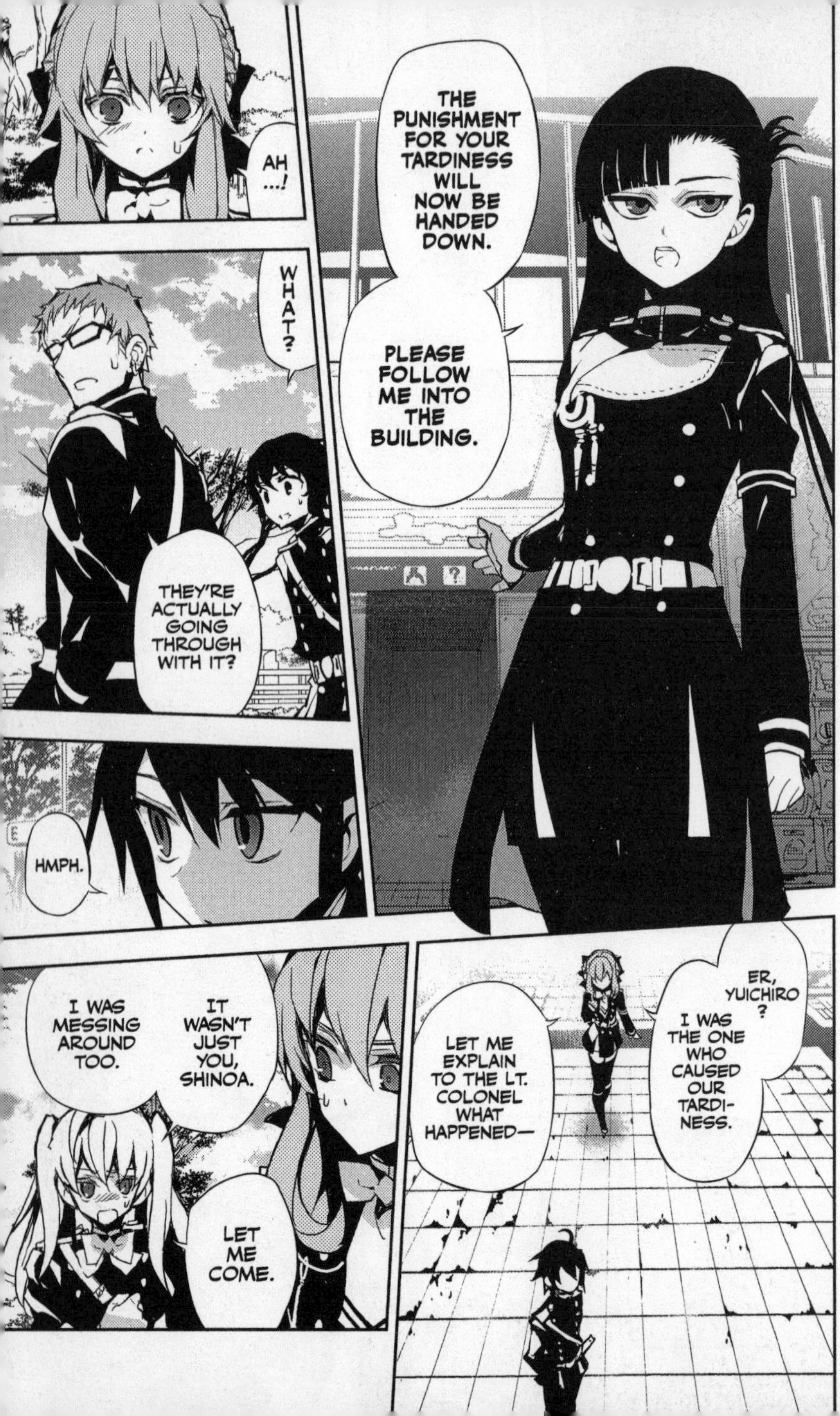
THE PUNISHMENT FOR YOUR TARDINESS WILL NOW BE HANDED DOWN.
PLEASE FOLLOW ME INTO THE BUILDING.
AH ...!
WHAT?
THEY'RE ACTUALLY GOING THROUGH WITH IT?
HMPH.
ER, YUICHIRO? I WAS THE ONE WHO CAUSED OUR TARDI-NESS.
LET ME EXPLAIN TO THE LT. COLONEL WHAT HAPPENED—
IT WASN'T JUST YOU, SHINOA.
I WAS MESSING AROUND TOO.
LET ME COME.

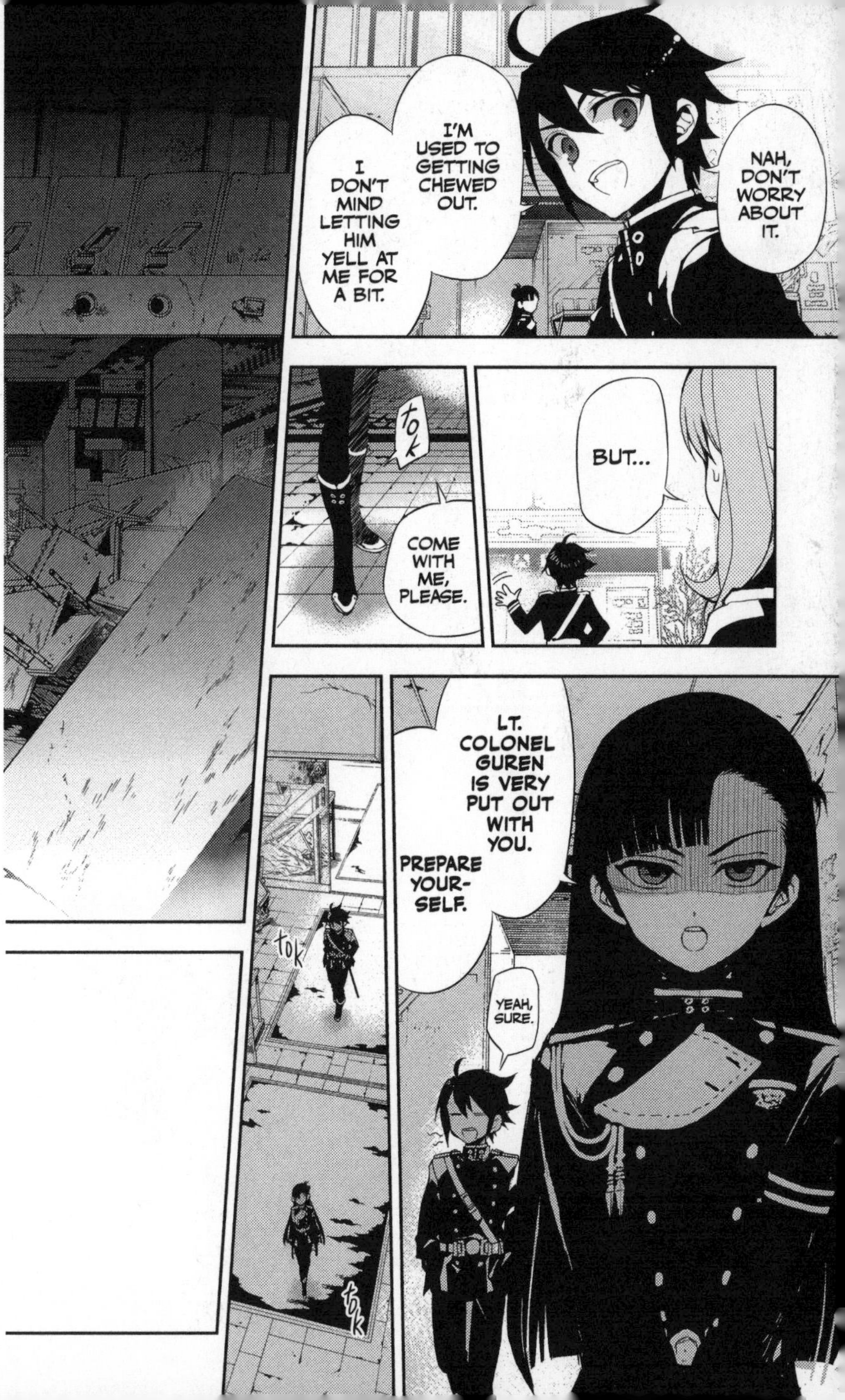
NAH, DON'T WORRY ABOUT IT.
I'M USED TO GETTING CHEWED OUT.
I DON'T MIND LETTING HIM YELL AT ME FOR A BIT.
BUT...
TOK
COME WITH ME, PLEASE.
LT. COLONEL GUREN IS VERY PUT OUT WITH YOU.
PREPARE YOUR-SELF.
YEAH, SURE.
TOK
TOK

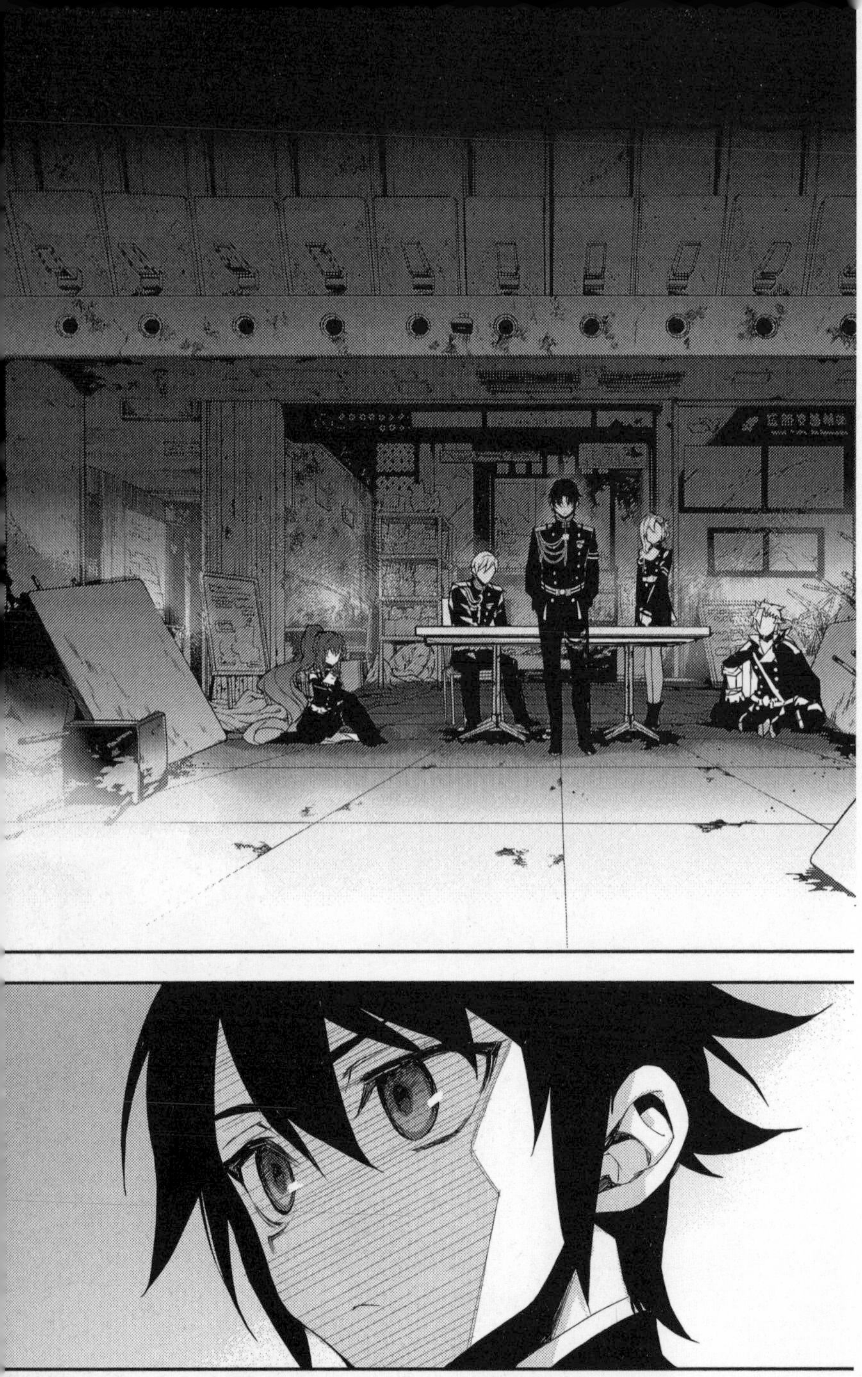

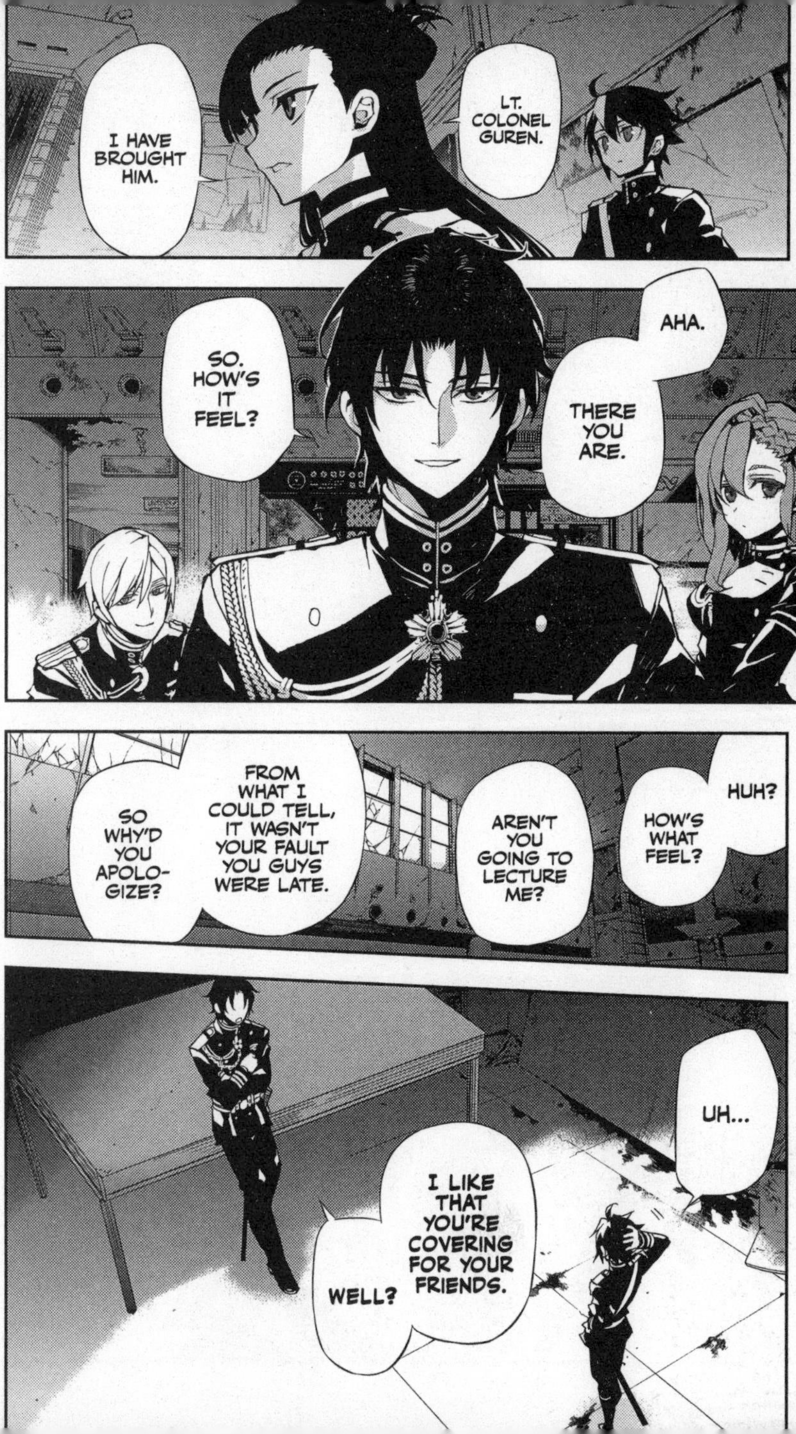
LT. COLONEL GUREN.
I HAVE BROUGHT HIM.
AHA.
THERE YOU ARE.
SO. HOW'S IT FEEL?
HUH?
HOW'S WHAT FEEL?
AREN'T YOU GOING TO LECTURE ME?
FROM WHAT I COULD TELL, IT WASN'T YOUR FAULT YOU GUYS WERE LATE.
SO WHY'D YOU APOLOGIZE?
UH...
I LIKE THAT YOU'RE COVERING FOR YOUR FRIENDS.
WELL?

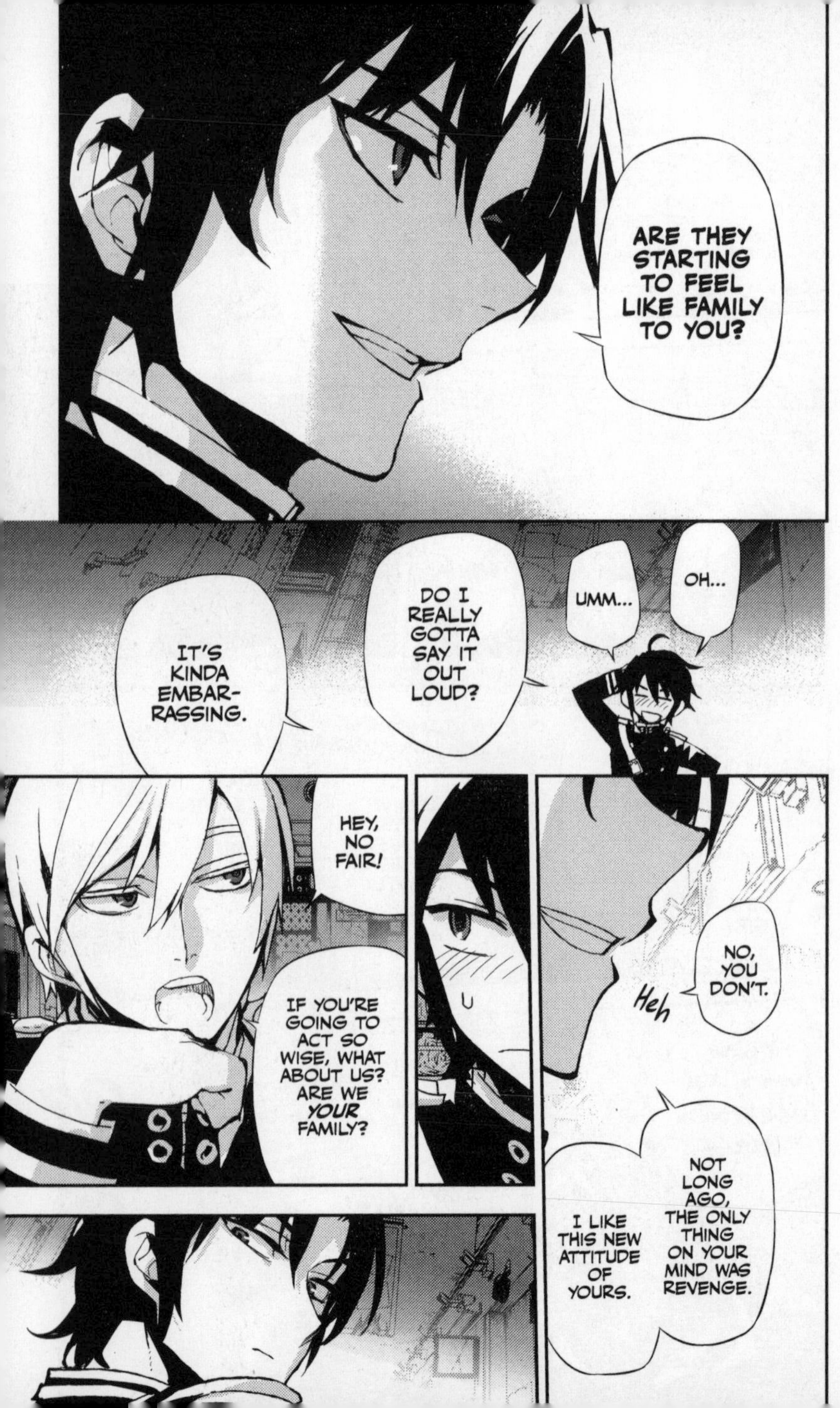
ARE THEY STARTING TO FEEL LIKE FAMILY TO YOU?
OH...
UMM...
DO I REALLY GOTTA SAY IT OUT LOUD?
IT'S KINDA EMBARRASSING.
Heh
NO, YOU DON'T.
NOT LONG AGO, THE ONLY THING ON YOUR MIND WAS REVENGE.
I LIKE THIS NEW ATTITUDE OF YOURS.
HEY, NO FAIR!
IF YOU'RE GOING TO ACT SO WISE, WHAT ABOUT US? ARE WE *YOUR* FAMILY?

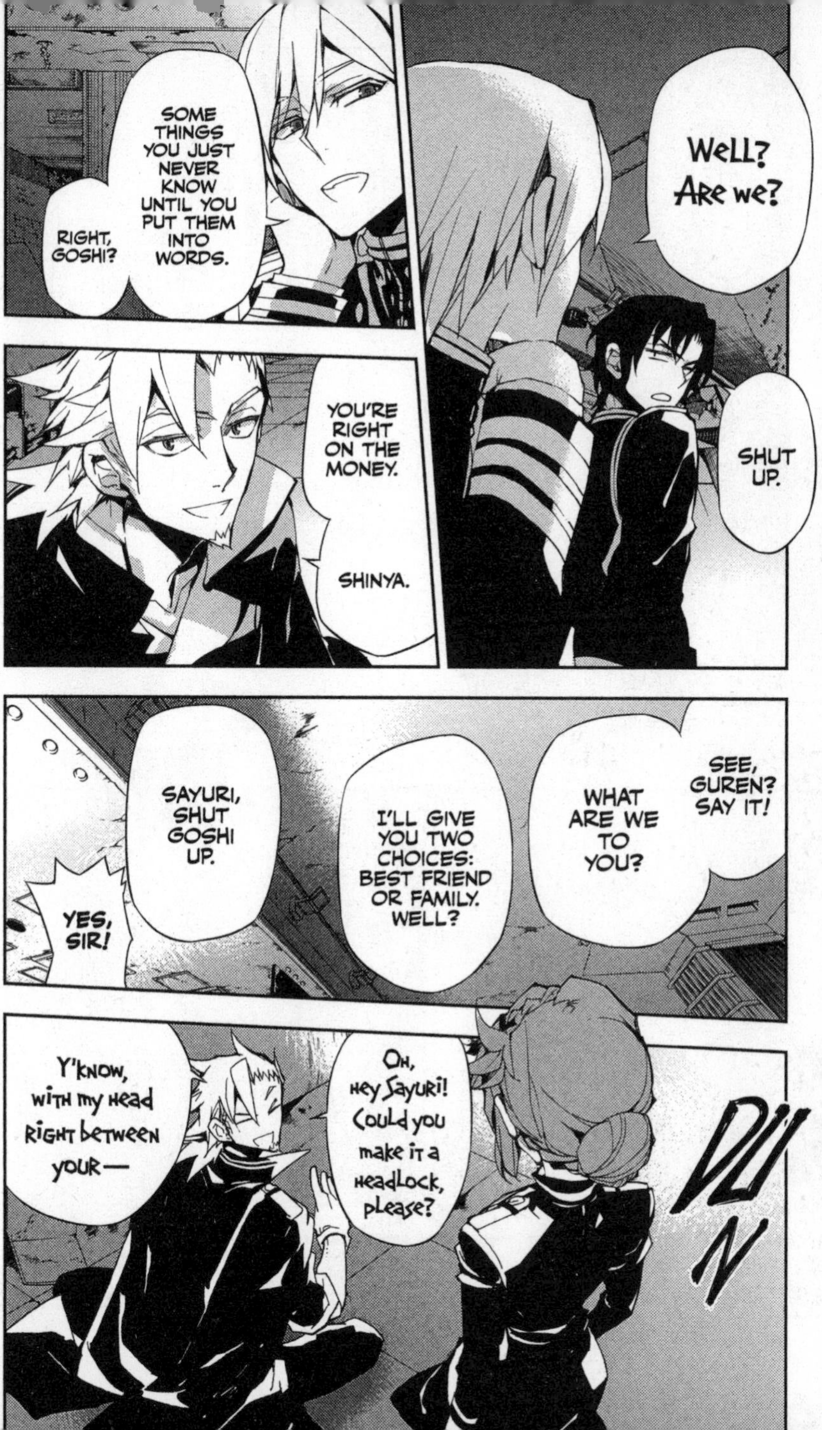
Well? Are we?
SHUT UP.
SOME THINGS YOU JUST NEVER KNOW UNTIL YOU PUT THEM INTO WORDS.
RIGHT, GOSHI?
YOU'RE RIGHT ON THE MONEY.
SHINYA.
SEE, GUREN? SAY IT!
WHAT ARE WE TO YOU?
I'LL GIVE YOU TWO CHOICES: BEST FRIEND OR FAMILY. WELL?
SAYURI, SHUT GOSHI UP.
YES, SIR!
DUN
Oh, hey Sayuri! Could you make it a headlock, please?
Y'know, with my head right between your—

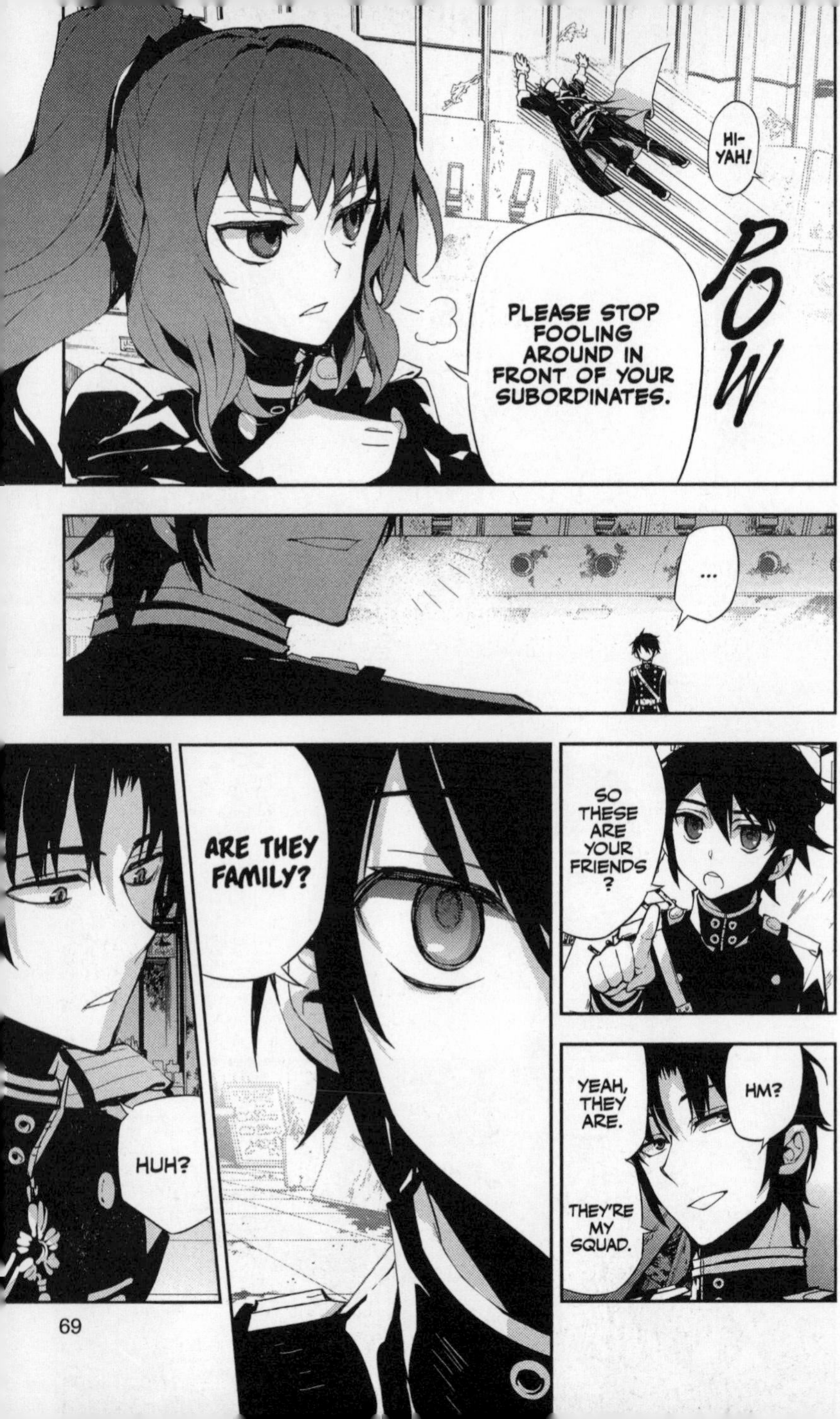
HI-YAH!
POW
PLEASE STOP FOOLING AROUND IN FRONT OF YOUR SUBORDINATES.
...
SO THESE ARE YOUR FRIENDS?
HM?
YEAH, THEY ARE.
THEY'RE MY SQUAD.
ARE THEY FAMILY?
HUH?

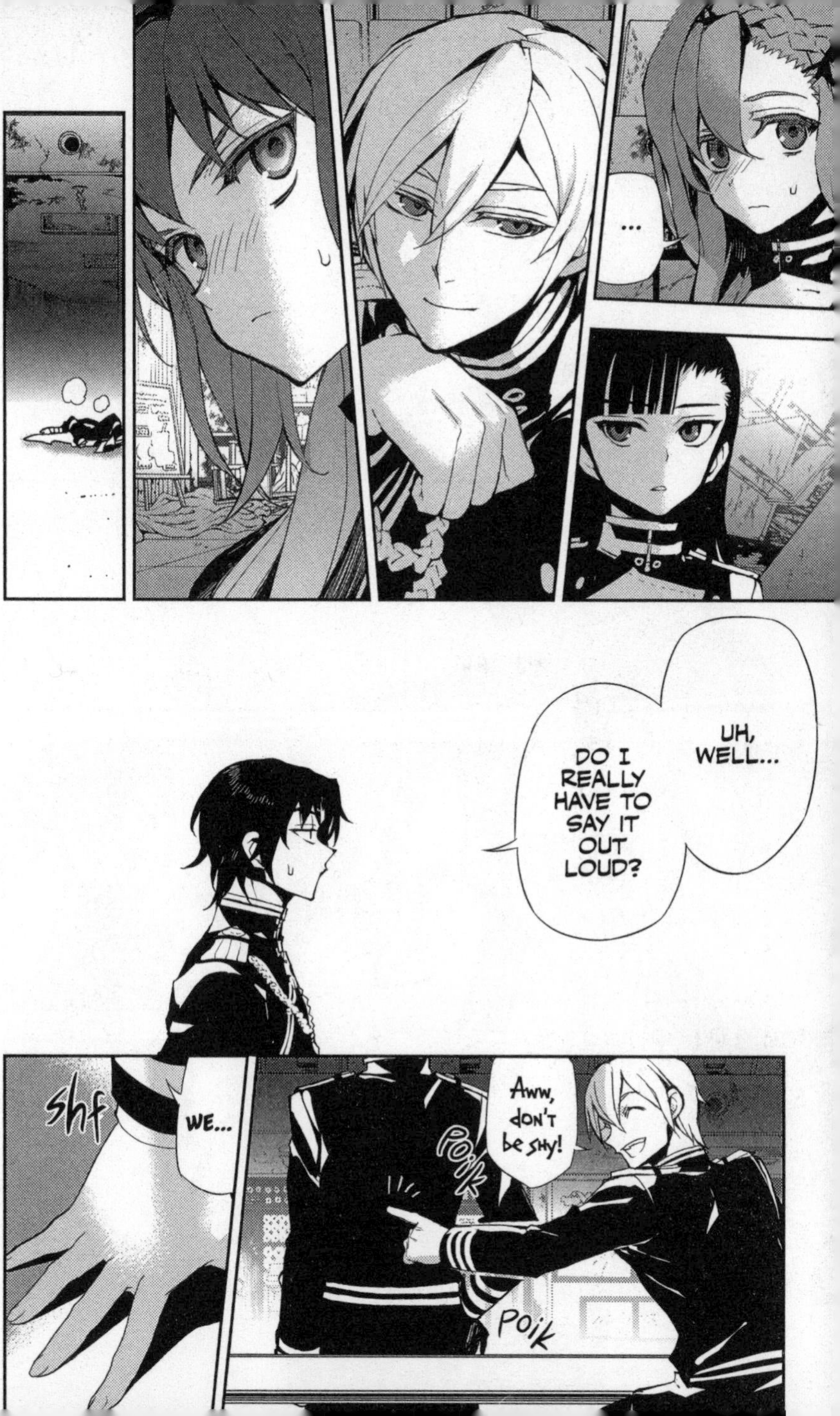
...
......
. . .
UH, WELL...
DO I REALLY HAVE TO SAY IT OUT LOUD?
Aww, don't be shy!
POIK
POIK
WE...
shf

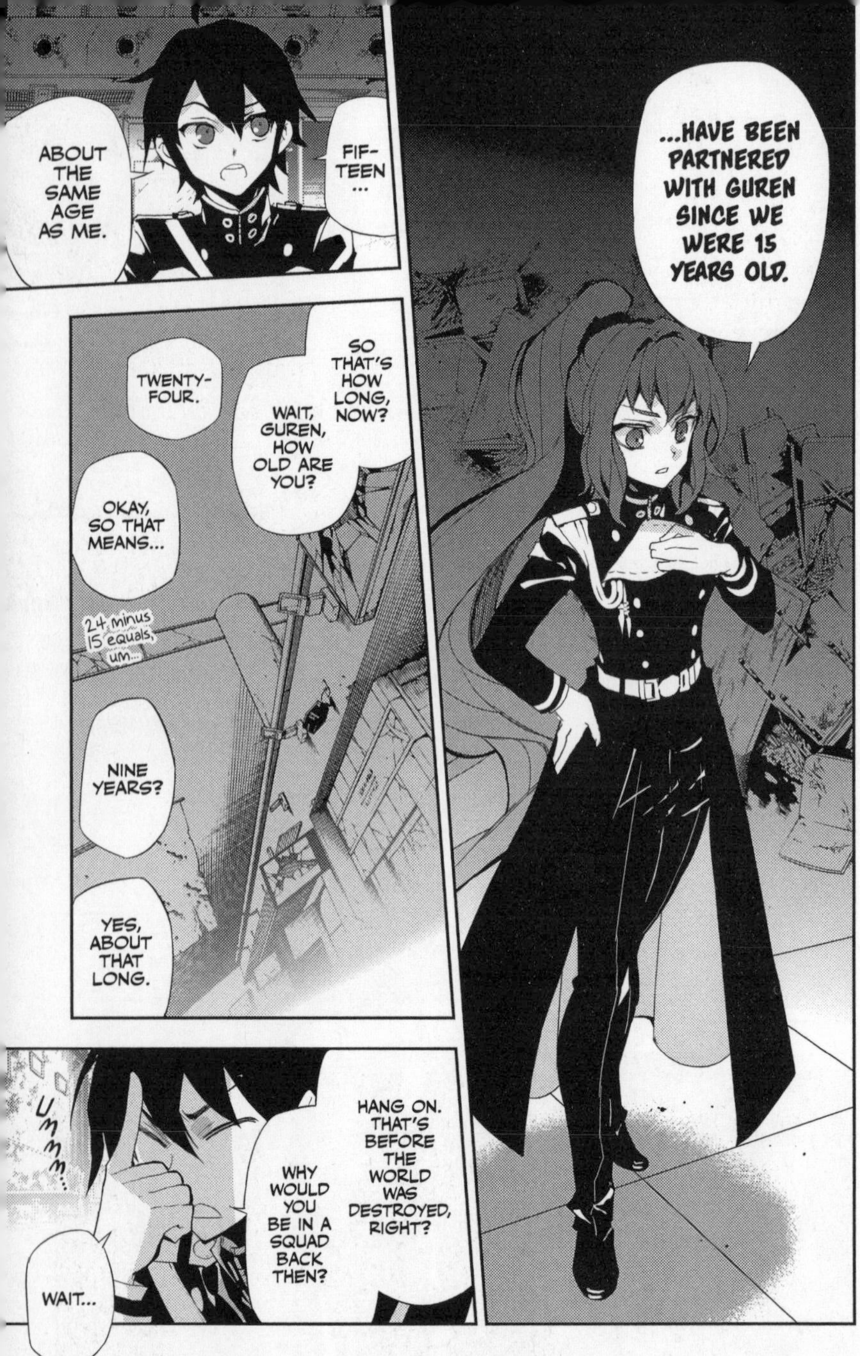
...HAVE BEEN PARTNERED WITH GUREN SINCE WE WERE 15 YEARS OLD.
FIF-TEEN...
ABOUT THE SAME AGE AS ME.
SO THAT'S HOW LONG, NOW?
WAIT, GUREN, HOW OLD ARE YOU?
TWENTY-FOUR.
OKAY, SO THAT MEANS...
24 minus 15 equals, um...
NINE YEARS?
YES, ABOUT THAT LONG.
HANG ON. THAT'S BEFORE THE WORLD WAS DESTROYED, RIGHT?
WHY WOULD YOU BE IN A SQUAD BACK THEN?
UMMM...
WAIT...

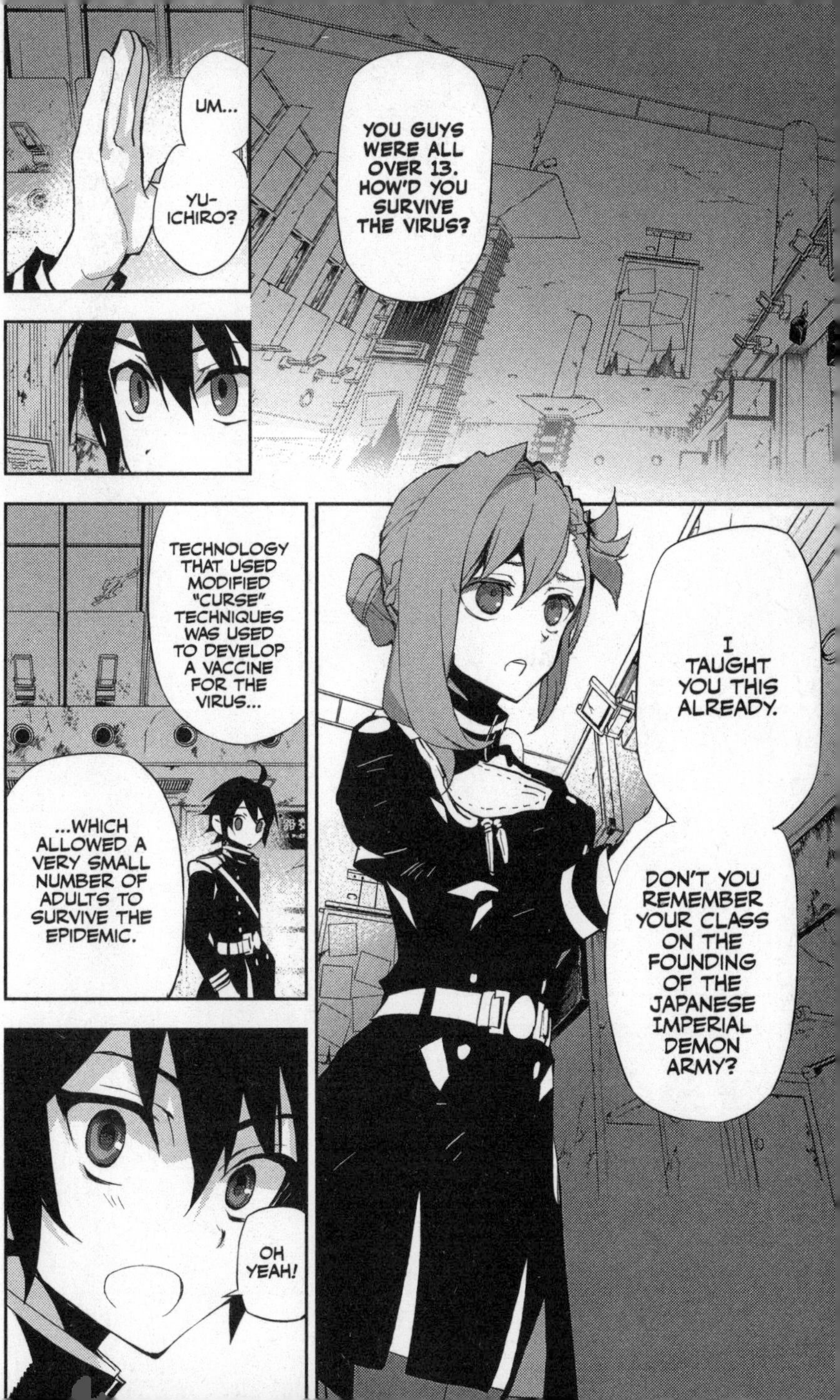
YOU GUYS WERE ALL OVER 13. HOW'D YOU SURVIVE THE VIRUS?
UM...
YU-ICHIRO?
I TAUGHT YOU THIS ALREADY.
DON'T YOU REMEMBER YOUR CLASS ON THE FOUNDING OF THE JAPANESE IMPERIAL DEMON ARMY?
TECHNOLOGY THAT USED MODIFIED "CURSE" TECHNIQUES WAS USED TO DEVELOP A VACCINE FOR THE VIRUS...
...WHICH ALLOWED A VERY SMALL NUMBER OF ADULTS TO SURVIVE THE EPIDEMIC.
OH YEAH!

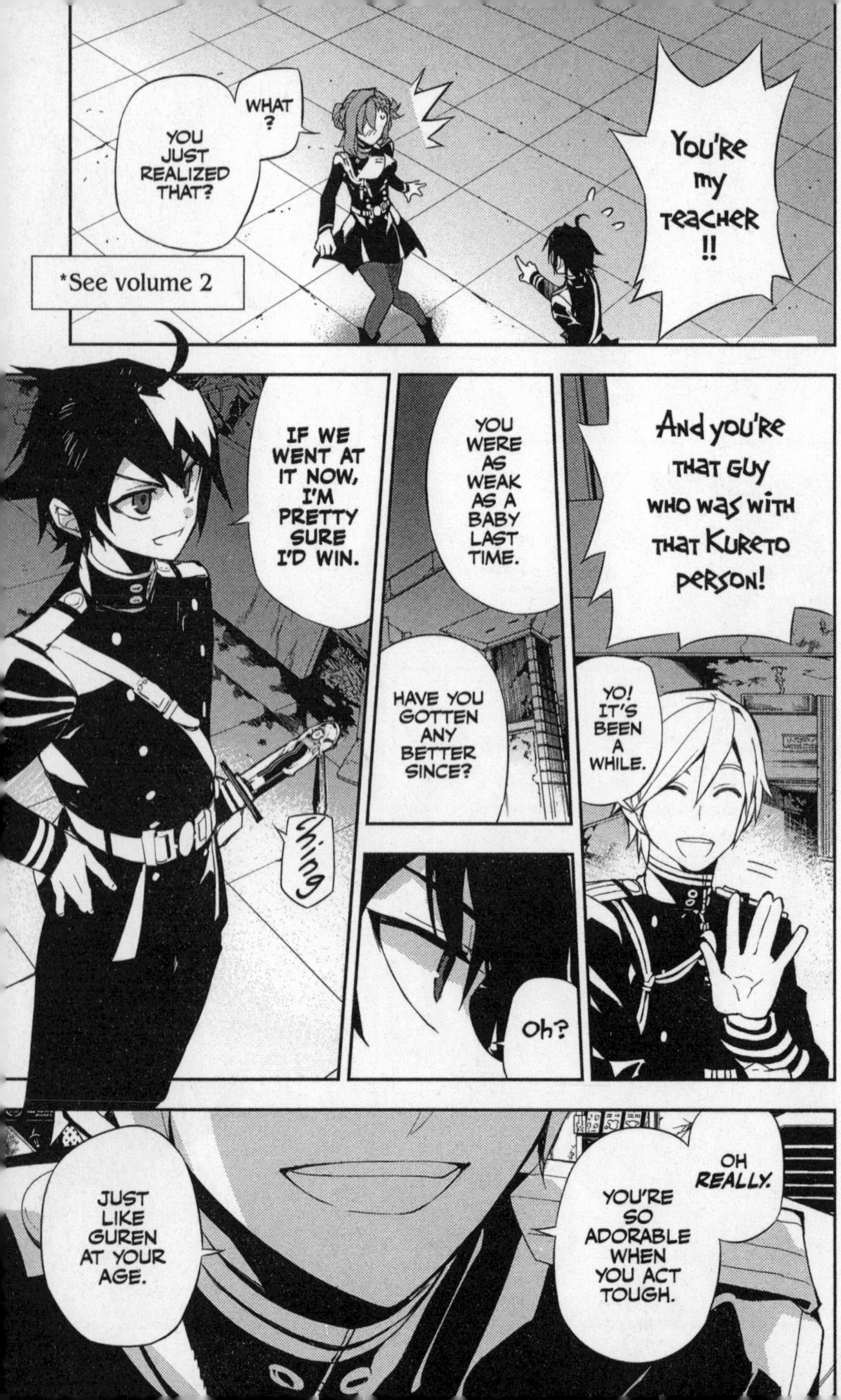
You're my teacher!!
WHAT?
YOU JUST REALIZED THAT?
*See volume 2
And you're that guy who was with that Kureto person!
YO! IT'S BEEN A WHILE.
YOU WERE AS WEAK AS A BABY LAST TIME.
HAVE YOU GOTTEN ANY BETTER SINCE?
Oh?
IF WE WENT AT IT NOW, I'M PRETTY SURE I'D WIN.
Ching
OH REALLY.
YOU'RE SO ADORABLE WHEN YOU ACT TOUGH.
JUST LIKE GUREN AT YOUR AGE.

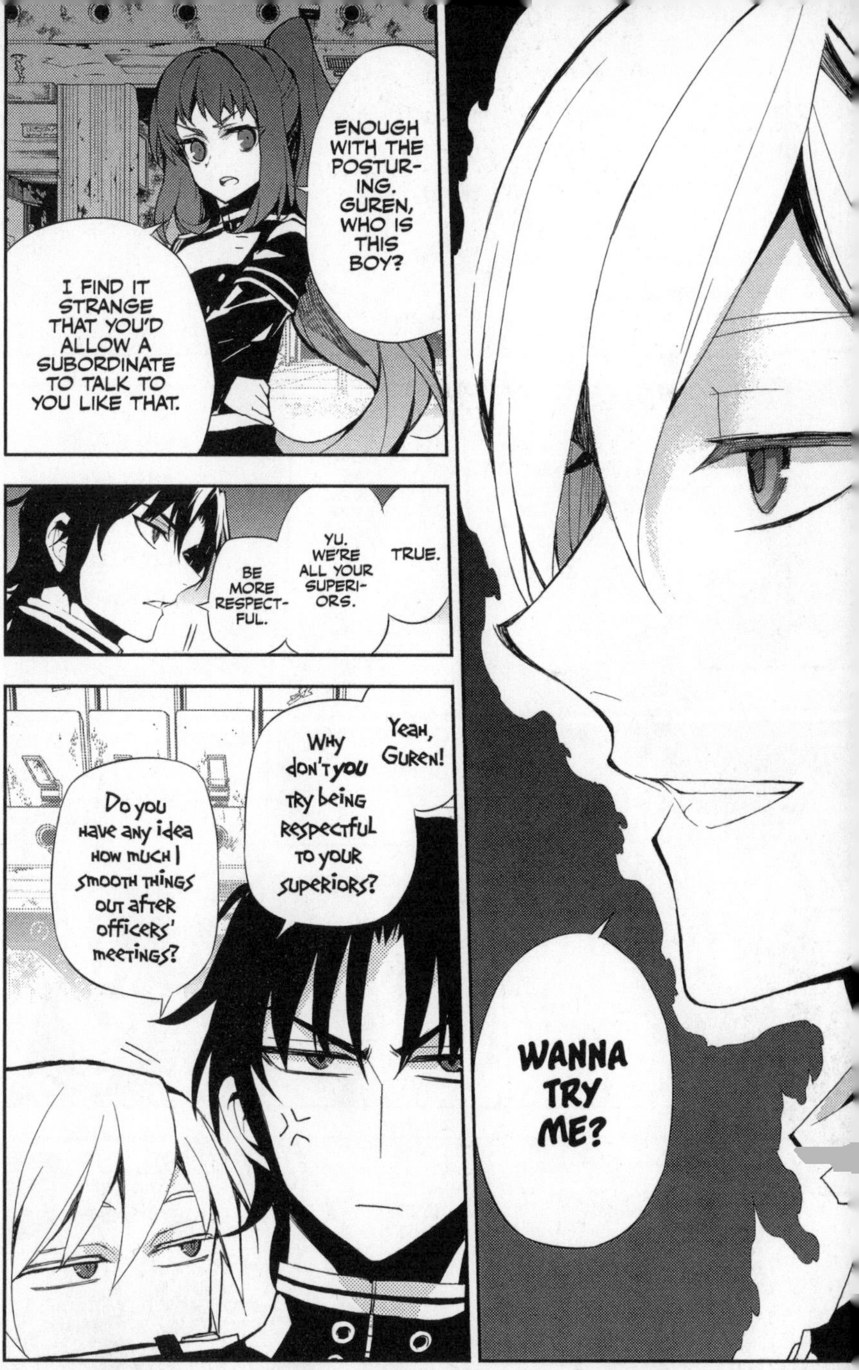
WANNA TRY ME?
ENOUGH WITH THE POSTURING. GUREN, WHO IS THIS BOY?
I FIND IT STRANGE THAT YOU'D ALLOW A SUBORDINATE TO TALK TO YOU LIKE THAT.
TRUE.
YU. WE'RE ALL YOUR SUPERIORS.
BE MORE RESPECTFUL.
Yeah, Guren!
Why don't you try being respectful to your superiors?
Do you have any idea how much I smooth things out after officers' meetings?

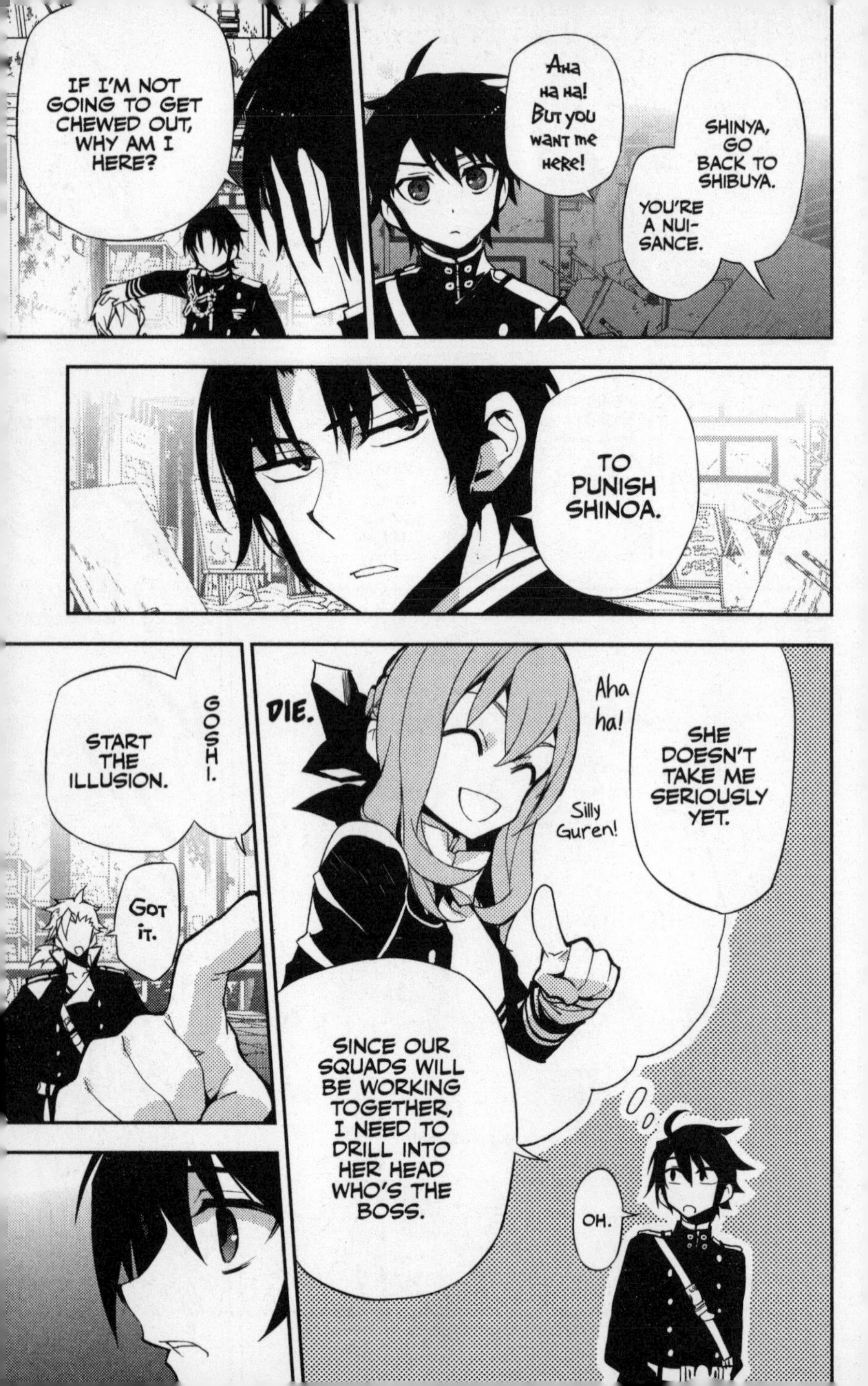
SHINYA, GO BACK TO SHIBUYA.
YOU'RE A NUI-SANCE.
Aha ha ha! But you want me here!
IF I'M NOT GOING TO GET CHEWED OUT, WHY AM I HERE?
TO PUNISH SHINOA.
SHE DOESN'T TAKE ME SERIOUSLY YET.
Aha ha!
Silly Guren!
DIE.
GOSHI.
START THE ILLUSION.
Got it.
SINCE OUR SQUADS WILL BE WORKING TOGETHER, I NEED TO DRILL INTO HER HEAD WHO'S THE BOSS.
OH.

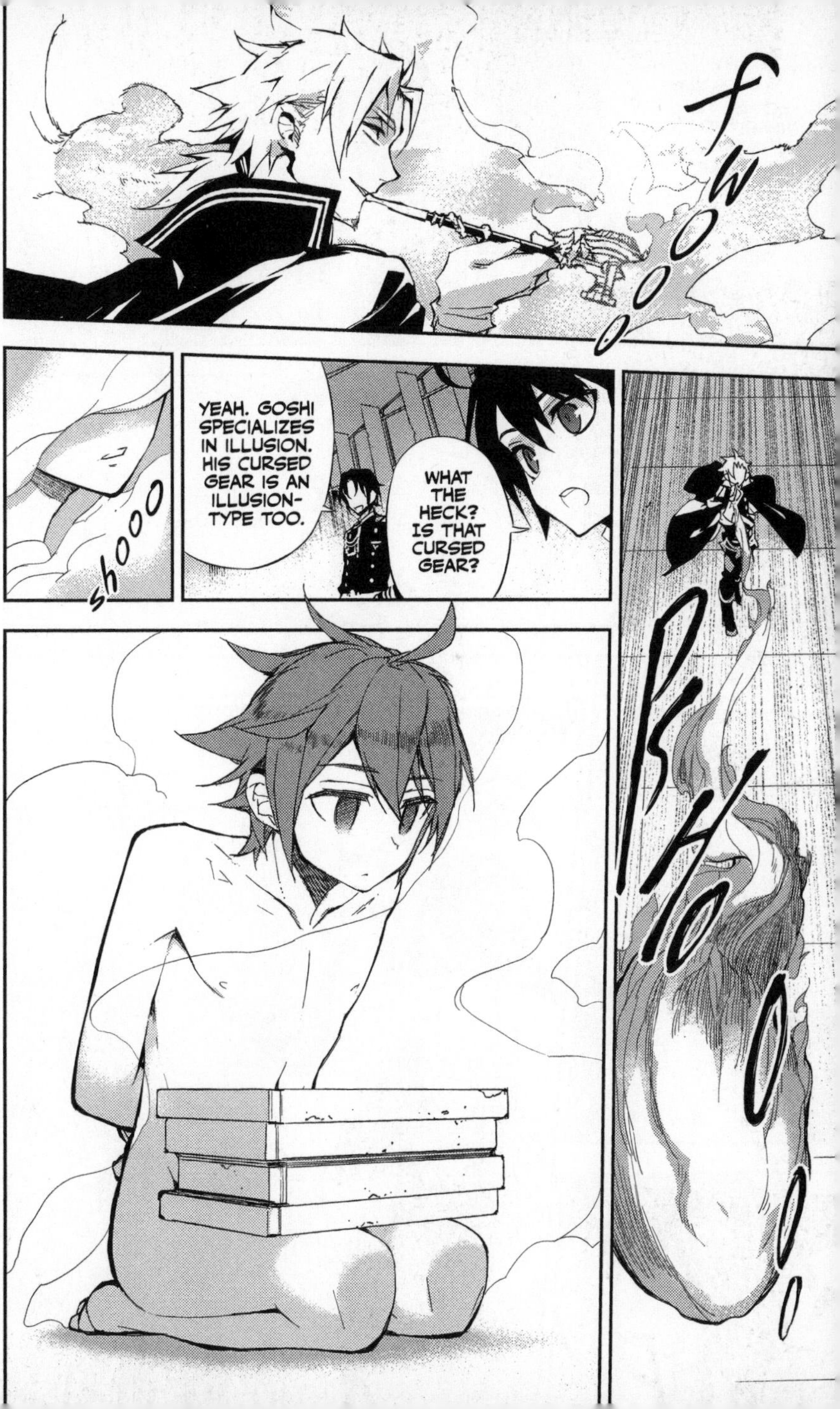
FWOOOO
PSHOOOOO
WHAT THE HECK? IS THAT CURSED GEAR?
YEAH. GOSHI SPECIALIZES IN ILLUSION. HIS CURSED GEAR IS AN ILLUSION-TYPE TOO.
shooo

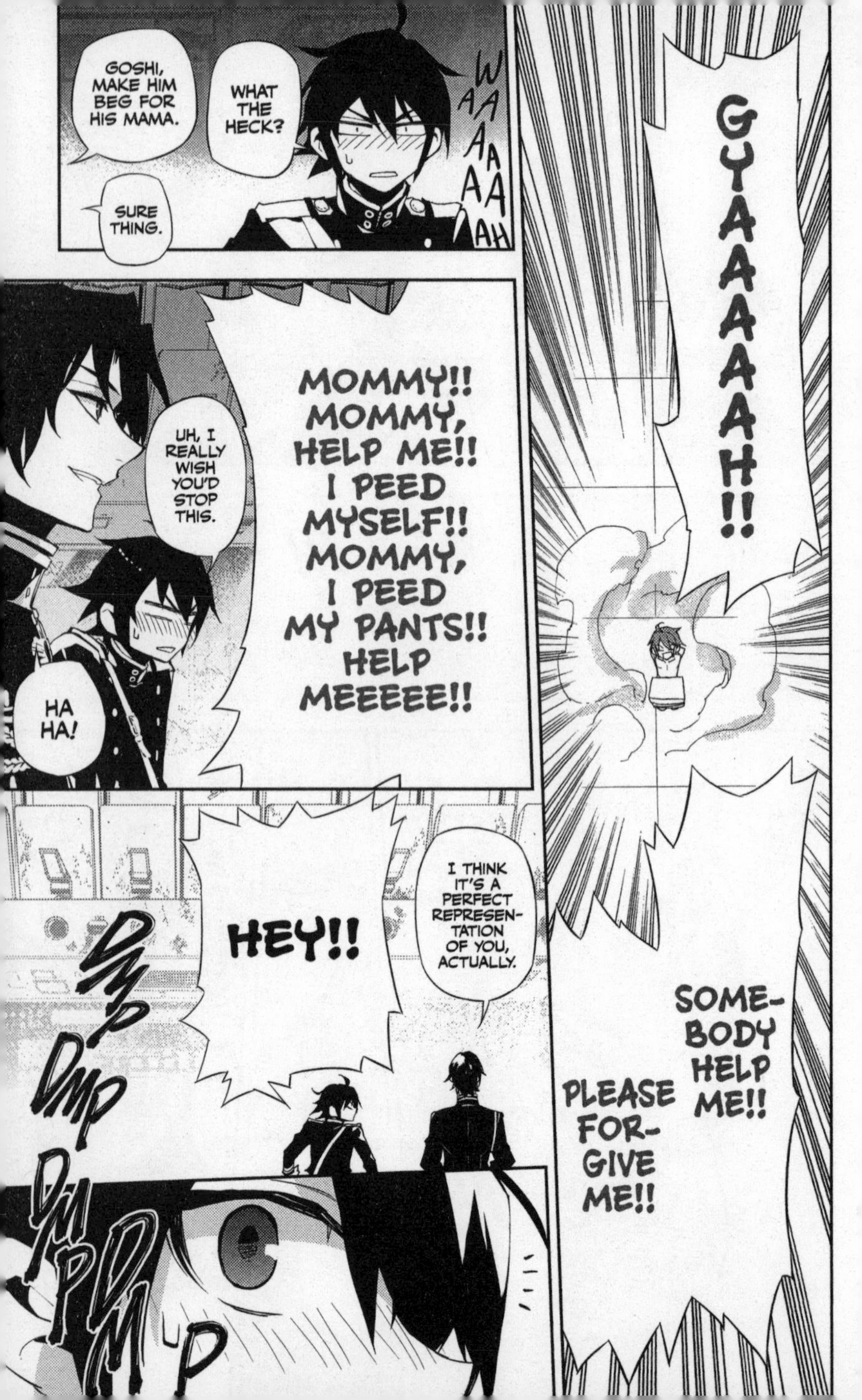
GYAAAAAAH!!
SOME-BODY HELP ME!!
PLEASE FOR-GIVE ME!!
WAAAAAAAH
WHAT THE HECK?
GOSHI, MAKE HIM BEG FOR HIS MAMA.
SURE THING.
MOMMY!! MOMMY, HELP ME!! I PEED MYSELF!! MOMMY, I PEED MY PANTS!! HELP MEEEEE!!
UH, I REALLY WISH YOU'D STOP THIS.
HA HA!
I THINK IT'S A PERFECT REPRESEN-TATION OF YOU, ACTUALLY.
HEY!!
DMP DMP DMP DMP

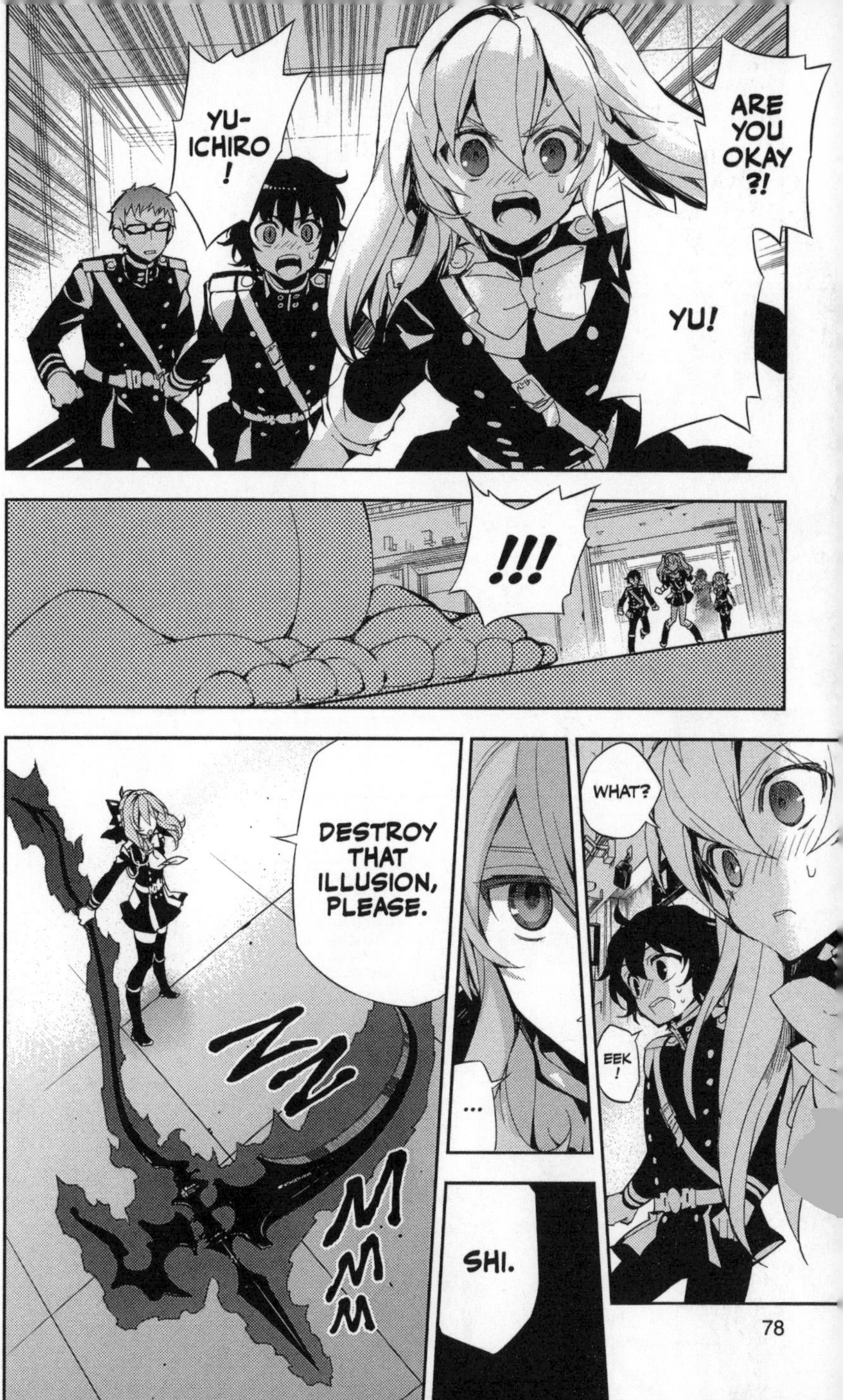
ARE YOU OKAY?!
YU!
YU-ICHIRO!
!!!
WHAT?
EEK!
...
SHI.
DESTROY THAT ILLUSION, PLEASE.
NN
MMM

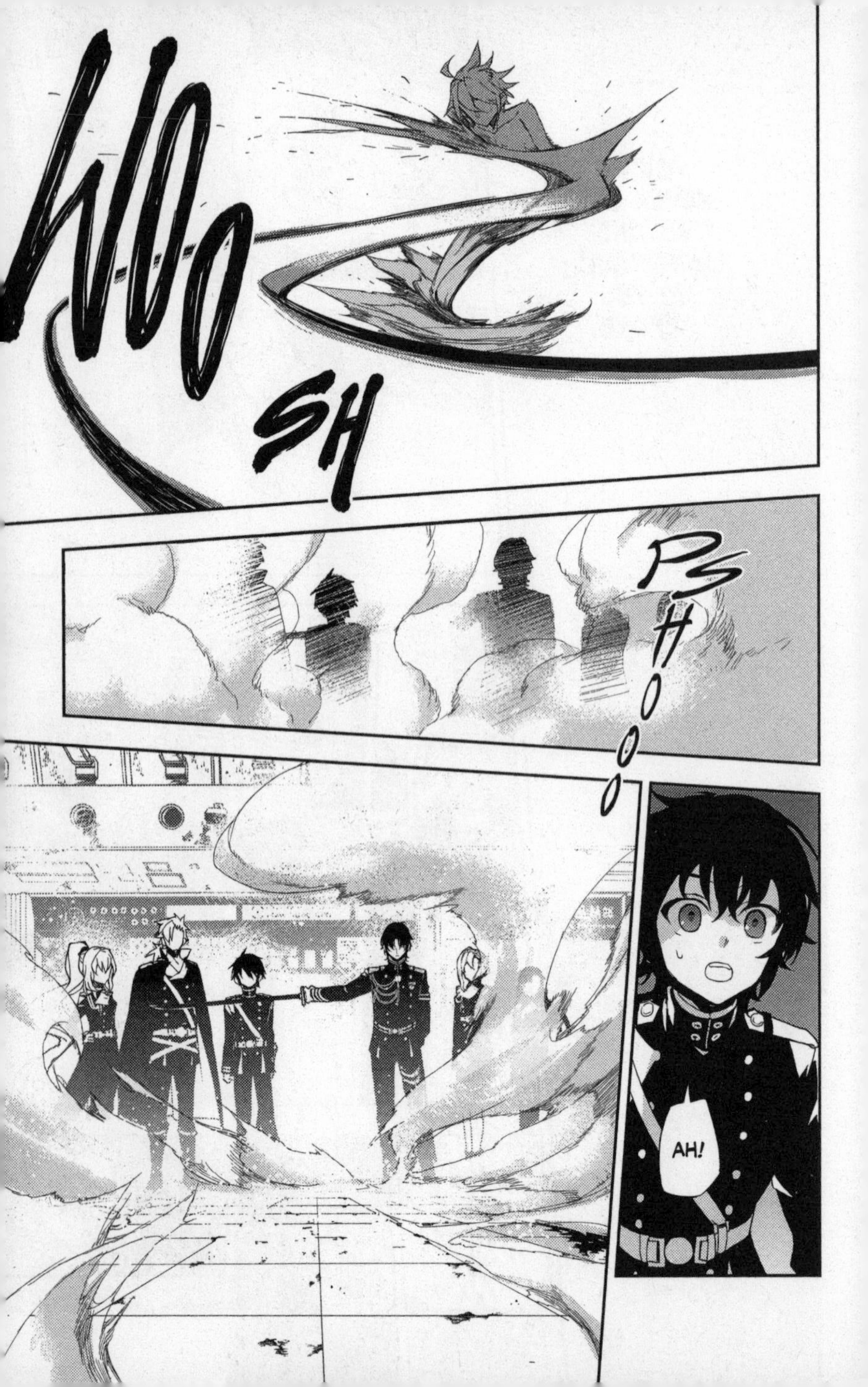
WHOOSH
PSHOOOO
AH!

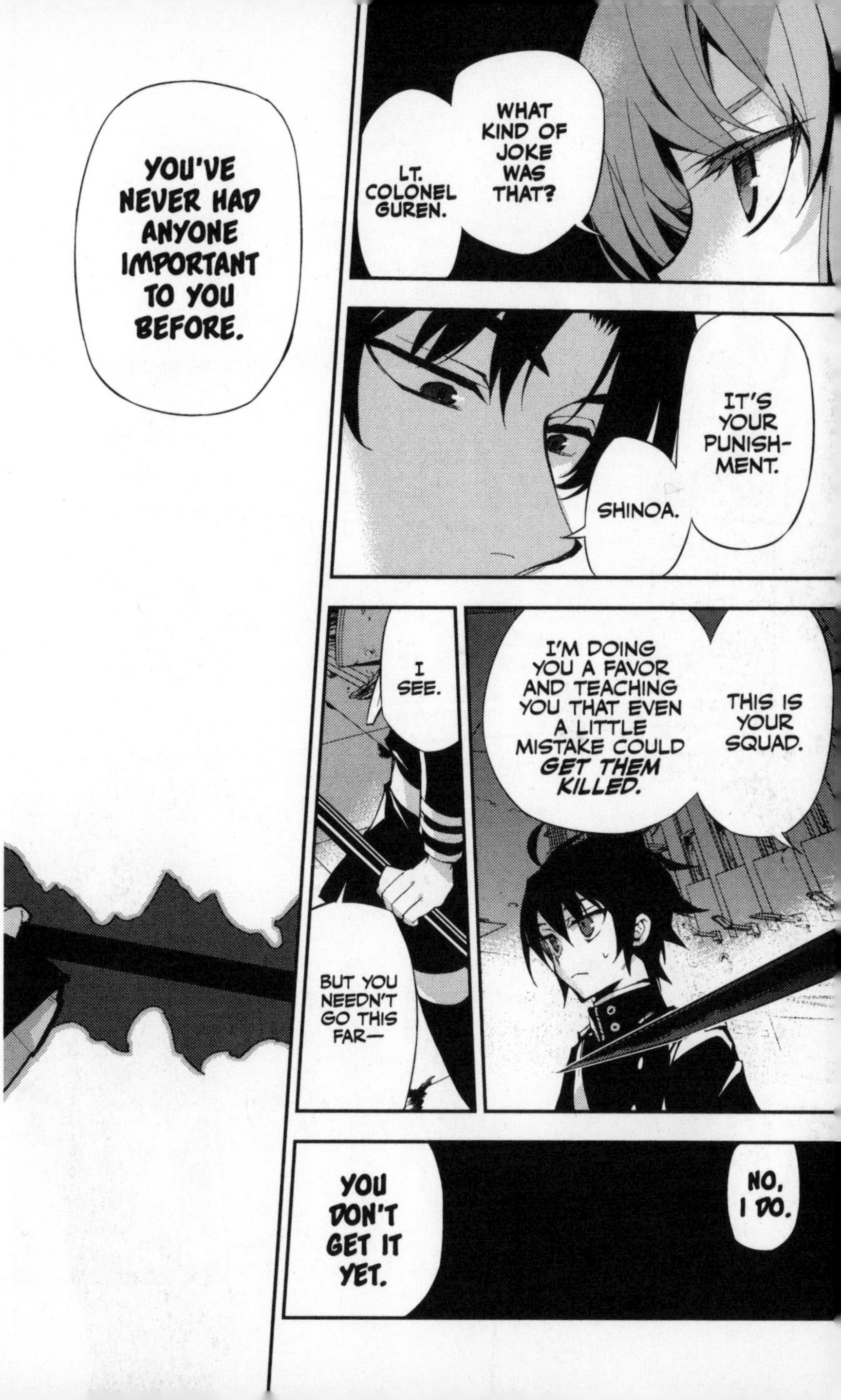
WHAT KIND OF JOKE WAS THAT?
LT. COLONEL GUREN.
IT'S YOUR PUNISH-MENT.
SHINOA.
THIS IS YOUR SQUAD.
I'M DOING YOU A FAVOR AND TEACHING YOU THAT EVEN A LITTLE MISTAKE COULD *GET THEM KILLED.*
I SEE.
BUT YOU NEEDN'T GO THIS FAR—
NO, I DO.
YOU DON'T GET IT YET.
YOU'VE NEVER HAD ANYONE IMPORTANT TO YOU BEFORE.

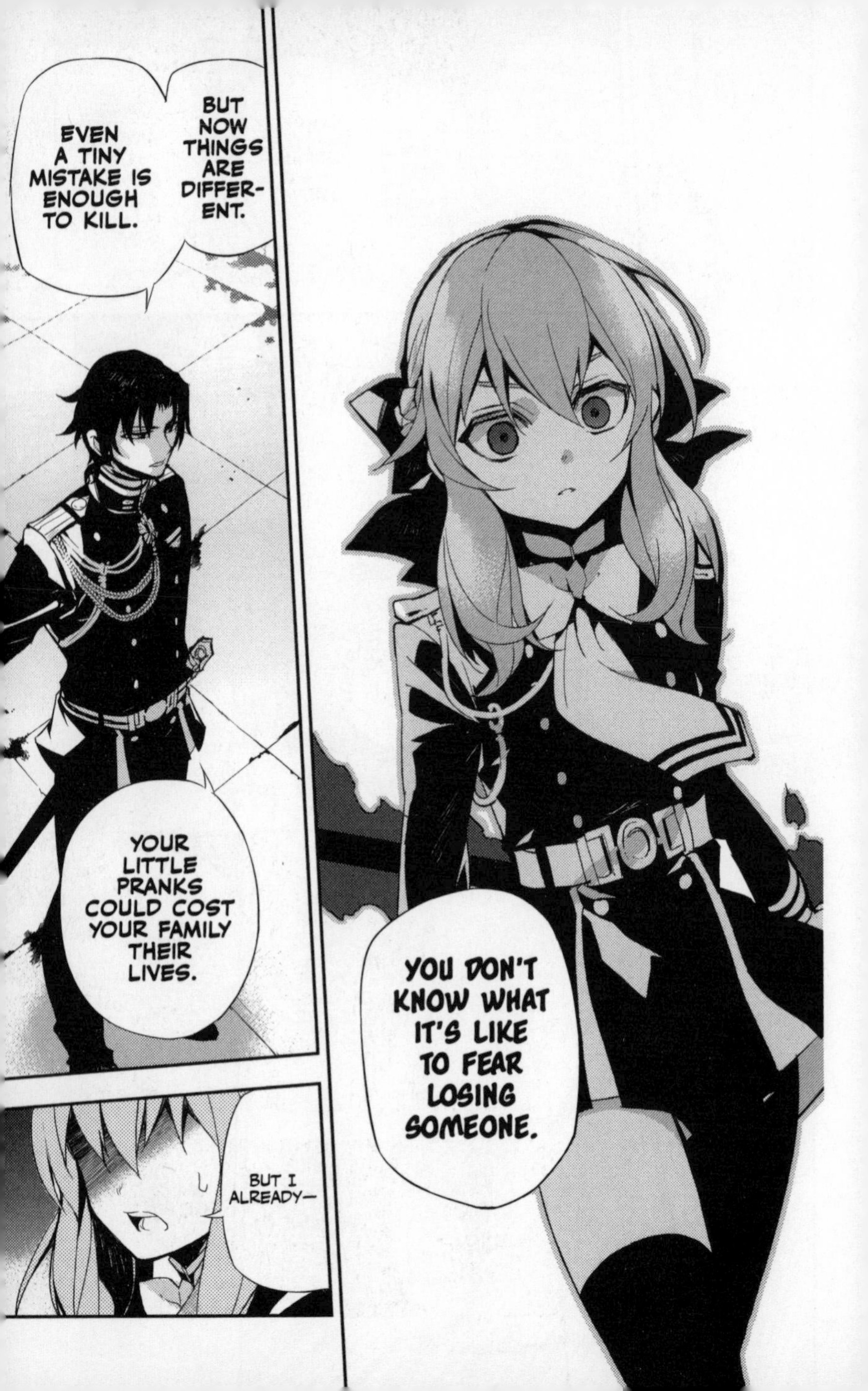
YOU DON'T KNOW WHAT IT'S LIKE TO FEAR LOSING SOMEONE.
BUT NOW THINGS ARE DIFFER-ENT.
EVEN A TINY MISTAKE IS ENOUGH TO KILL.
YOUR LITTLE PRANKS COULD COST YOUR FAMILY THEIR LIVES.
BUT I ALREADY—

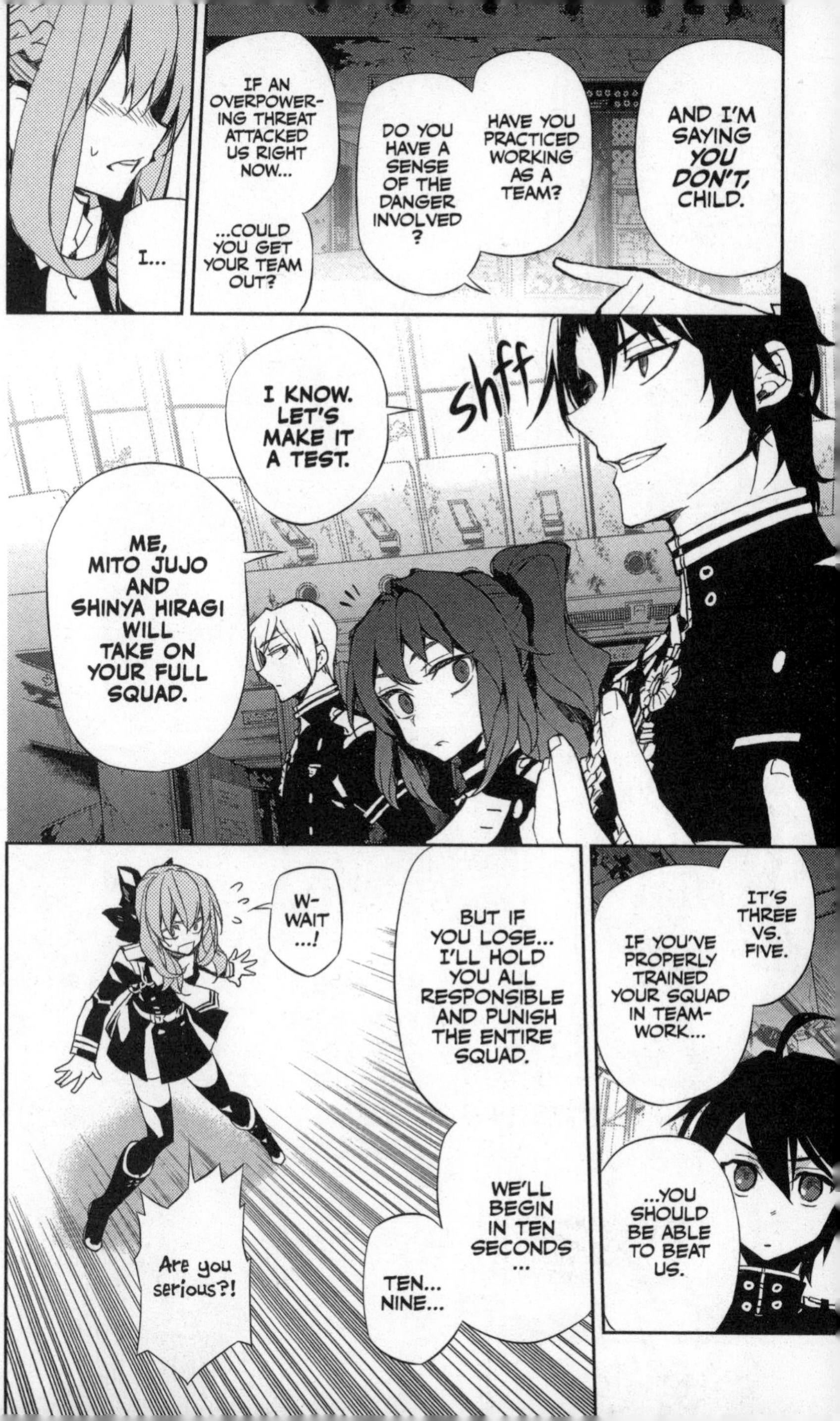
AND I'M SAYING *YOU DON'T*, CHILD.
HAVE YOU PRACTICED WORKING AS A TEAM?
DO YOU HAVE A SENSE OF THE DANGER INVOLVED?
IF AN OVERPOWERING THREAT ATTACKED US RIGHT NOW...
...COULD YOU GET YOUR TEAM OUT?
I...
shff
I KNOW. LET'S MAKE IT A TEST.
ME, MITO JUJO AND SHINYA HIRAGI WILL TAKE ON YOUR FULL SQUAD.
IT'S THREE VS. FIVE.
IF YOU'VE PROPERLY TRAINED YOUR SQUAD IN TEAMWORK...
...YOU SHOULD BE ABLE TO BEAT US.
BUT IF YOU LOSE... I'LL HOLD YOU ALL RESPONSIBLE AND PUNISH THE ENTIRE SQUAD.
W-WAIT...!
WE'LL BEGIN IN TEN SECONDS...
TEN... NINE...
Are you serious?!

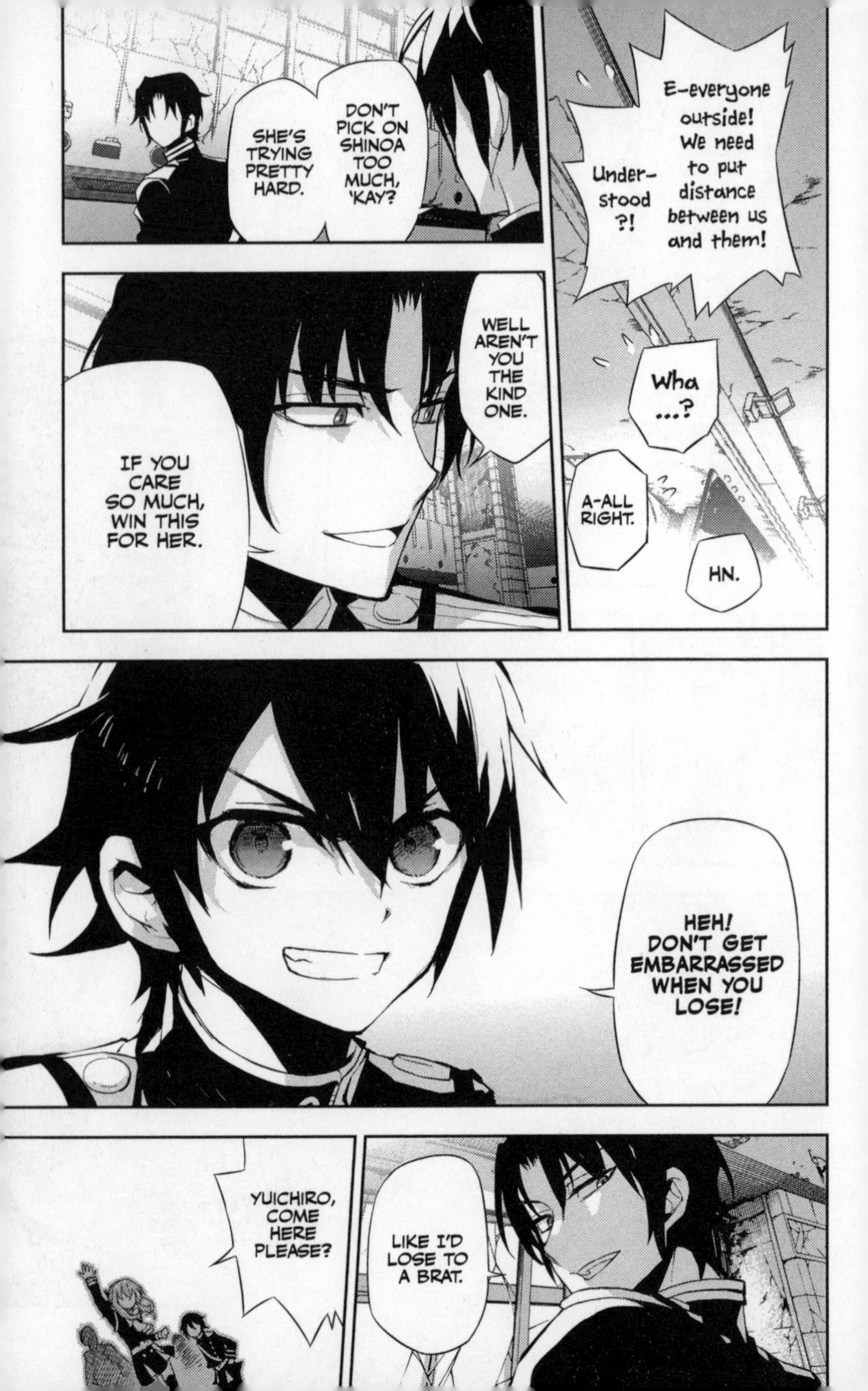
E-everyone outside! We need to put distance between us and them!
Under-stood?!
Wha...?
A-ALL RIGHT.
HN.
DON'T PICK ON SHINOA TOO MUCH, 'KAY?
SHE'S TRYING PRETTY HARD.
WELL AREN'T YOU THE KIND ONE.
IF YOU CARE SO MUCH, WIN THIS FOR HER.
HEH! DON'T GET EMBARRASSED WHEN YOU LOSE!
LIKE I'D LOSE TO A BRAT.
YUICHIRO, COME HERE PLEASE?

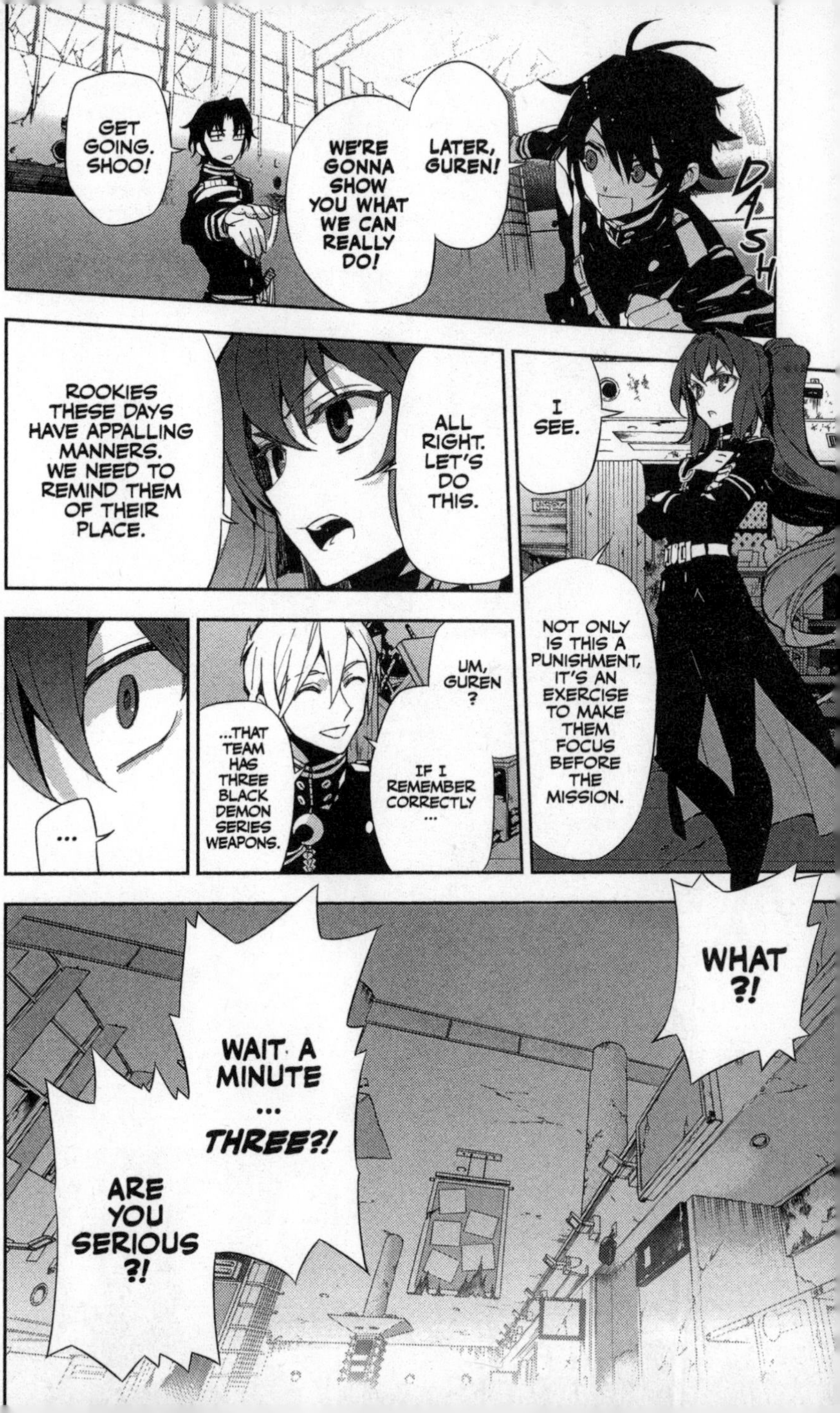
DASH
LATER, GUREN!
WE'RE GONNA SHOW YOU WHAT WE CAN REALLY DO!
GET GOING. SHOO!
I SEE.
NOT ONLY IS THIS A PUNISHMENT, IT'S AN EXERCISE TO MAKE THEM FOCUS BEFORE THE MISSION.
ALL RIGHT. LET'S DO THIS.
ROOKIES THESE DAYS HAVE APPALLING MANNERS. WE NEED TO REMIND THEM OF THEIR PLACE.
UM, GUREN?
IF I REMEMBER CORRECTLY...
...THAT TEAM HAS THREE BLACK DEMON SERIES WEAPONS.
...
WHAT?!
WAIT A MINUTE... THREE?!
ARE YOU SERIOUS?!

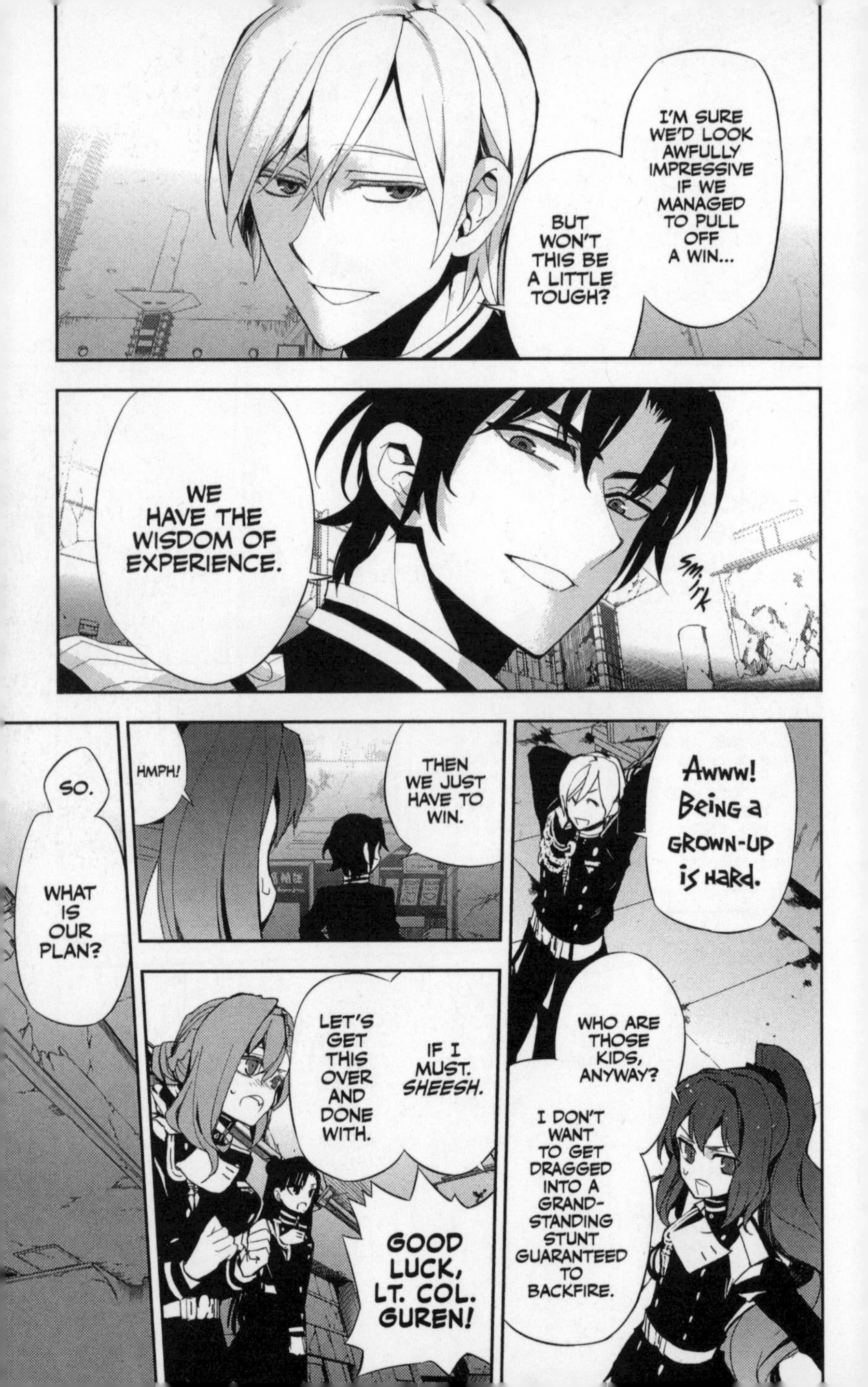
I'M SURE WE'D LOOK AWFULLY IMPRESSIVE IF WE MANAGED TO PULL OFF A WIN...
BUT WON'T THIS BE A LITTLE TOUGH?
WE HAVE THE WISDOM OF EXPERIENCE.
smirk
Awww! Being a GROWN-UP is hard.
THEN WE JUST HAVE TO WIN.
HMPH!
SO.
WHAT IS OUR PLAN?
WHO ARE THOSE KIDS, ANYWAY?
I DON'T WANT TO GET DRAGGED INTO A GRAND-STANDING STUNT GUARANTEED TO BACKFIRE.
IF I MUST. SHEESH.
LET'S GET THIS OVER AND DONE WITH.
GOOD LUCK, LT. COL. GUREN!

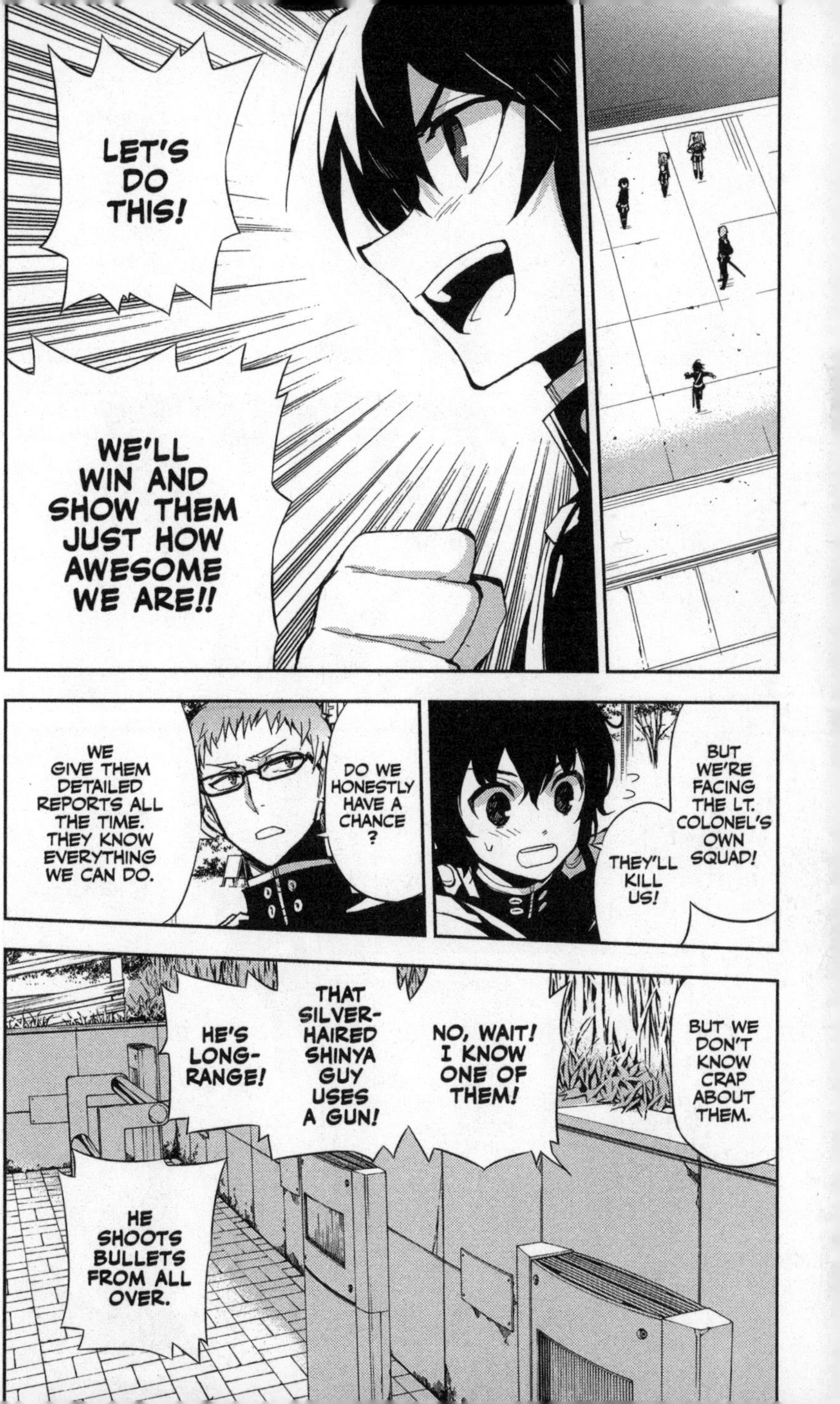
LET'S DO THIS!
WE'LL WIN AND SHOW THEM JUST HOW AWESOME WE ARE!!
BUT WE'RE FACING THE LT. COLONEL'S OWN SQUAD!
THEY'LL KILL US!
DO WE HONESTLY HAVE A CHANCE?
WE GIVE THEM DETAILED REPORTS ALL THE TIME. THEY KNOW EVERYTHING WE CAN DO.
BUT WE DON'T KNOW CRAP ABOUT THEM.
NO, WAIT! I KNOW ONE OF THEM!
THAT SILVER-HAIRED SHINYA GUY USES A GUN!
HE'S LONG-RANGE!
HE SHOOTS BULLETS FROM ALL OVER.

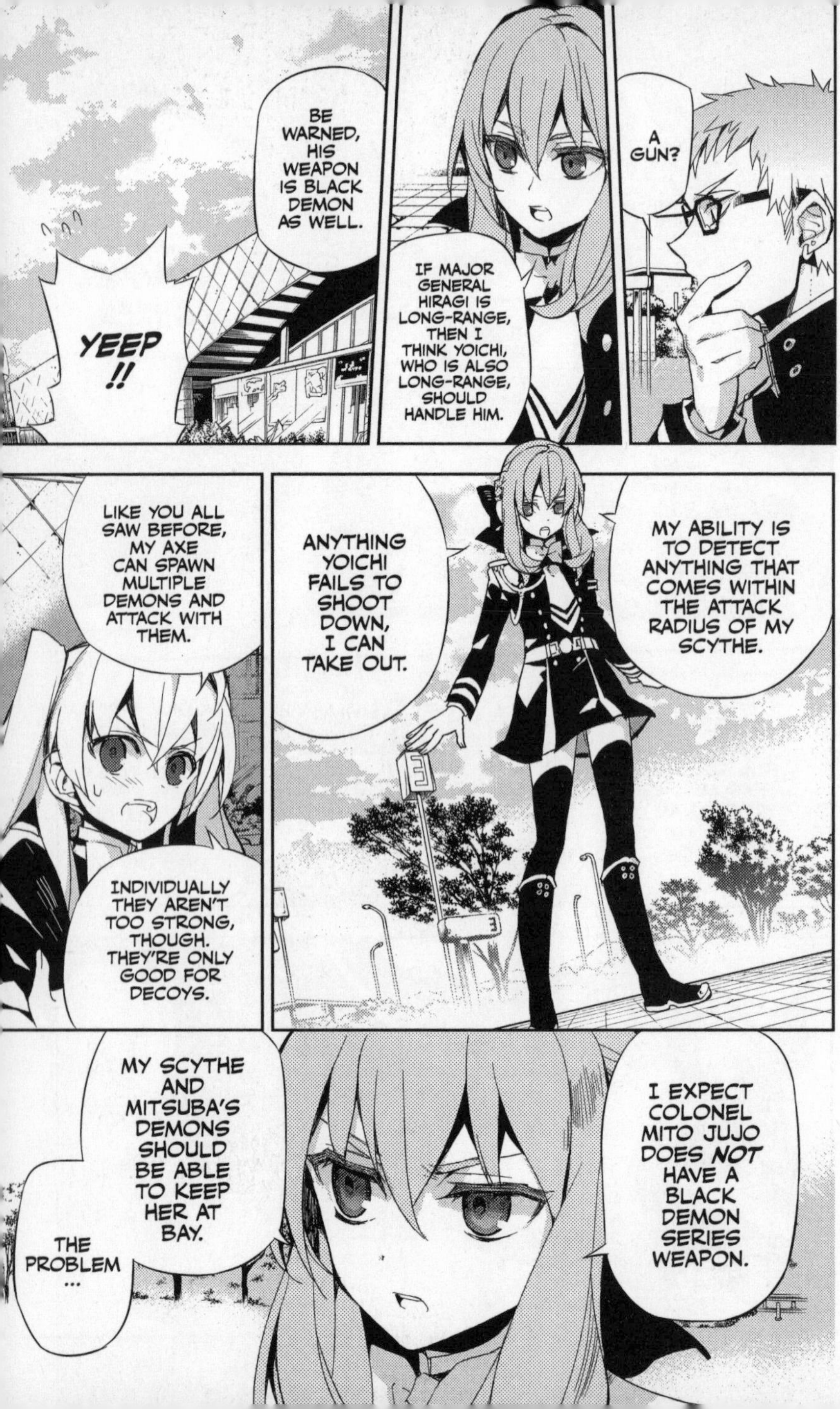
A GUN?
BE WARNED, HIS WEAPON IS BLACK DEMON AS WELL.
IF MAJOR GENERAL HIRAGI IS LONG-RANGE, THEN I THINK YOICHI, WHO IS ALSO LONG-RANGE, SHOULD HANDLE HIM.
YEEP!!
MY ABILITY IS TO DETECT ANYTHING THAT COMES WITHIN THE ATTACK RADIUS OF MY SCYTHE.
ANYTHING YOICHI FAILS TO SHOOT DOWN, I CAN TAKE OUT.
LIKE YOU ALL SAW BEFORE, MY AXE CAN SPAWN MULTIPLE DEMONS AND ATTACK WITH THEM.
INDIVIDUALLY THEY AREN'T TOO STRONG, THOUGH. THEY'RE ONLY GOOD FOR DECOYS.
I EXPECT COLONEL MITO JUJO DOES *NOT* HAVE A BLACK DEMON SERIES WEAPON.
MY SCYTHE AND MITSUBA'S DEMONS SHOULD BE ABLE TO KEEP HER AT BAY.
THE PROBLEM...

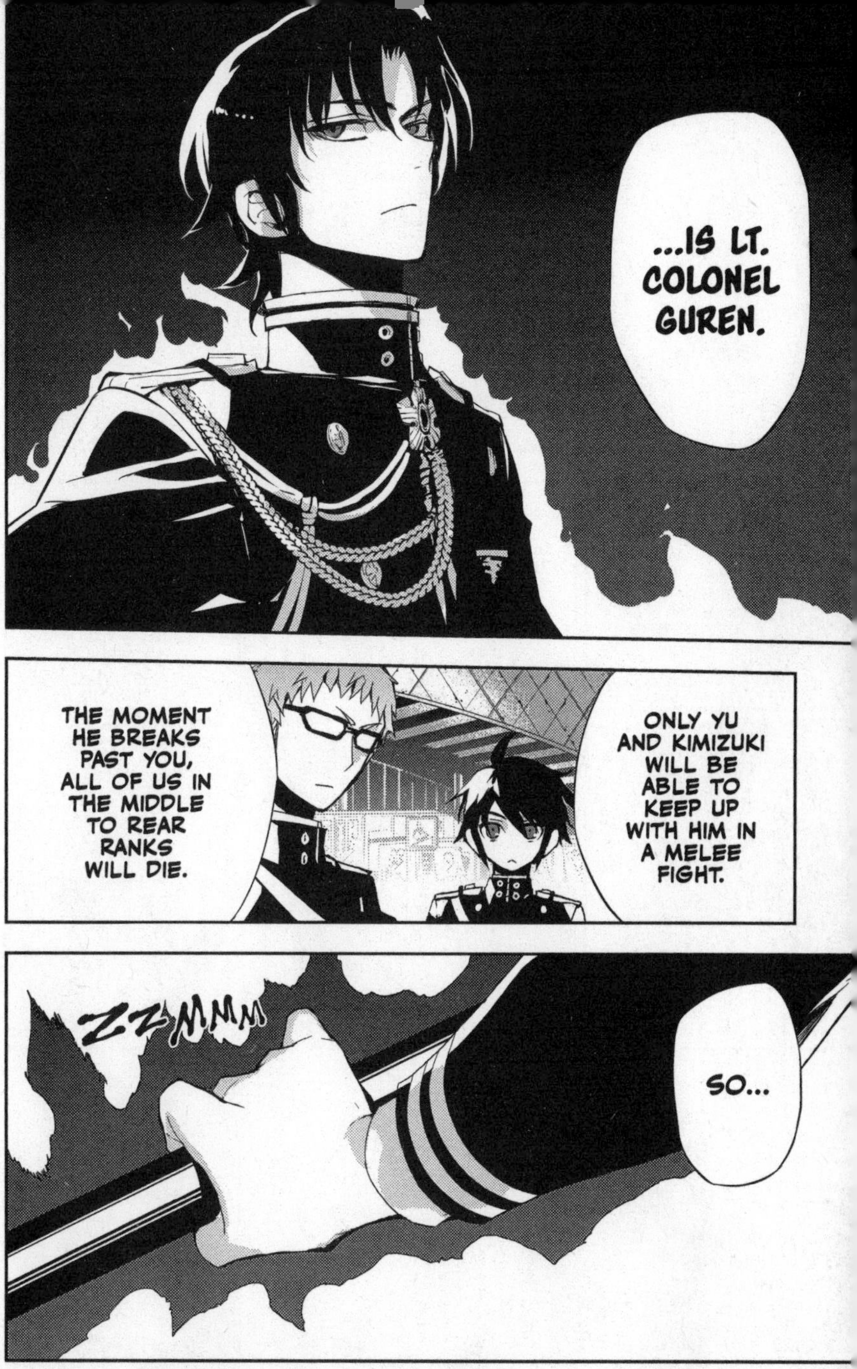
...IS LT. COLONEL GUREN.
ONLY YU AND KIMIZUKI WILL BE ABLE TO KEEP UP WITH HIM IN A MELEE FIGHT.
THE MOMENT HE BREAKS PAST YOU, ALL OF US IN THE MIDDLE TO REAR RANKS WILL DIE.
SO...
ZZMMM

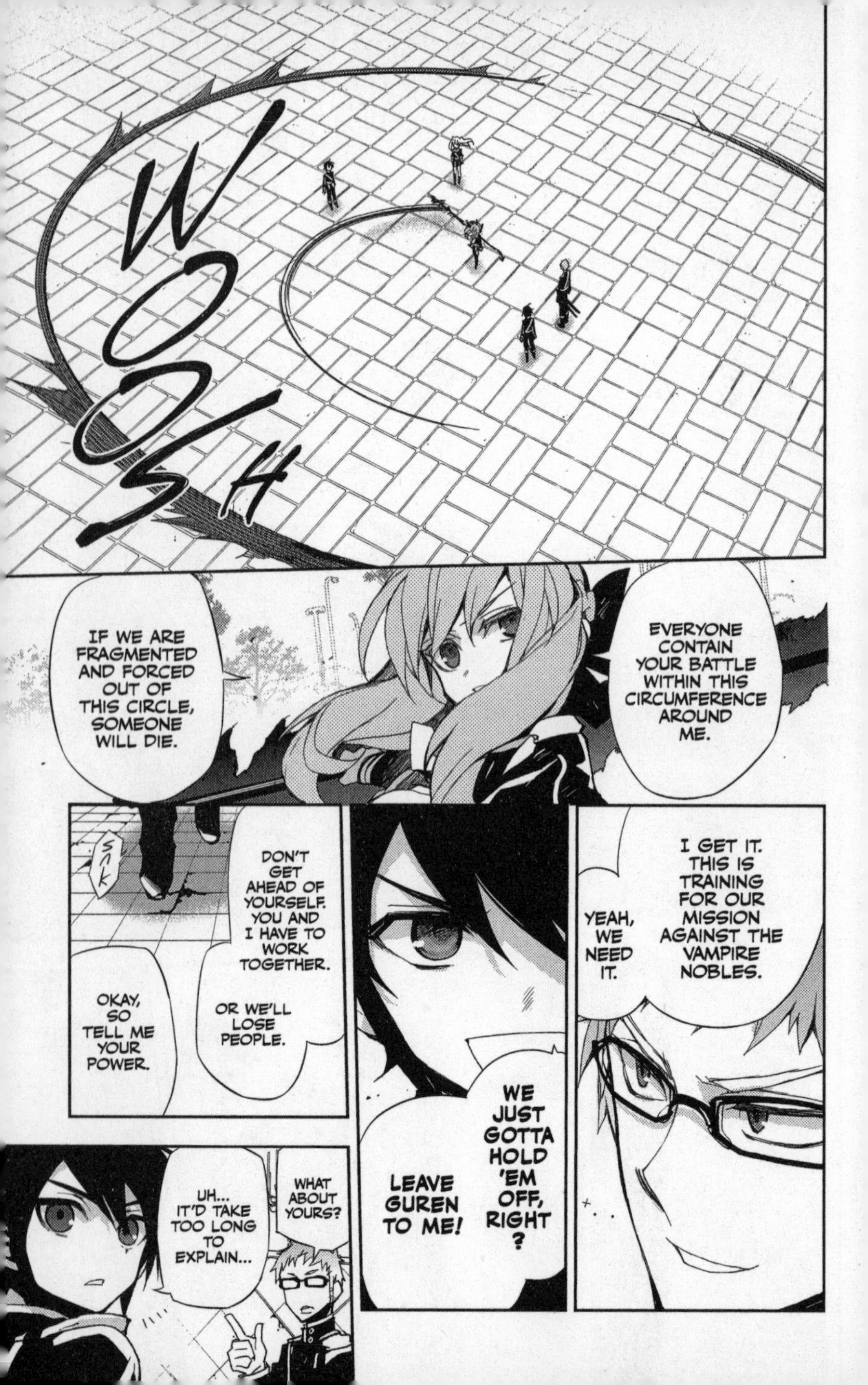
WOOSH
EVERYONE CONTAIN YOUR BATTLE WITHIN THIS CIRCUMFERENCE AROUND ME.
IF WE ARE FRAGMENTED AND FORCED OUT OF THIS CIRCLE, SOMEONE WILL DIE.
I GET IT. THIS IS TRAINING FOR OUR MISSION AGAINST THE VAMPIRE NOBLES.
YEAH, WE NEED IT.
WE JUST GOTTA HOLD 'EM OFF, RIGHT?
LEAVE GUREN TO ME!
DON'T GET AHEAD OF YOURSELF. YOU AND I HAVE TO WORK TOGETHER.
OR WE'LL LOSE PEOPLE.
OKAY, SO TELL ME YOUR POWER.
WHAT ABOUT YOURS?
UH... IT'D TAKE TOO LONG TO EXPLAIN...

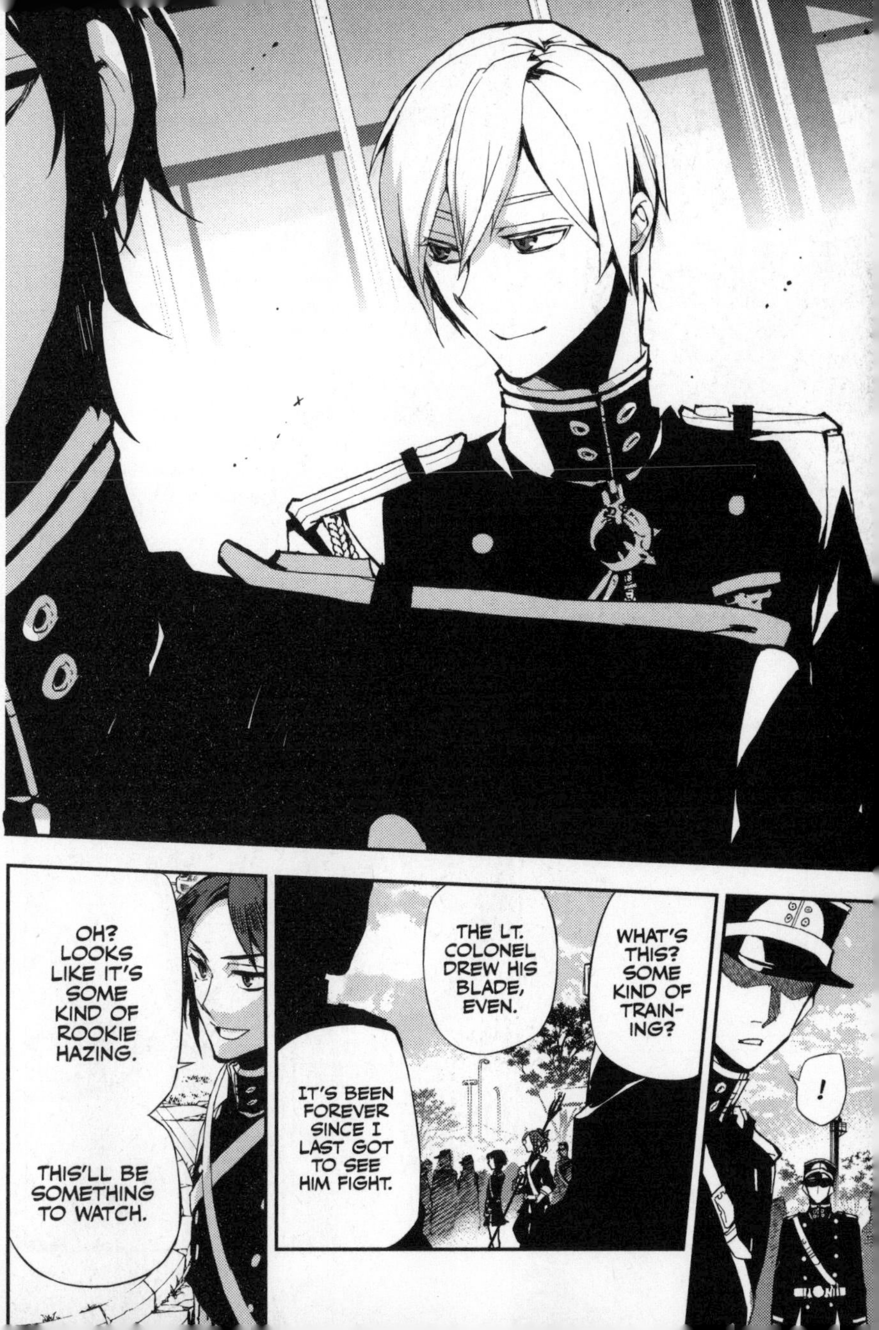
!
WHAT'S THIS? SOME KIND OF TRAINING?
THE LT. COLONEL DREW HIS BLADE, EVEN.
IT'S BEEN FOREVER SINCE I LAST GOT TO SEE HIM FIGHT.
OH? LOOKS LIKE IT'S SOME KIND OF ROOKIE HAZING.
THIS'LL BE SOMETHING TO WATCH.

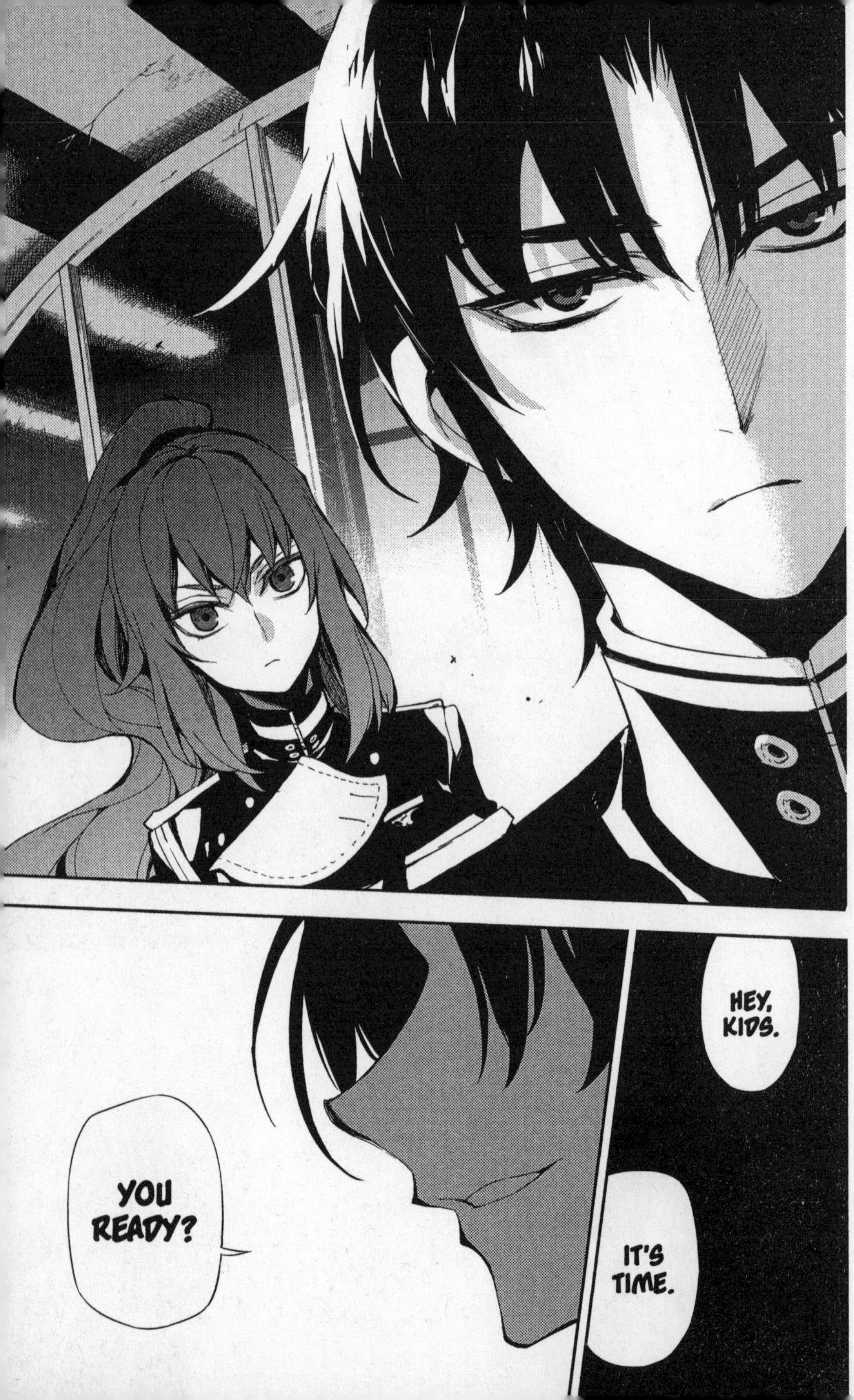
HEY, KIDS.
IT'S TIME.
YOU READY?

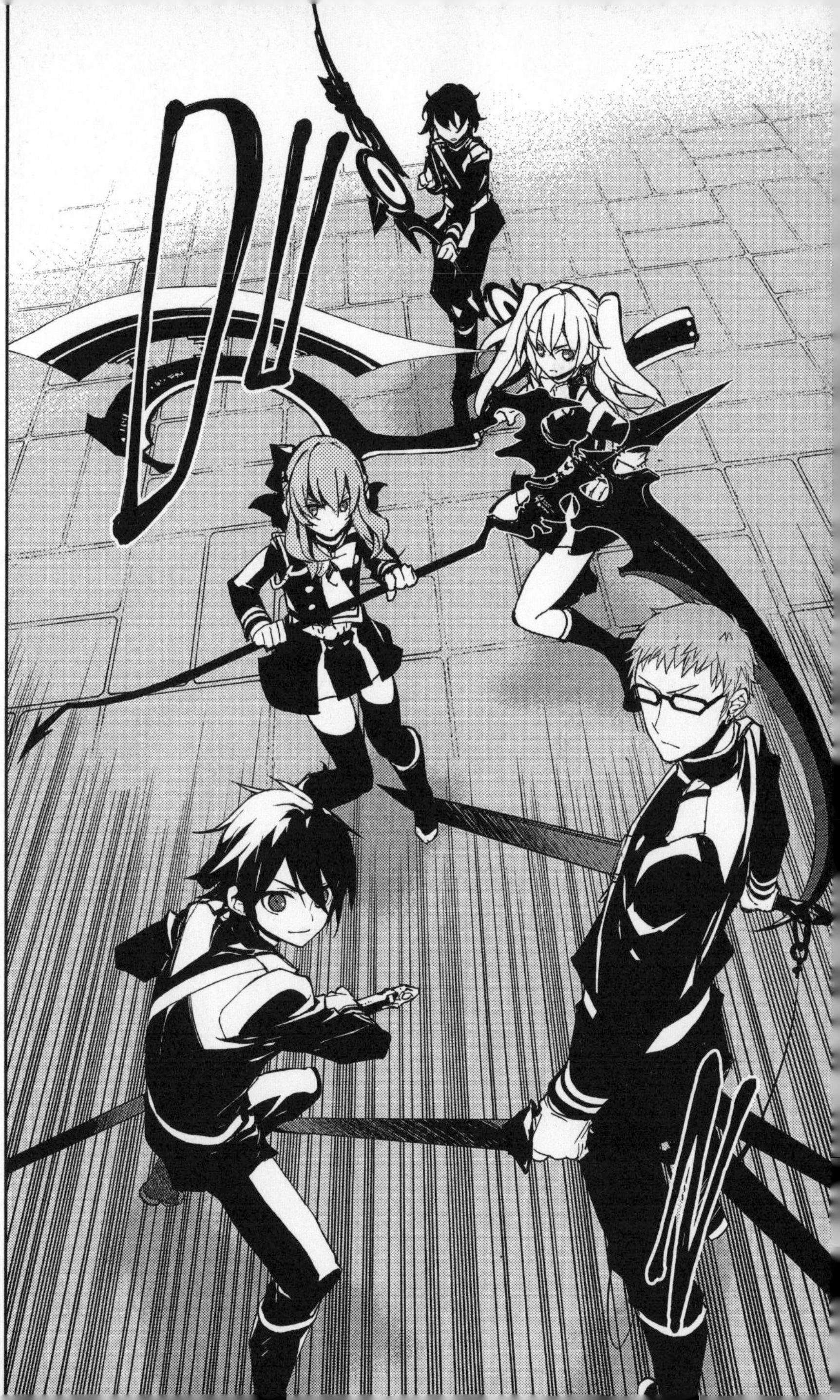
DU

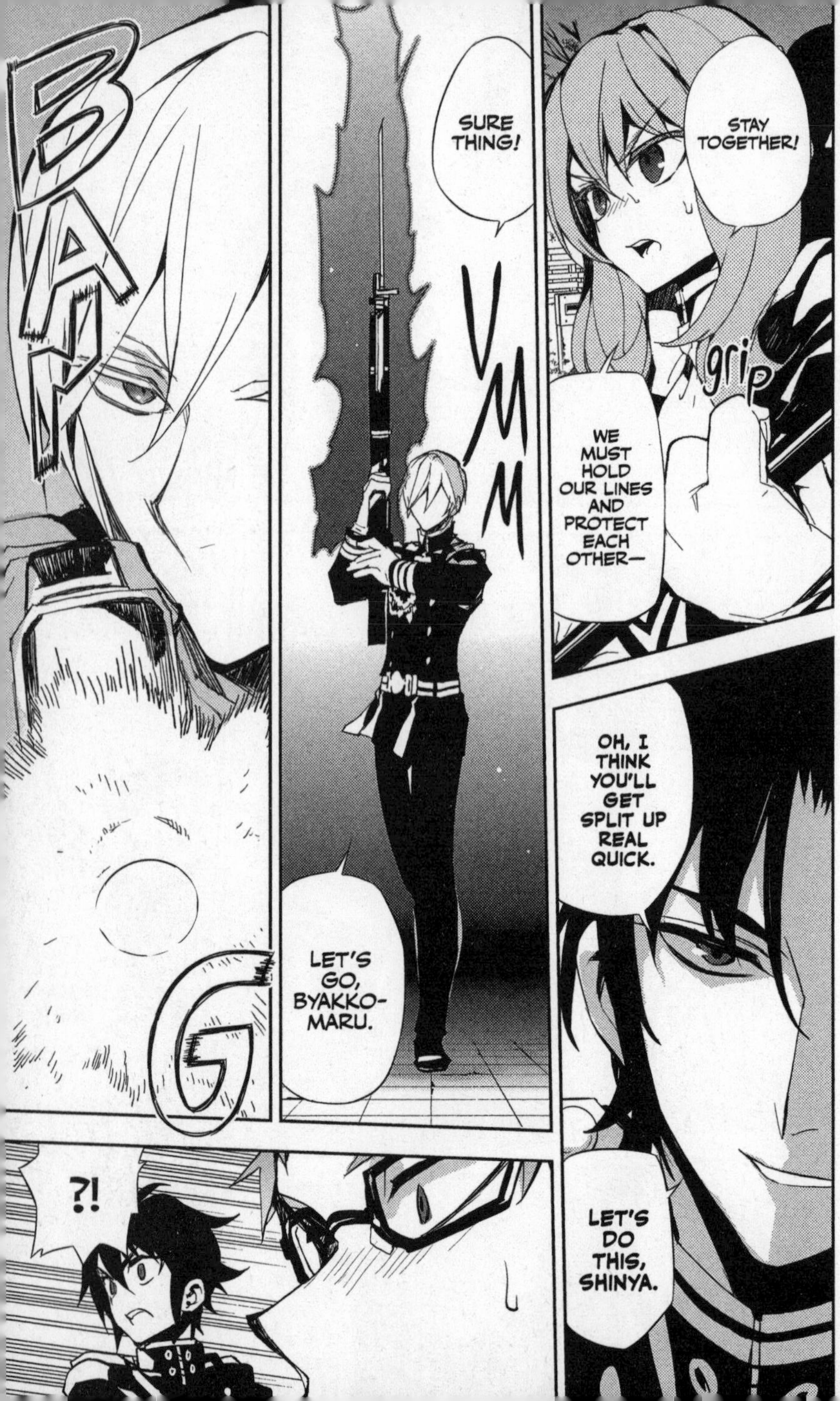

STAY TOGETHER!
grip
WE MUST HOLD OUR LINES AND PROTECT EACH OTHER—
OH, I THINK YOU'LL GET SPLIT UP REAL QUICK.
LET'S DO THIS, SHINYA.
SURE THING!
VMMM
LET'S GO, BYAKKO-MARU.
BANG
?!

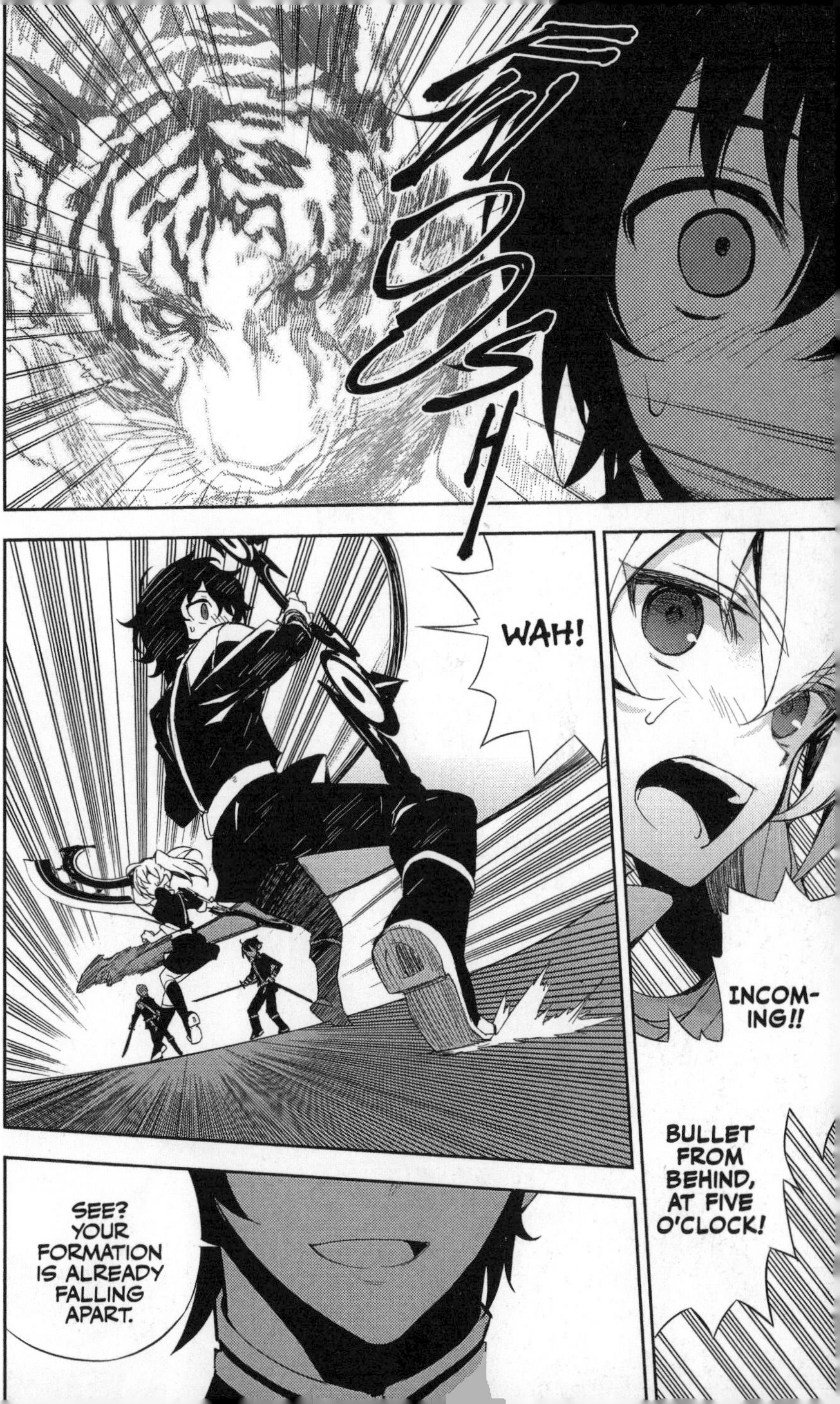
FWOOSH
INCOM-
ING!!
BULLET FROM BEHIND, AT FIVE O'CLOCK!
WAH!
SEE? YOUR FORMATION IS ALREADY FALLING APART.

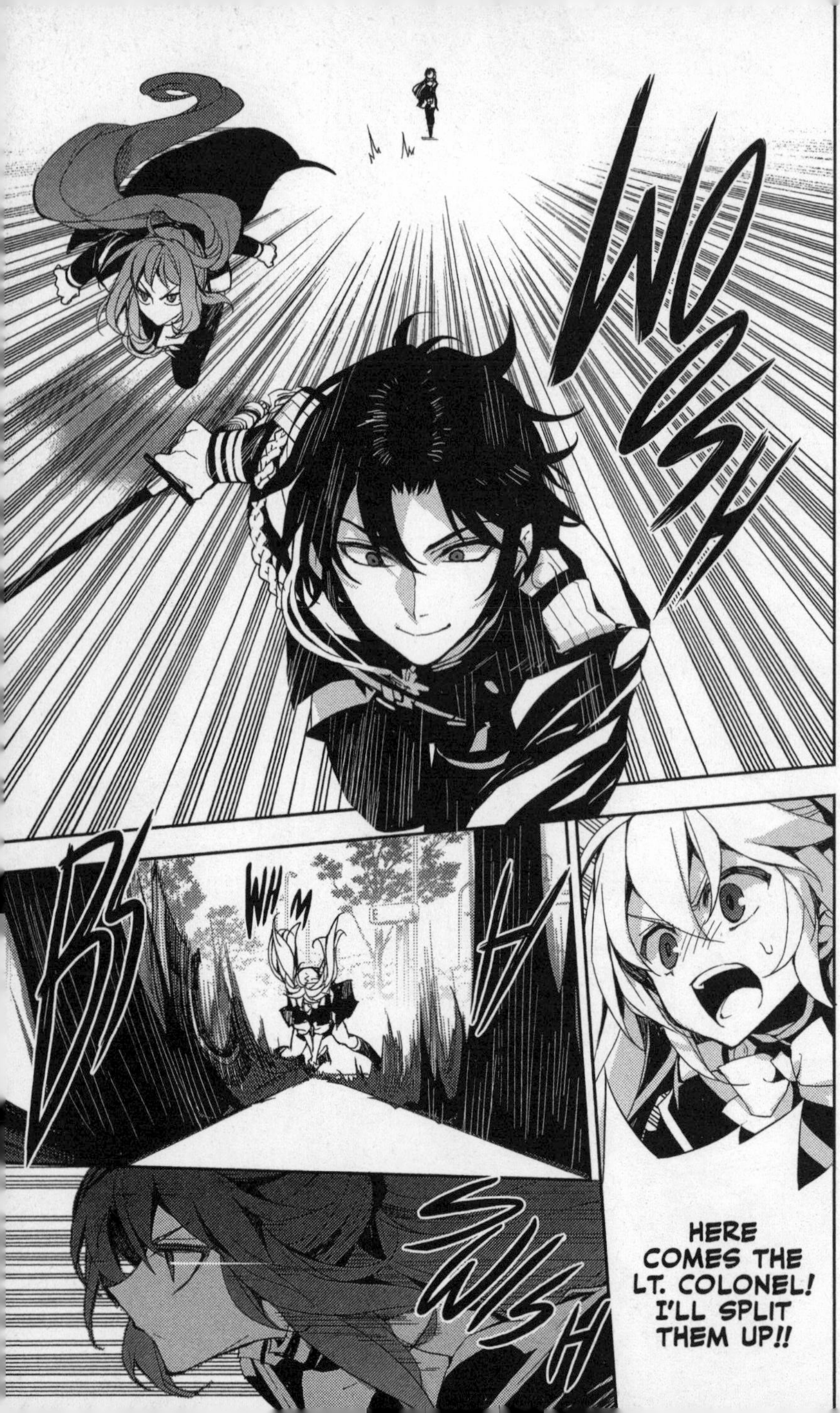
WOOSH
HERE COMES THE LT. COLONEL! I'LL SPLIT THEM UP!!
SWISH

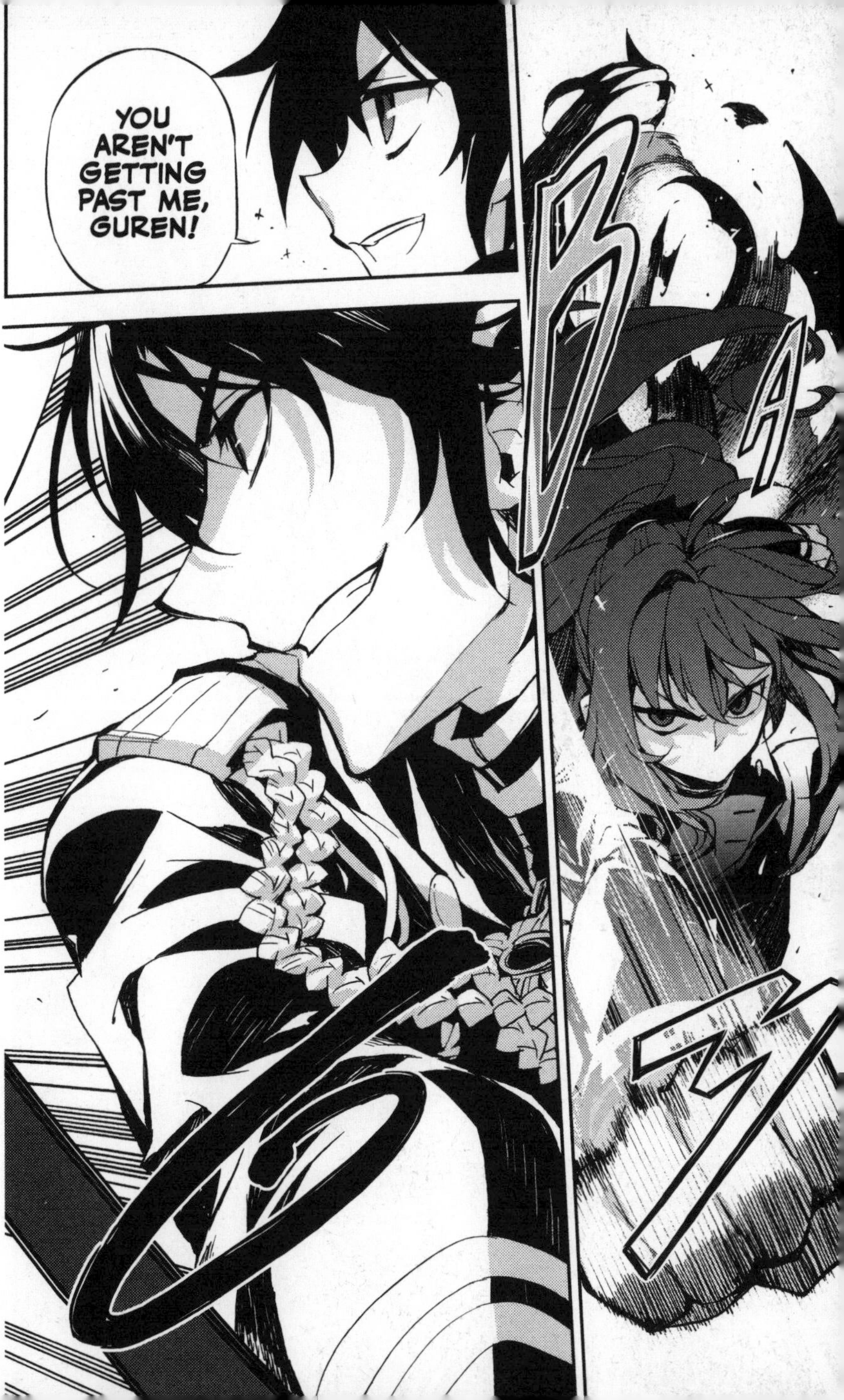
YOU AREN'T GETTING PAST ME, GUREN!

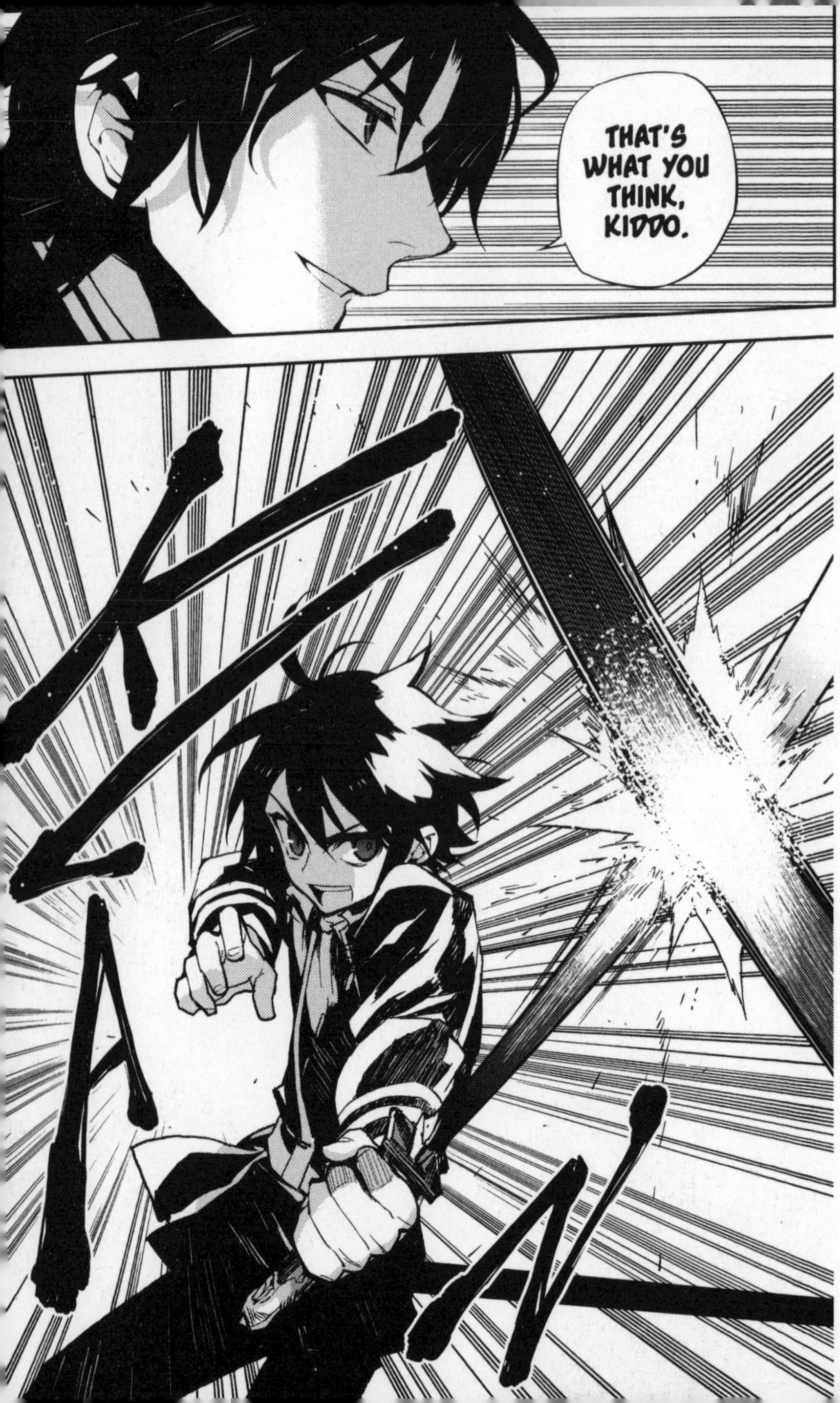
THAT'S WHAT YOU THINK, KIDDO.

Seraph of the End

—VAMPIRE REIGN—

CHAPTER 25 Thirst Logic

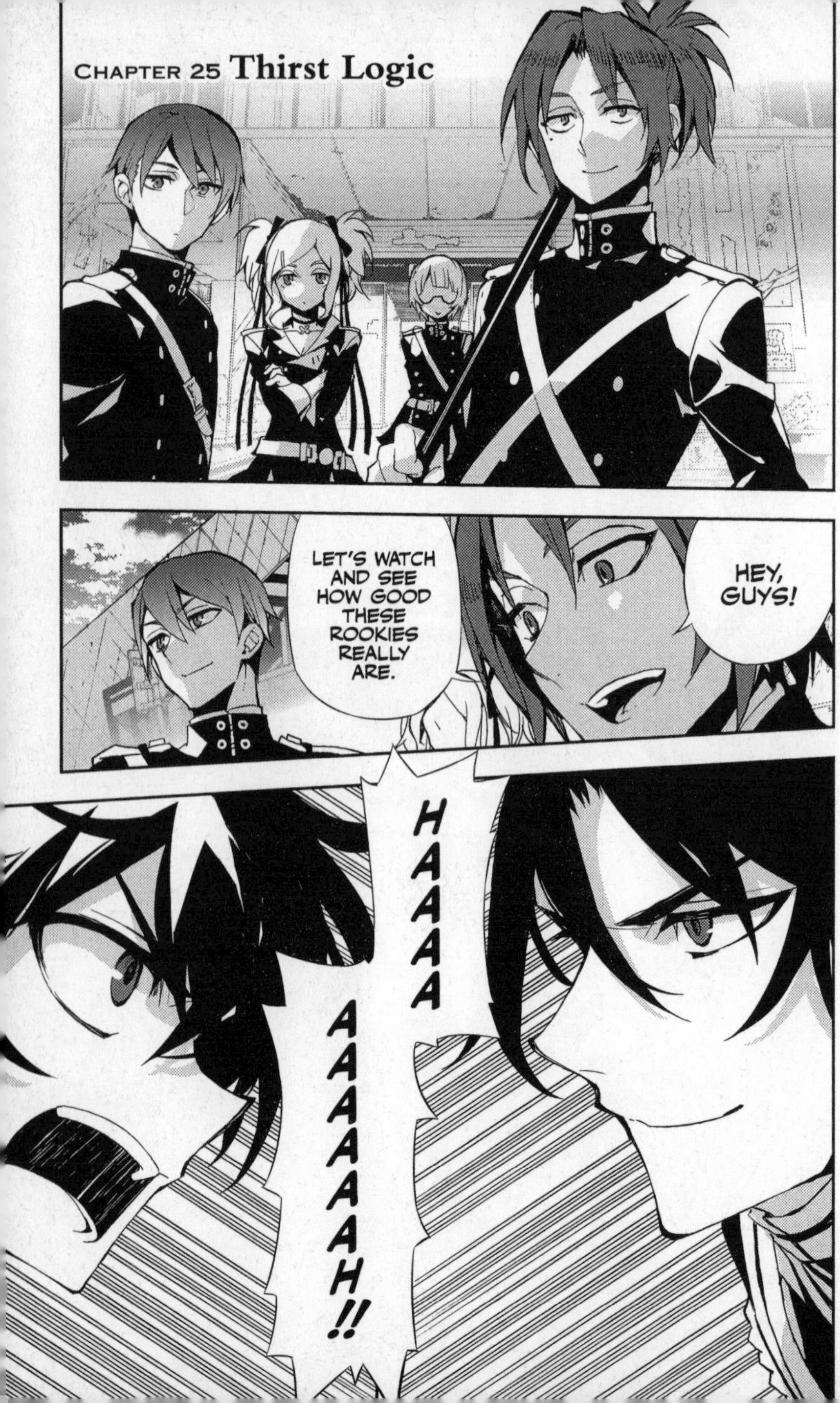
HEY, GUYS!
LET'S WATCH AND SEE HOW GOOD THESE ROOKIES REALLY ARE.
HAAAAAAAAAAAAAH!!

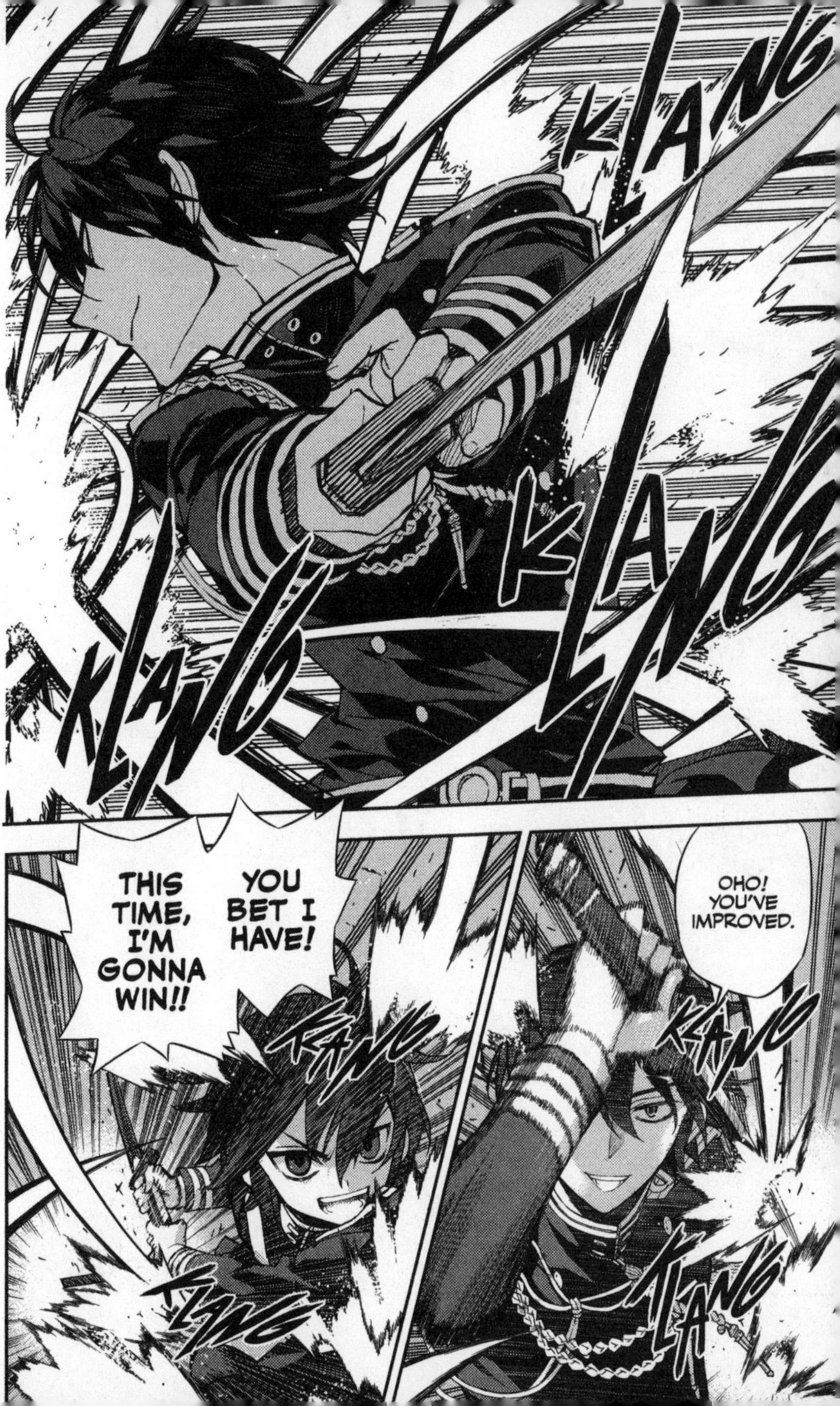
KLANG
KLANG
KLANG
OHO! YOU'VE IMPROVED.
KANG
YOU BET I HAVE!
THIS TIME, I'M GONNA WIN!!
KANG
KLANG

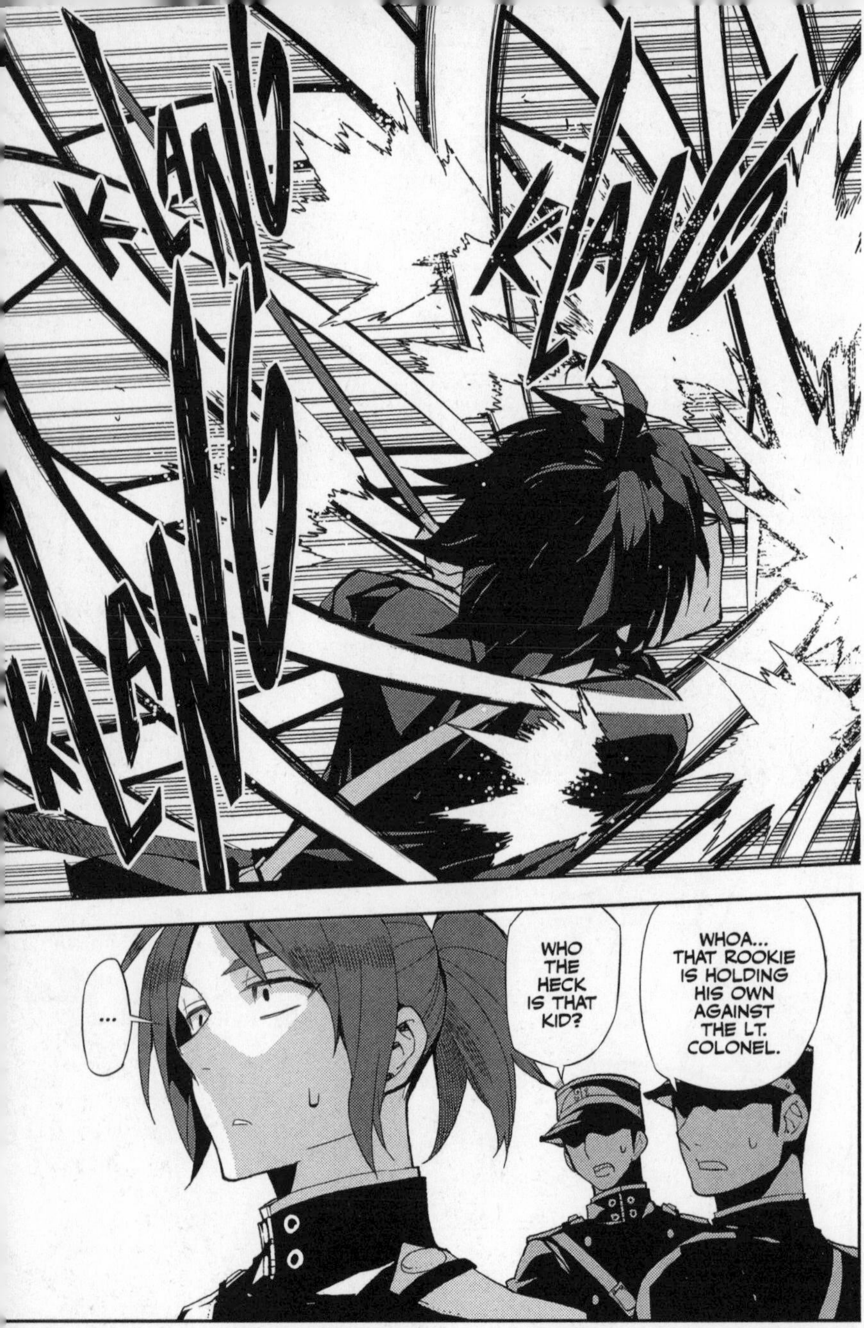
KLANG
KLANG
KLANG
KLANG
WHOA... THAT ROOKIE IS HOLDING HIS OWN AGAINST THE LT. COLONEL.
WHO THE HECK IS THAT KID?
...

Chapter 25 Thirst Logic

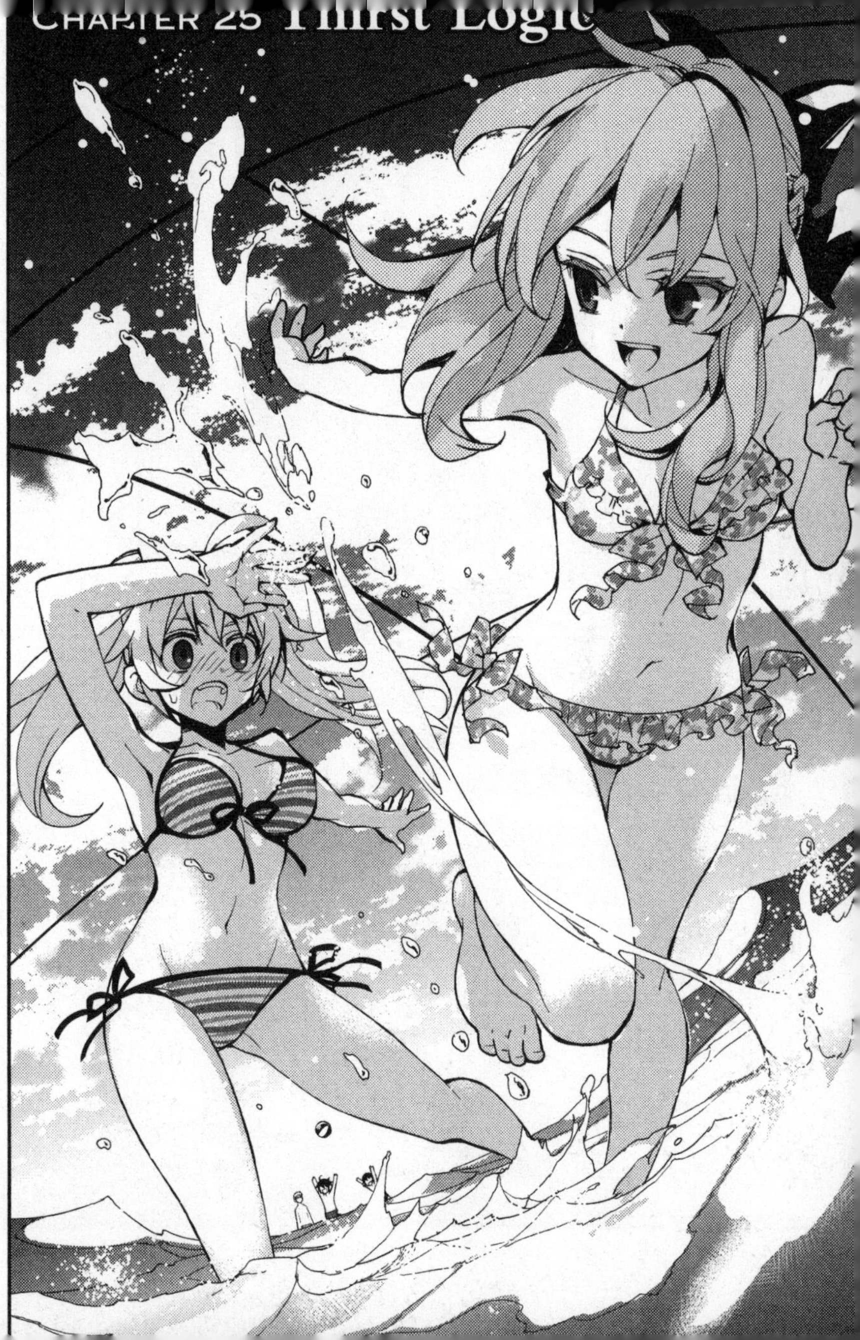

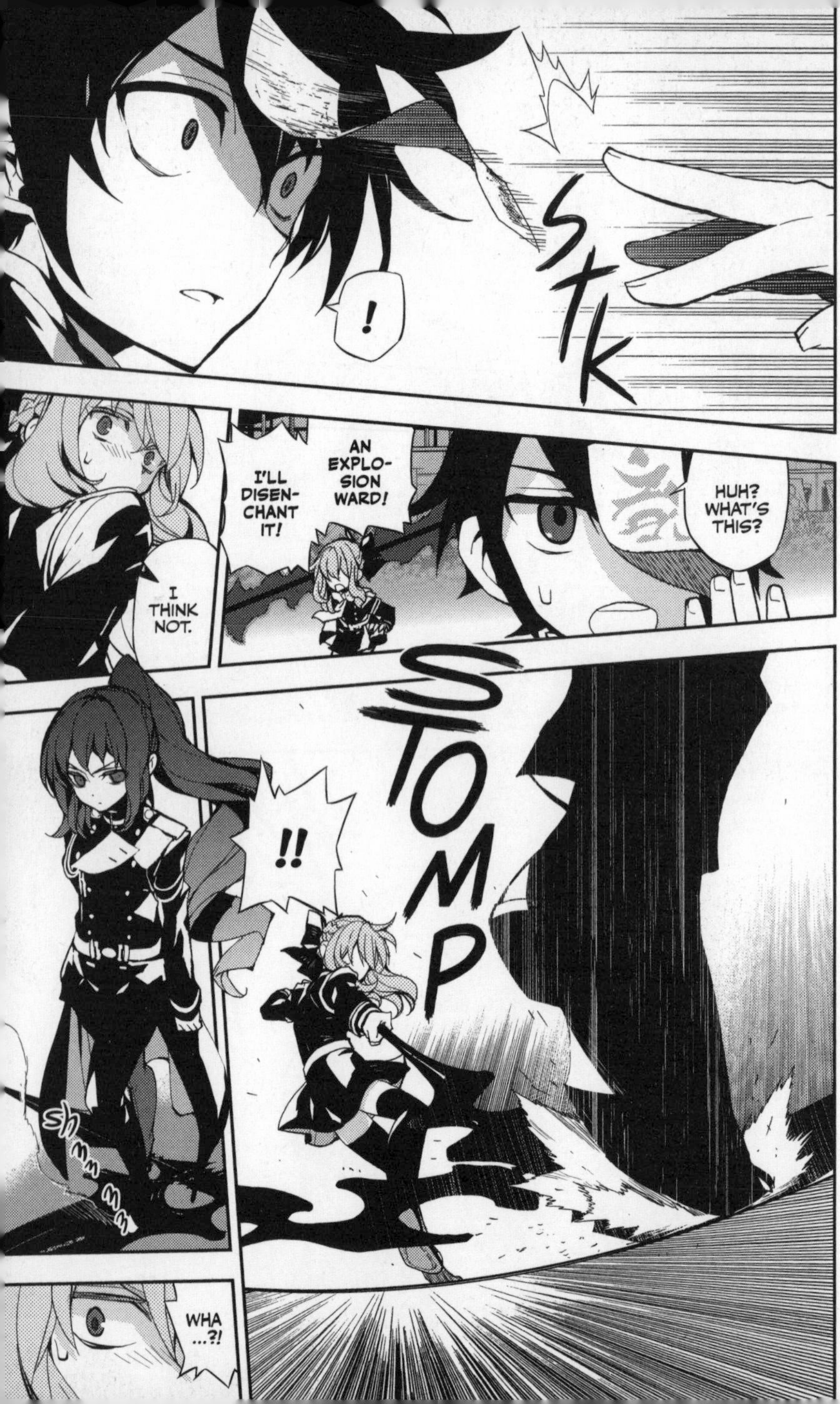
STK
!
HUH? WHAT'S THIS?
AN EXPLOSION WARD!
I'LL DISENCHANT IT!
I THINK NOT.
STOMP
!!
shmm mm mm
WHA ...?!

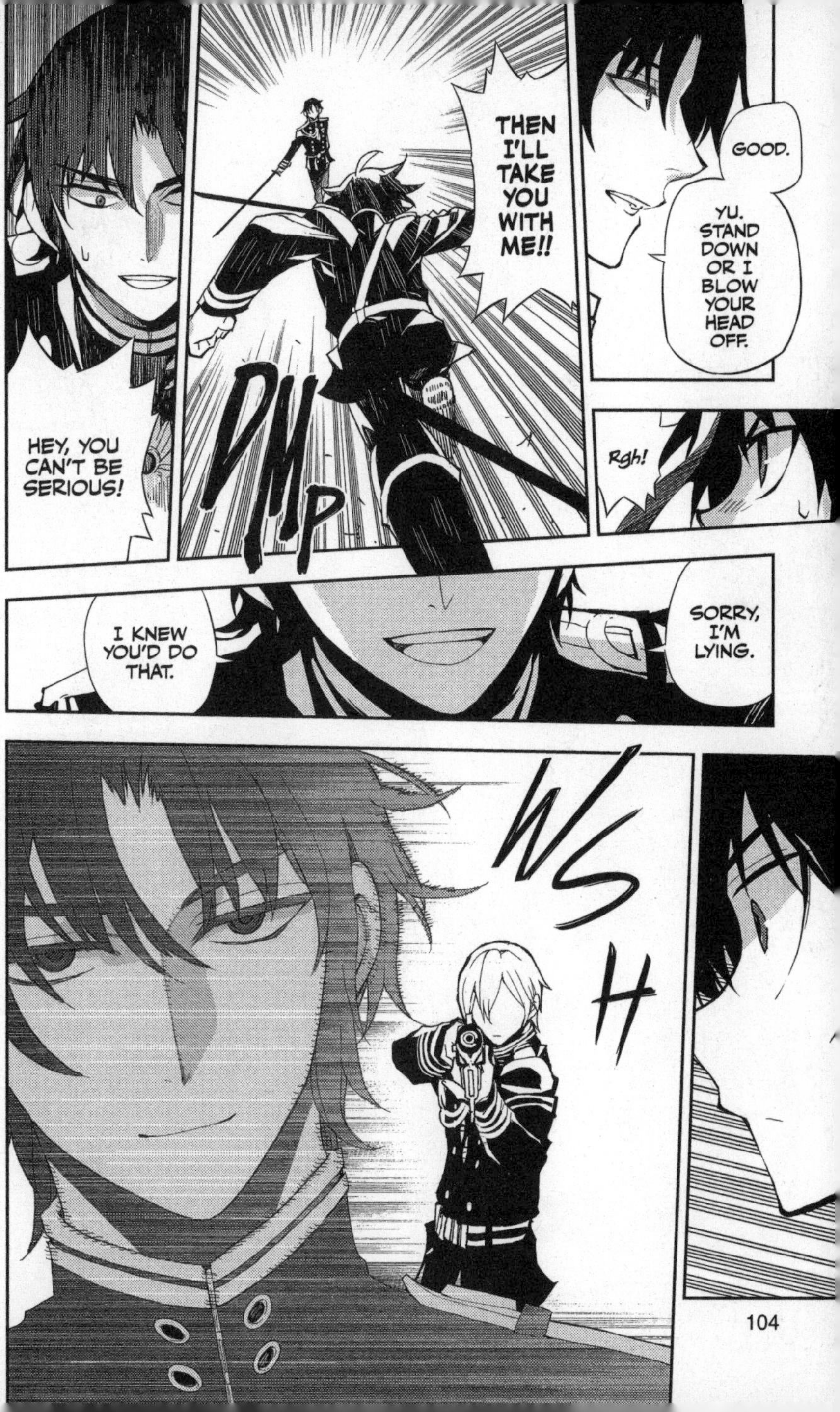
GOOD.
YU. STAND DOWN OR I BLOW YOUR HEAD OFF.
Rgh!
THEN I'LL TAKE YOU WITH ME!!
DMP
HEY, YOU CAN'T BE SERIOUS!
SORRY, I'M LYING.
I KNEW YOU'D DO THAT.
WSH

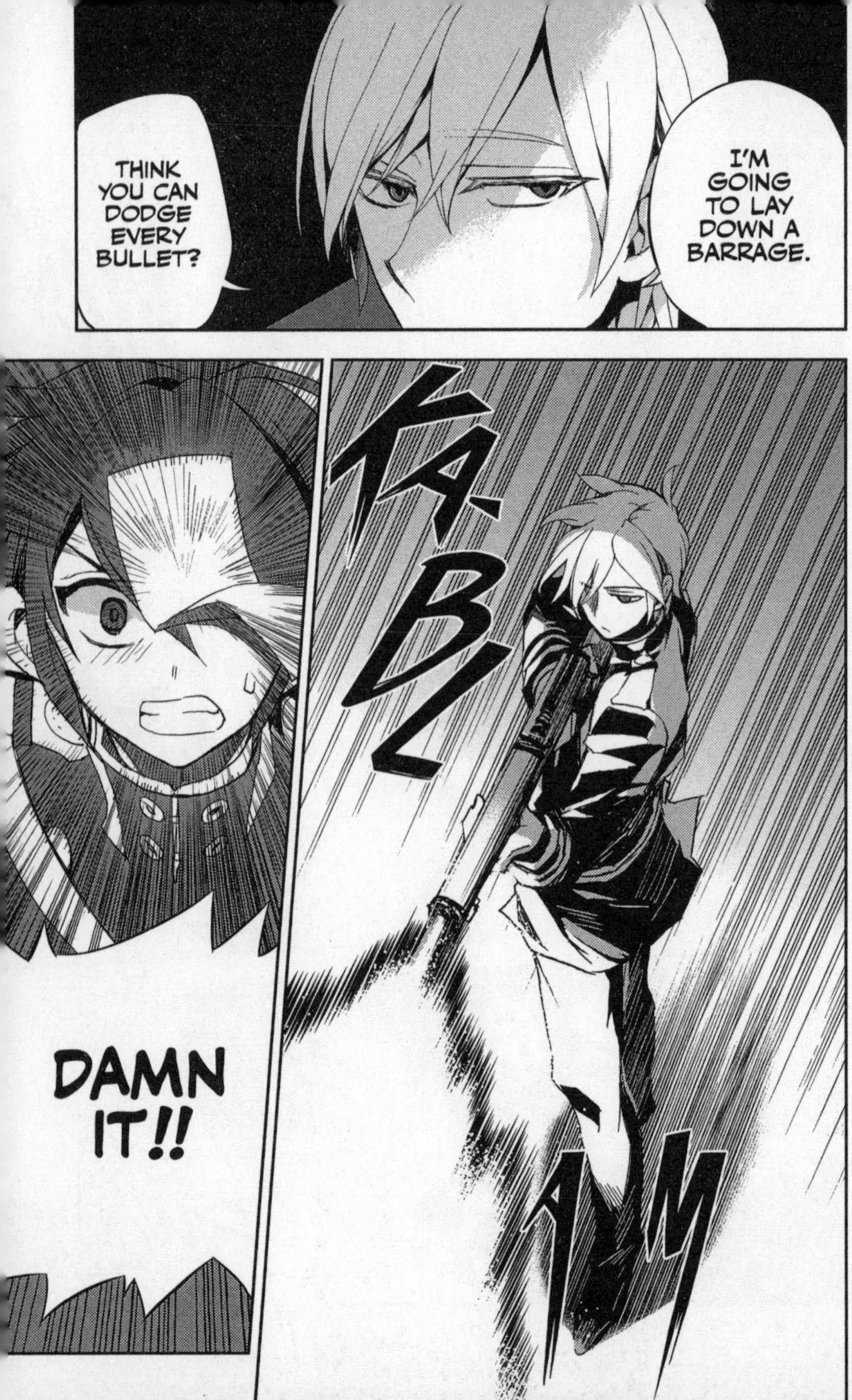
I'M GOING TO LAY DOWN A BARRAGE.
THINK YOU CAN DODGE EVERY BULLET?
KA-BLAM
DAMN IT!!

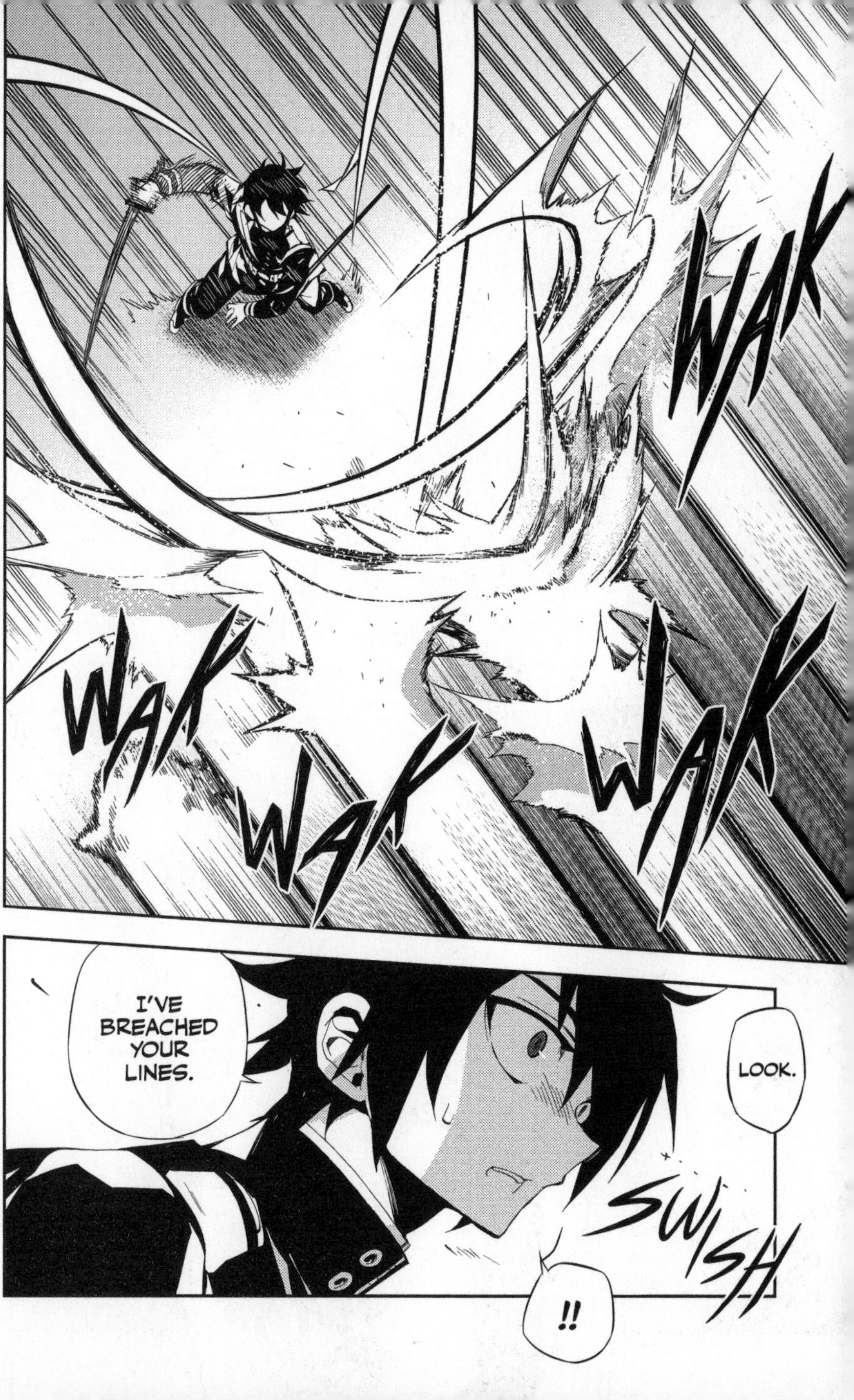
WAK
WAK
WAK
WAK
LOOK.
I'VE BREACHED YOUR LINES.
SWISH
!!

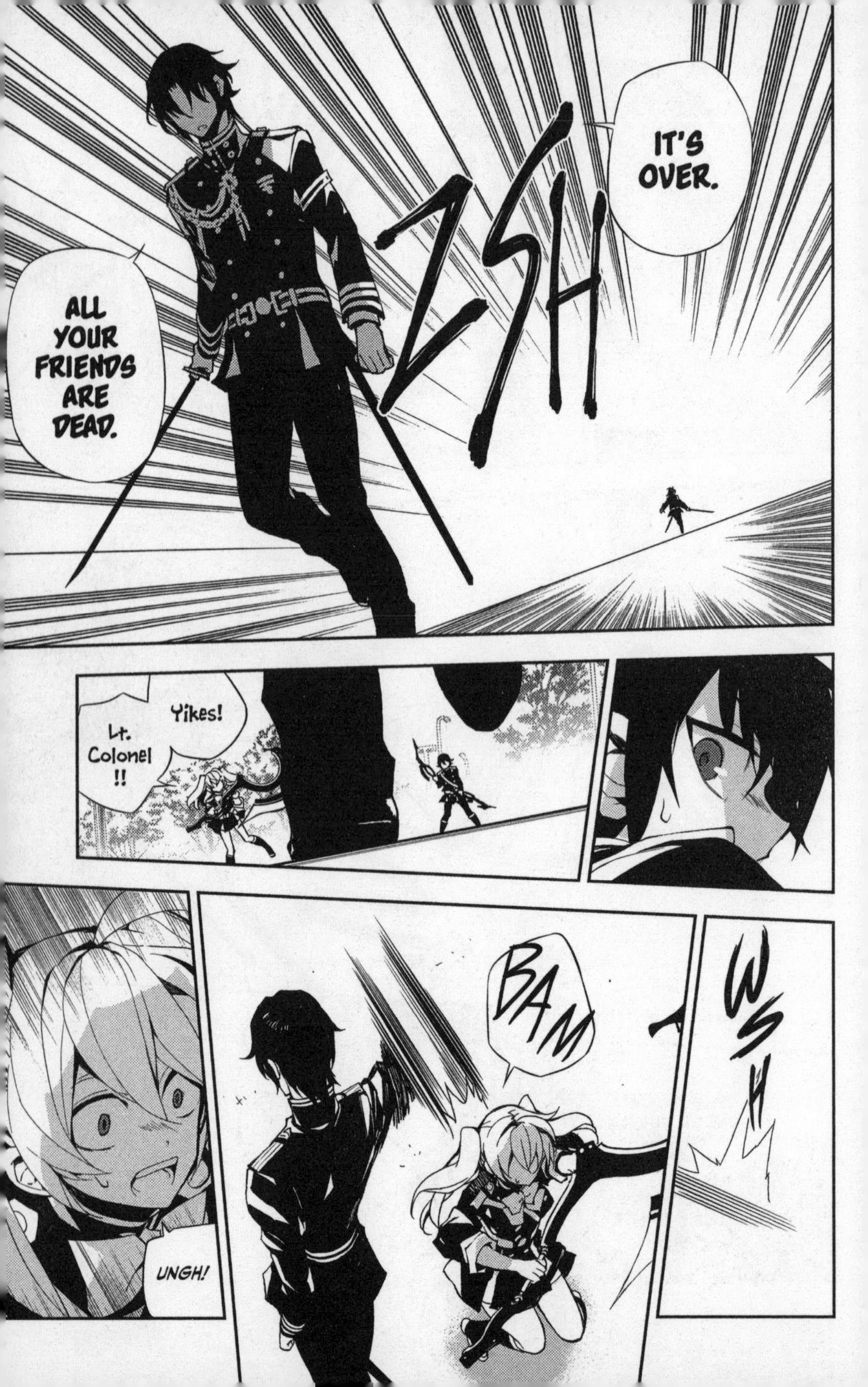
IT'S OVER.
ZSH
ALL YOUR FRIENDS ARE DEAD.
Yikes!
Lt. Colonel!!
WSH
BAM
UNGH!

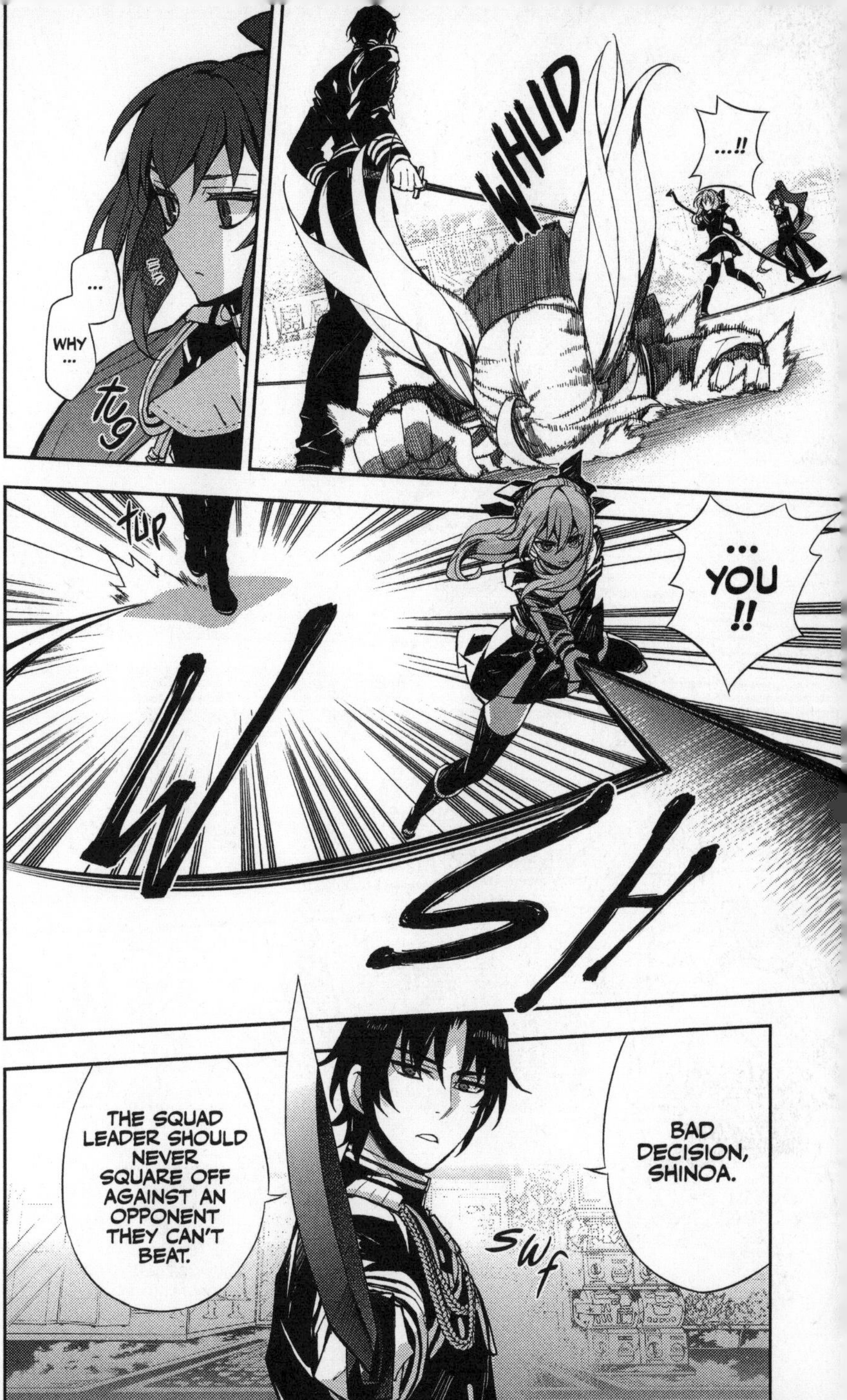
WHUD
...!!
...
WHY ...
tug
...
YOU !!
tup
WHSH
BAD DECISION, SHINOA.
THE SQUAD LEADER SHOULD NEVER SQUARE OFF AGAINST AN OPPONENT THEY CAN'T BEAT.
SWf

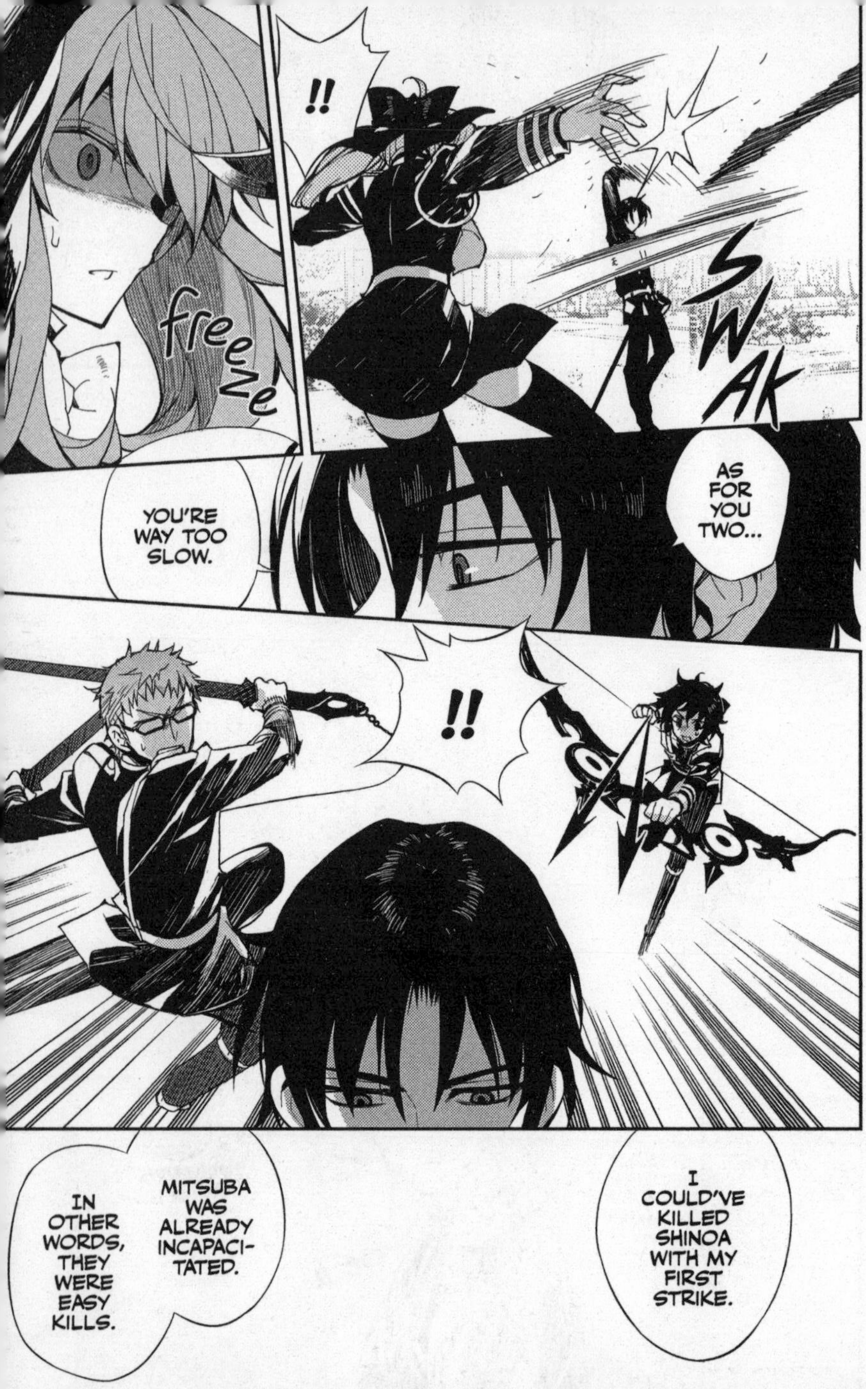
!!
SWAK
freeze
AS FOR YOU TWO...
YOU'RE WAY TOO SLOW.
!!
I COULD'VE KILLED SHINOA WITH MY FIRST STRIKE.
MITSUBA WAS ALREADY INCAPACITATED.
IN OTHER WORDS, THEY WERE EASY KILLS.

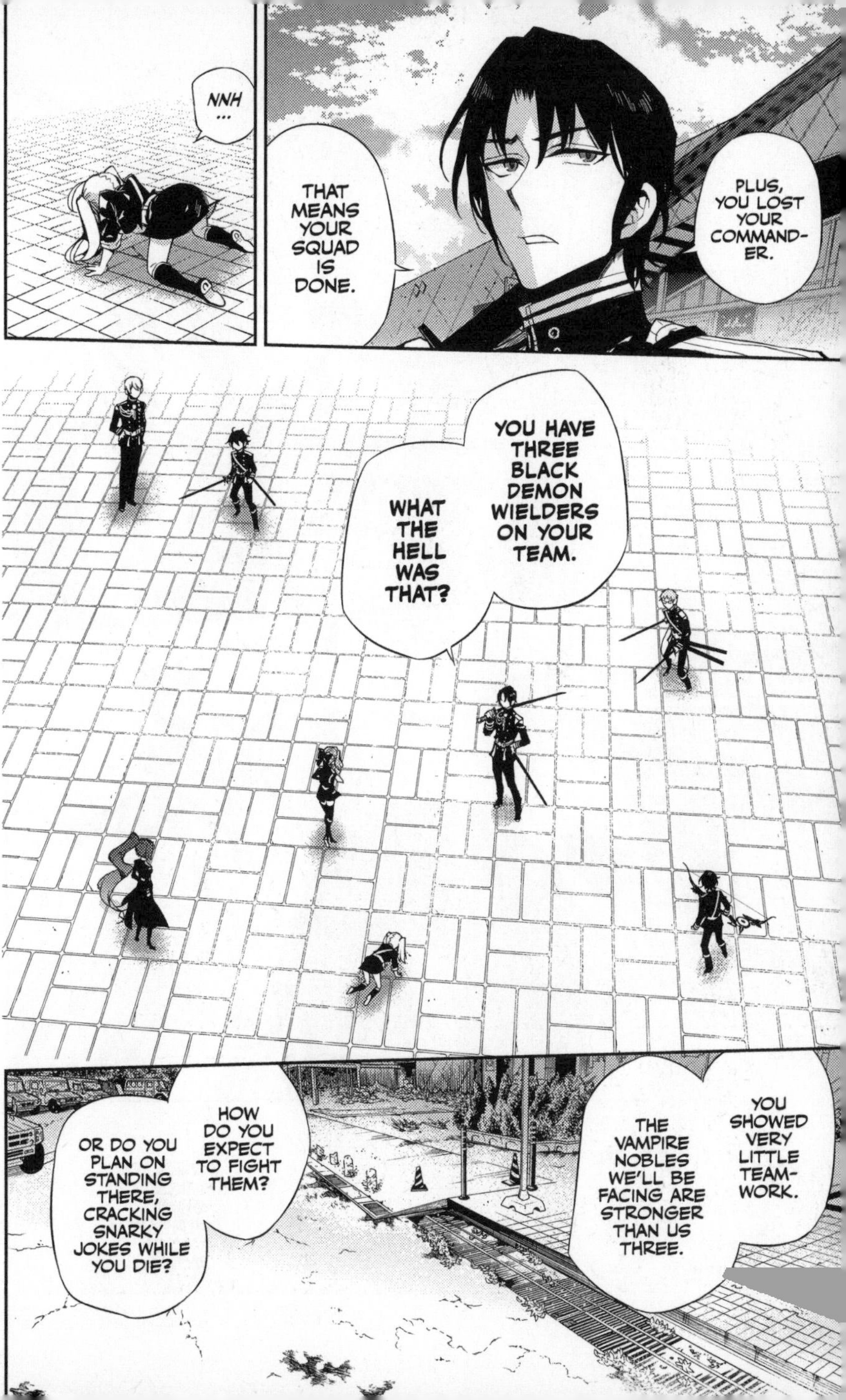
PLUS, YOU LOST YOUR COMMANDER.
THAT MEANS YOUR SQUAD IS DONE.
NNH...
YOU HAVE THREE BLACK DEMON WIELDERS ON YOUR TEAM.
WHAT THE HELL WAS THAT?
YOU SHOWED VERY LITTLE TEAMWORK.
THE VAMPIRE NOBLES WE'LL BE FACING ARE STRONGER THAN US THREE.
HOW DO YOU EXPECT TO FIGHT THEM?
OR DO YOU PLAN ON STANDING THERE, CRACKING SNARKY JOKES WHILE YOU DIE?

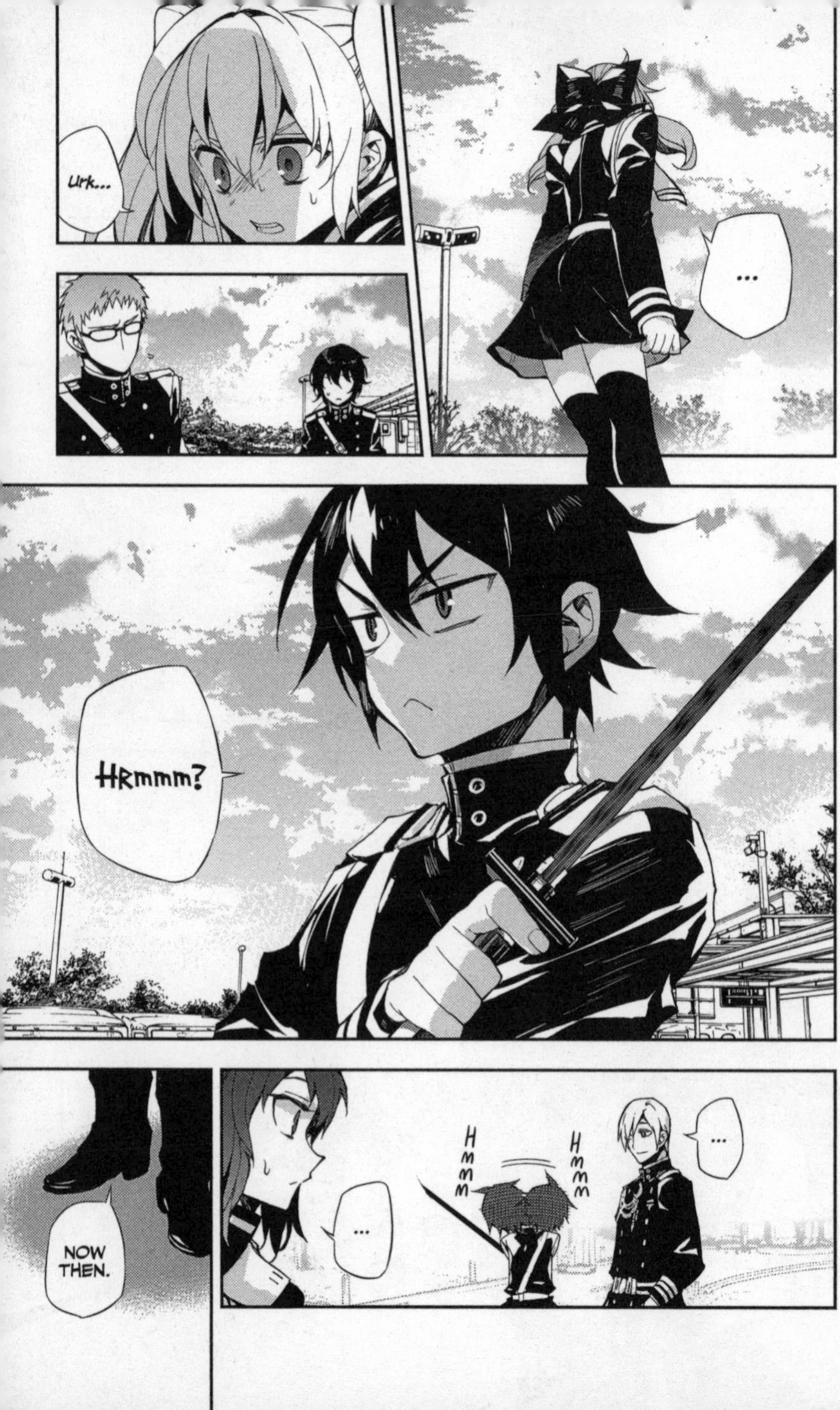
...
Urk...
HRmmm?
...
HMMM
HMMM
...
NOW THEN.

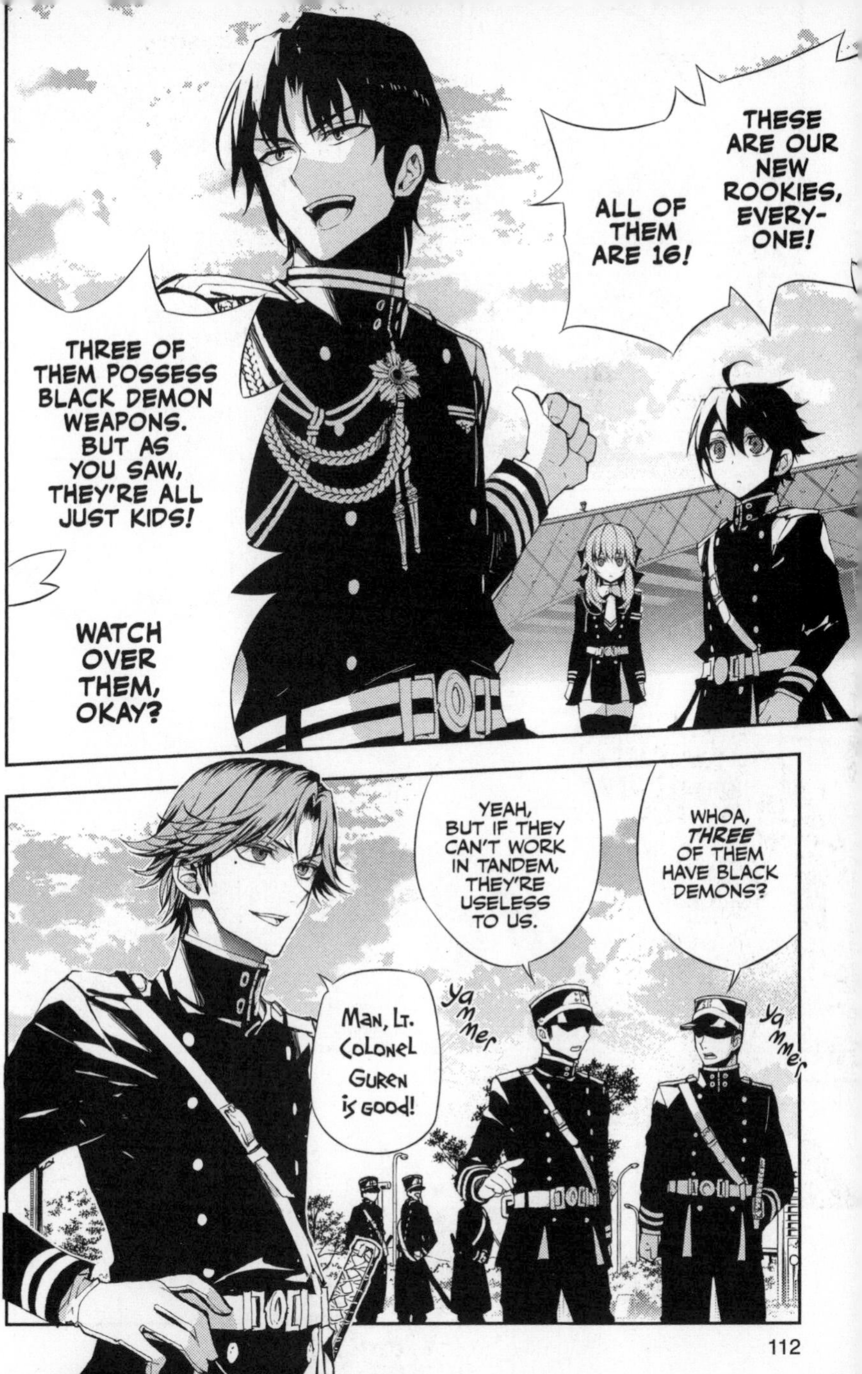
THESE ARE OUR NEW ROOKIES, EVERYONE!
ALL OF THEM ARE 16!
THREE OF THEM POSSESS BLACK DEMON WEAPONS. BUT AS YOU SAW, THEY'RE ALL JUST KIDS!
WATCH OVER THEM, OKAY?
WHOA, *THREE* OF THEM HAVE BLACK DEMONS?
YEAH, BUT IF THEY CAN'T WORK IN TANDEM, THEY'RE USELESS TO US.
yammer
yammer
Man, Lt. Colonel Guren is good!

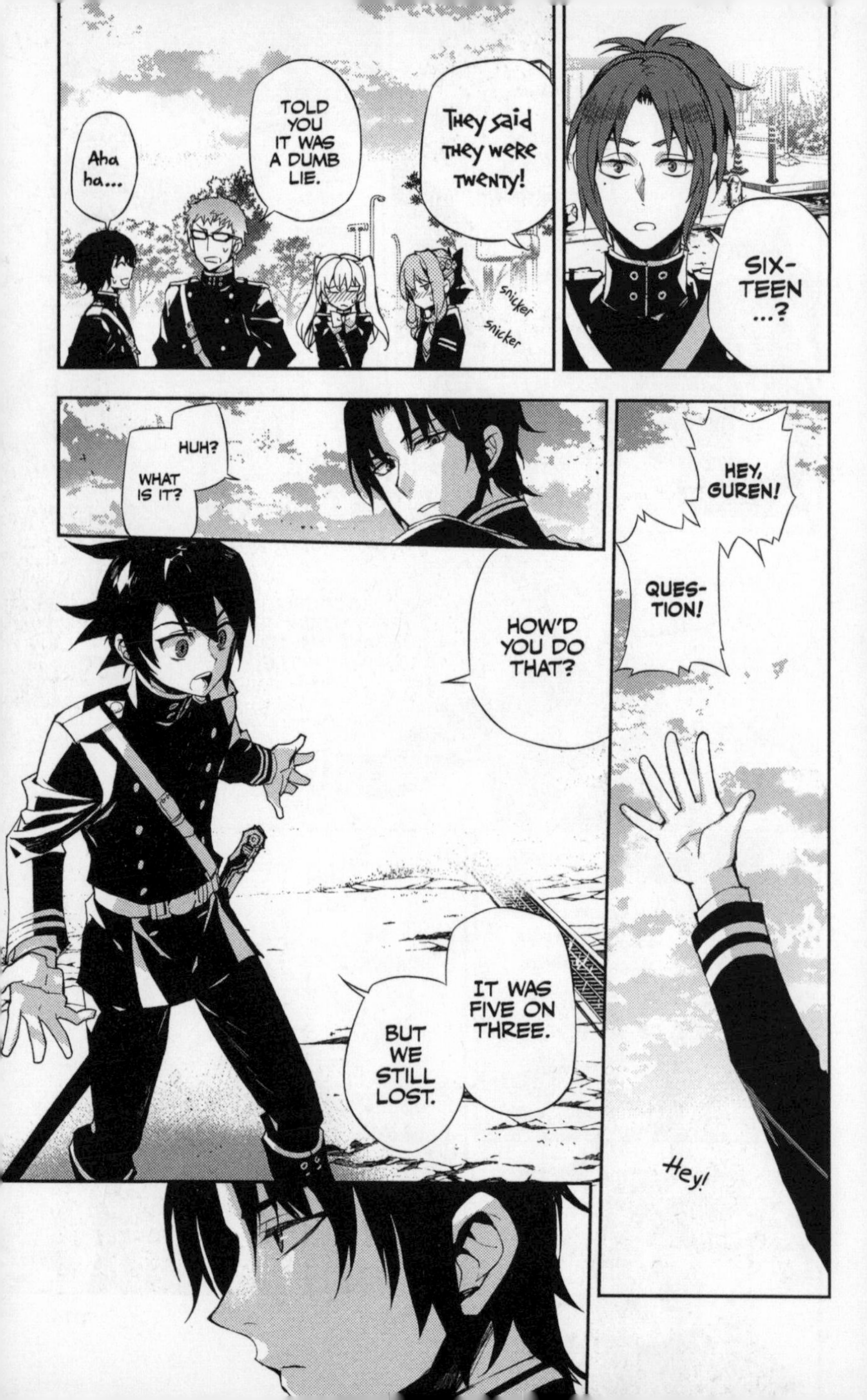
SIX-
TEEN
...?
They said they were twenty!
snicker
snicker
TOLD YOU IT WAS A DUMB LIE.
Aha ha...
HEY, GUREN!
QUES-
TION!
Hey!
HUH?
WHAT IS IT?
HOW'D YOU DO THAT?
IT WAS FIVE ON THREE.
BUT WE STILL LOST.

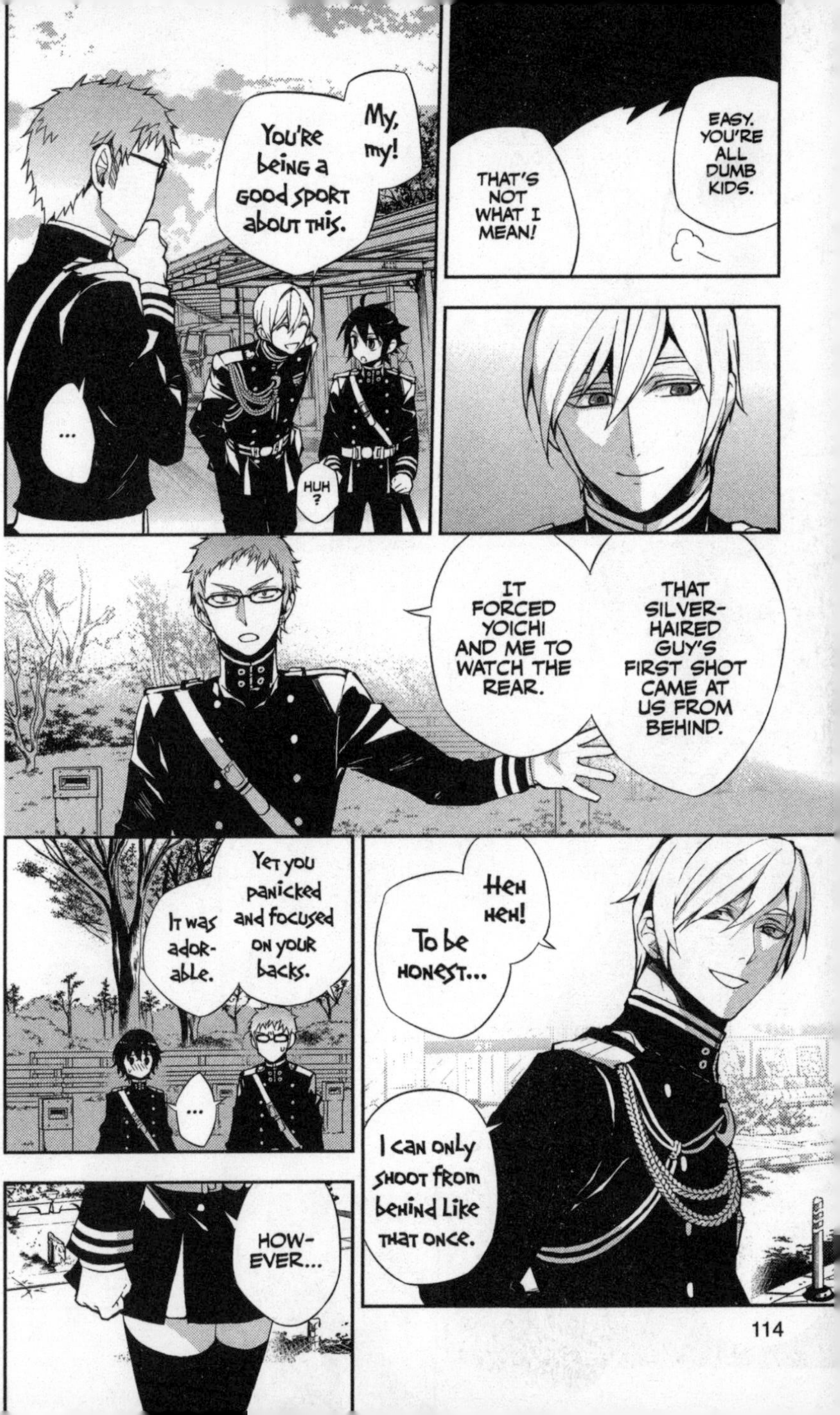
EASY. YOU'RE ALL DUMB KIDS.
THAT'S NOT WHAT I MEAN!
My, my!
You're being a good sport about this.
...
HUH?
THAT SILVER-HAIRED GUY'S FIRST SHOT CAME AT US FROM BEHIND.
IT FORCED YOICHI AND ME TO WATCH THE REAR.
Heh heh!
To be honest...
I can only shoot from behind like that once.
Yet you panicked and focused on your backs.
It was adorable.
...
HOW-EVER...

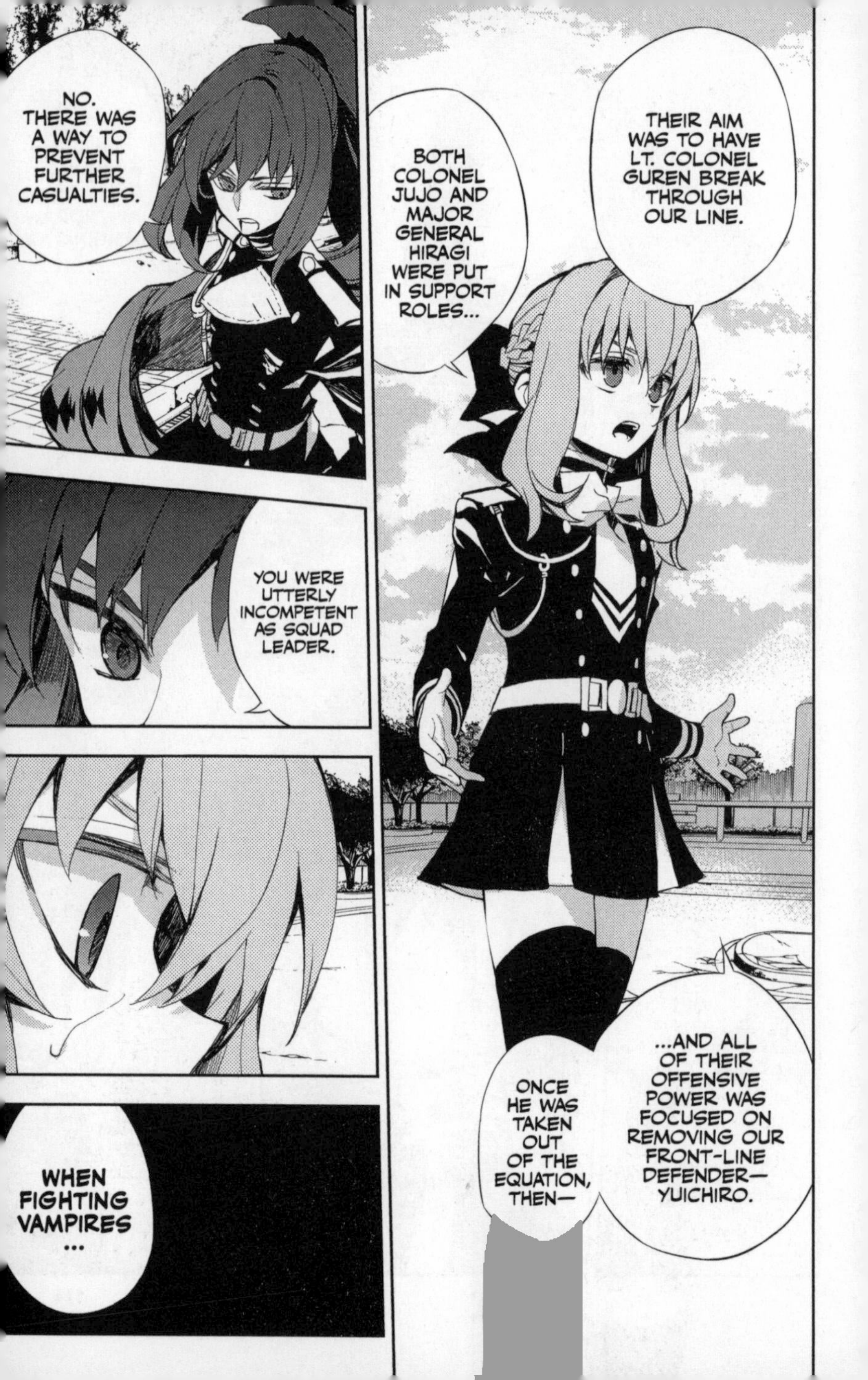
THEIR AIM WAS TO HAVE LT. COLONEL GUREN BREAK THROUGH OUR LINE.
BOTH COLONEL JUJO AND MAJOR GENERAL HIRAGI WERE PUT IN SUPPORT ROLES...
...AND ALL OF THEIR OFFENSIVE POWER WAS FOCUSED ON REMOVING OUR FRONT-LINE DEFENDER—YUICHIRO.
ONCE HE WAS TAKEN OUT OF THE EQUATION, THEN—
NO. THERE WAS A WAY TO PREVENT FURTHER CASUALTIES.
YOU WERE UTTERLY INCOMPETENT AS SQUAD LEADER.
WHEN FIGHTING VAMPIRES ...

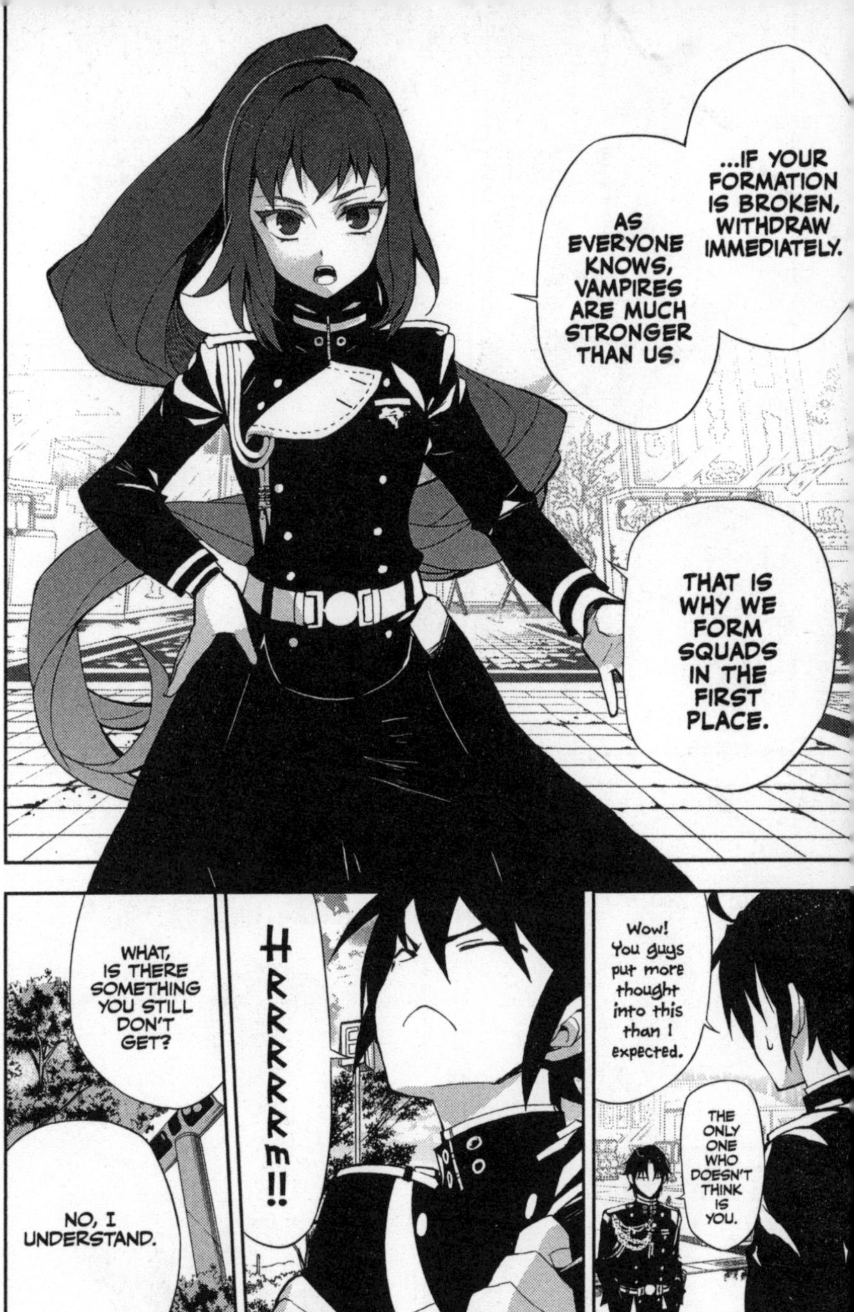
...IF YOUR FORMATION IS BROKEN, WITHDRAW IMMEDIATELY.
AS EVERYONE KNOWS, VAMPIRES ARE MUCH STRONGER THAN US.
THAT IS WHY WE FORM SQUADS IN THE FIRST PLACE.
Wow! You guys put more thought into this than I expected.
THE ONLY ONE WHO DOESN'T THINK IS YOU.
HRRRRRRm!!
WHAT, IS THERE SOMETHING YOU STILL DON'T GET?
NO, I UNDERSTAND.

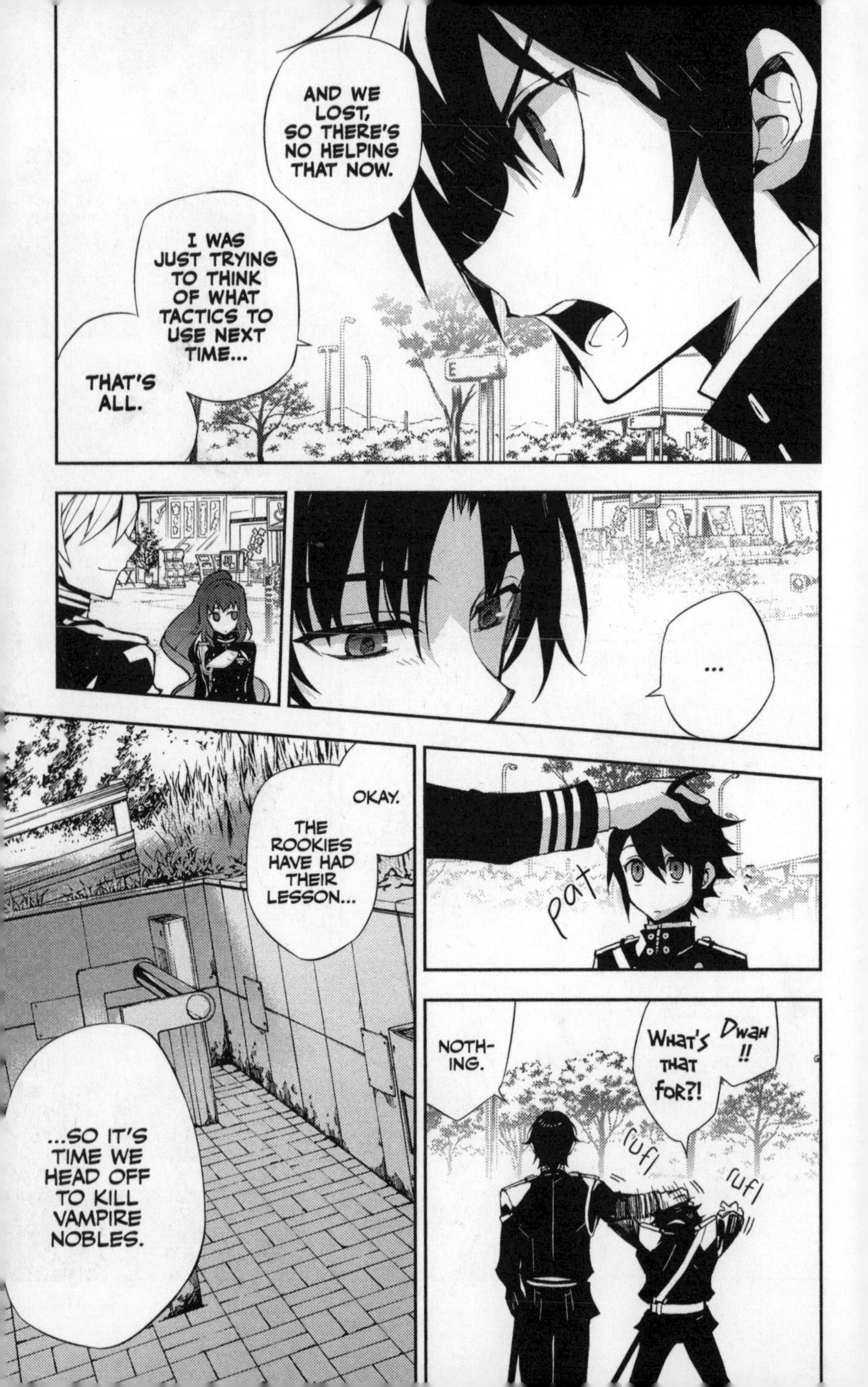
AND WE LOST, SO THERE'S NO HELPING THAT NOW.
I WAS JUST TRYING TO THINK OF WHAT TACTICS TO USE NEXT TIME...
THAT'S ALL.
...
pat
Dwah!!
What's that for?!
rufl
rufl
NOTHING.
OKAY.
THE ROOKIES HAVE HAD THEIR LESSON...
...SO IT'S TIME WE HEAD OFF TO KILL VAMPIRE NOBLES.

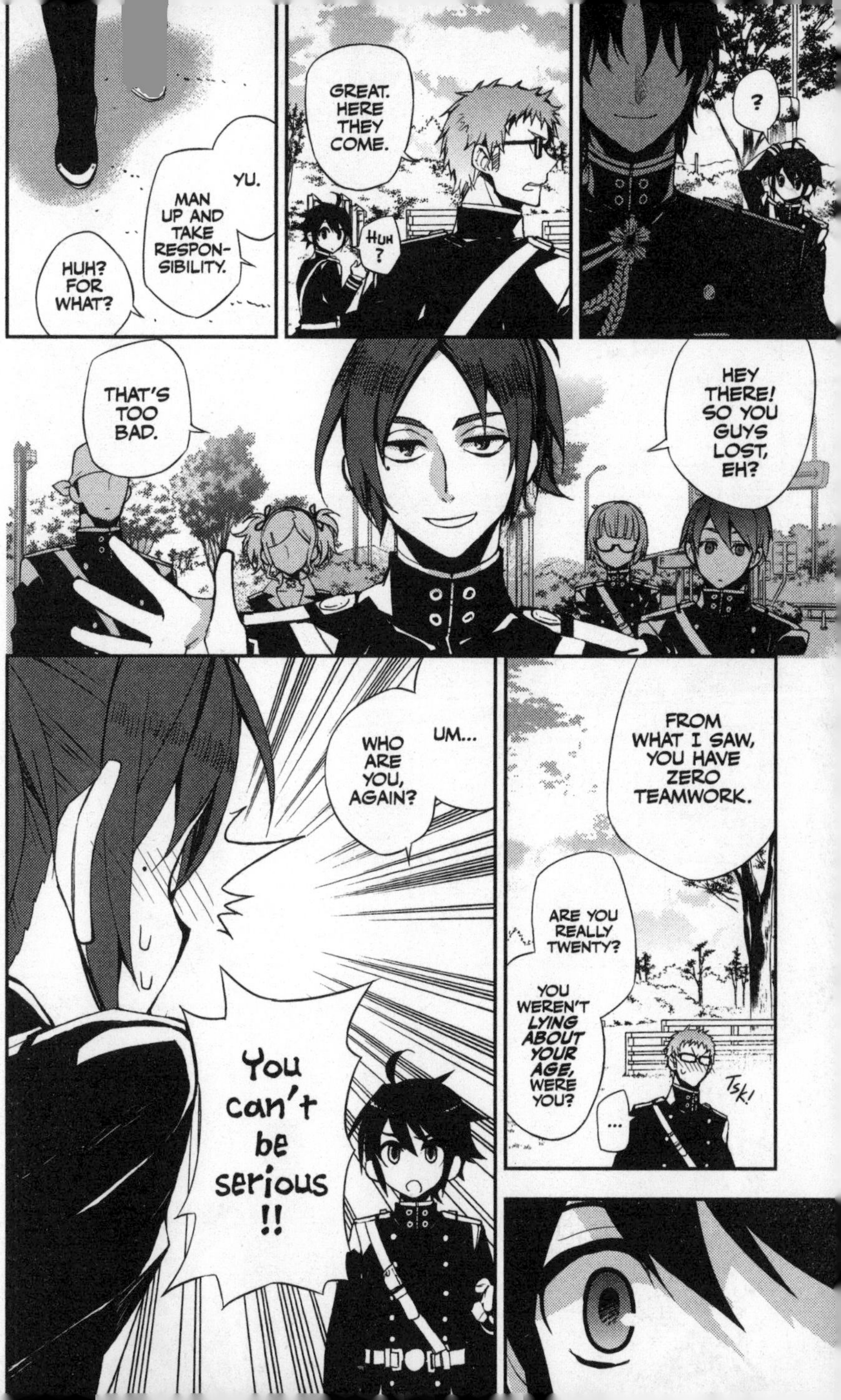
?
GREAT. HERE THEY COME.
HUH?
YU.
MAN UP AND TAKE RESPON-SIBILITY.
HUH? FOR WHAT?
HEY THERE! SO YOU GUYS LOST, EH?
THAT'S TOO BAD.
FROM WHAT I SAW, YOU HAVE ZERO TEAMWORK.
ARE YOU REALLY TWENTY?
YOU WEREN'T *LYING ABOUT YOUR AGE*, WERE YOU?
...
TSK!
UM...
WHO ARE YOU, AGAIN?
You can't be serious!!

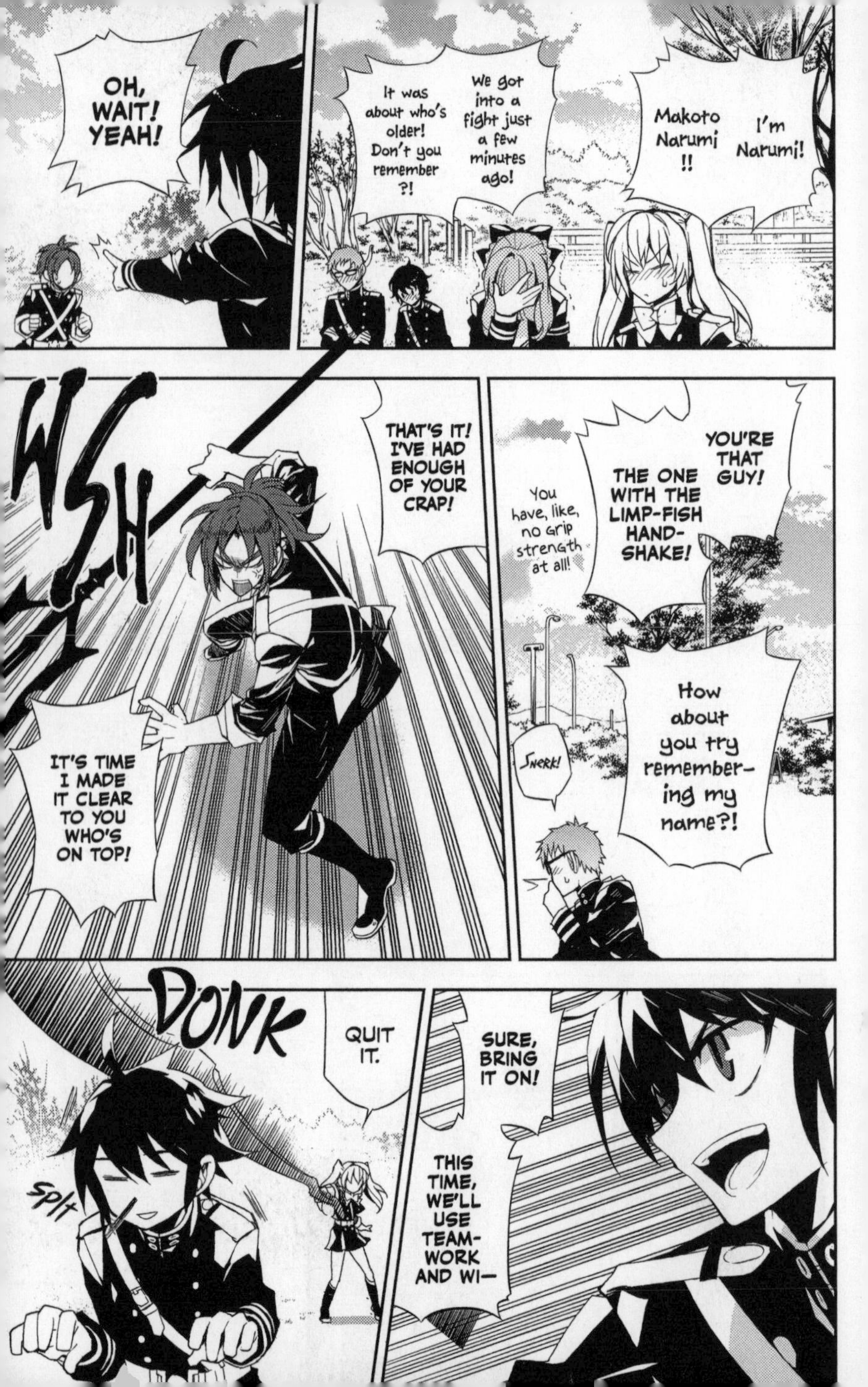
I'm Narumi!
Makoto Narumi!!
We got into a fight just a few minutes ago!
It was about who's older! Don't you remember?!
OH, WAIT! YEAH!
YOU'RE THAT GUY!
THE ONE WITH THE LIMP-FISH HANDSHAKE!
You have, like, no grip strength at all!
How about you try remembering my name?!
SNERK!
WSH
THAT'S IT! I'VE HAD ENOUGH OF YOUR CRAP!
IT'S TIME I MADE IT CLEAR TO YOU WHO'S ON TOP!
SURE, BRING IT ON!
THIS TIME, WE'LL USE TEAMWORK AND WI—
DONK
QUIT IT.
splt

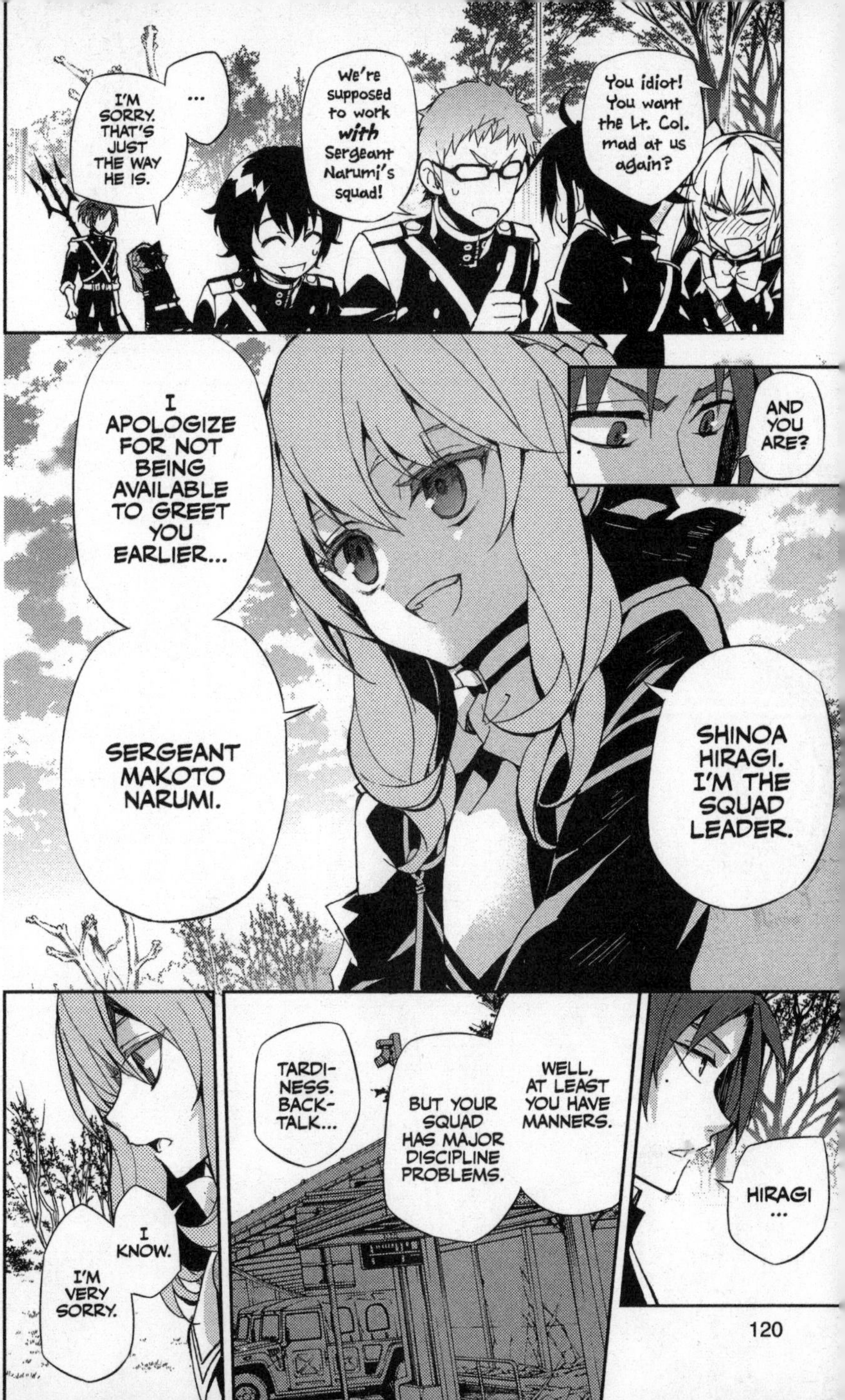
You idiot! You want the Lt. Col. mad at us again?
We're supposed to work *with* Sergeant Narumi's squad!
...
I'M SORRY. THAT'S JUST THE WAY HE IS.
AND YOU ARE?
SHINOA HIRAGI. I'M THE SQUAD LEADER.
I APOLOGIZE FOR NOT BEING AVAILABLE TO GREET YOU EARLIER...
SERGEANT MAKOTO NARUMI.
HIRAGI ...
WELL, AT LEAST YOU HAVE MANNERS.
BUT YOUR SQUAD HAS MAJOR DISCIPLINE PROBLEMS.
TARDI-NESS. BACK-TALK...
I KNOW.
I'M VERY SORRY.

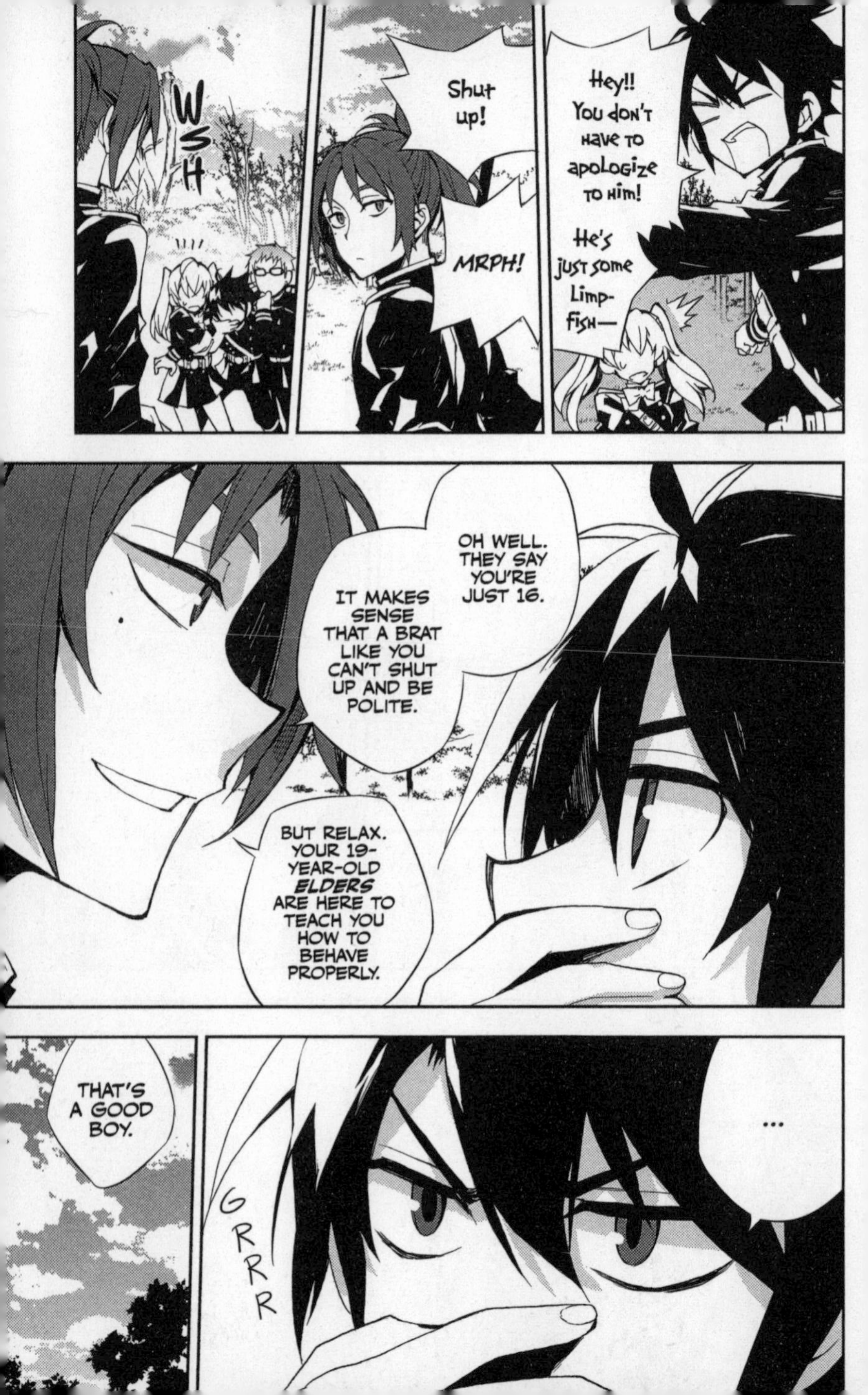
Hey!! You don't have to apologize to him!
He's just some Limp-fish—
Shut up!
MRPH!
WSH
!!!
OH WELL. THEY SAY YOU'RE JUST 16.
IT MAKES SENSE THAT A BRAT LIKE YOU CAN'T SHUT UP AND BE POLITE.
BUT RELAX. YOUR 19-YEAR-OLD *ELDERS* ARE HERE TO TEACH YOU HOW TO BEHAVE PROPERLY.
...
GRRR
THAT'S A GOOD BOY.

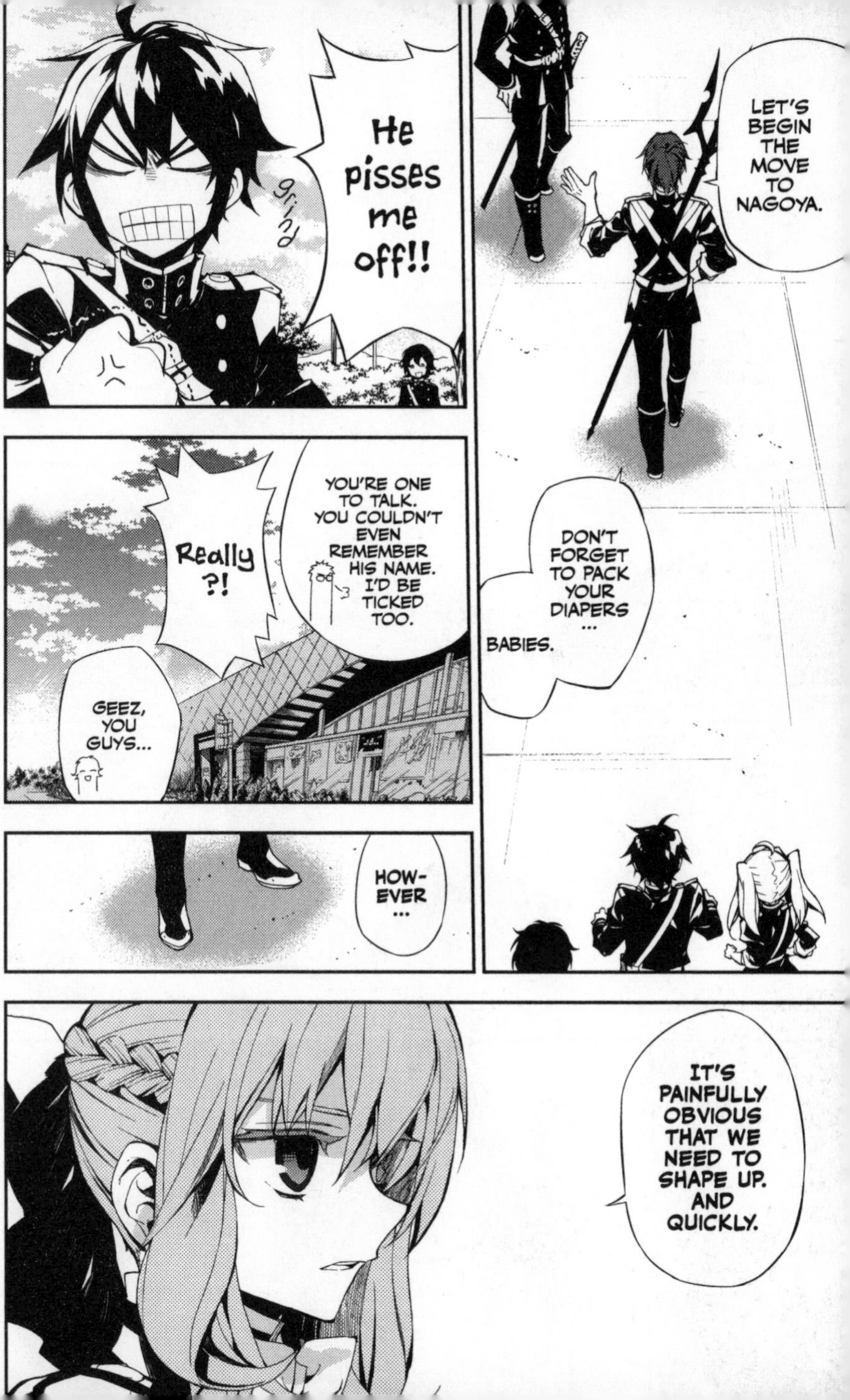
LET'S BEGIN THE MOVE TO NAGOYA.
DON'T FORGET TO PACK YOUR DIAPERS...
BABIES.
He pisses me off!!
grind
YOU'RE ONE TO TALK. YOU COULDN'T EVEN REMEMBER HIS NAME. I'D BE TICKED TOO.
Really?!
GEEZ, YOU GUYS...
HOW-EVER...
IT'S PAINFULLY OBVIOUS THAT WE NEED TO SHAPE UP. AND QUICKLY.

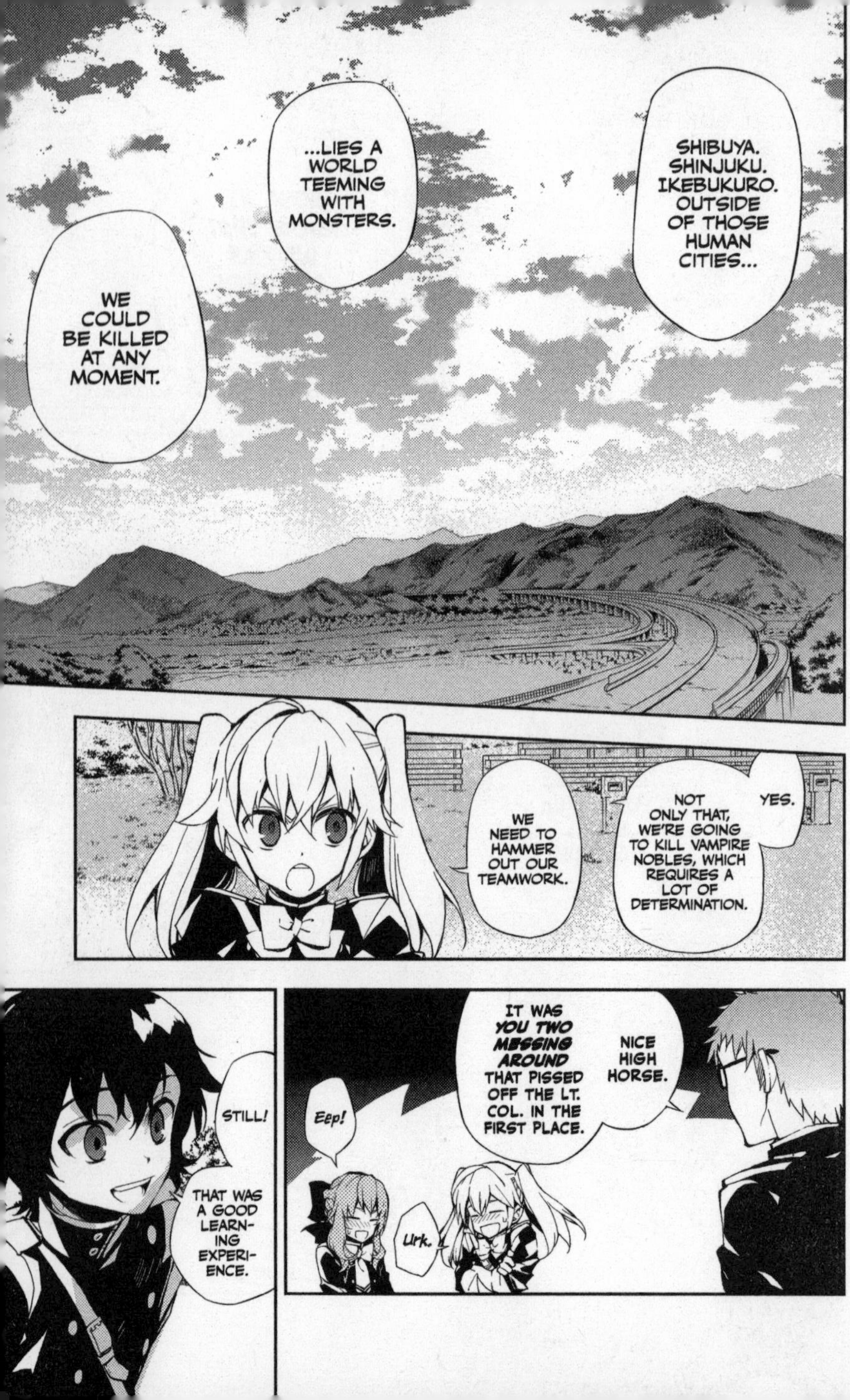
SHIBUYA. SHINJUKU. IKEBUKURO. OUTSIDE OF THOSE HUMAN CITIES...
...LIES A WORLD TEEMING WITH MONSTERS.
WE COULD BE KILLED AT ANY MOMENT.
YES.
NOT ONLY THAT, WE'RE GOING TO KILL VAMPIRE NOBLES, WHICH REQUIRES A LOT OF DETERMINATION.
WE NEED TO HAMMER OUT OUR TEAMWORK.
NICE HIGH HORSE.
IT WAS *YOU TWO MESSING AROUND* THAT PISSED OFF THE LT. COL. IN THE FIRST PLACE.
Eep!
Urk.
STILL!
THAT WAS A GOOD LEARNING EXPERIENCE.

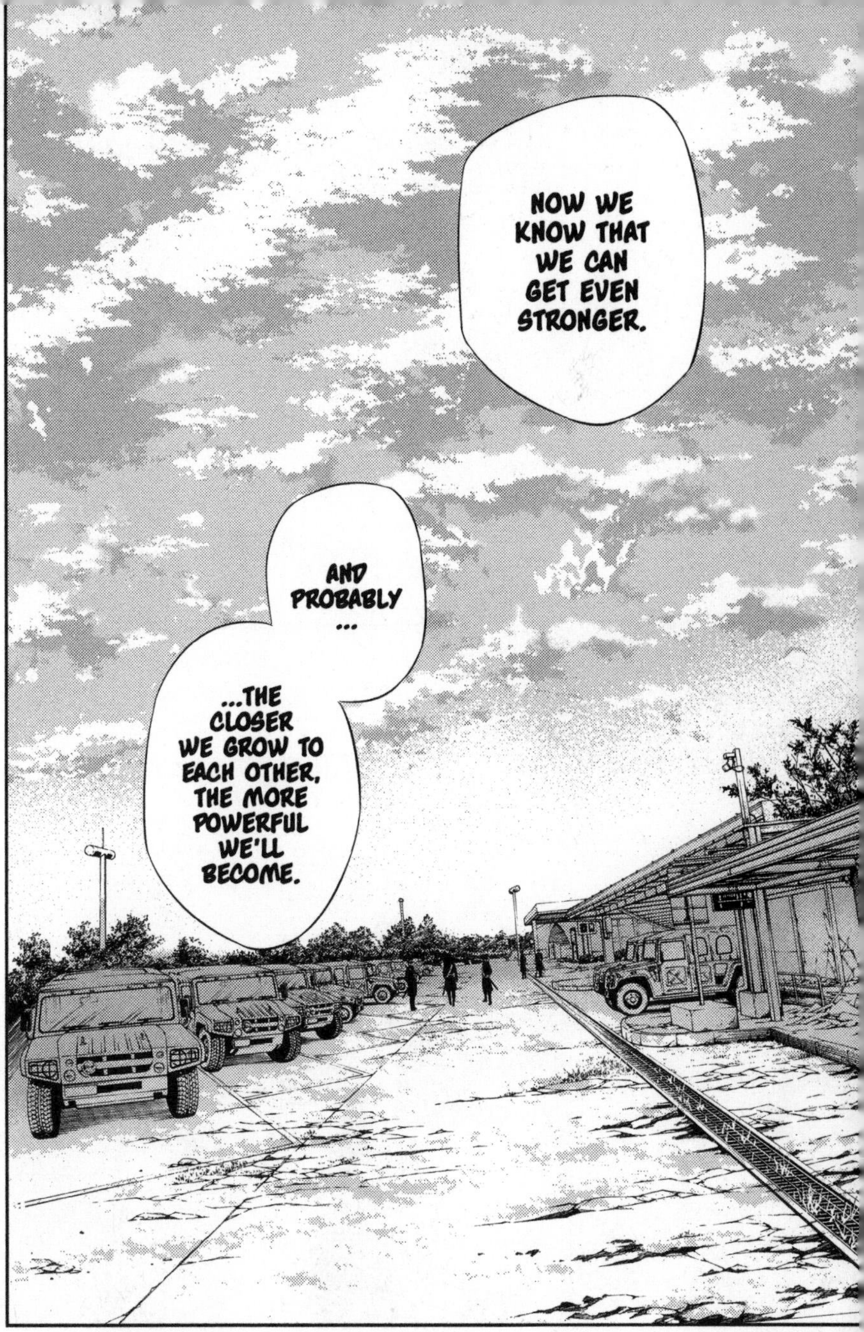
NOW WE KNOW THAT WE CAN GET EVEN STRONGER.
AND PROBABLY ...
...THE CLOSER WE GROW TO EACH OTHER, THE MORE POWERFUL WE'LL BECOME.

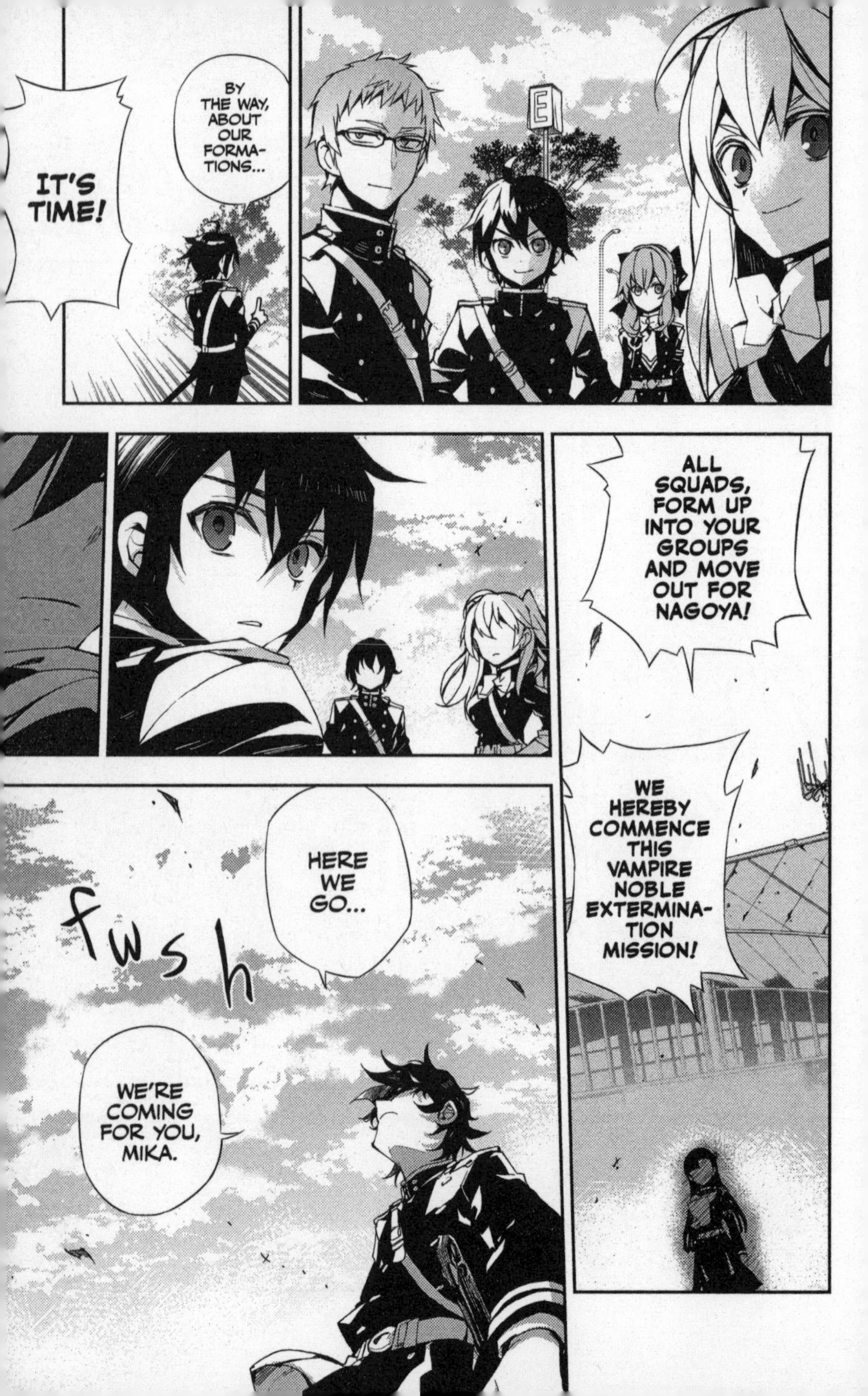
E
BY THE WAY, ABOUT OUR FORMATIONS...
IT'S TIME!
ALL SQUADS, FORM UP INTO YOUR GROUPS AND MOVE OUT FOR NAGOYA!
WE HEREBY COMMENCE THIS VAMPIRE NOBLE EXTERMINATION MISSION!
HERE WE GO...
fwsh
WE'RE COMING FOR YOU, MIKA.

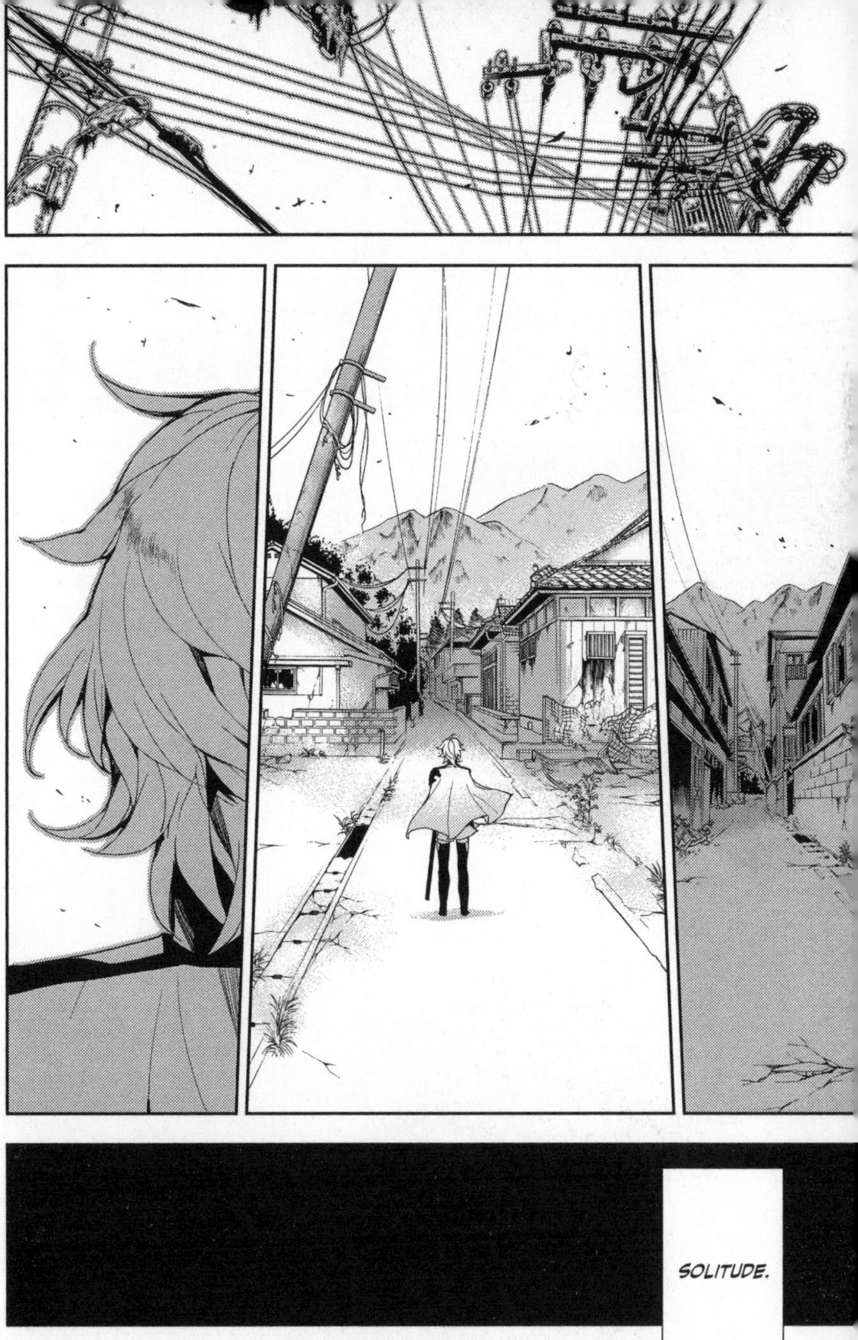
SOLITUDE.

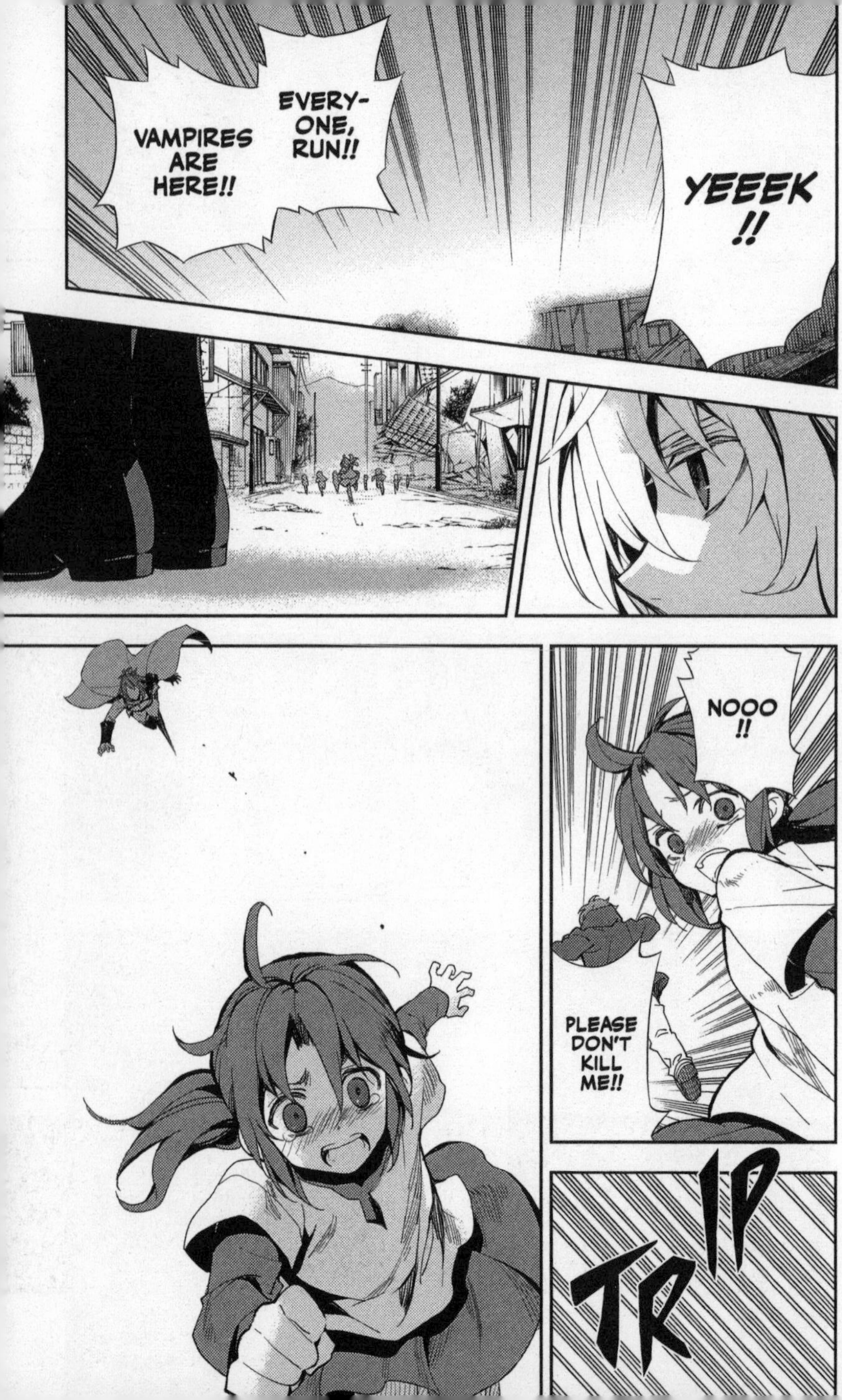
YEEEK!!
EVERY-ONE, RUN!!
VAMPIRES ARE HERE!!
NOOO!!
PLEASE DON'T KILL ME!!
TRIP

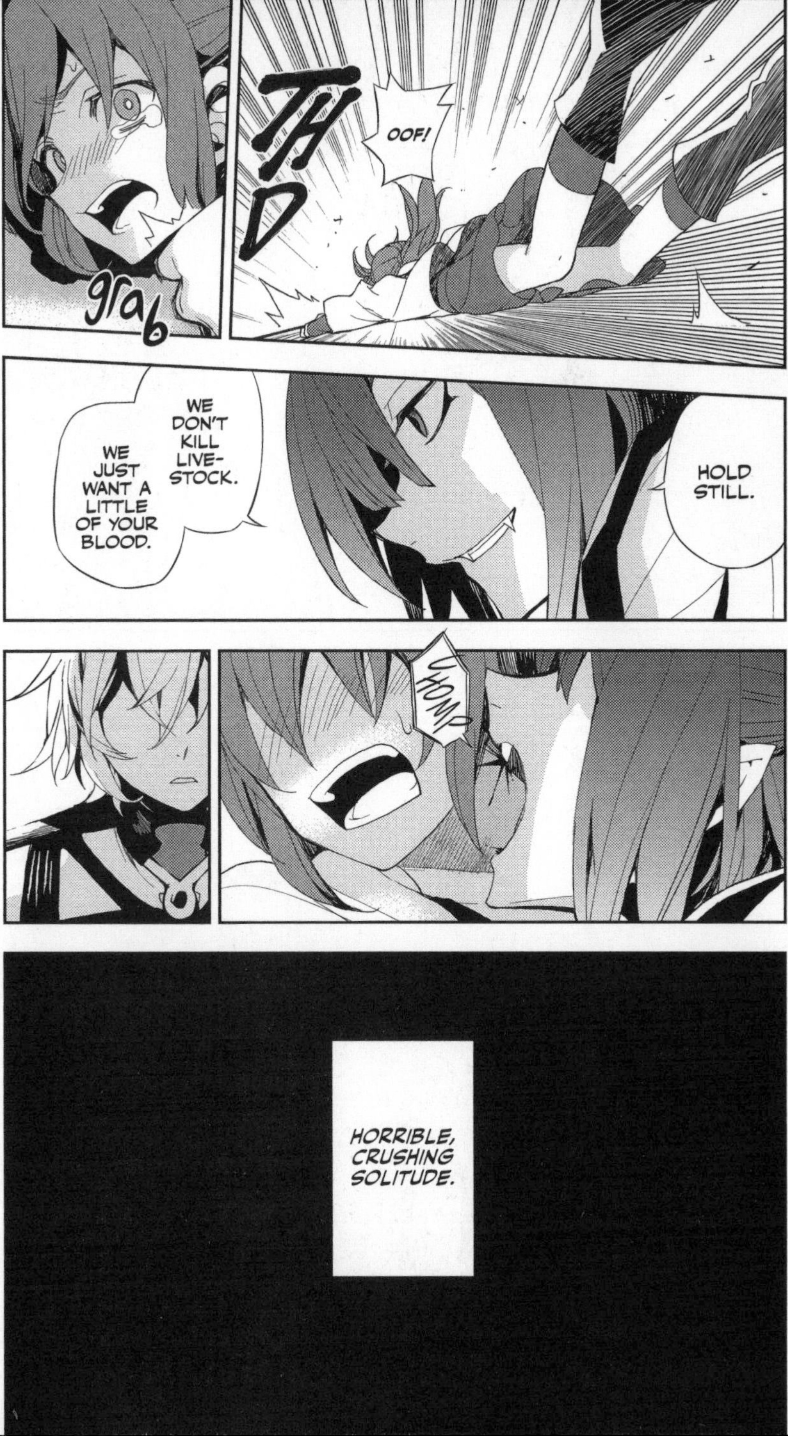
THD
OOF!
grab
HOLD STILL.
WE DON'T KILL LIVE-STOCK.
WE JUST WANT A LITTLE OF YOUR BLOOD.
CHOMP!
HORRIBLE, CRUSHING SOLITUDE.

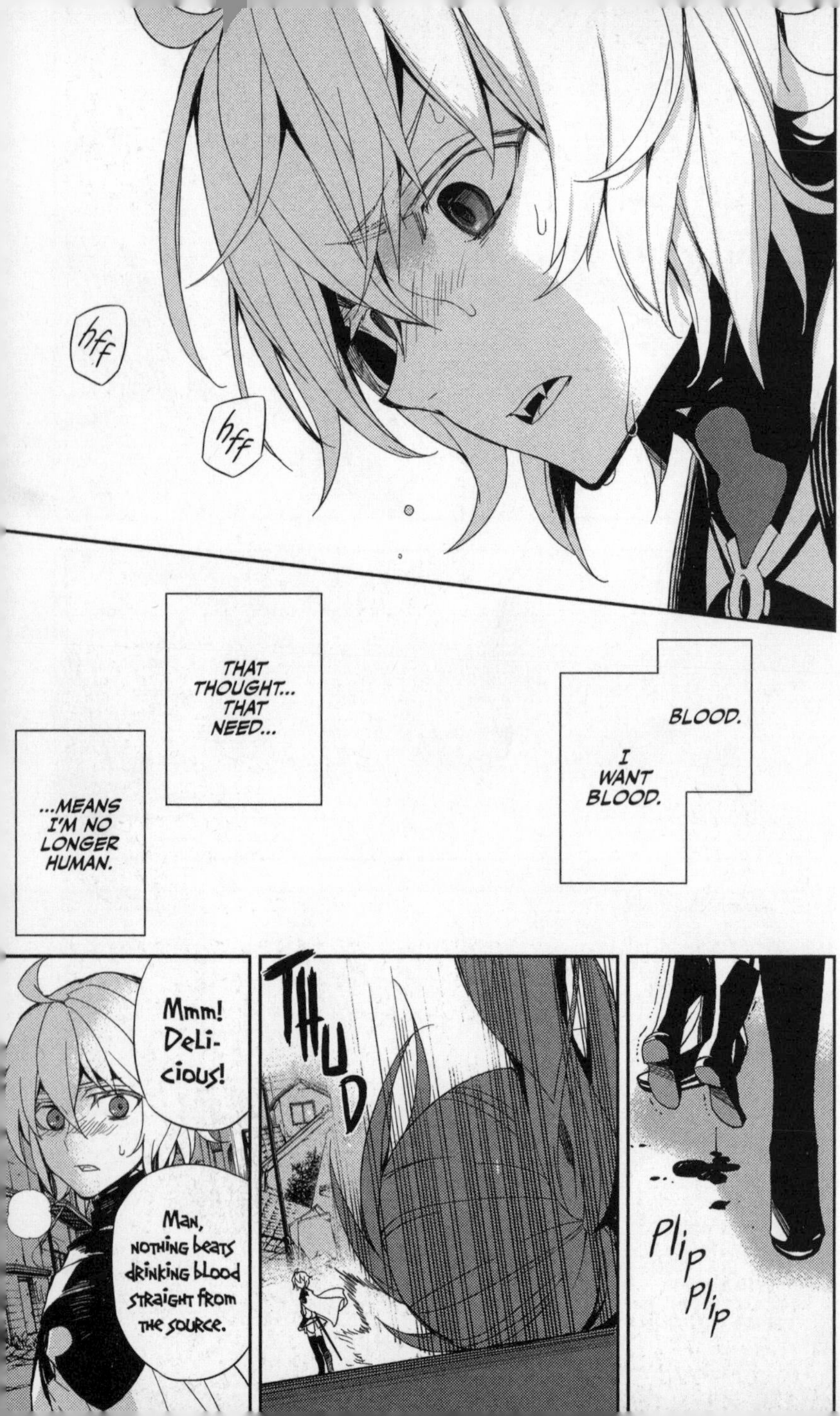
hff
hff
BLOOD.
I WANT BLOOD.
THAT THOUGHT... THAT NEED...
...MEANS I'M NO LONGER HUMAN.
Plip plip
THUD
Mmm! Deli-cious!
Man, nothing beats drinking blood straight from the source.

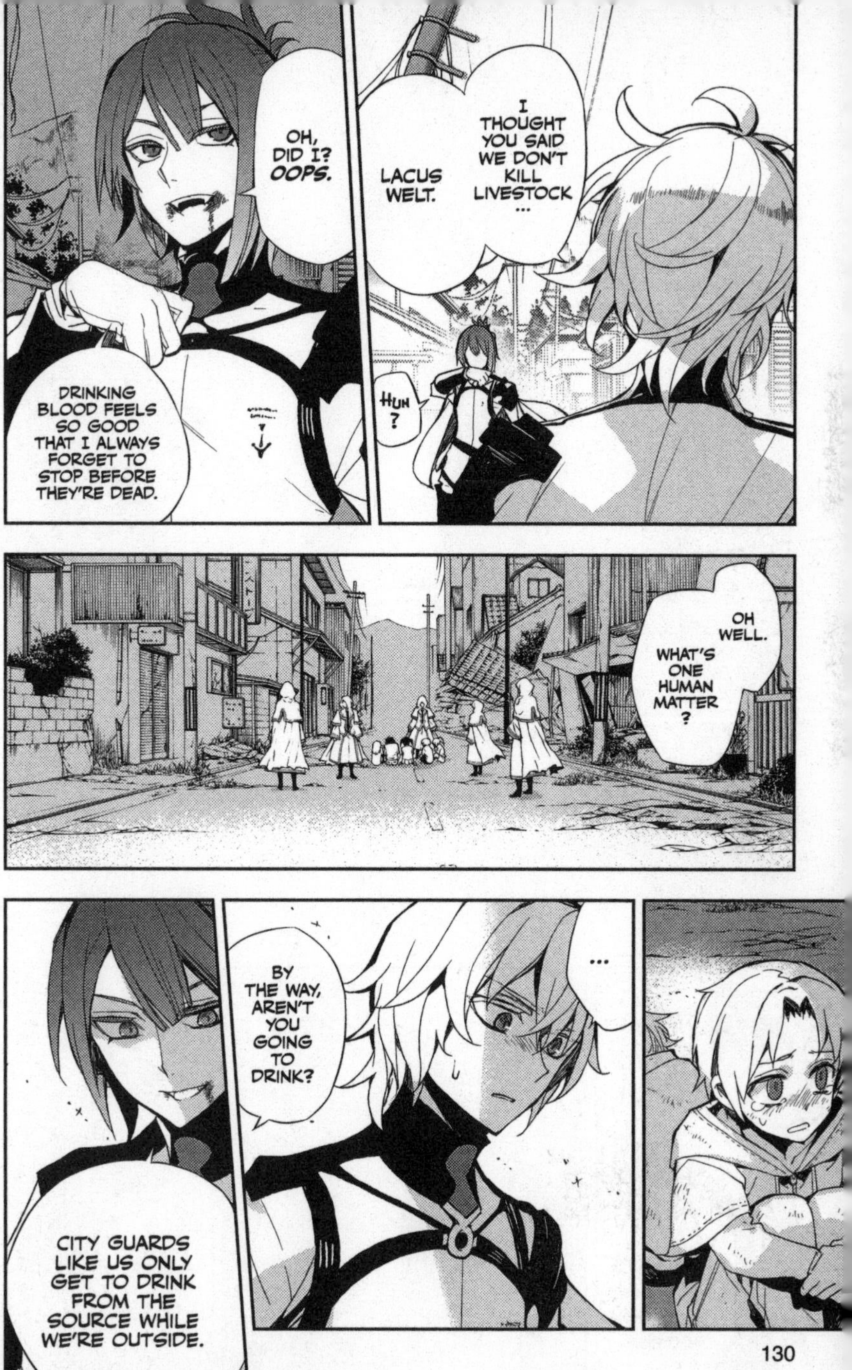
I THOUGHT YOU SAID WE DON'T KILL LIVESTOCK ...
LACUS WELT.
HUH ?
OH, DID I? OOPS.
DRINKING BLOOD FEELS SO GOOD THAT I ALWAYS FORGET TO STOP BEFORE THEY'RE DEAD.
OH WELL. WHAT'S ONE HUMAN MATTER ?
...
BY THE WAY, AREN'T YOU GOING TO DRINK?
CITY GUARDS LIKE US ONLY GET TO DRINK FROM THE SOURCE WHILE WE'RE OUTSIDE.

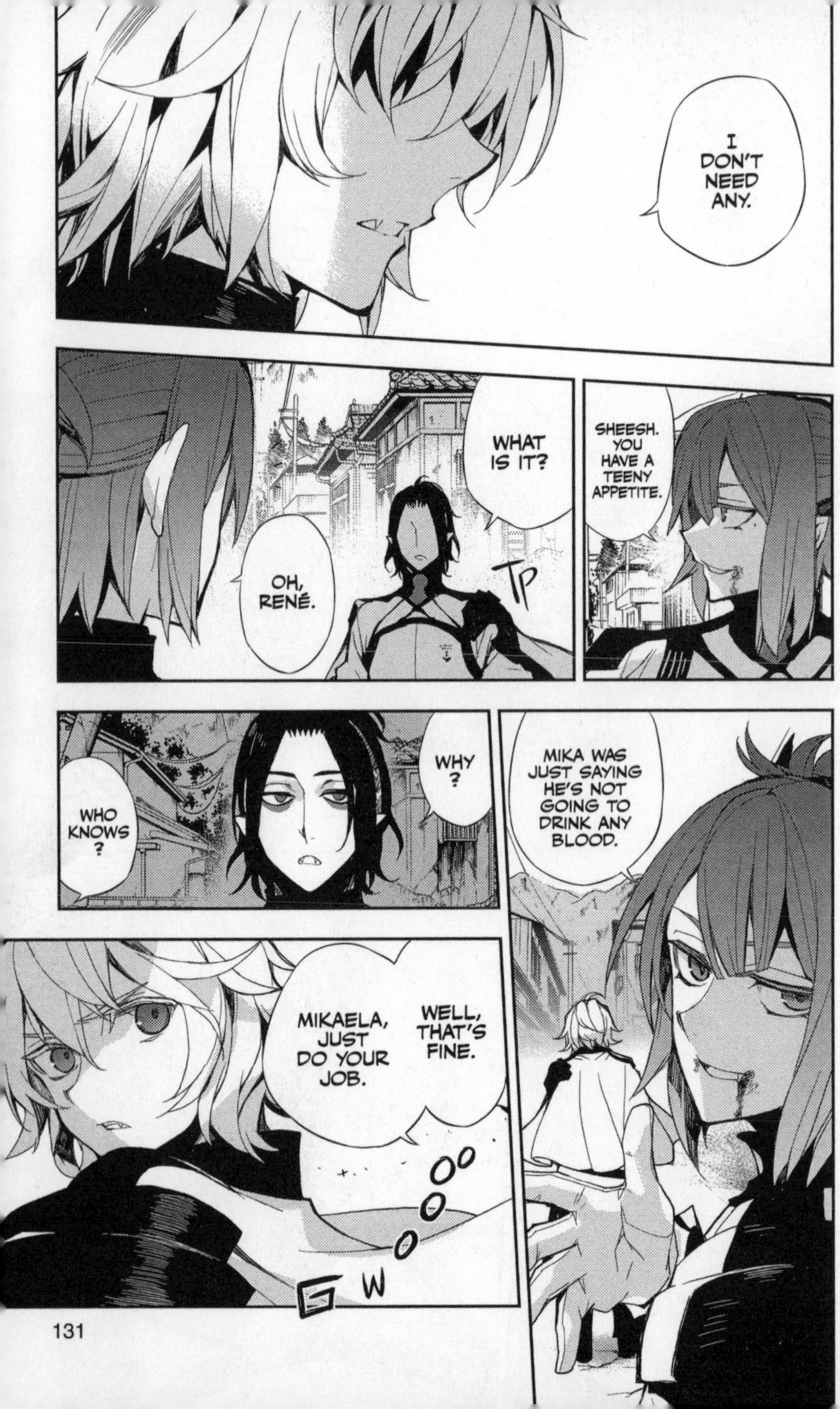
I DON'T NEED ANY.
SHEESH. YOU HAVE A TEENY APPETITE.
WHAT IS IT?
TP
OH, RENÉ.
MIKA WAS JUST SAYING HE'S NOT GOING TO DRINK ANY BLOOD.
WHY?
WHO KNOWS?
WELL, THAT'S FINE.
MIKAELA, JUST DO YOUR JOB.
GWOOOO

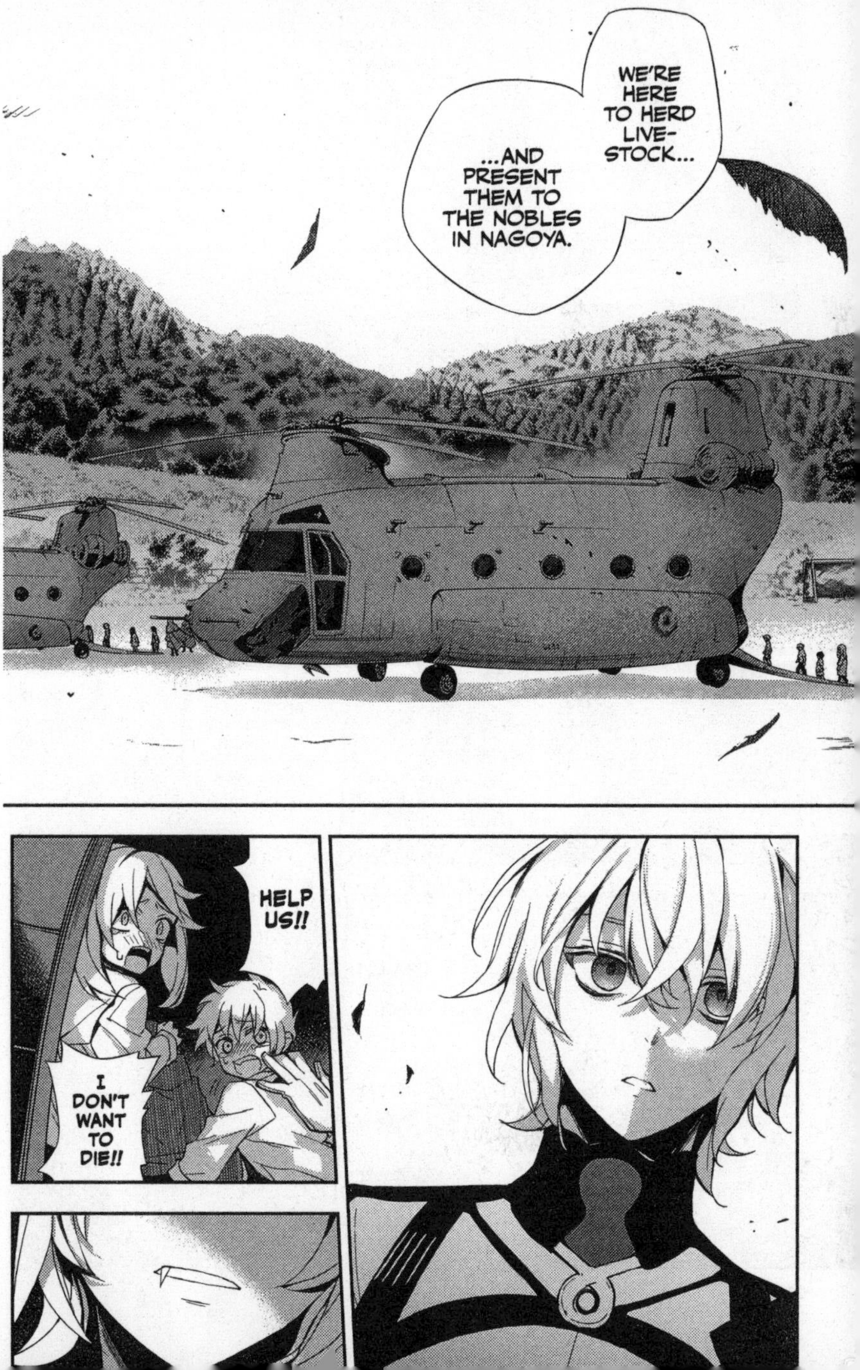
WE'RE HERE TO HERD LIVE-STOCK...
...AND PRESENT THEM TO THE NOBLES IN NAGOYA.
HELP US!!
I DON'T WANT TO DIE!!

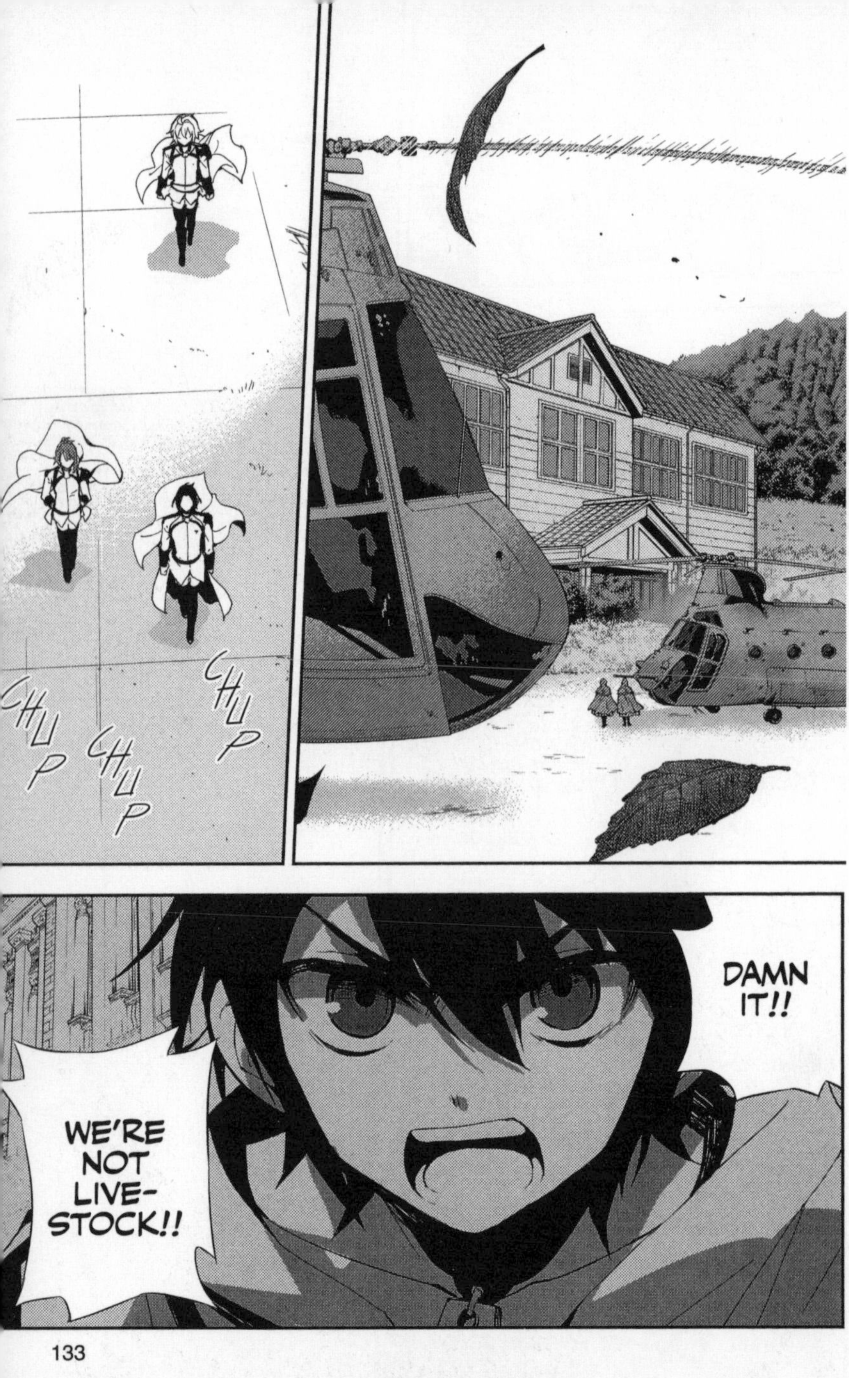
CHUP
CHUP
CHUP
DAMN IT!!
WE'RE NOT LIVE-STOCK!!

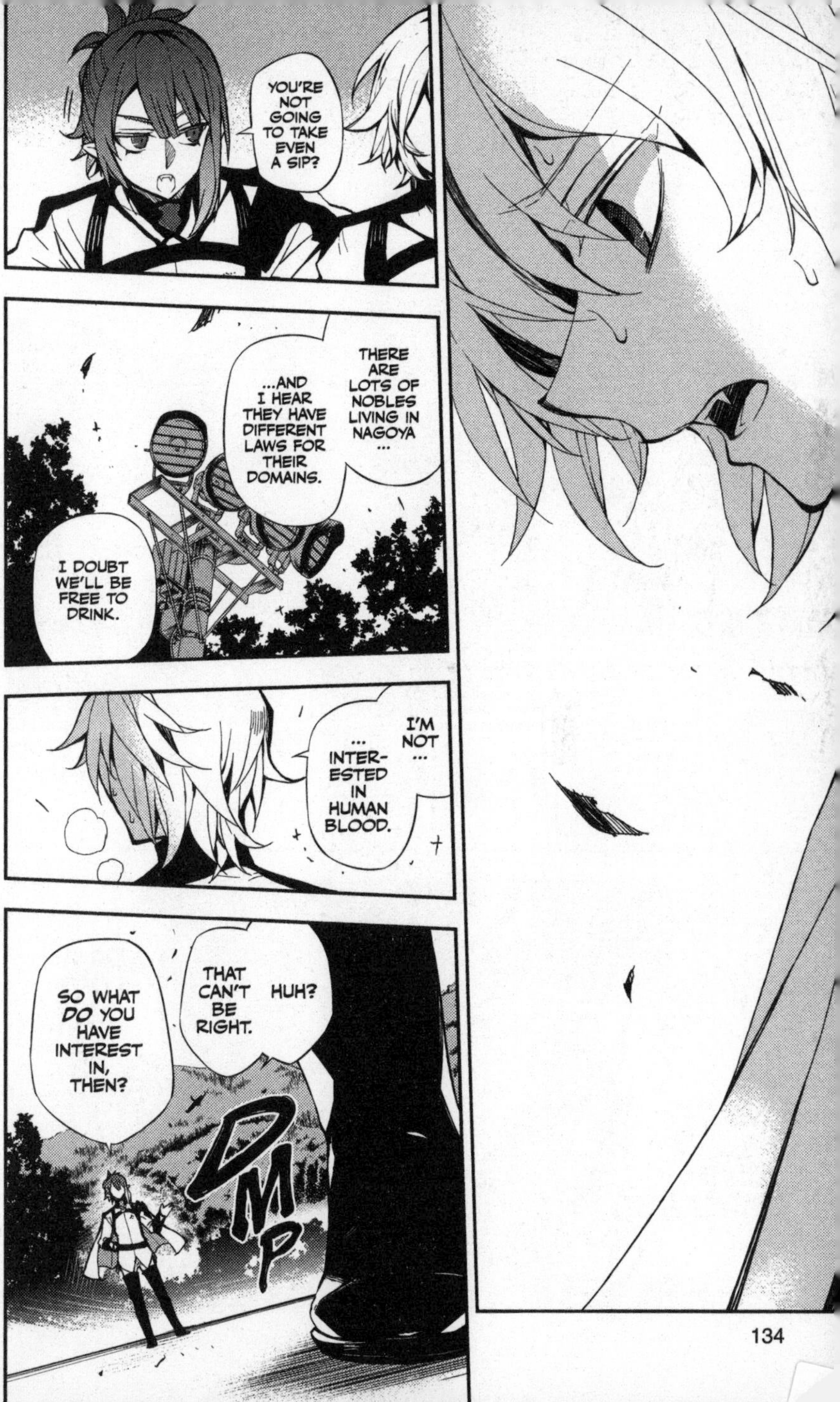
YOU'RE NOT GOING TO TAKE EVEN A SIP?
THERE ARE LOTS OF NOBLES LIVING IN NAGOYA...
...AND I HEAR THEY HAVE DIFFERENT LAWS FOR THEIR DOMAINS.
I DOUBT WE'LL BE FREE TO DRINK.
I'M NOT...
...INTERESTED IN HUMAN BLOOD.
HUH?
THAT CAN'T BE RIGHT.
SO WHAT *DO* YOU HAVE INTEREST IN, THEN?
DMP

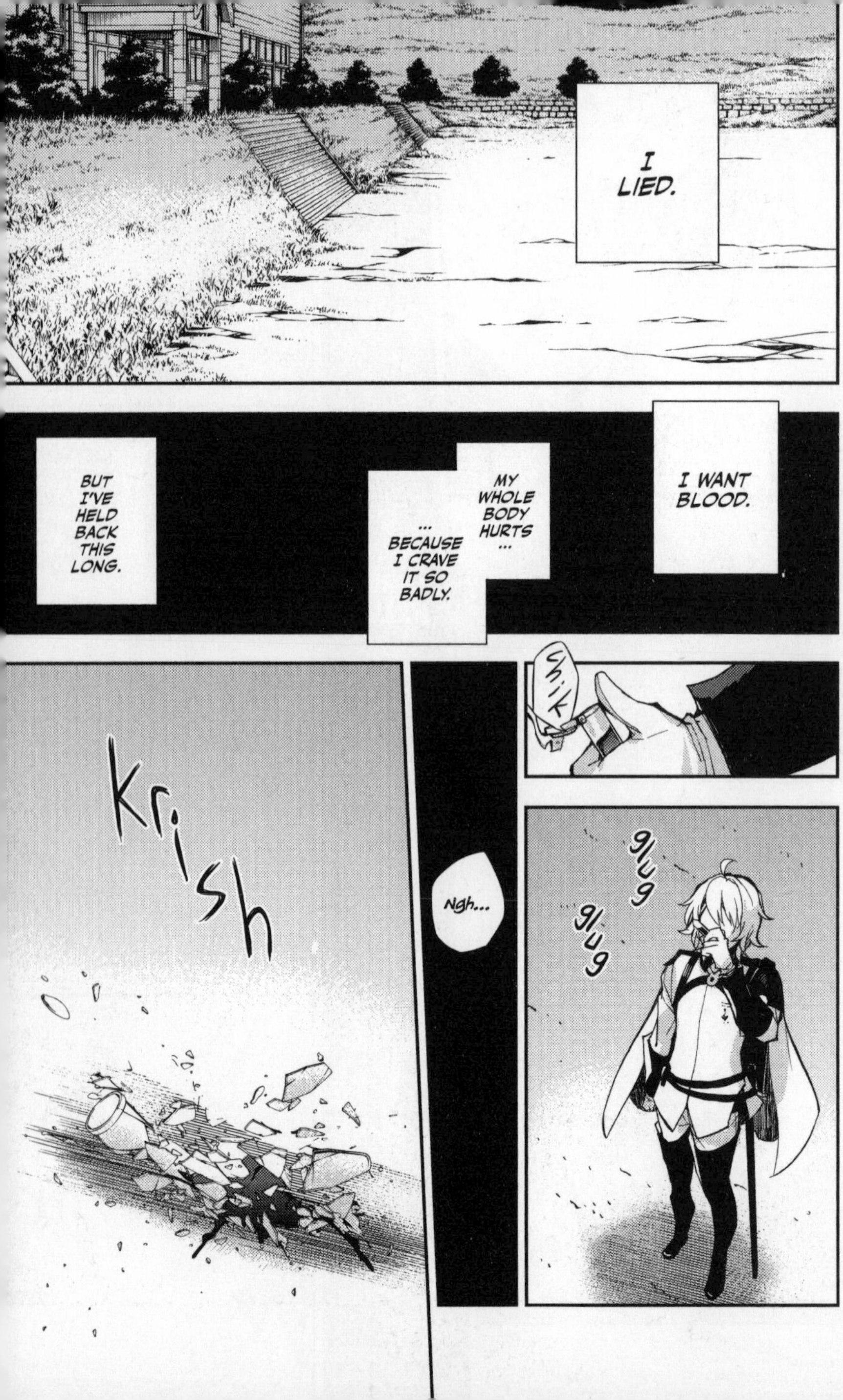
I LIED.
I WANT BLOOD.
MY WHOLE BODY HURTS...
...BECAUSE I CRAVE IT SO BADLY.
BUT I'VE HELD BACK THIS LONG.
chik
glug glug
Ngh...
Krish

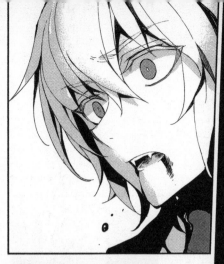

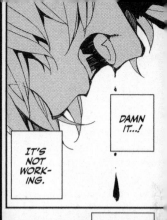

DAMN IT...!

IT'S NOT WORK-ING.

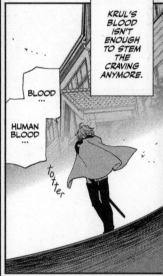

KRUL'S BLOOD ISN'T ENOUGH TO STEM THE CRAVING ANYMORE.

BLOOD...

HUMAN BLOOD...

totter

I WANT HUMAN BLOOD!

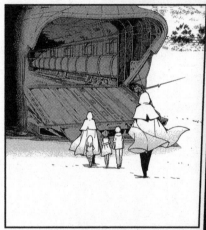

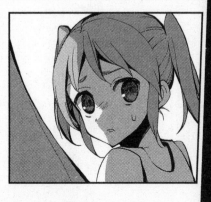

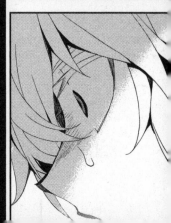

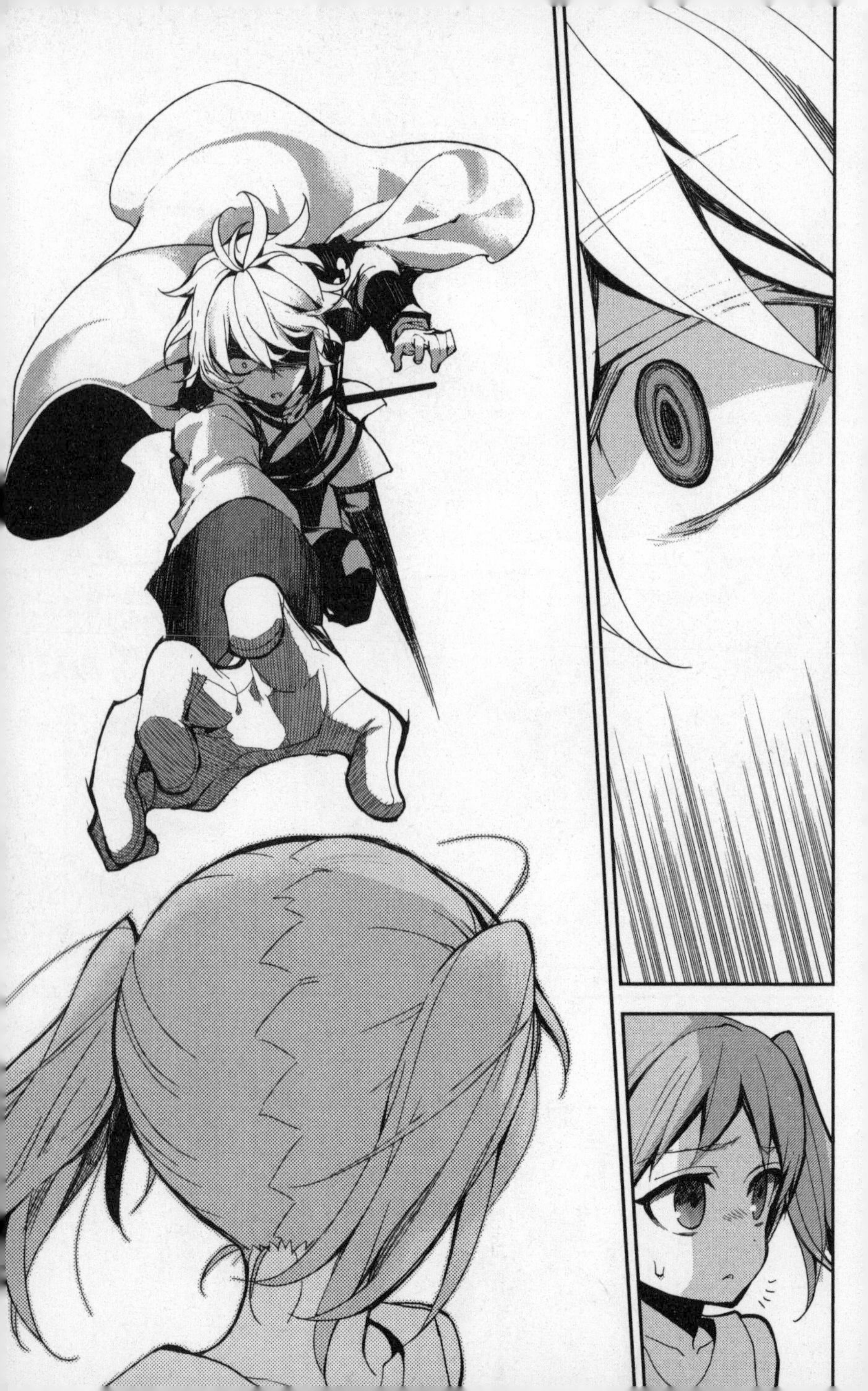

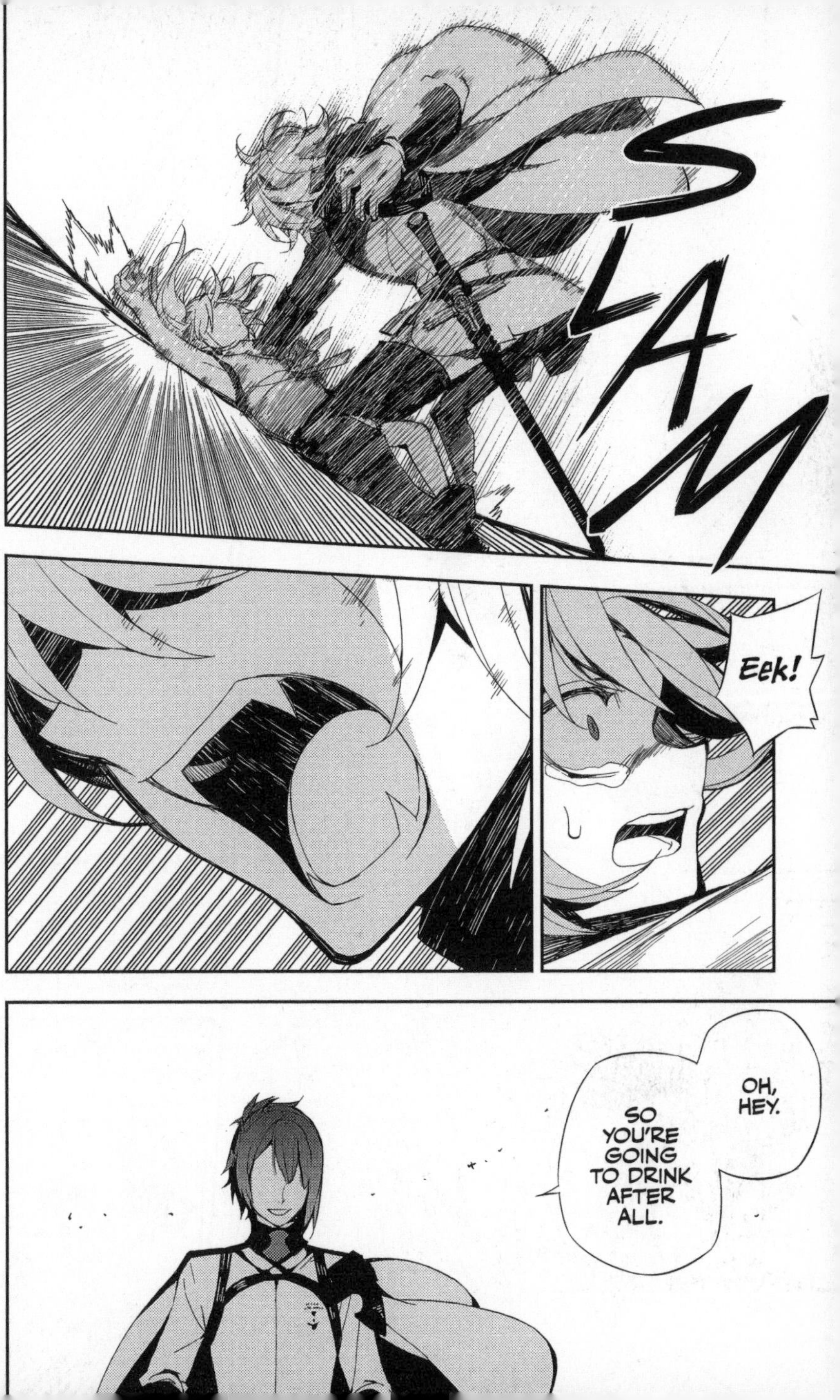
SLAM
Eek!
OH, HEY.
SO YOU'RE GOING TO DRINK AFTER ALL.

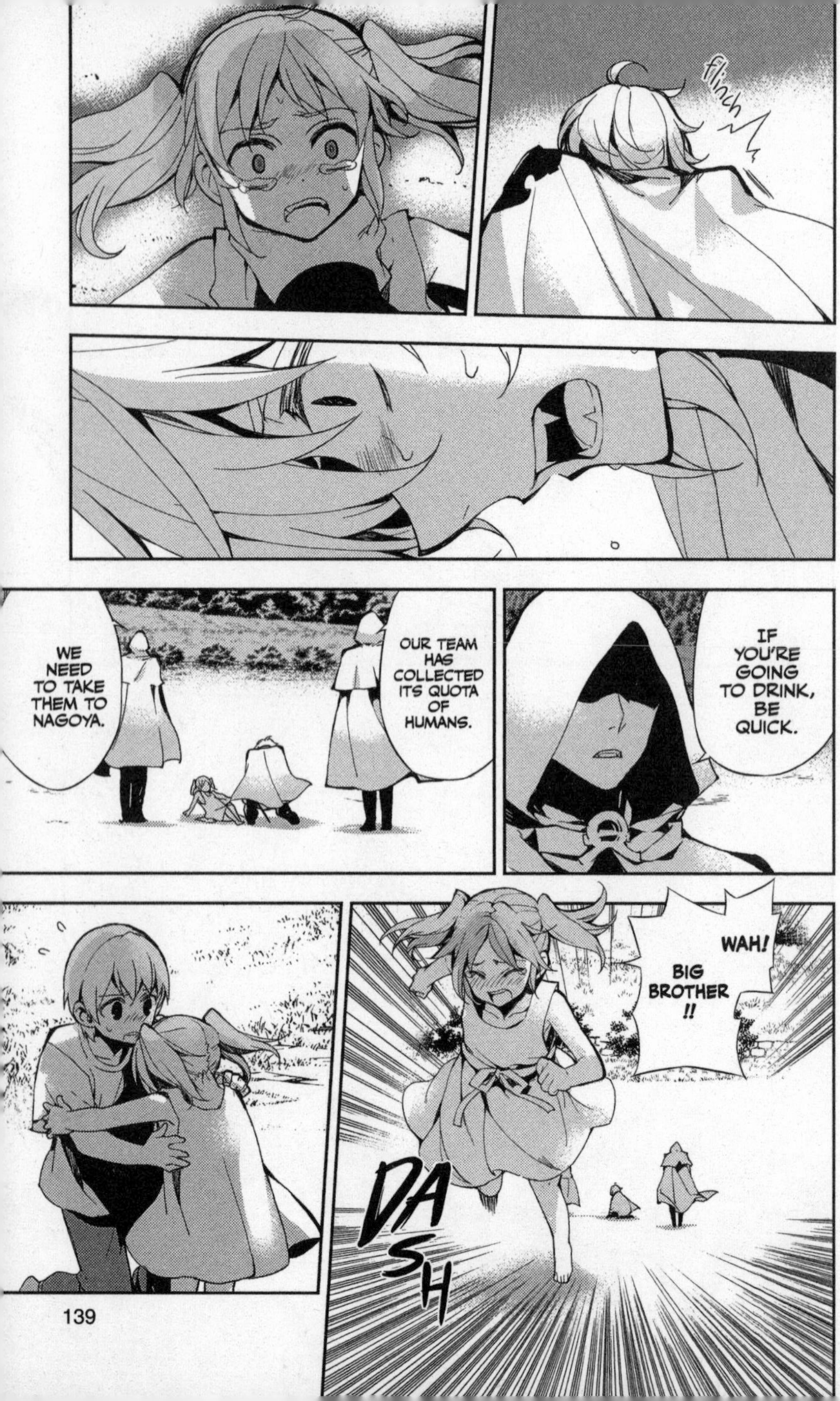
flinch
IF YOU'RE GOING TO DRINK, BE QUICK.
OUR TEAM HAS COLLECTED ITS QUOTA OF HUMANS.
WE NEED TO TAKE THEM TO NAGOYA.
WAH!
BIG BROTHER !!
DASH

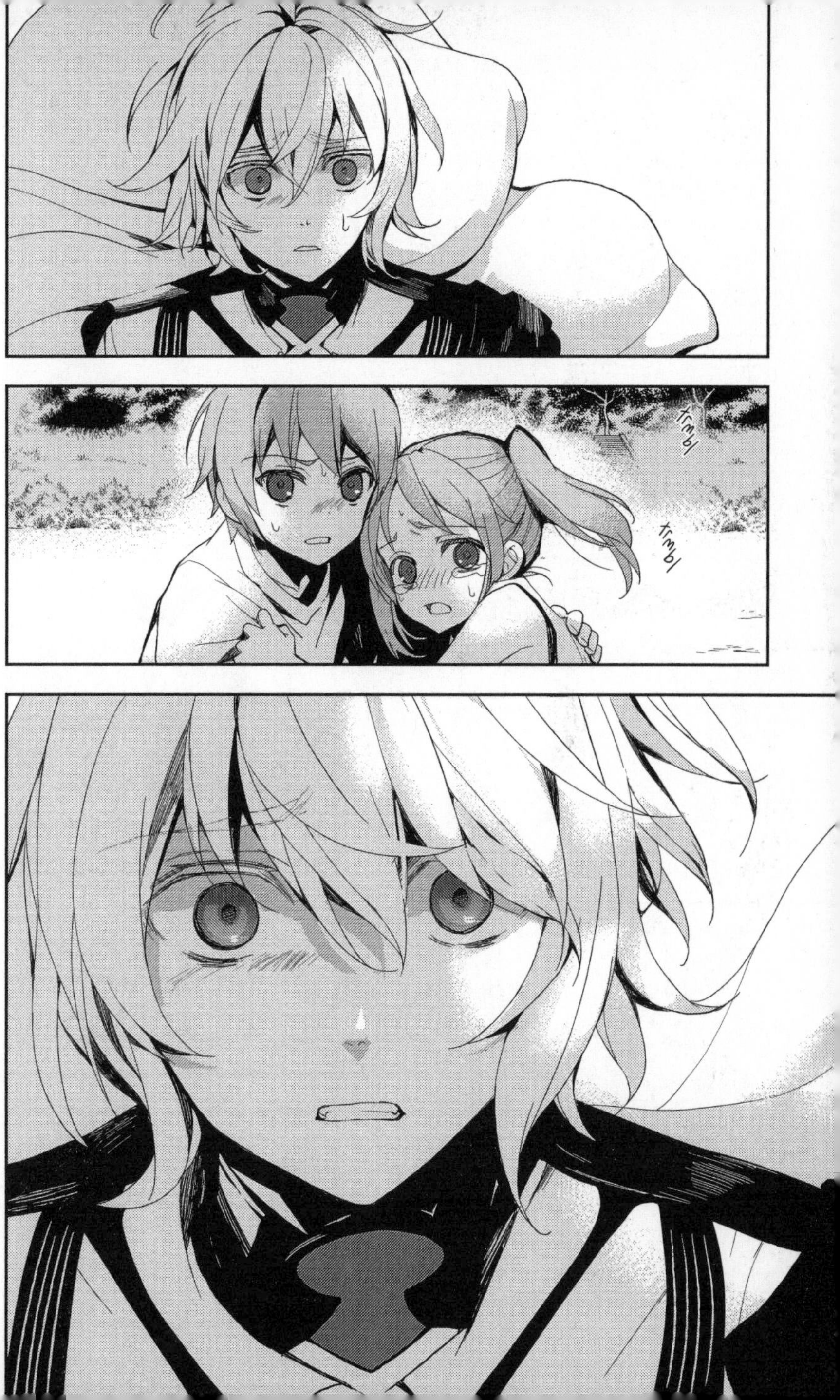
trmbl
trmbl

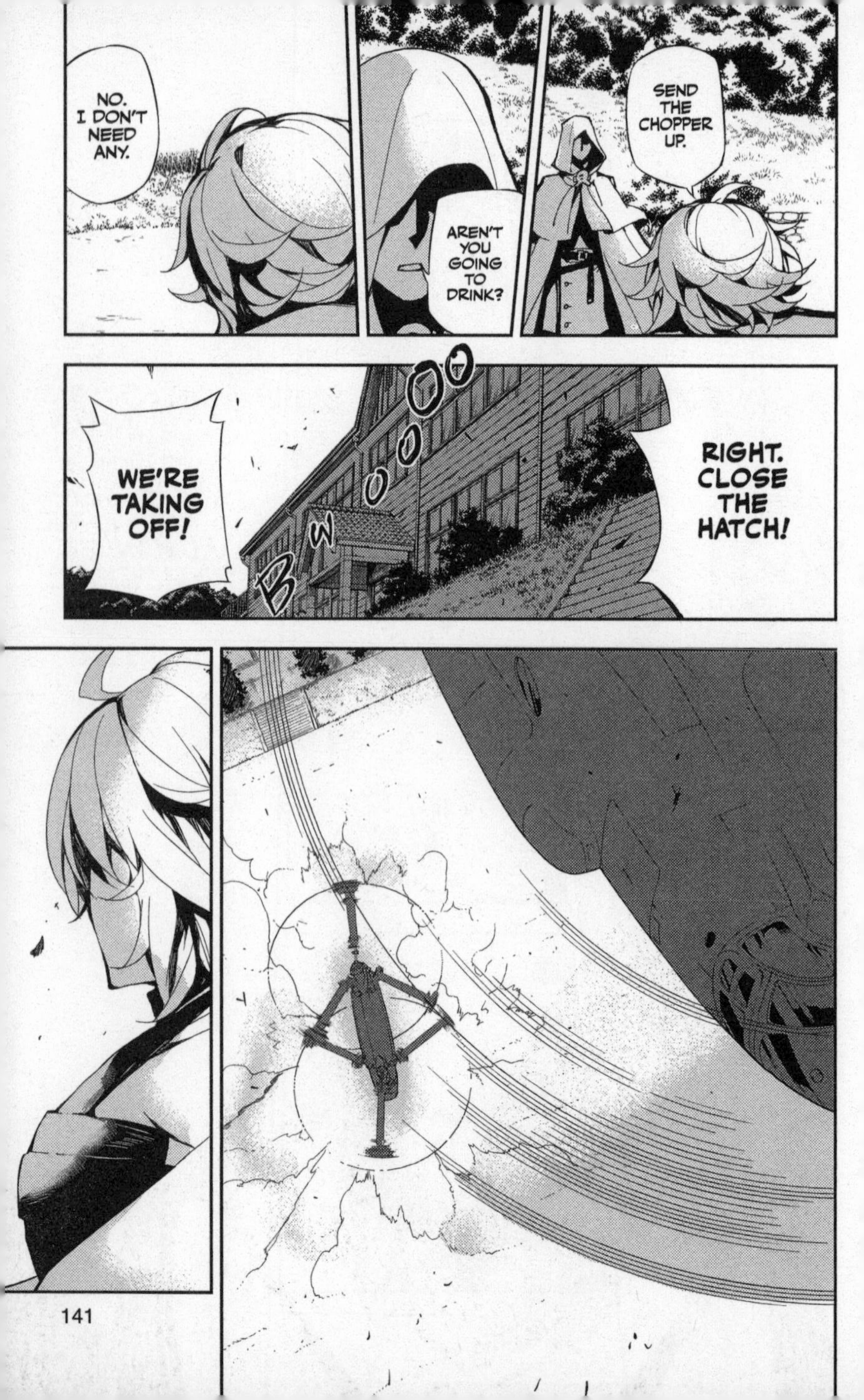
SEND THE CHOPPER UP.
AREN'T YOU GOING TO DRINK?
NO. I DON'T NEED ANY.
RIGHT. CLOSE THE HATCH!
WE'RE TAKING OFF!
BWOOOOO

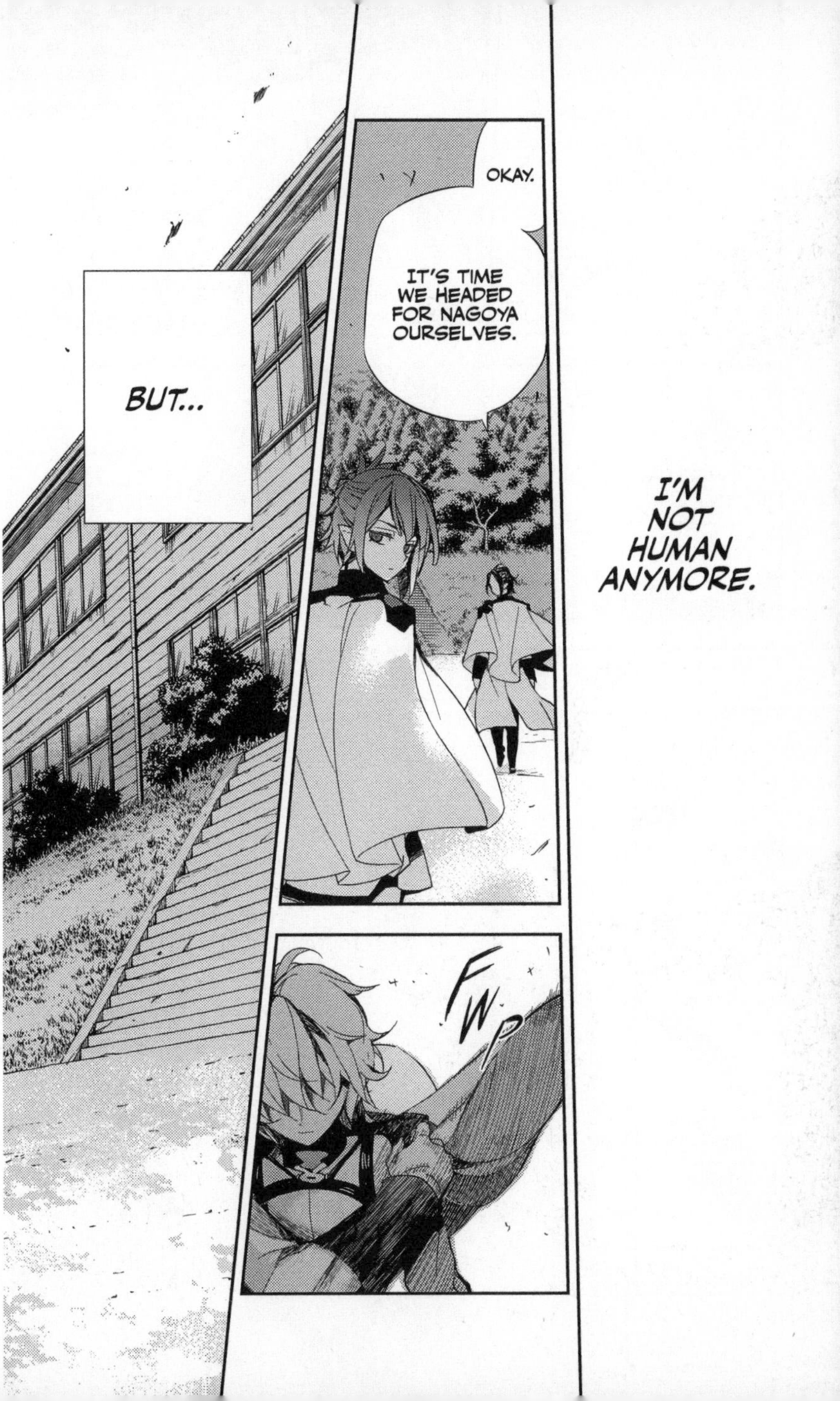
OKAY.
IT'S TIME WE HEADED FOR NAGOYA OURSELVES.
FWP
BUT...
I'M NOT HUMAN ANYMORE.

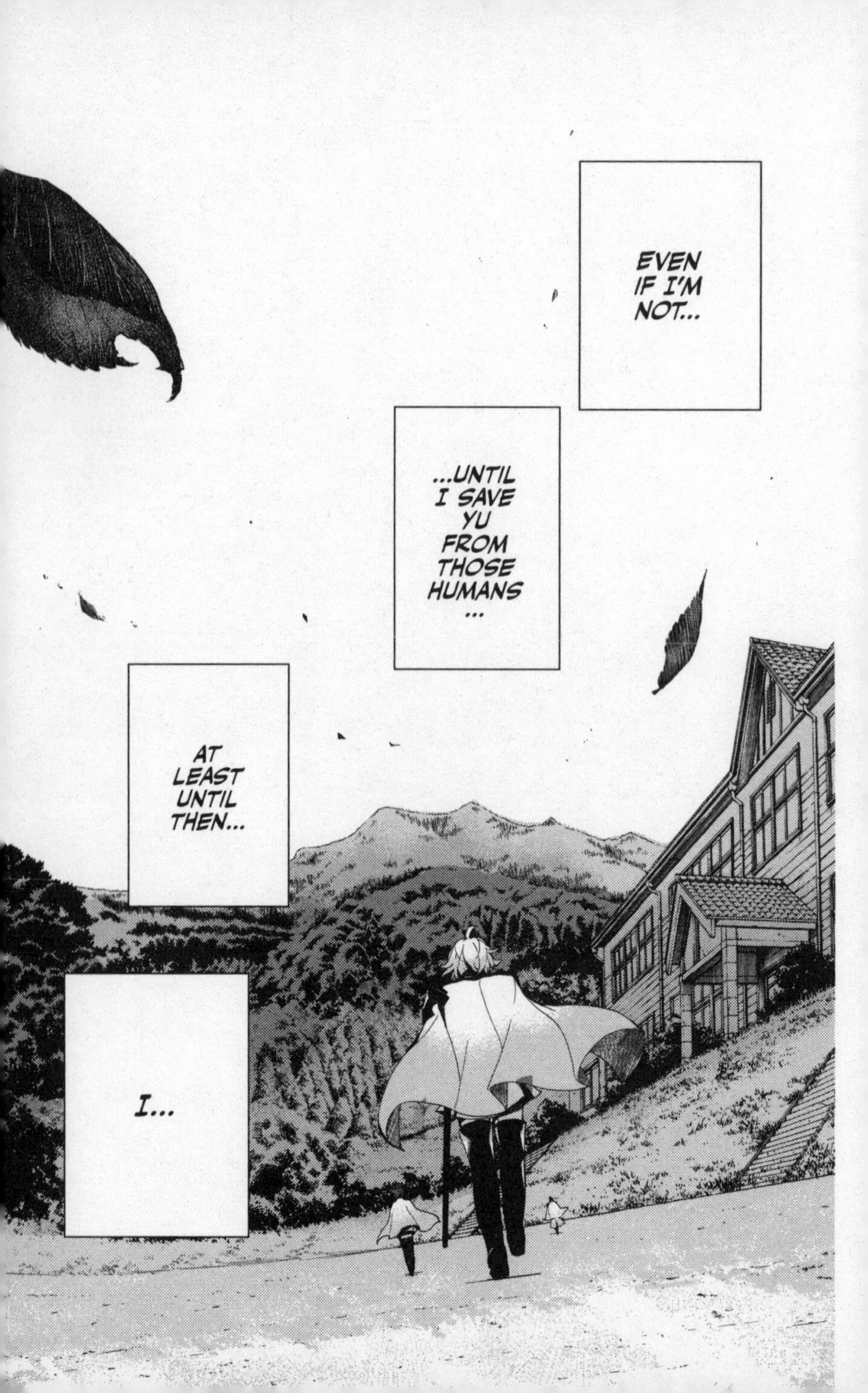
EVEN IF I'M NOT...
...UNTIL I SAVE YU FROM THOSE HUMANS...
AT LEAST UNTIL THEN...
I...

Seraph of the End

VAMPIRE REIGN

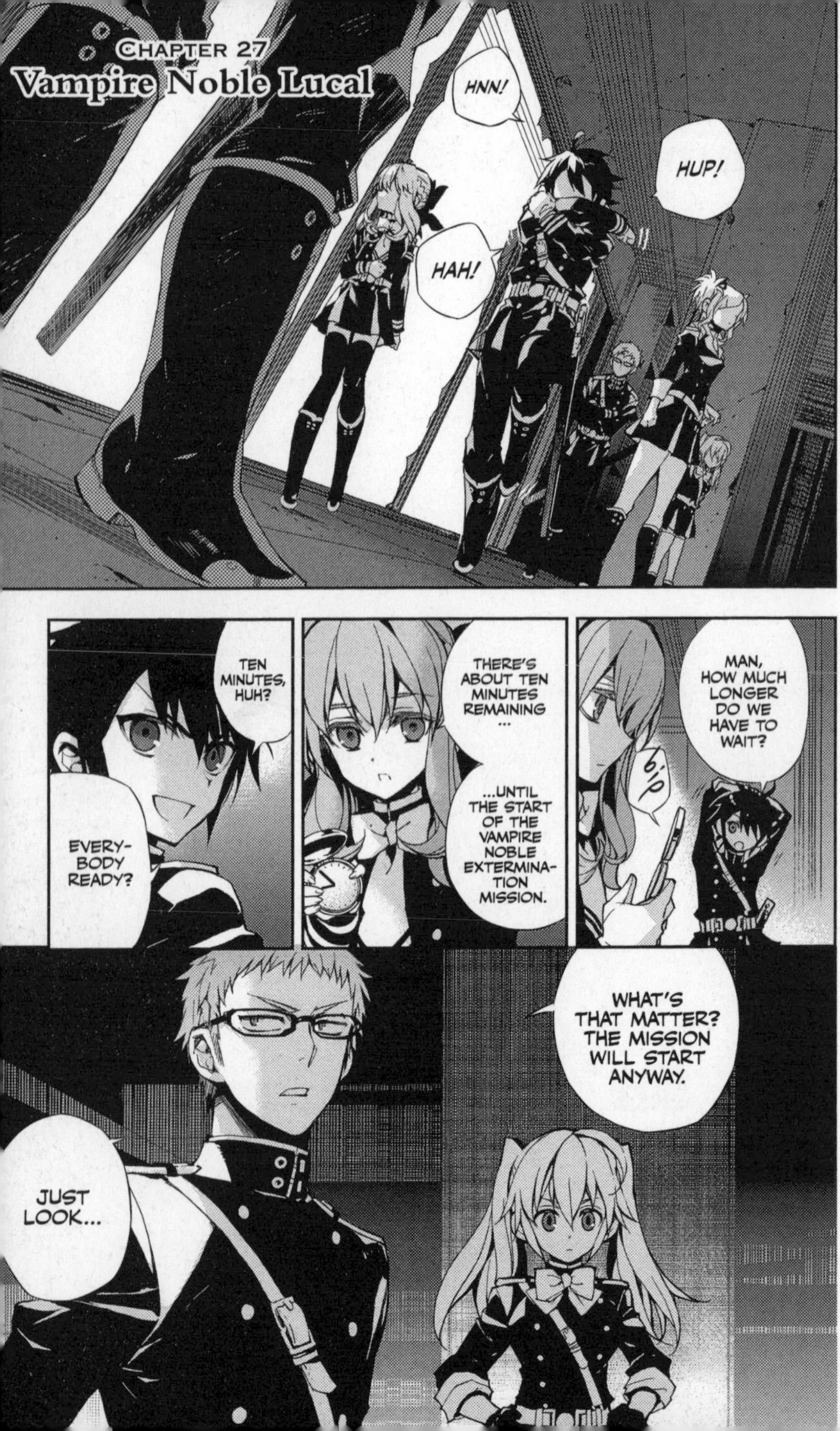
CHAPTER 27
Vampire Noble Lucal
HNN!
HUP!
HAH!
MAN, HOW MUCH LONGER DO WE HAVE TO WAIT?
BIP
THERE'S ABOUT TEN MINUTES REMAINING...
...UNTIL THE START OF THE VAMPIRE NOBLE EXTERMINATION MISSION.
TEN MINUTES, HUH?
EVERYBODY READY?
WHAT'S THAT MATTER? THE MISSION WILL START ANYWAY.
JUST LOOK...

Chapter 27
Vampire Noble Lucal

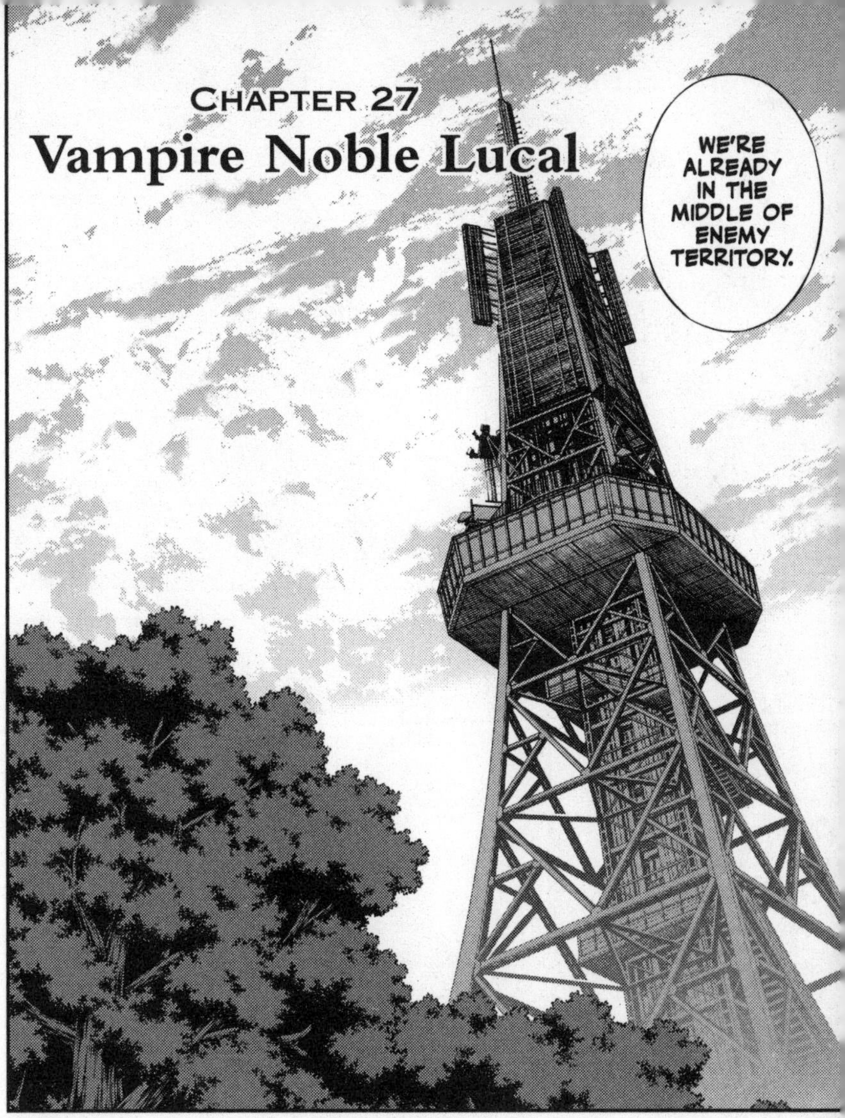
WE'RE ALREADY IN THE MIDDLE OF ENEMY TERRITORY.

Nagoya

Vampire Noble Lucal Wesker's ward

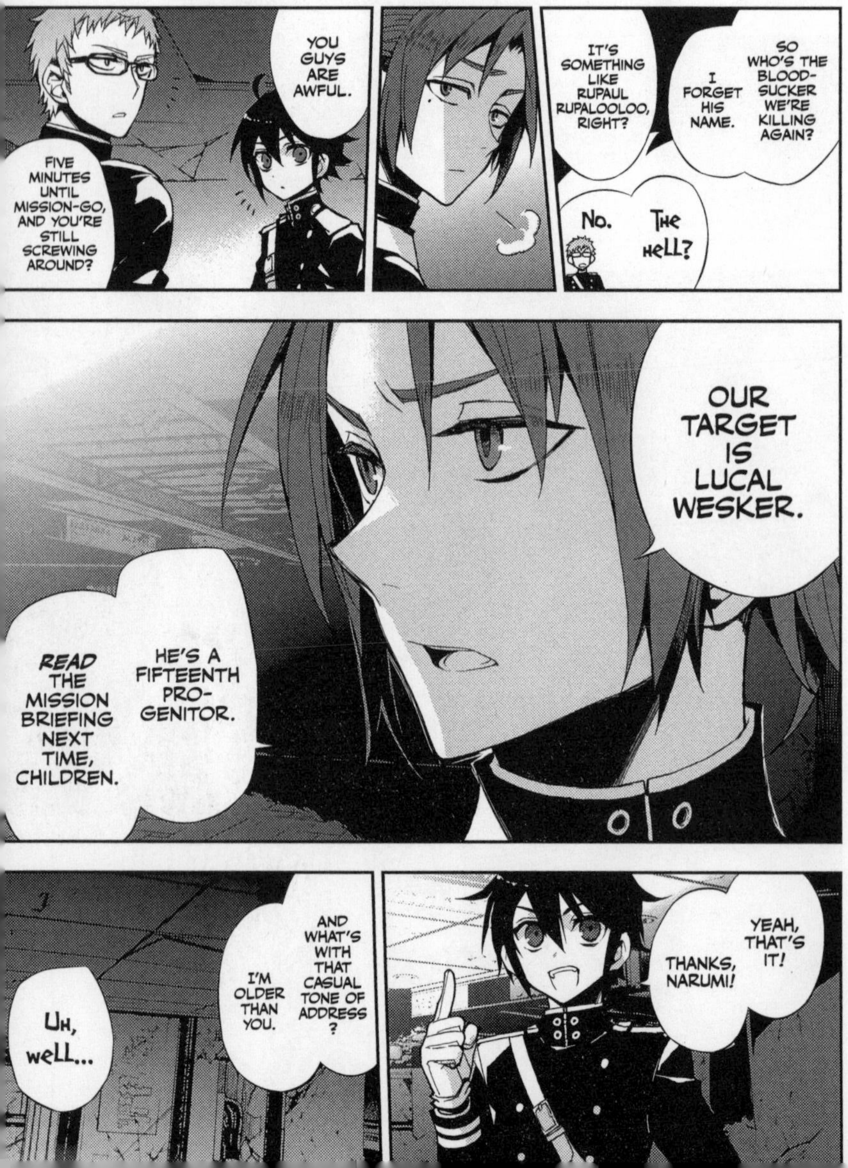
SO WHO'S THE BLOOD-SUCKER WE'RE KILLING AGAIN?
I FORGET HIS NAME.
IT'S SOMETHING LIKE RUPAUL RUPALOOLOO, RIGHT?
THE HELL?
NO.
YOU GUYS ARE AWFUL.
FIVE MINUTES UNTIL MISSION-GO, AND YOU'RE STILL SCREWING AROUND?
OUR TARGET IS LUCAL WESKER.
HE'S A FIFTEENTH PRO-GENITOR.
READ THE MISSION BRIEFING NEXT TIME, CHILDREN.
YEAH, THAT'S IT!
THANKS, NARUMI!
AND WHAT'S WITH THAT CASUAL TONE OF ADDRESS?
I'M OLDER THAN YOU.
UH, WELL...

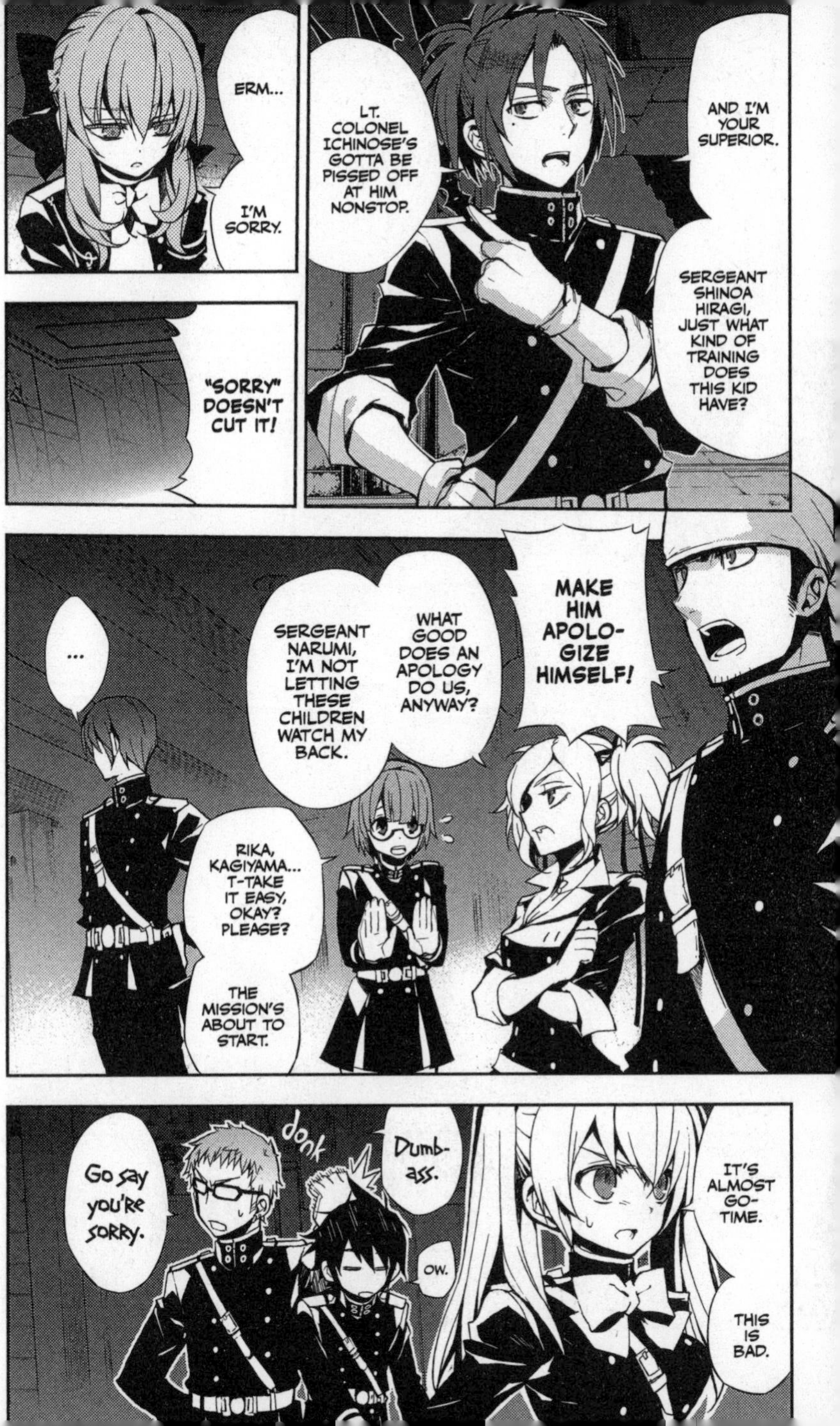
AND I'M YOUR SUPERIOR.
LT. COLONEL ICHINOSE'S GOTTA BE PISSED OFF AT HIM NONSTOP.
SERGEANT SHINOA HIRAGI, JUST WHAT KIND OF TRAINING DOES THIS KID HAVE?
ERM...
I'M SORRY.
"SORRY" DOESN'T CUT IT!
MAKE HIM APOLO-GIZE HIMSELF!
WHAT GOOD DOES AN APOLOGY DO US, ANYWAY?
SERGEANT NARUMI, I'M NOT LETTING THESE CHILDREN WATCH MY BACK.
...
RIKA, KAGIYAMA... T-TAKE IT EASY, OKAY? PLEASE?
THE MISSION'S ABOUT TO START.
IT'S ALMOST GO-TIME.
THIS IS BAD.
Dumb-ass.
donk
OW.
Go say you're sorry.

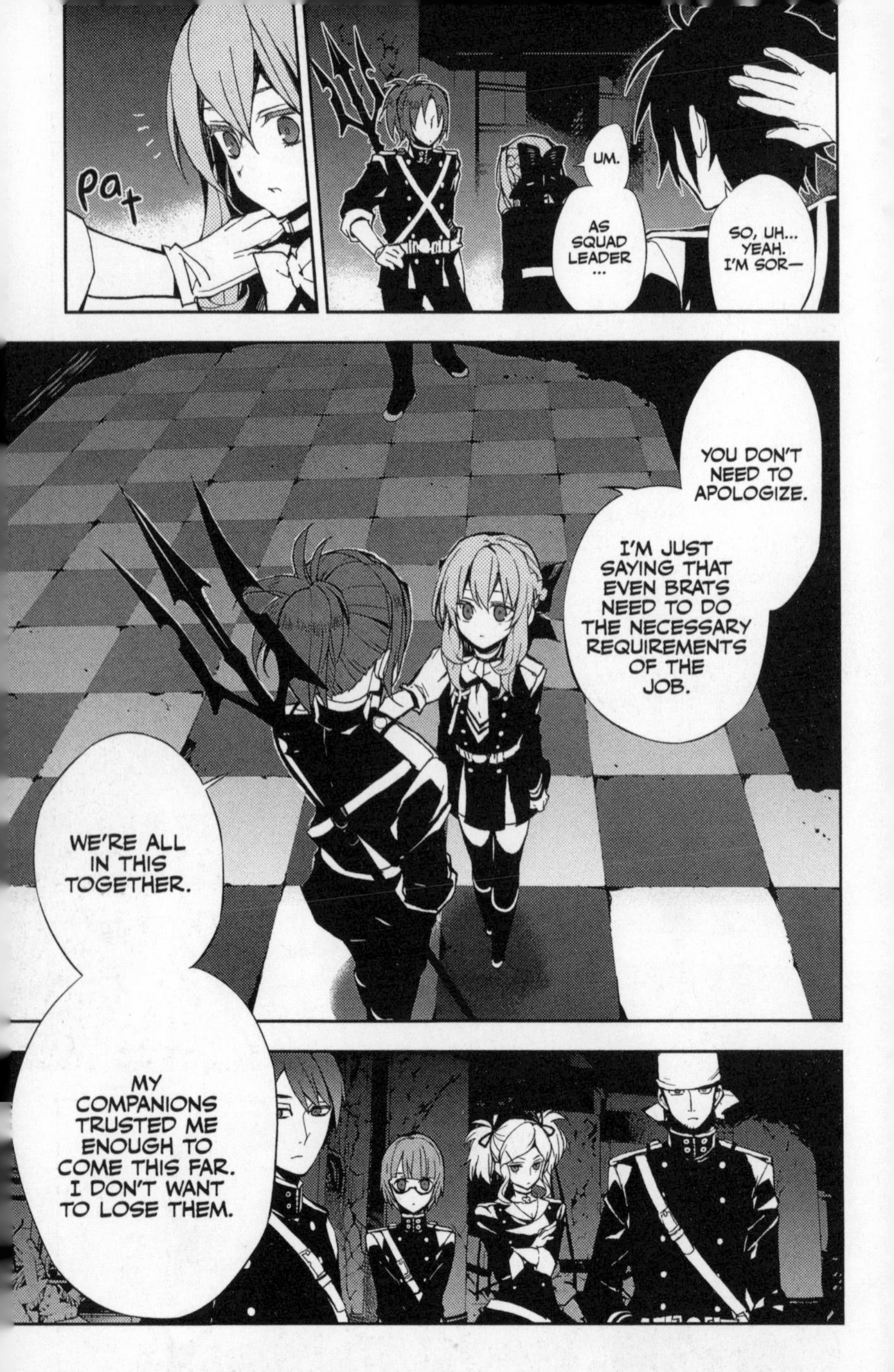
SO, UH... YEAH. I'M SOR—
UM.
AS SQUAD LEADER ...
pat
YOU DON'T NEED TO APOLOGIZE.
I'M JUST SAYING THAT EVEN BRATS NEED TO DO THE NECESSARY REQUIREMENTS OF THE JOB.
WE'RE ALL IN THIS TOGETHER.
MY COMPANIONS TRUSTED ME ENOUGH TO COME THIS FAR. I DON'T WANT TO LOSE THEM.

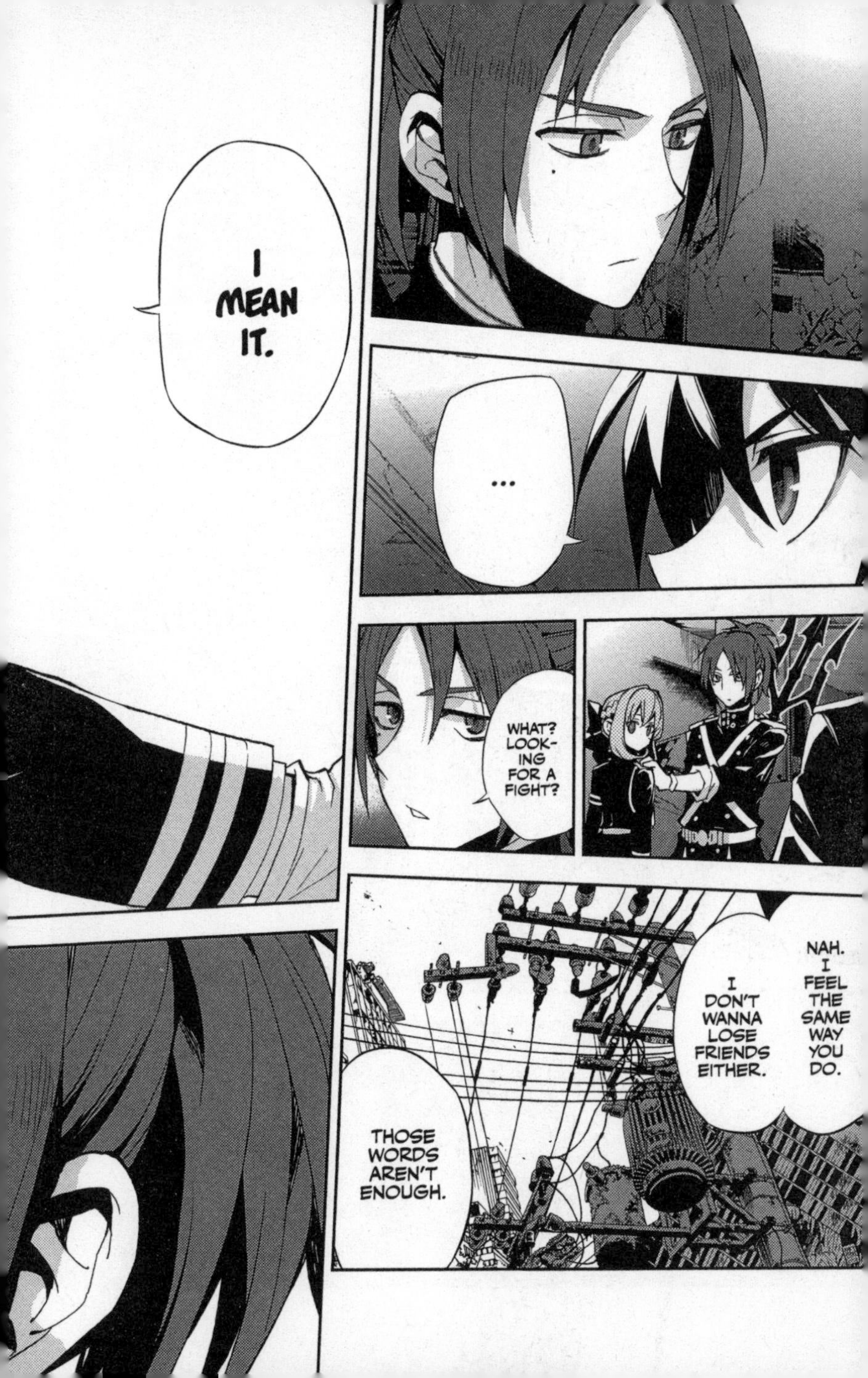
...
WHAT? LOOKING FOR A FIGHT?
I MEAN IT.
NAH. I FEEL THE SAME WAY YOU DO.
I DON'T WANNA LOSE FRIENDS EITHER.
THOSE WORDS AREN'T ENOUGH.

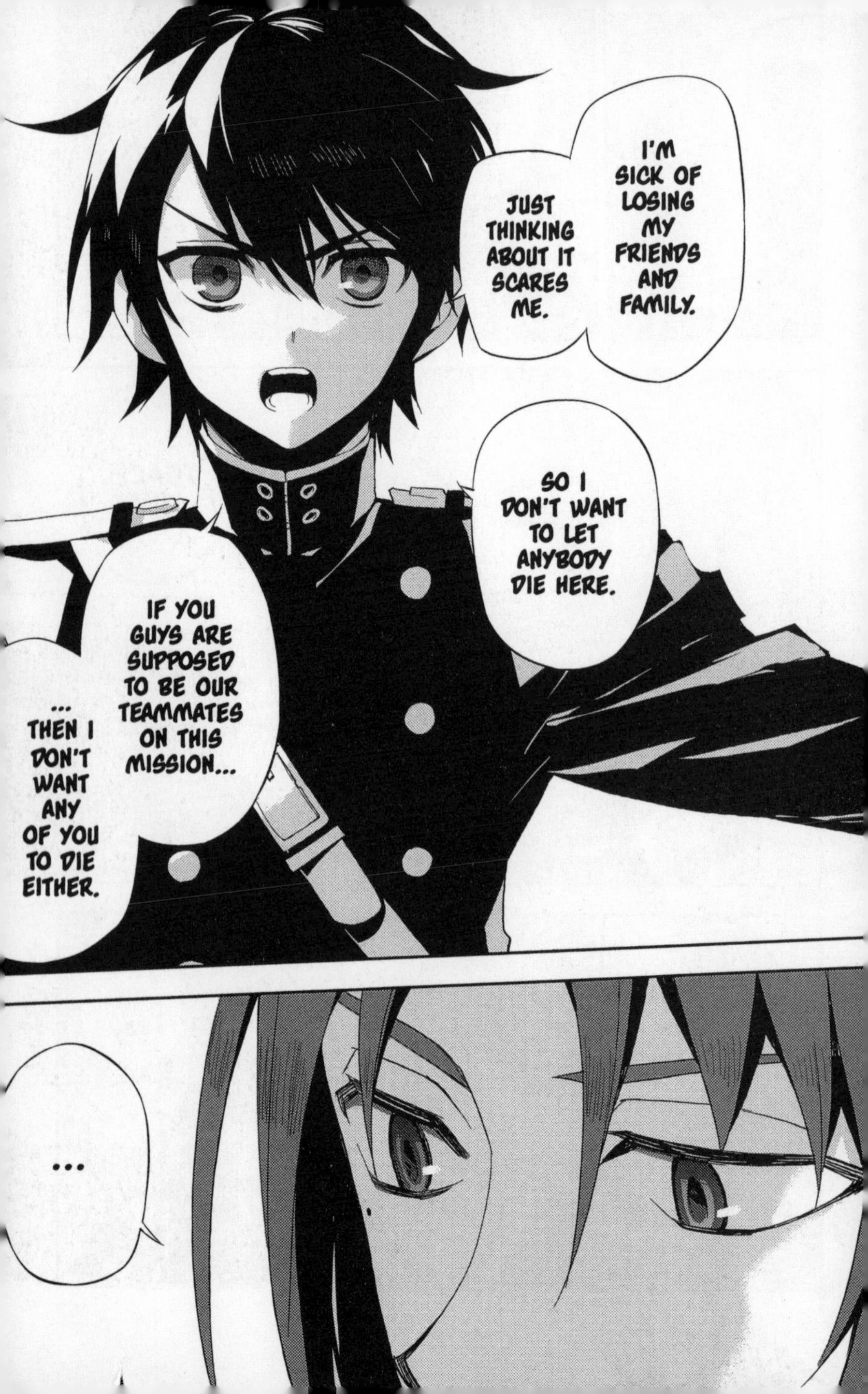
I'M SICK OF LOSING MY FRIENDS AND FAMILY.
JUST THINKING ABOUT IT SCARES ME.
SO I DON'T WANT TO LET ANYBODY DIE HERE.
IF YOU GUYS ARE SUPPOSED TO BE OUR TEAMMATES ON THIS MISSION...
...THEN I DON'T WANT ANY OF YOU TO DIE EITHER.
...

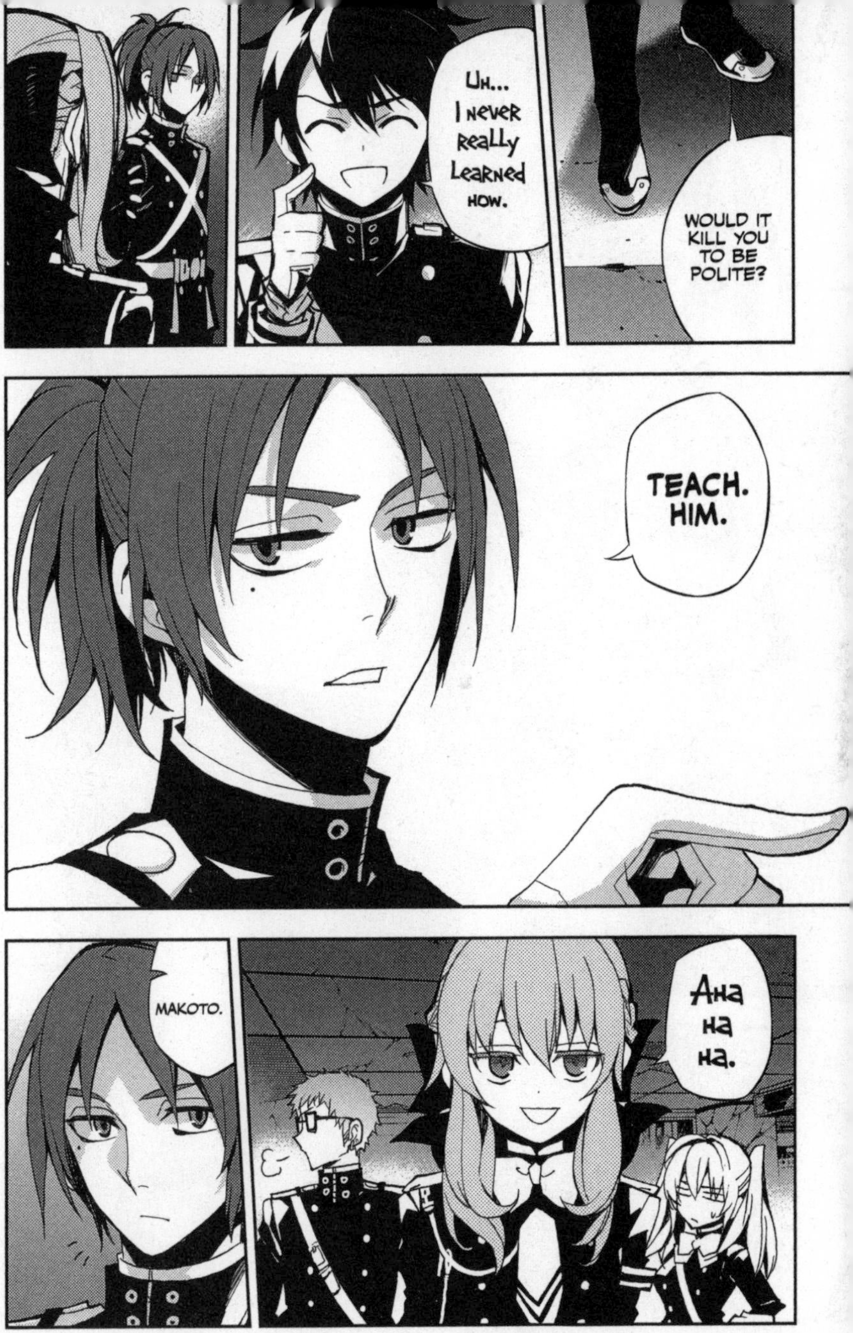
WOULD IT KILL YOU TO BE POLITE?
Uh... I never really learned how.
TEACH. HIM.
Aha ha ha.
MAKOTO.

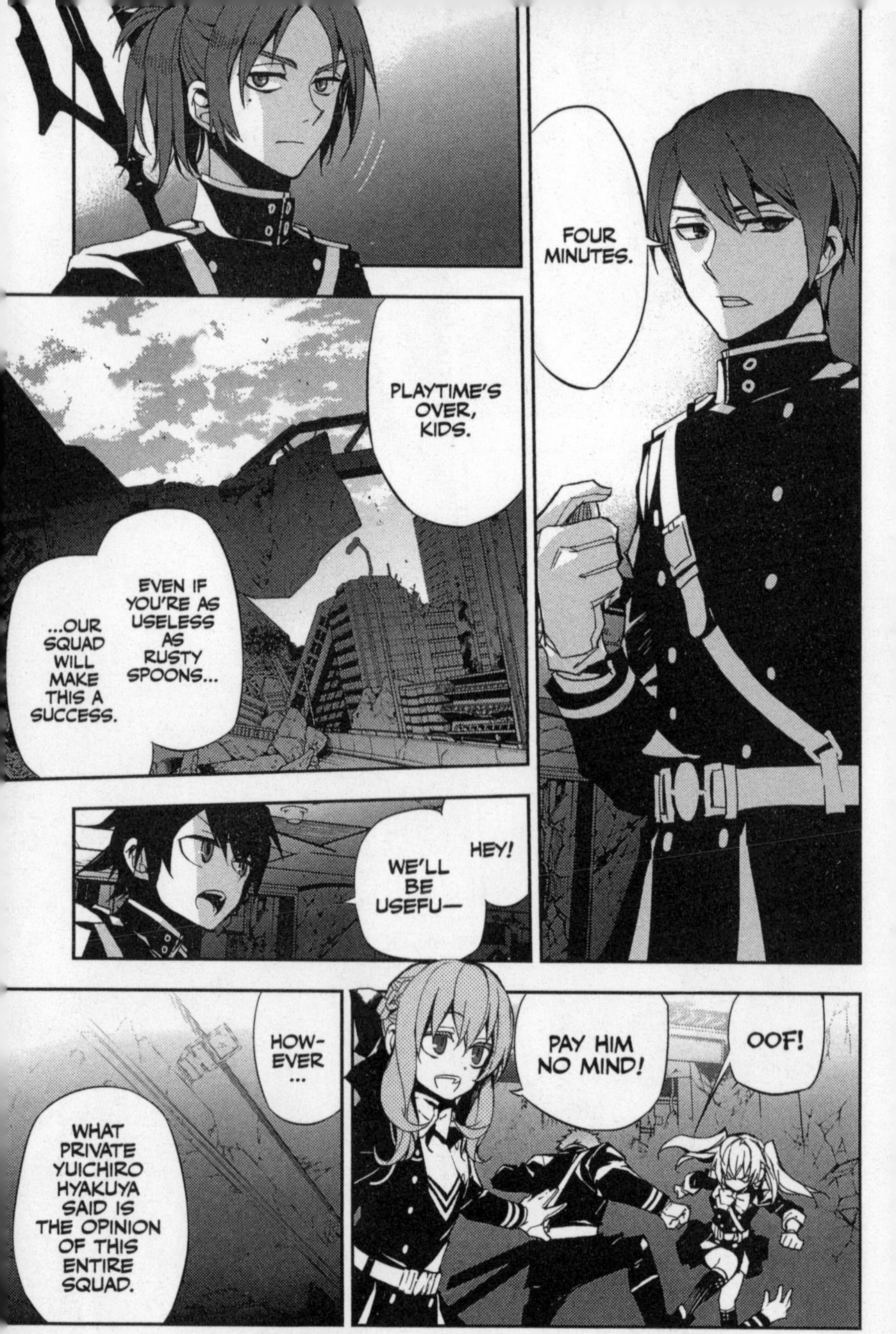
FOUR MINUTES.
PLAYTIME'S OVER, KIDS.
EVEN IF YOU'RE AS USELESS AS RUSTY SPOONS...
...OUR SQUAD WILL MAKE THIS A SUCCESS.
HEY!
WE'LL BE USEFU—
OOF!
PAY HIM NO MIND!
HOW-EVER...
WHAT PRIVATE YUICHIRO HYAKUYA SAID IS THE OPINION OF THIS ENTIRE SQUAD.

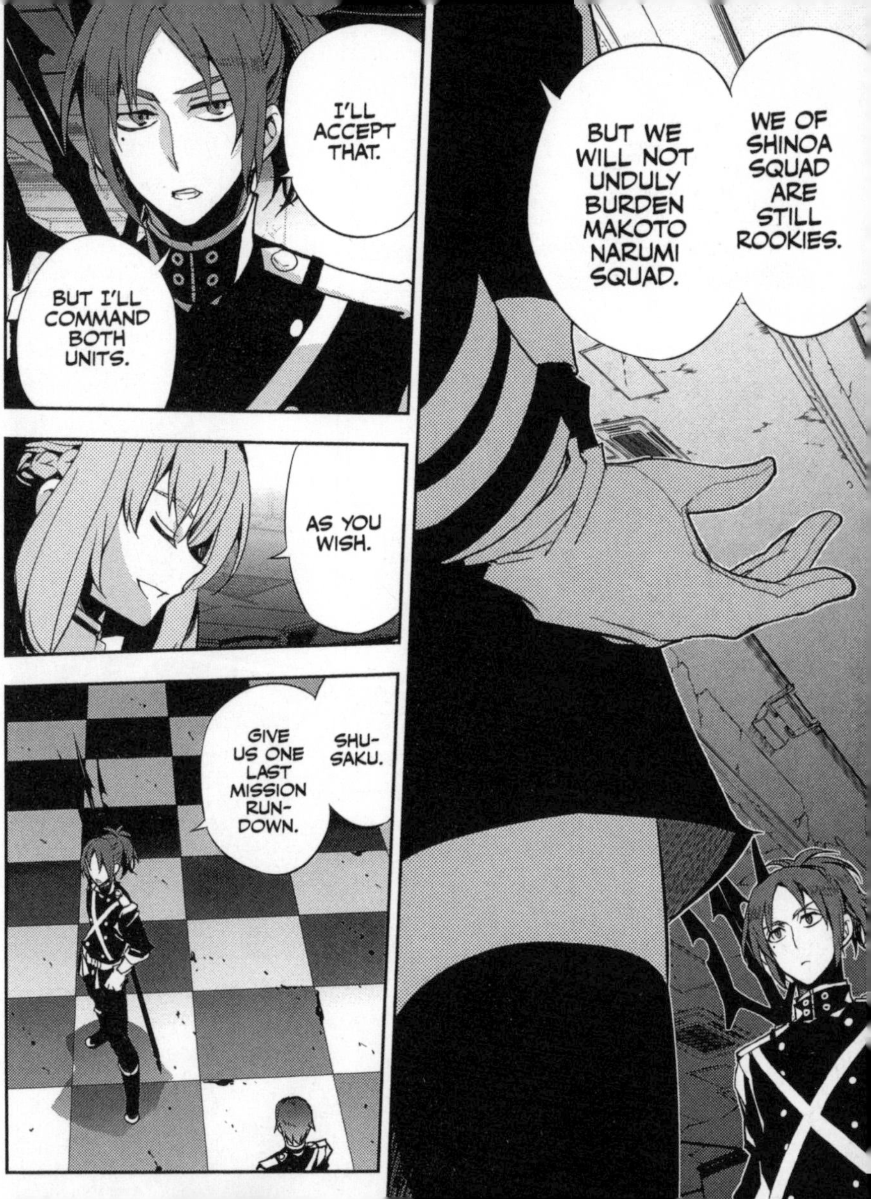
WE OF SHINOA SQUAD ARE STILL ROOKIES.
BUT WE WILL NOT UNDULY BURDEN MAKOTO NARUMI SQUAD.
I'LL ACCEPT THAT.
BUT I'LL COMMAND BOTH UNITS.
AS YOU WISH.
SHU-SAKU.
GIVE US ONE LAST MISSION RUN-DOWN.

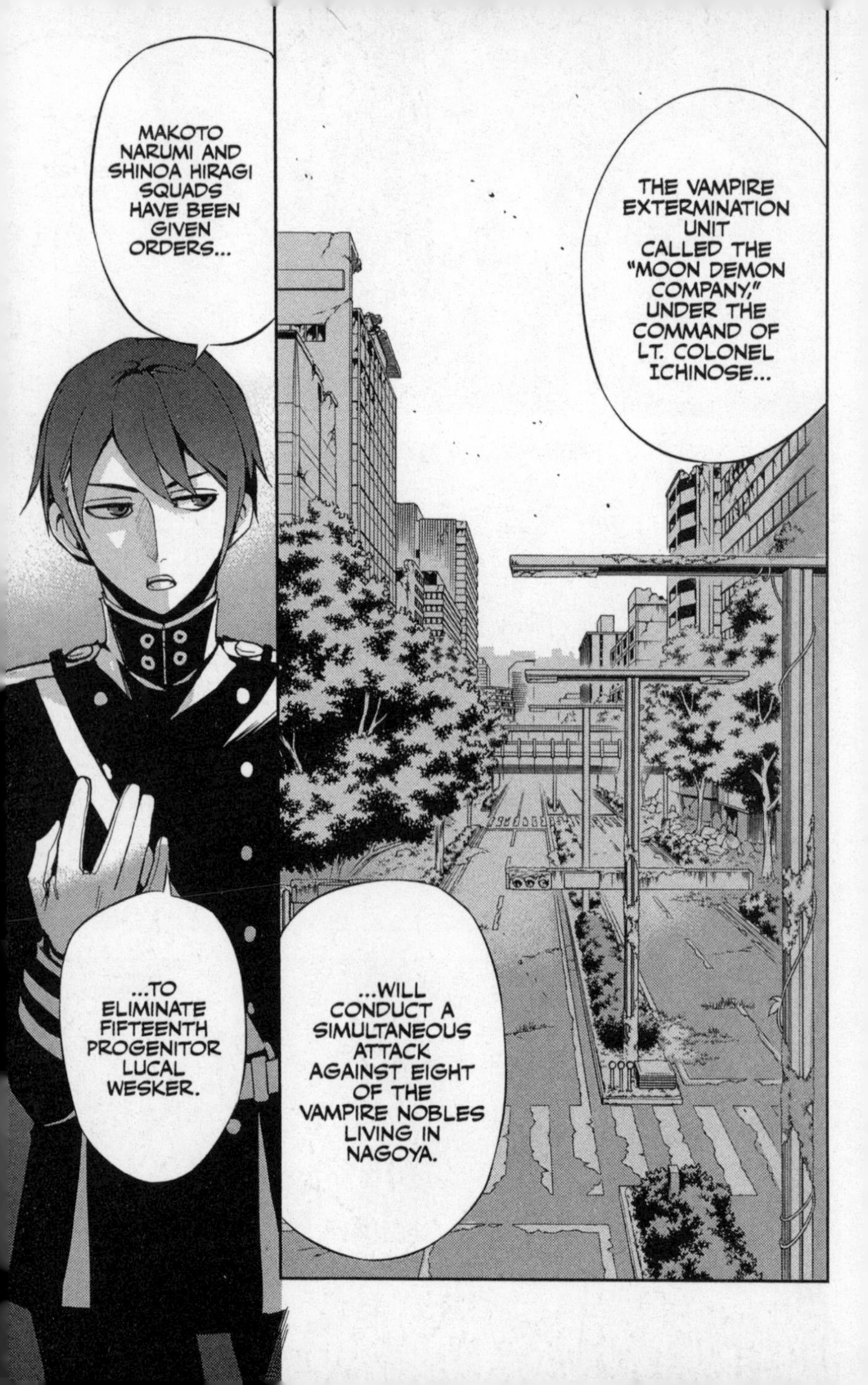
THE VAMPIRE EXTERMINATION UNIT CALLED THE "MOON DEMON COMPANY," UNDER THE COMMAND OF LT. COLONEL ICHINOSE...
...WILL CONDUCT A SIMULTANEOUS ATTACK AGAINST EIGHT OF THE VAMPIRE NOBLES LIVING IN NAGOYA.
MAKOTO NARUMI AND SHINOA HIRAGI SQUADS HAVE BEEN GIVEN ORDERS...
...TO ELIMINATE FIFTEENTH PROGENITOR LUCAL WESKER.

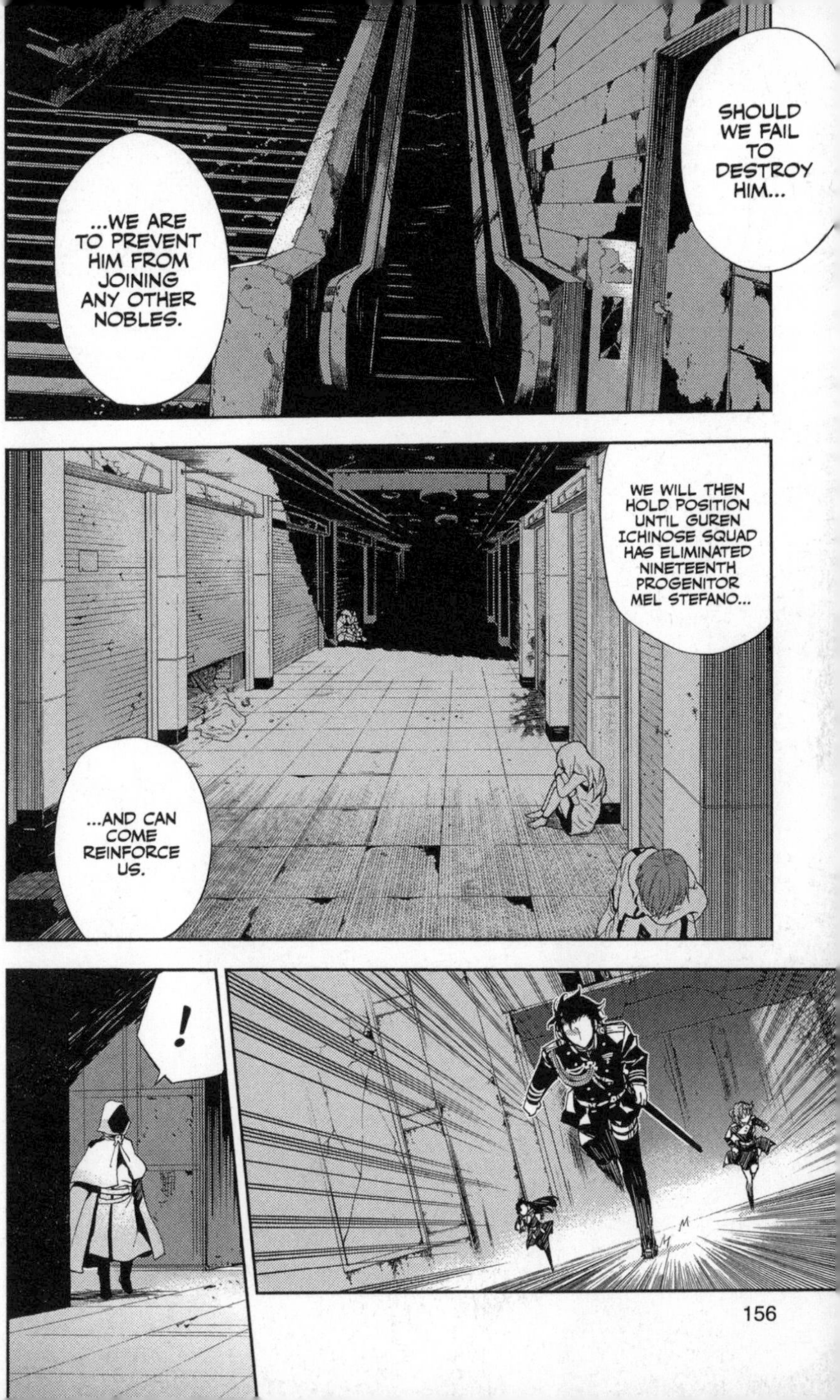
SHOULD WE FAIL TO DESTROY HIM...
...WE ARE TO PREVENT HIM FROM JOINING ANY OTHER NOBLES.
WE WILL THEN HOLD POSITION UNTIL GUREN ICHINOSE SQUAD HAS ELIMINATED NINETEENTH PROGENITOR MEL STEFANO...
...AND CAN COME REINFORCE US.
!

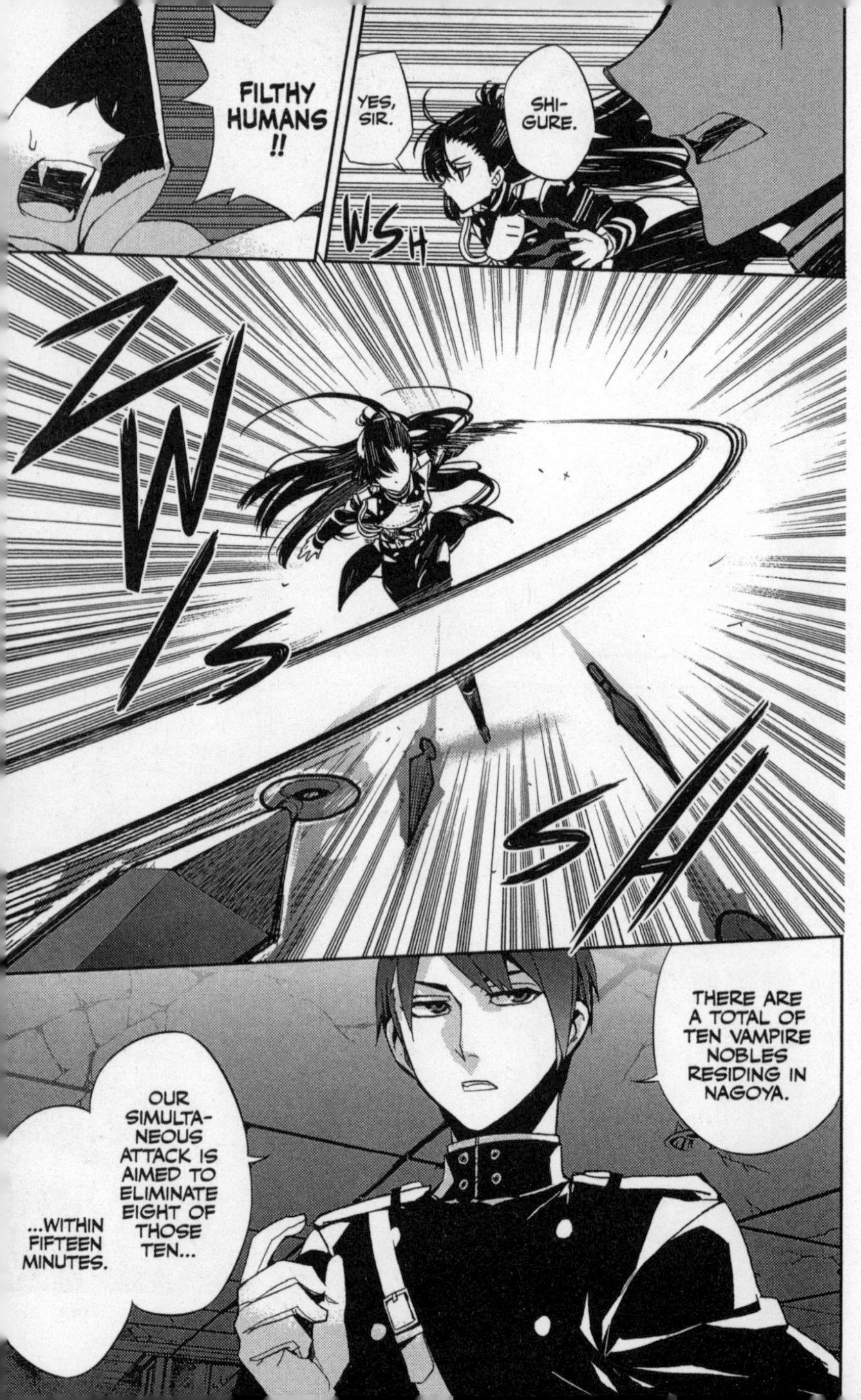
SHI-GURE.
YES, SIR.
WSH
FILTHY HUMANS!!
ZWIS
SH
THERE ARE A TOTAL OF TEN VAMPIRE NOBLES RESIDING IN NAGOYA.
OUR SIMULTA-NEOUS ATTACK IS AIMED TO ELIMINATE EIGHT OF THOSE TEN...
...WITHIN FIFTEEN MINUTES.

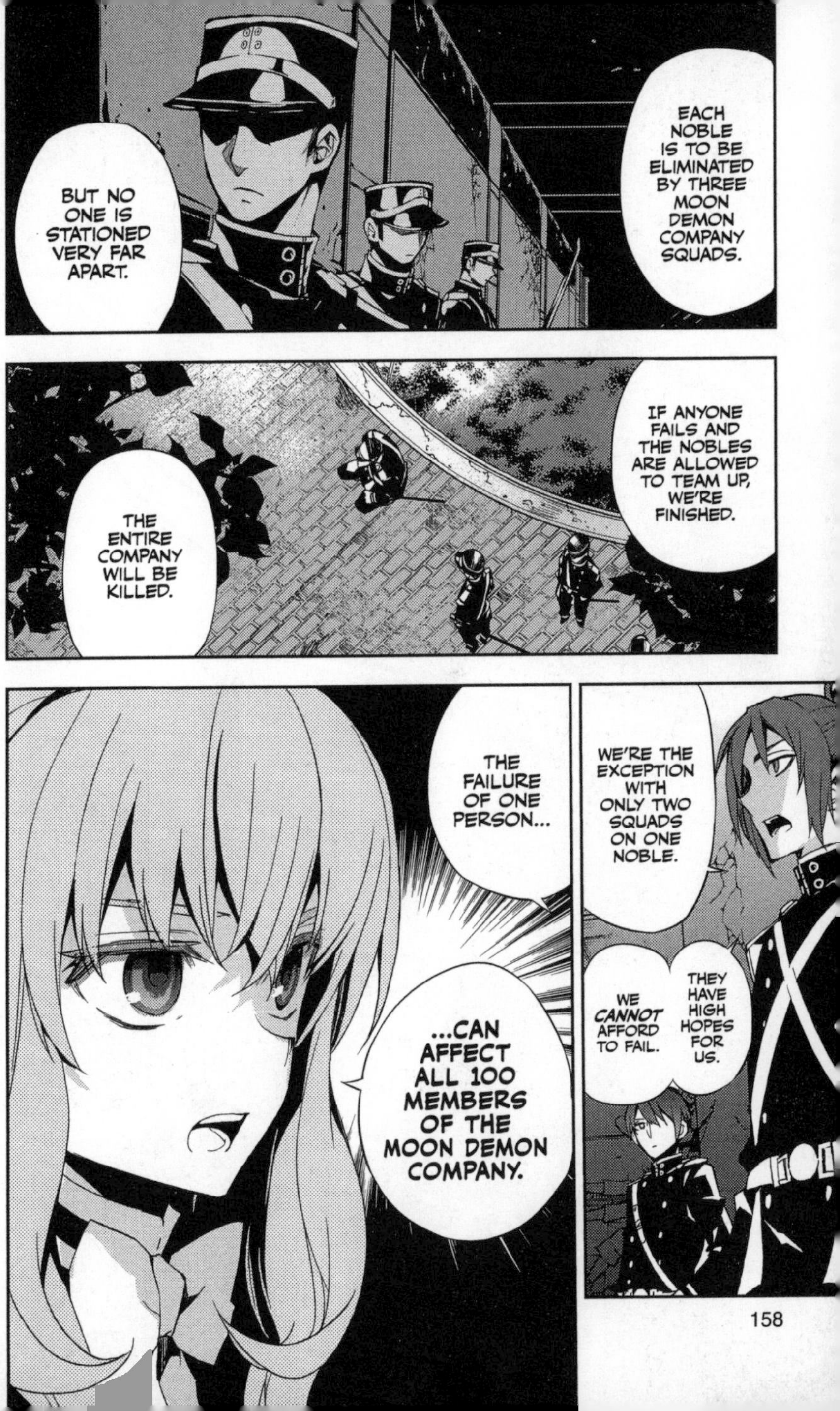
EACH NOBLE IS TO BE ELIMINATED BY THREE MOON DEMON COMPANY SQUADS.
BUT NO ONE IS STATIONED VERY FAR APART.
IF ANYONE FAILS AND THE NOBLES ARE ALLOWED TO TEAM UP, WE'RE FINISHED.
THE ENTIRE COMPANY WILL BE KILLED.
WE'RE THE EXCEPTION WITH ONLY TWO SQUADS ON ONE NOBLE.
THEY HAVE HIGH HOPES FOR US.
WE *CANNOT* AFFORD TO FAIL.
THE FAILURE OF ONE PERSON...
...CAN AFFECT ALL 100 MEMBERS OF THE MOON DEMON COMPANY.

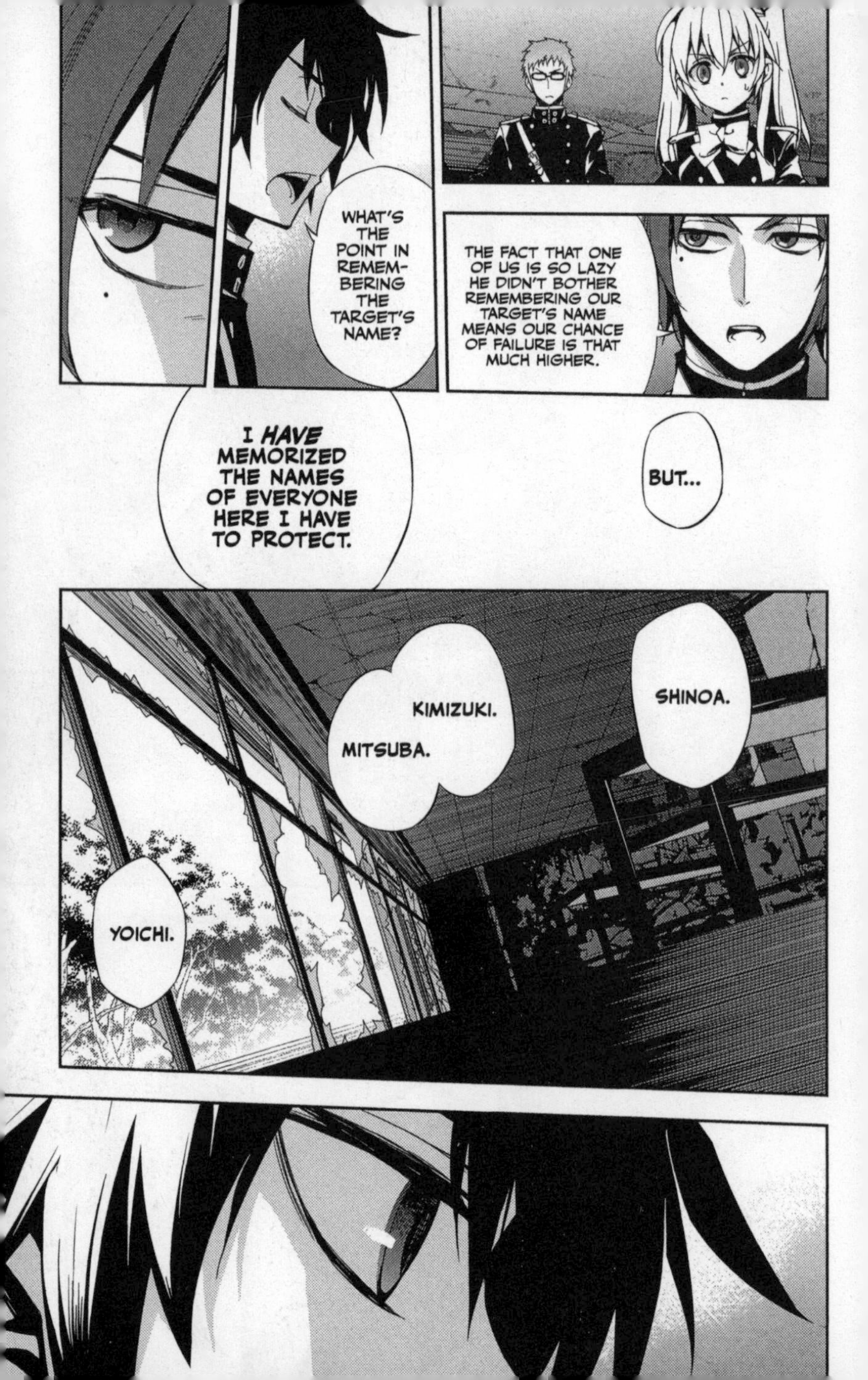
THE FACT THAT ONE OF US IS SO LAZY HE DIDN'T BOTHER REMEMBERING OUR TARGET'S NAME MEANS OUR CHANCE OF FAILURE IS THAT MUCH HIGHER.
WHAT'S THE POINT IN REMEMBERING THE TARGET'S NAME?
BUT...
I *HAVE* MEMORIZED THE NAMES OF EVERYONE HERE I HAVE TO PROTECT.
SHINOA.
KIMIZUKI.
MITSUBA.
YOICHI.

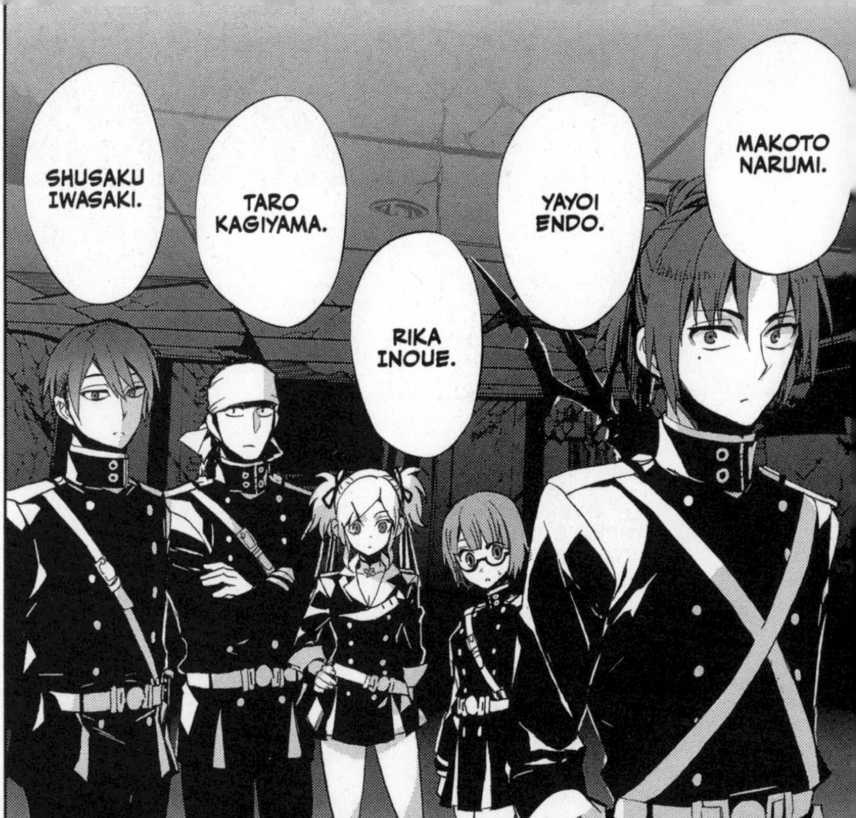
MAKOTO NARUMI.
YAYOI ENDO.
RIKA INOUE.
TARO KAGIYAMA.
SHUSAKU IWASAKI.

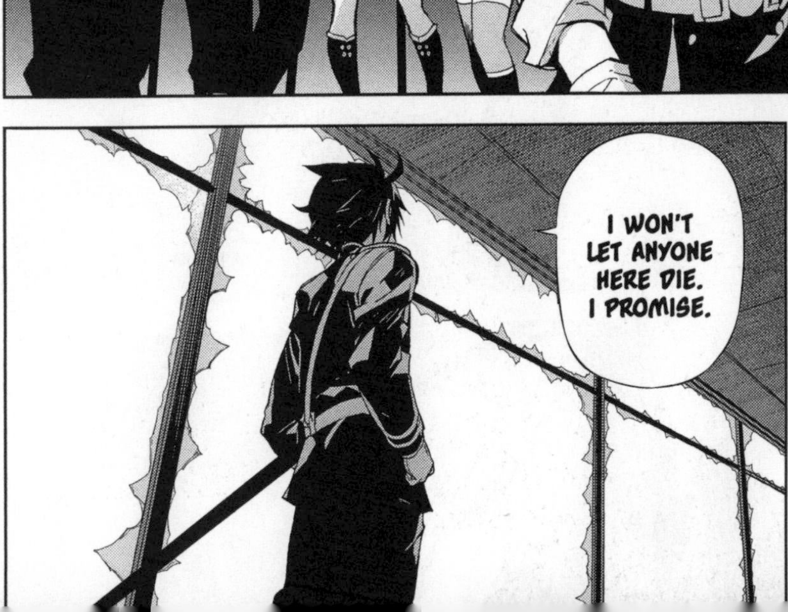
I WON'T LET ANYONE HERE DIE. I PROMISE.

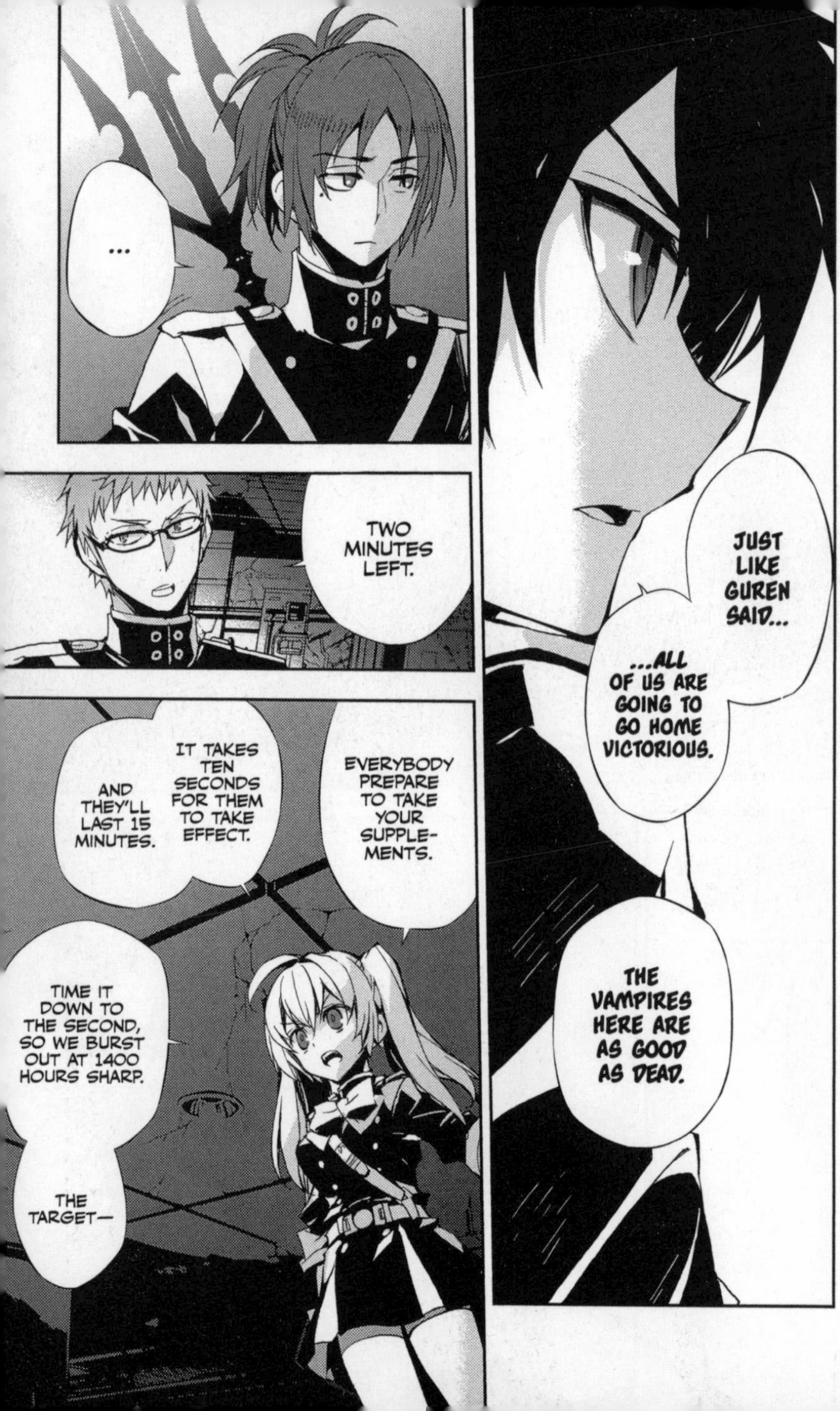
JUST LIKE GUREN SAID...
...ALL OF US ARE GOING TO GO HOME VICTORIOUS.
THE VAMPIRES HERE ARE AS GOOD AS DEAD.
...
TWO MINUTES LEFT.
EVERYBODY PREPARE TO TAKE YOUR SUPPLEMENTS.
IT TAKES TEN SECONDS FOR THEM TO TAKE EFFECT.
AND THEY'LL LAST 15 MINUTES.
TIME IT DOWN TO THE SECOND, SO WE BURST OUT AT 1400 HOURS SHARP.
THE TARGET—

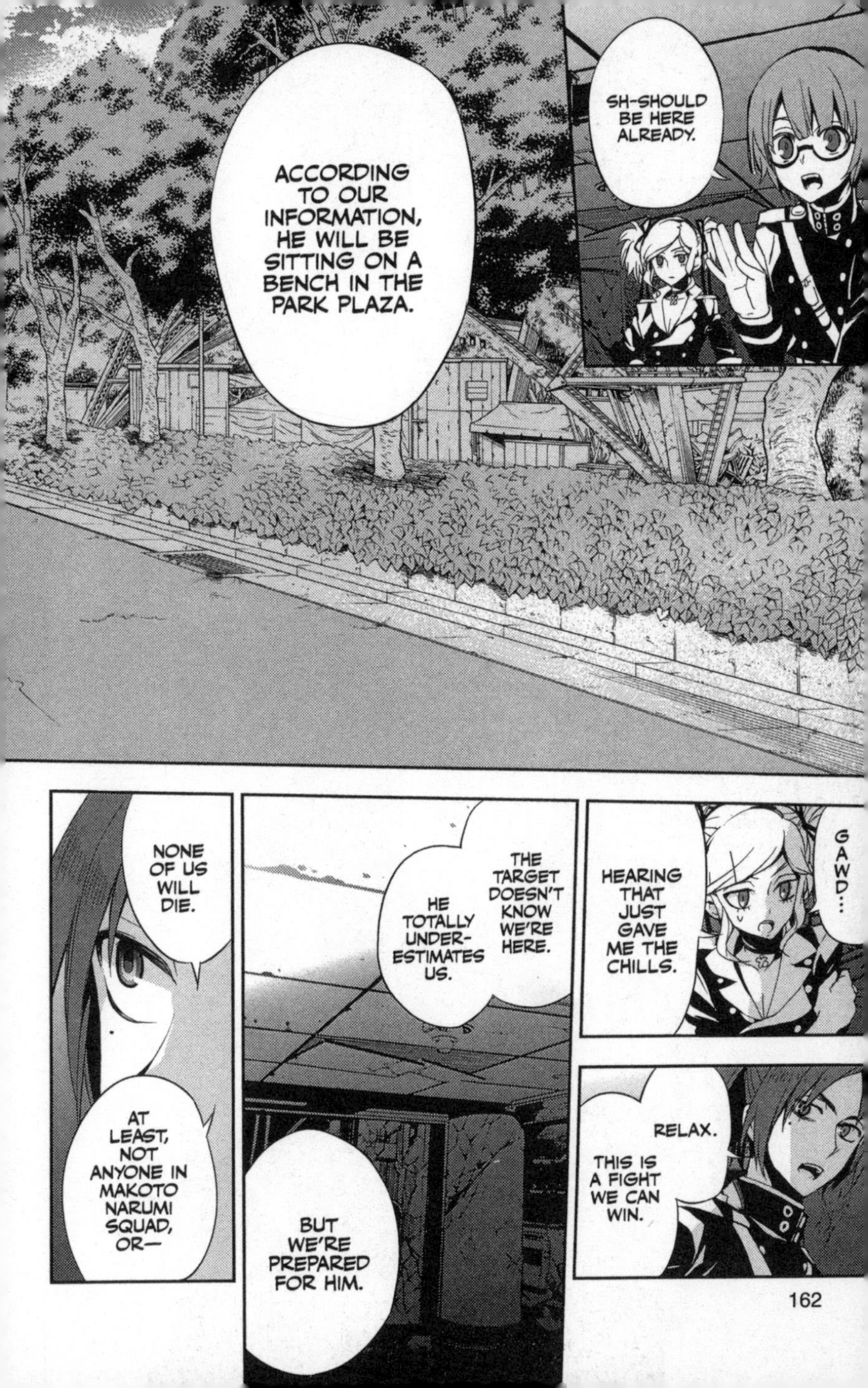
SH-SHOULD BE HERE ALREADY.
ACCORDING TO OUR INFORMATION, HE WILL BE SITTING ON A BENCH IN THE PARK PLAZA.
GAWD...
HEARING THAT JUST GAVE ME THE CHILLS.
RELAX.
THIS IS A FIGHT WE CAN WIN.
THE TARGET DOESN'T KNOW WE'RE HERE.
HE TOTALLY UNDER-ESTIMATES US.
BUT WE'RE PREPARED FOR HIM.
NONE OF US WILL DIE.
AT LEAST, NOT ANYONE IN MAKOTO NARUMI SQUAD, OR—

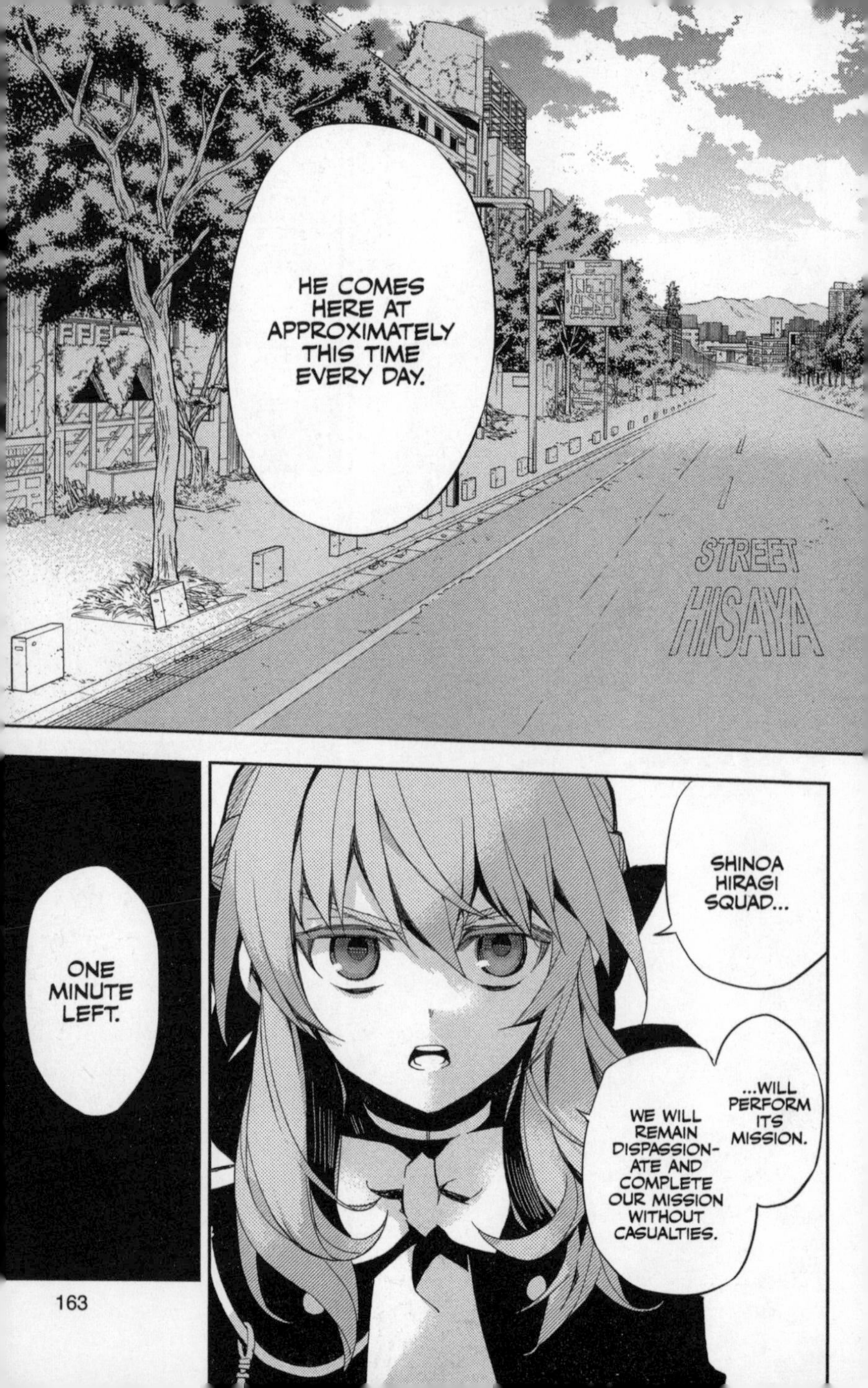
HE COMES HERE AT APPROXIMATELY THIS TIME EVERY DAY.
STREET
HISAYA
SHINOA HIRAGI SQUAD...
...WILL PERFORM ITS MISSION.
WE WILL REMAIN DISPASSIONATE AND COMPLETE OUR MISSION WITHOUT CASUALTIES.
ONE MINUTE LEFT.

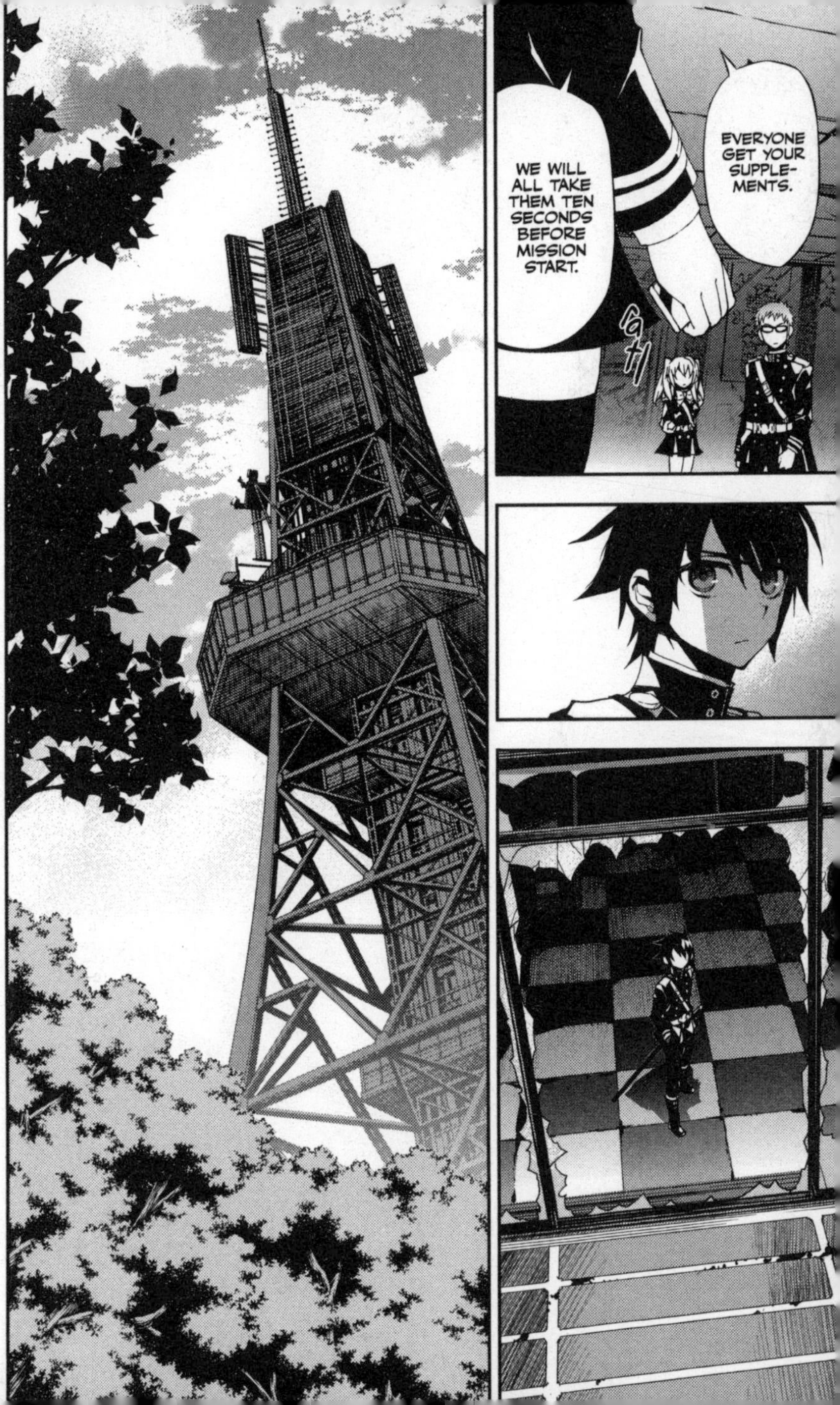
EVERYONE GET YOUR SUPPLE-MENTS.
WE WILL ALL TAKE THEM TEN SECONDS BEFORE MISSION START.
PAT

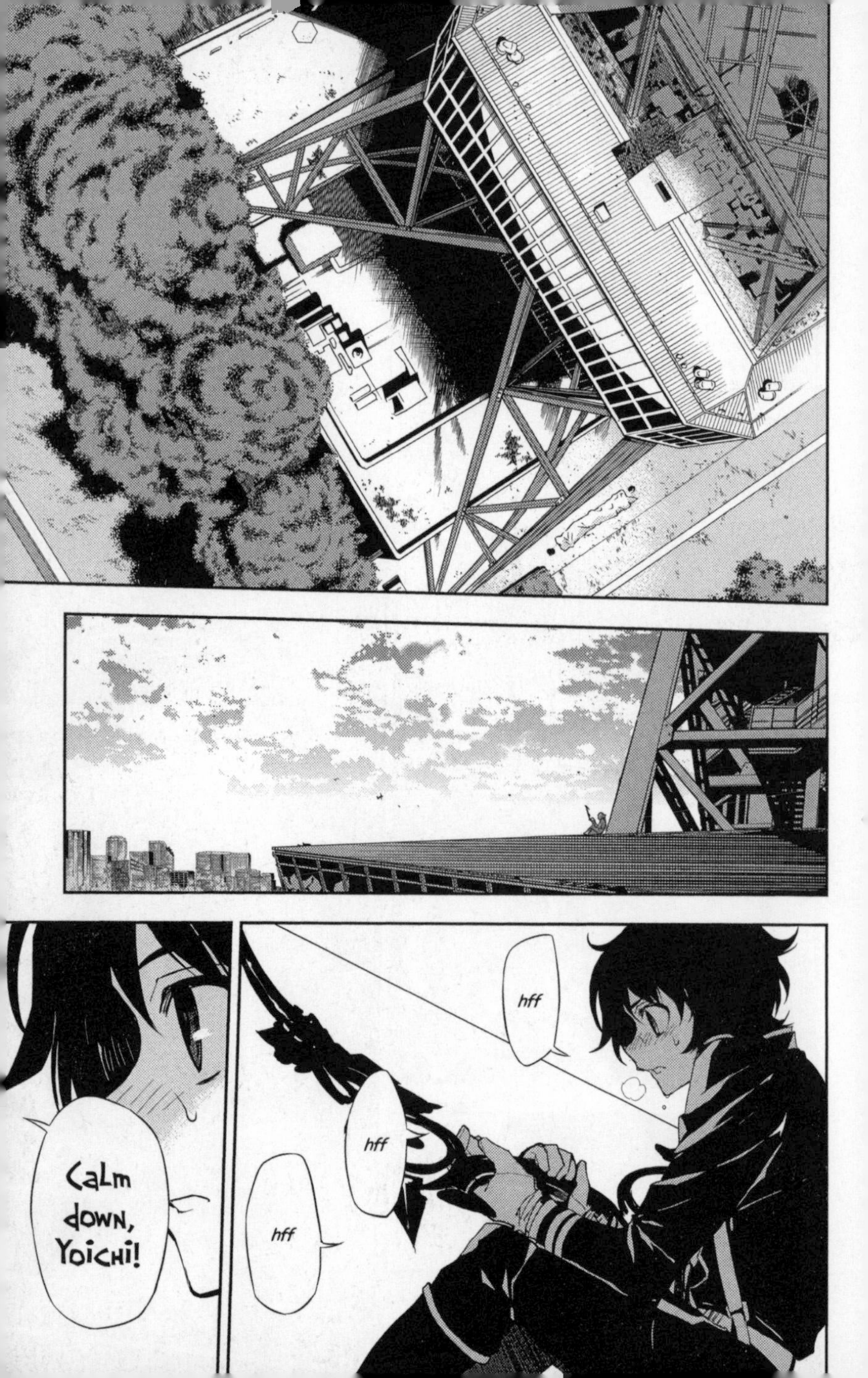
hff
hff
hff
Calm down, Yoichi!

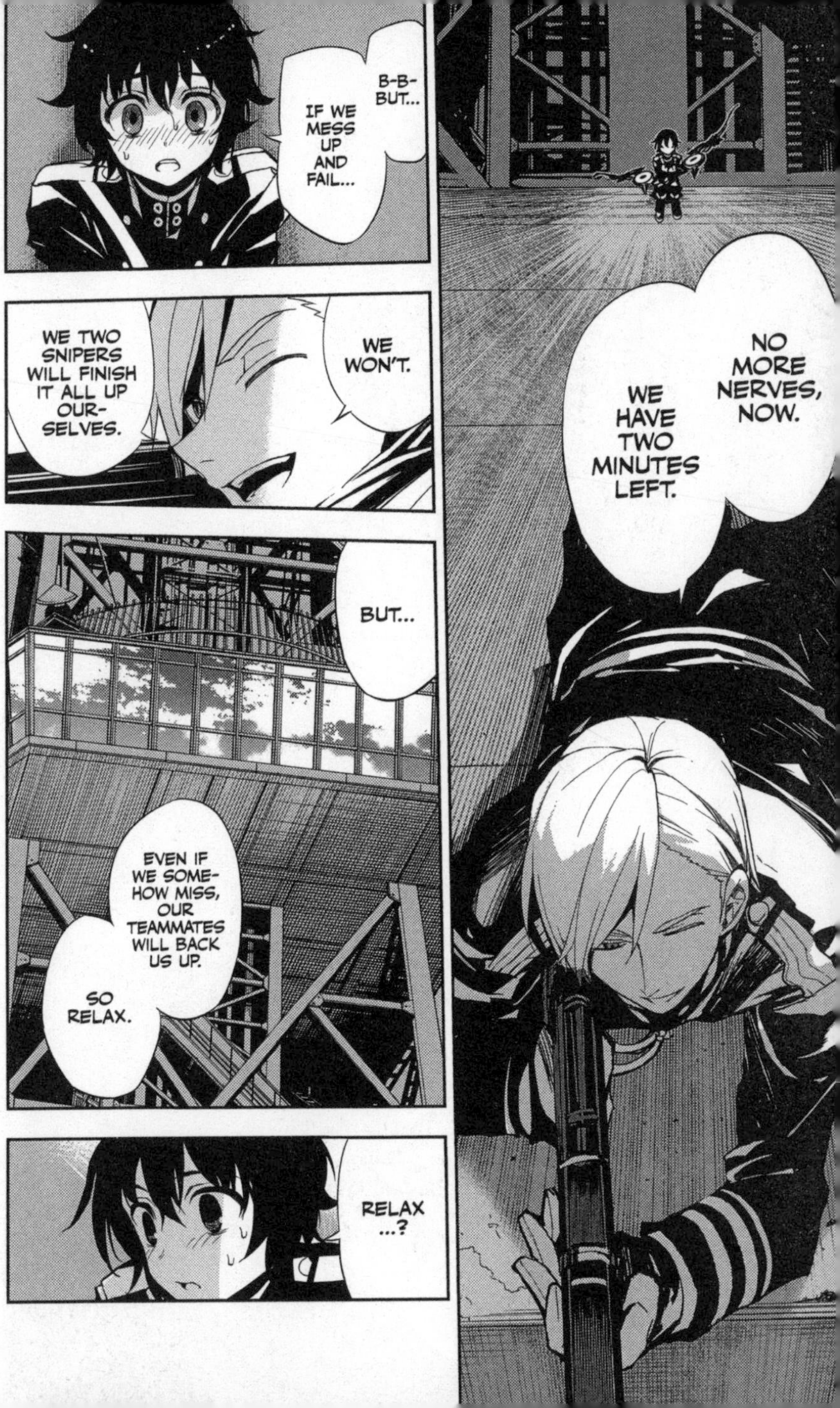
NO MORE NERVES, NOW.
WE HAVE TWO MINUTES LEFT.
B-B-BUT...
IF WE MESS UP AND FAIL...
WE WON'T.
WE TWO SNIPERS WILL FINISH IT ALL UP OUR-SELVES.
BUT...
EVEN IF WE SOME-HOW MISS, OUR TEAMMATES WILL BACK US UP.
SO RELAX.
RELAX ...?

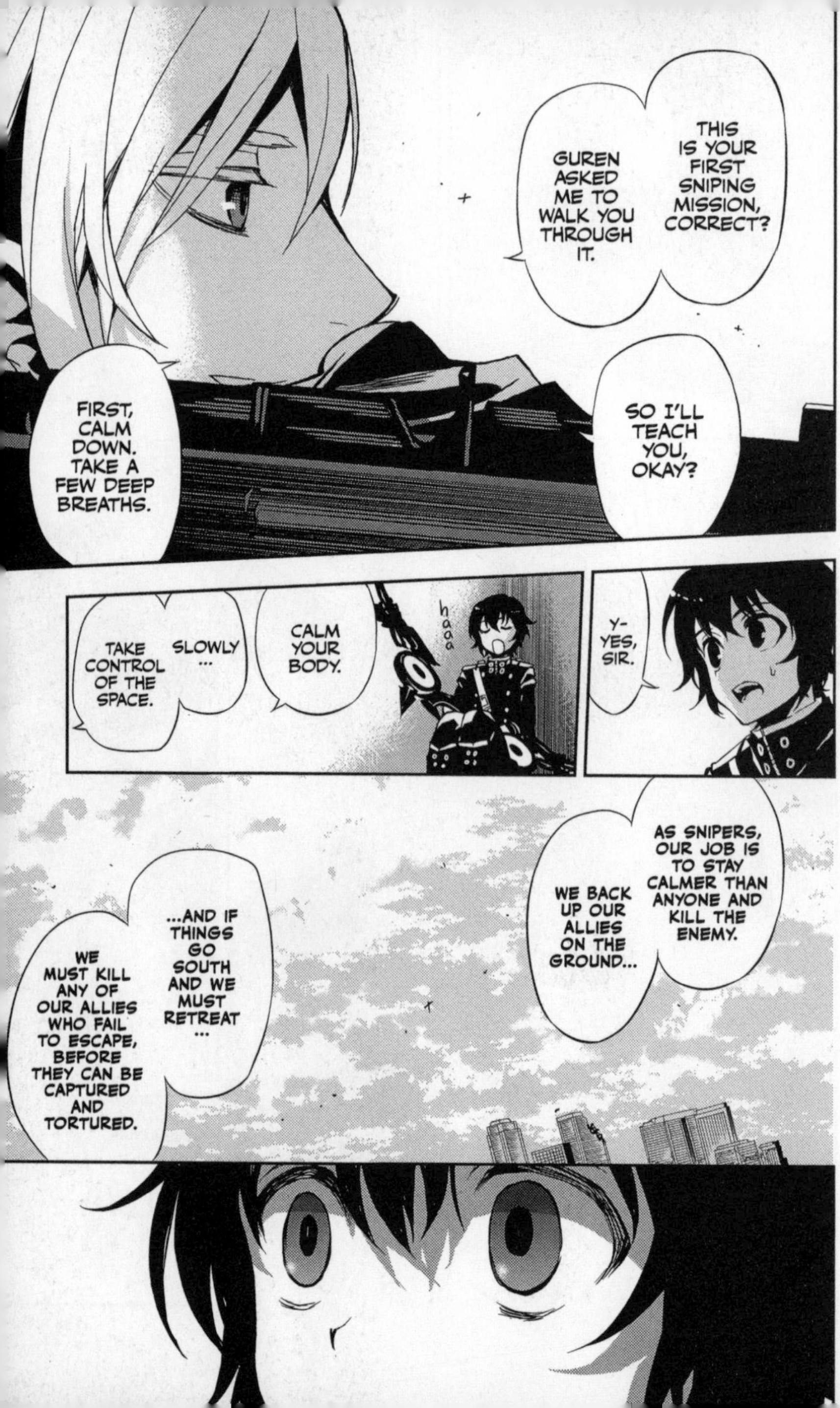
THIS IS YOUR FIRST SNIPING MISSION, CORRECT?
GUREN ASKED ME TO WALK YOU THROUGH IT.
SO I'LL TEACH YOU, OKAY?
FIRST, CALM DOWN. TAKE A FEW DEEP BREATHS.
Y-YES, SIR.
haaa
CALM YOUR BODY.
SLOWLY...
TAKE CONTROL OF THE SPACE.
AS SNIPERS, OUR JOB IS TO STAY CALMER THAN ANYONE AND KILL THE ENEMY.
WE BACK UP OUR ALLIES ON THE GROUND...
...AND IF THINGS GO SOUTH AND WE MUST RETREAT...
WE MUST KILL ANY OF OUR ALLIES WHO FAIL TO ESCAPE, BEFORE THEY CAN BE CAPTURED AND TORTURED.

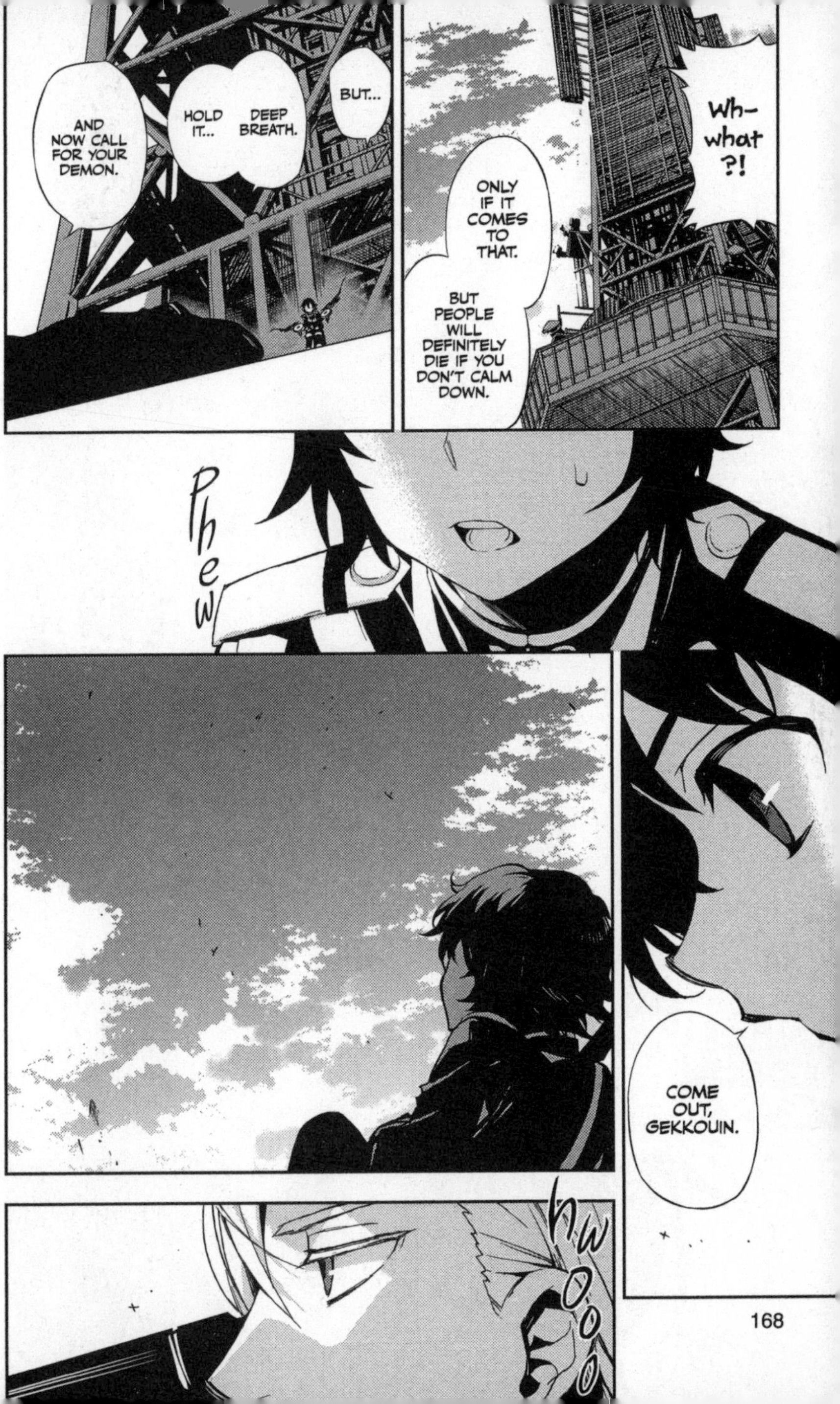
Wh-what?!
ONLY IF IT COMES TO THAT.
BUT PEOPLE WILL DEFINITELY DIE IF YOU DON'T CALM DOWN.
BUT...
DEEP BREATH.
HOLD IT...
AND NOW CALL FOR YOUR DEMON.
Phew
COME OUT, GEKKOUIN.
hwooo

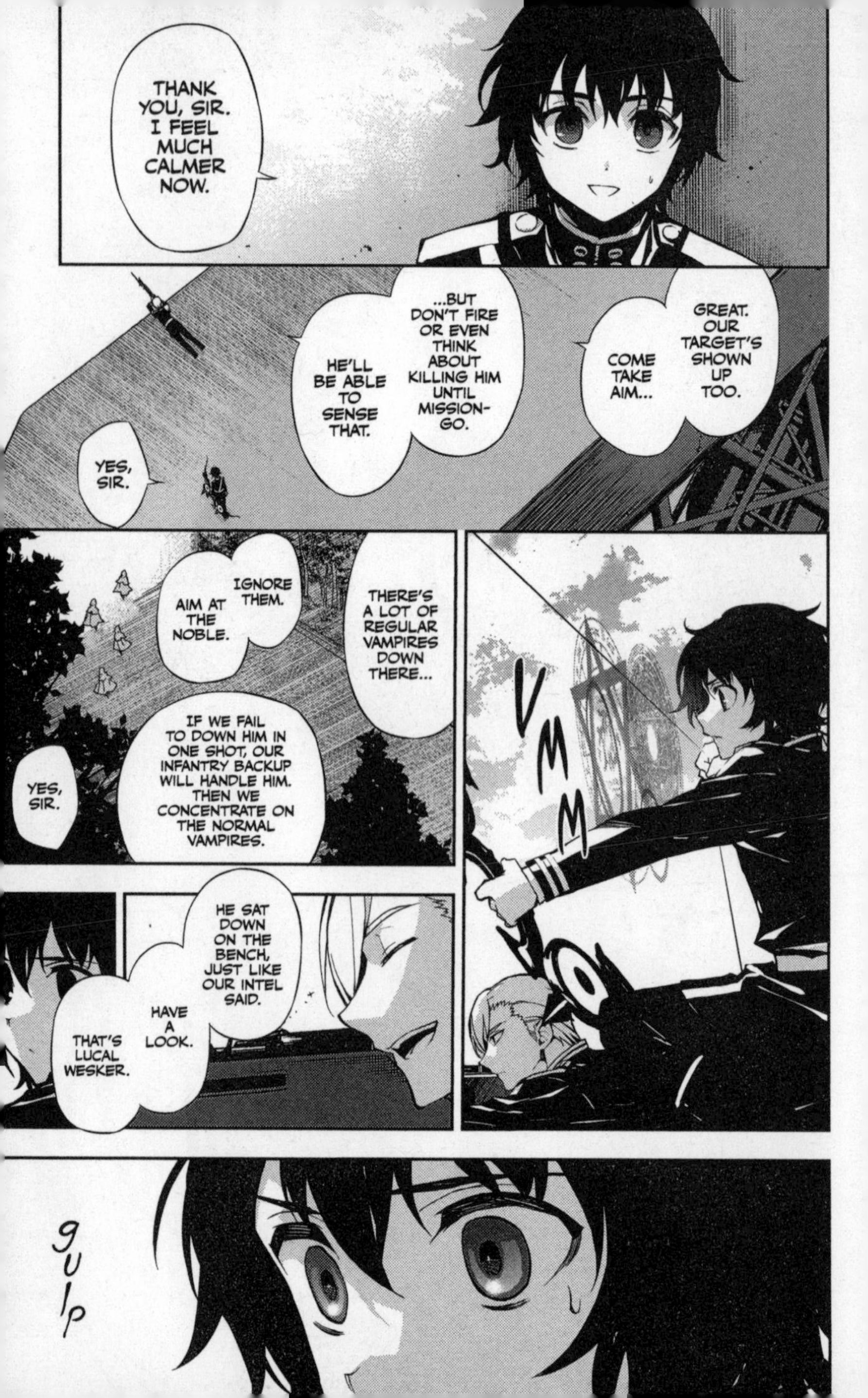
THANK YOU, SIR. I FEEL MUCH CALMER NOW.
GREAT. OUR TARGET'S SHOWN UP TOO.
COME TAKE AIM...
...BUT DON'T FIRE OR EVEN THINK ABOUT KILLING HIM UNTIL MISSION-GO.
HE'LL BE ABLE TO SENSE THAT.
YES, SIR.
VMMM
THERE'S A LOT OF REGULAR VAMPIRES DOWN THERE...
IGNORE THEM.
AIM AT THE NOBLE.
IF WE FAIL TO DOWN HIM IN ONE SHOT, OUR INFANTRY BACKUP WILL HANDLE HIM. THEN WE CONCENTRATE ON THE NORMAL VAMPIRES.
YES, SIR.
HE SAT DOWN ON THE BENCH, JUST LIKE OUR INTEL SAID.
HAVE A LOOK.
THAT'S LUCAL WESKER.
gulp

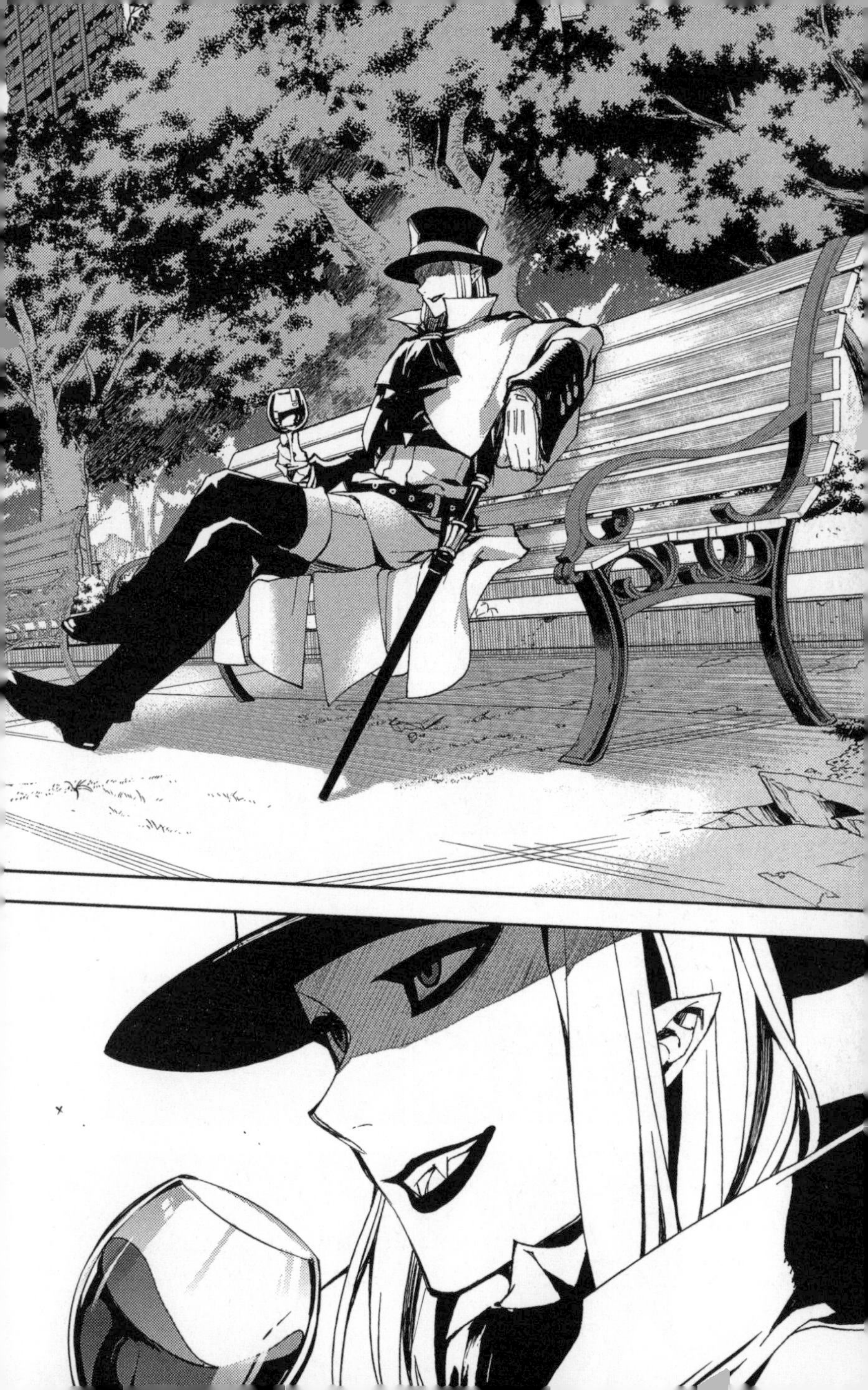

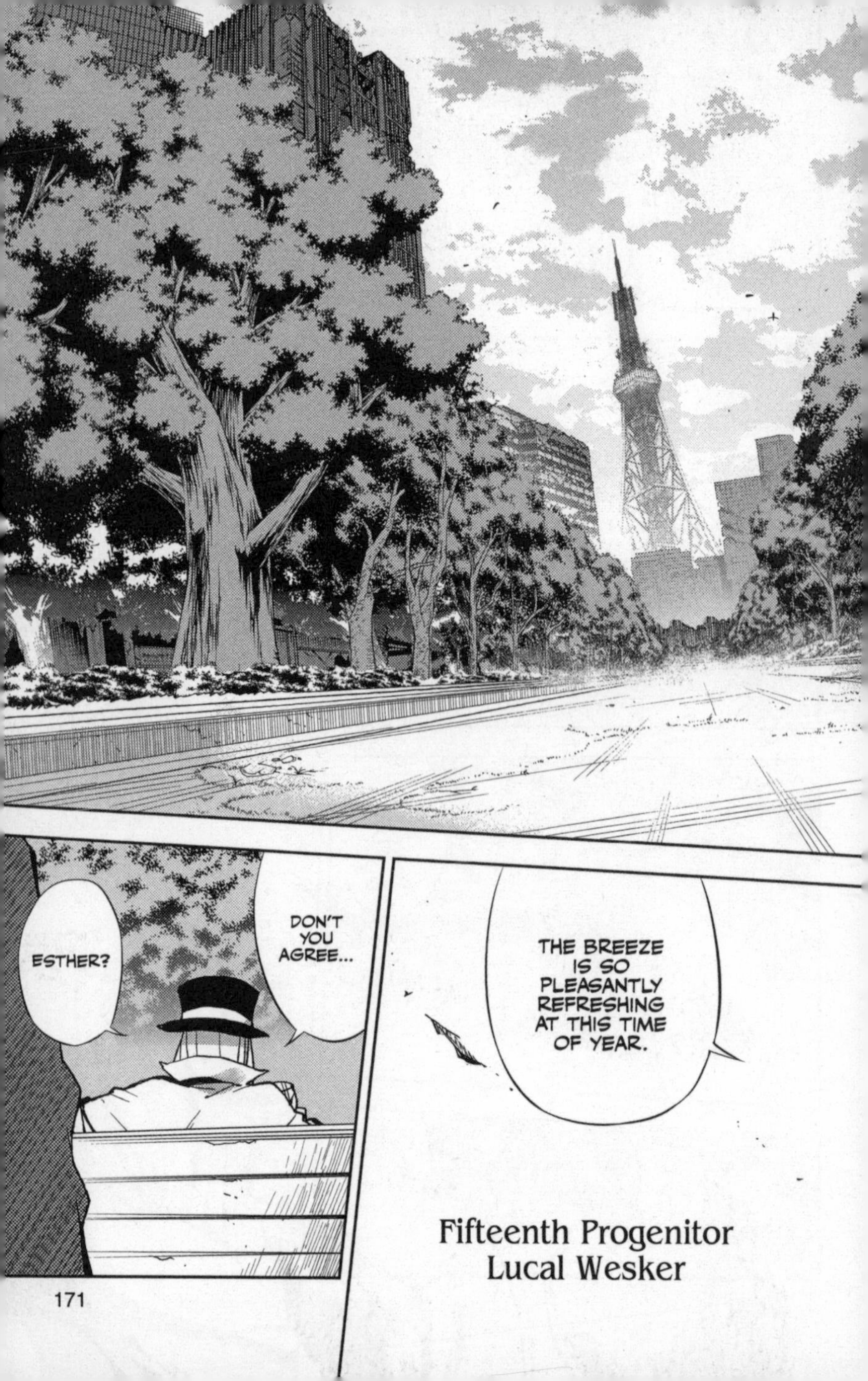
THE BREEZE IS SO PLEASANTLY REFRESHING AT THIS TIME OF YEAR.
Fifteenth Progenitor Lucal Wesker
DON'T YOU AGREE...
ESTHER?

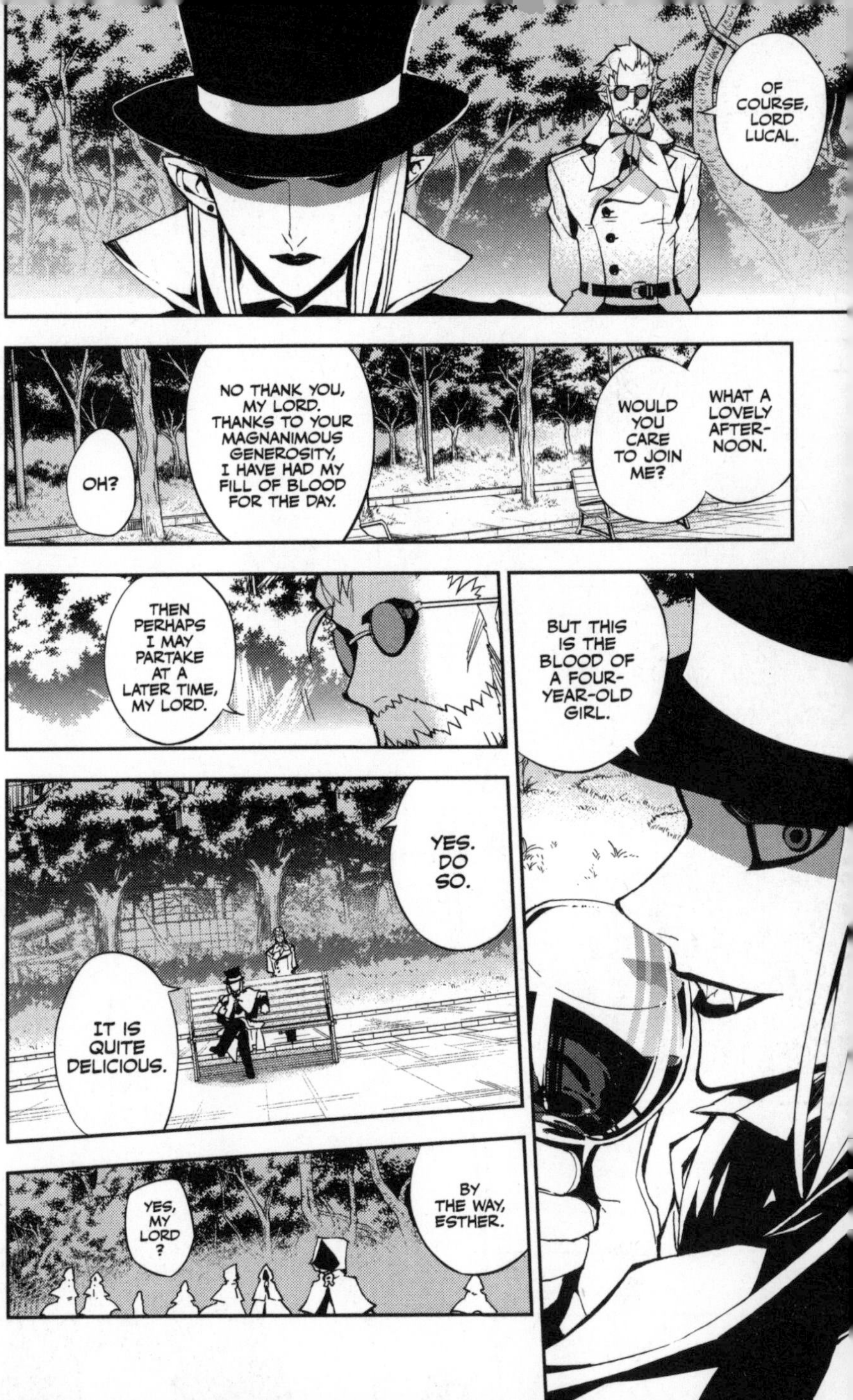
OF COURSE, LORD LUCAL.
WHAT A LOVELY AFTERNOON.
WOULD YOU CARE TO JOIN ME?
NO THANK YOU, MY LORD. THANKS TO YOUR MAGNANIMOUS GENEROSITY, I HAVE HAD MY FILL OF BLOOD FOR THE DAY.
OH?
BUT THIS IS THE BLOOD OF A FOUR-YEAR-OLD GIRL.
THEN PERHAPS I MAY PARTAKE AT A LATER TIME, MY LORD.
YES. DO SO.
IT IS QUITE DELICIOUS.
BY THE WAY, ESTHER.
YES, MY LORD?

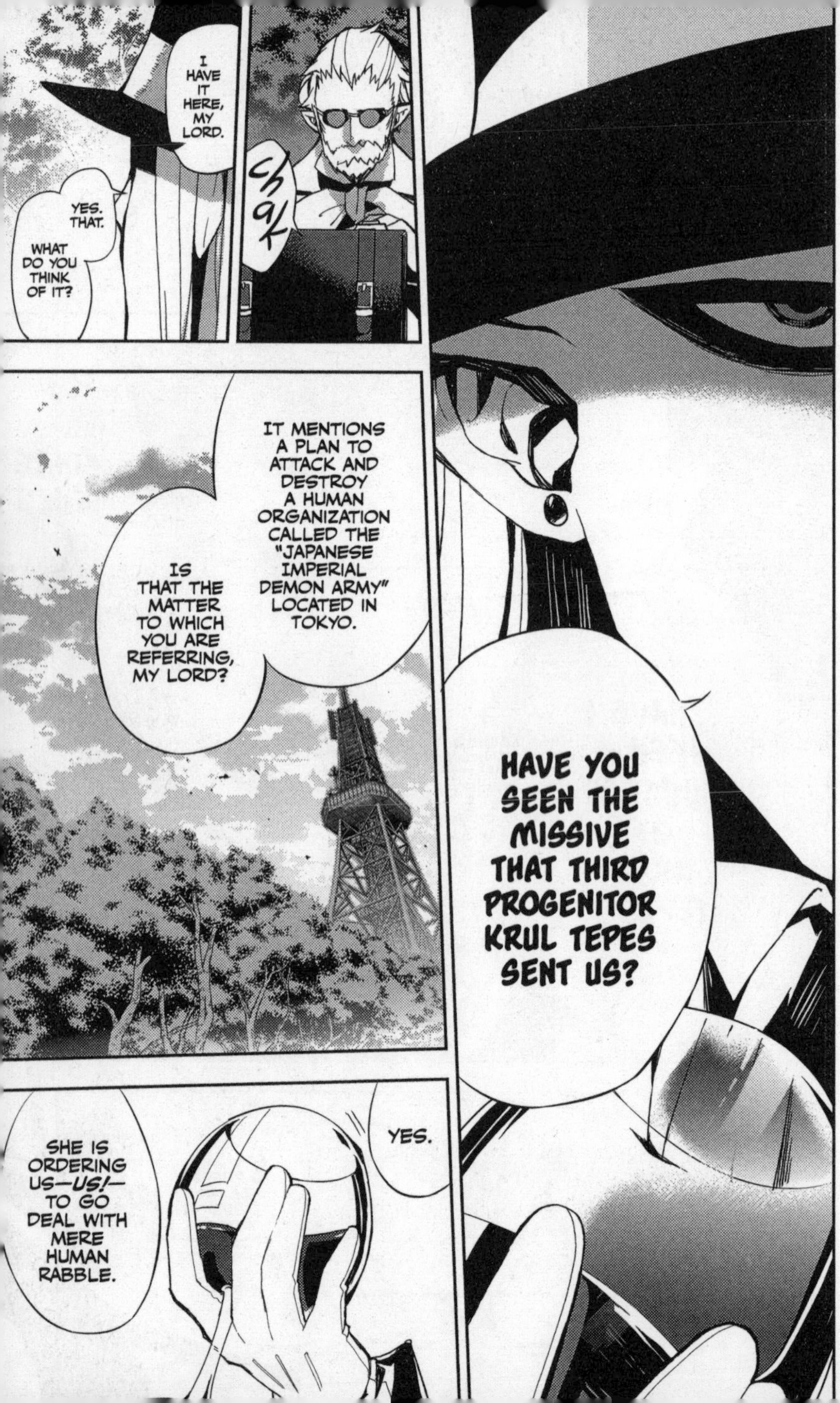
HAVE YOU SEEN THE MISSIVE THAT THIRD PROGENITOR KRUL TEPES SENT US?
I HAVE IT HERE, MY LORD.
CHAK
YES. THAT.
WHAT DO YOU THINK OF IT?
IT MENTIONS A PLAN TO ATTACK AND DESTROY A HUMAN ORGANIZATION CALLED THE "JAPANESE IMPERIAL DEMON ARMY" LOCATED IN TOKYO.
IS THAT THE MATTER TO WHICH YOU ARE REFERRING, MY LORD?
YES.
SHE IS ORDERING US—*US!*—TO GO DEAL WITH MERE HUMAN RABBLE.

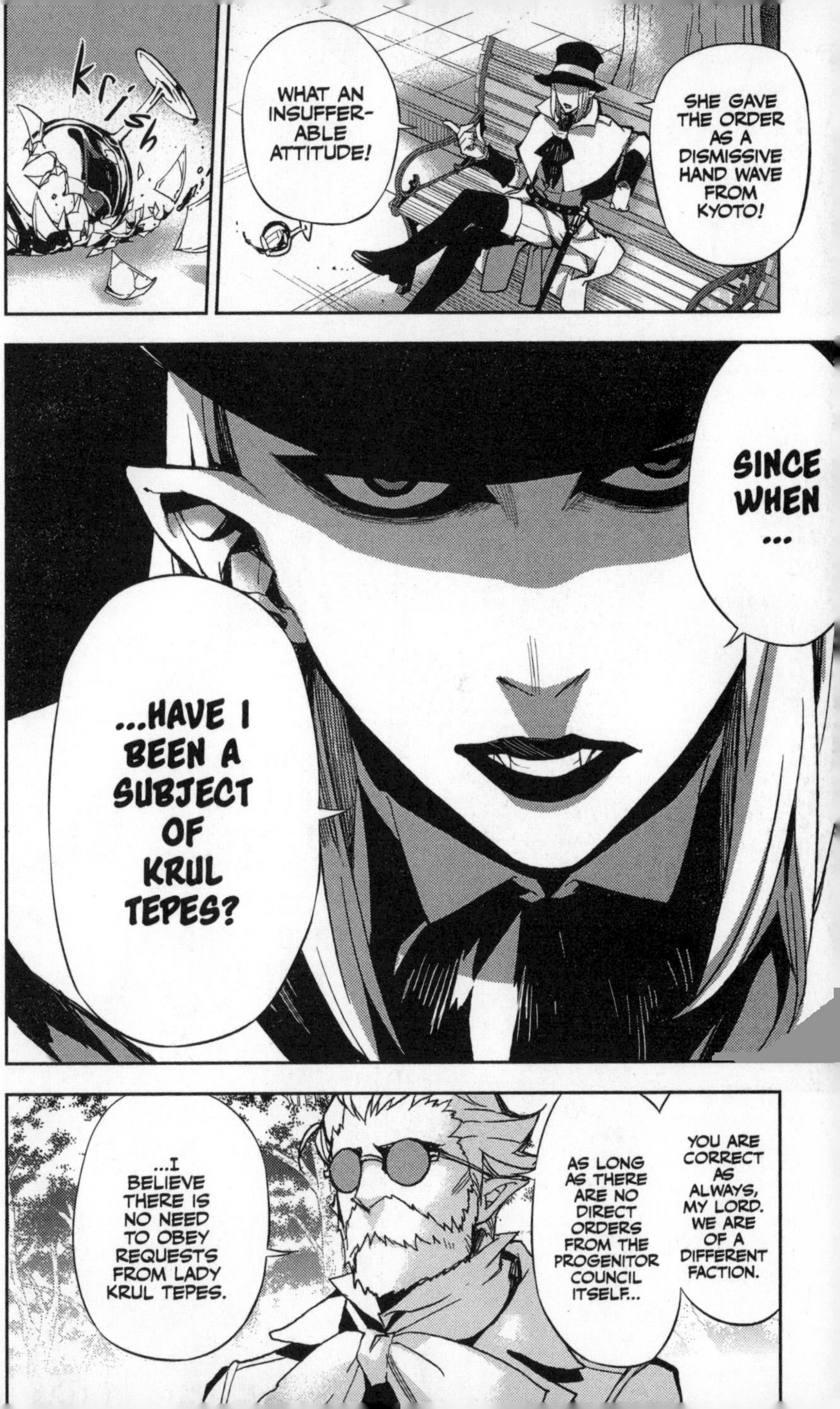
SHE GAVE THE ORDER AS A DISMISSIVE HAND WAVE FROM KYOTO!
WHAT AN INSUFFER-ABLE ATTITUDE!
krish
SINCE WHEN...
...HAVE I BEEN A SUBJECT OF KRUL TEPES?
YOU ARE CORRECT AS ALWAYS, MY LORD. WE ARE OF A DIFFERENT FACTION.
AS LONG AS THERE ARE NO DIRECT ORDERS FROM THE PROGENITOR COUNCIL ITSELF...
...I BELIEVE THERE IS NO NEED TO OBEY REQUESTS FROM LADY KRUL TEPES.

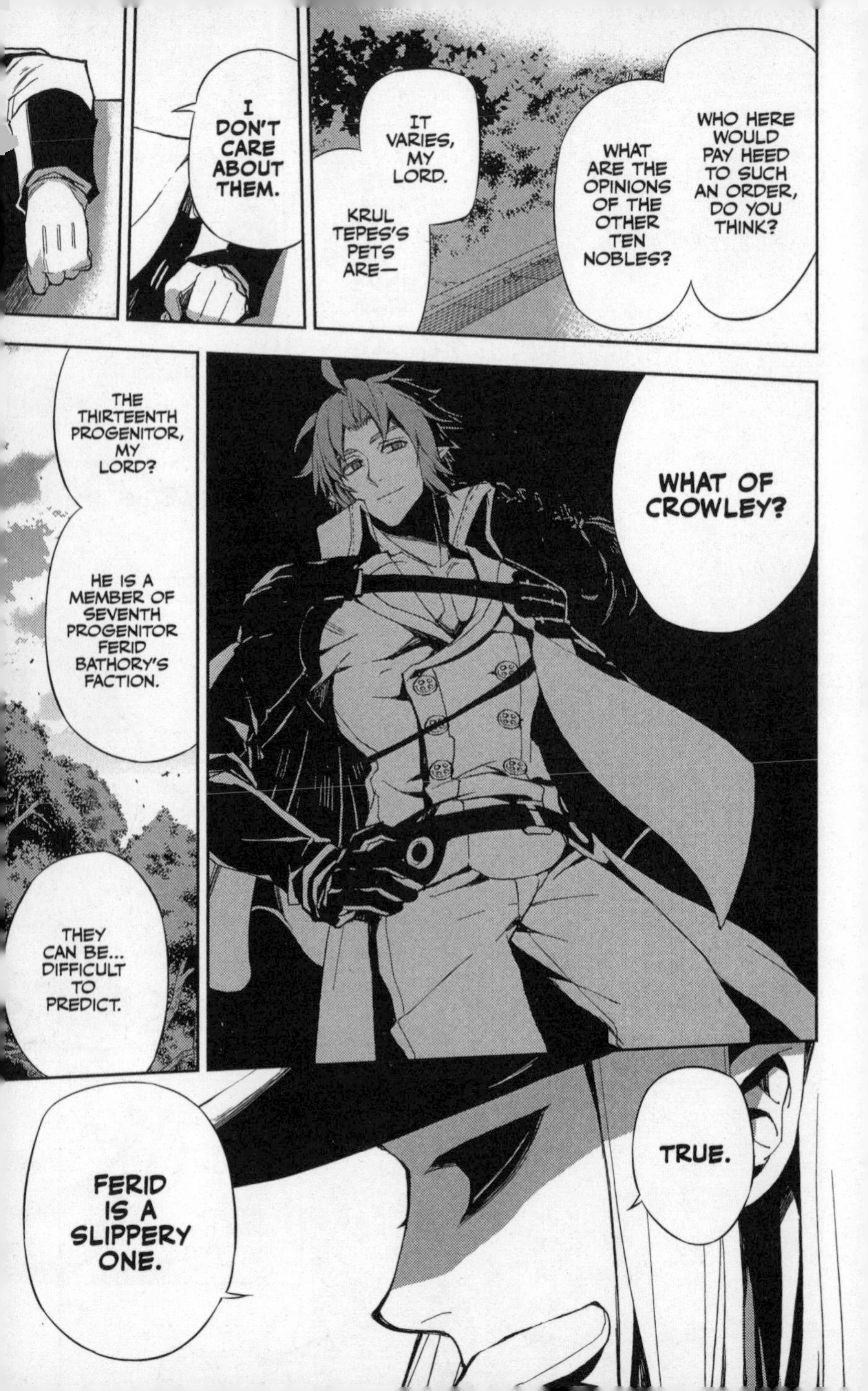
WHO HERE WOULD PAY HEED TO SUCH AN ORDER, DO YOU THINK?
WHAT ARE THE OPINIONS OF THE OTHER TEN NOBLES?
IT VARIES, MY LORD.
KRUL TEPES'S PETS ARE—
I DON'T CARE ABOUT THEM.
WHAT OF CROWLEY?
THE THIRTEENTH PROGENITOR, MY LORD?
HE IS A MEMBER OF SEVENTH PROGENITOR FERID BATHORY'S FACTION.
THEY CAN BE... DIFFICULT TO PREDICT.
TRUE.
FERID IS A SLIPPERY ONE.

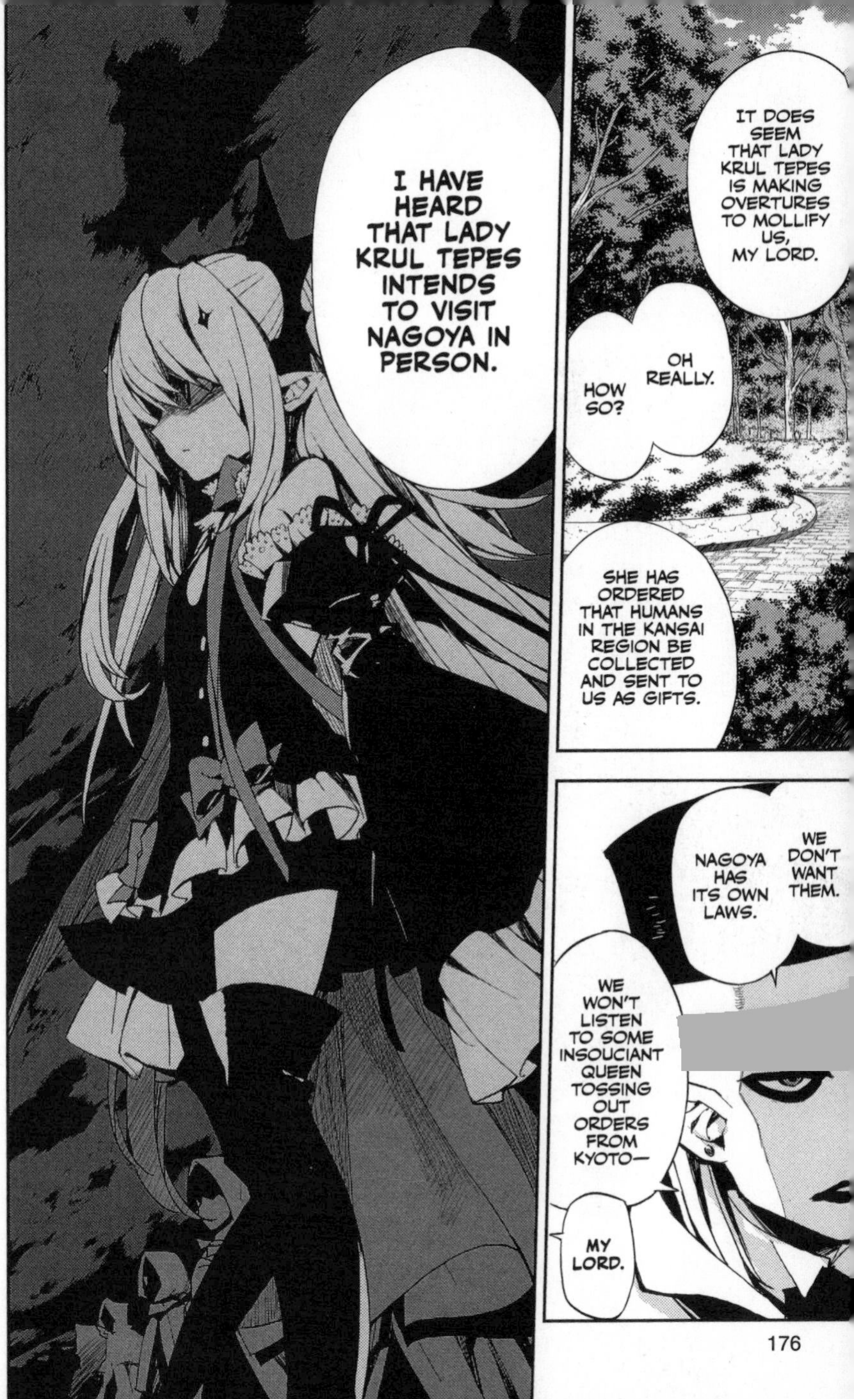
IT DOES SEEM THAT LADY KRUL TEPES IS MAKING OVERTURES TO MOLLIFY US, MY LORD.
OH REALLY.
HOW SO?
SHE HAS ORDERED THAT HUMANS IN THE KANSAI REGION BE COLLECTED AND SENT TO US AS GIFTS.
WE DON'T WANT THEM.
NAGOYA HAS ITS OWN LAWS.
WE WON'T LISTEN TO SOME INSOUCIANT QUEEN TOSSING OUT ORDERS FROM KYOTO—
MY LORD.
I HAVE HEARD THAT LADY KRUL TEPES INTENDS TO VISIT NAGOYA IN PERSON.

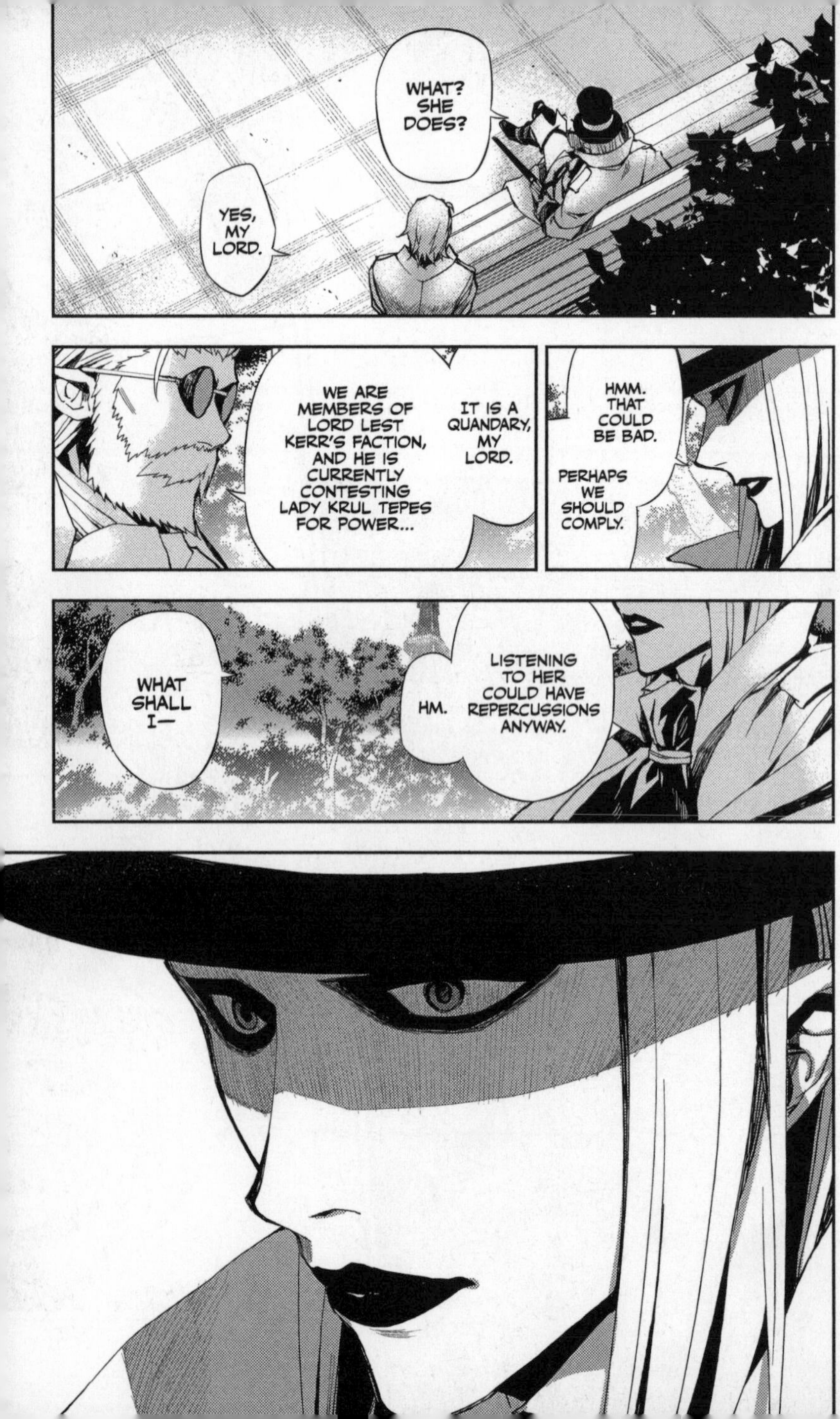
WHAT? SHE DOES?
YES, MY LORD.
HMM. THAT COULD BE BAD.
PERHAPS WE SHOULD COMPLY.
IT IS A QUANDARY, MY LORD.
WE ARE MEMBERS OF LORD LEST KERR'S FACTION, AND HE IS CURRENTLY CONTESTING LADY KRUL TEPES FOR POWER...
LISTENING TO HER COULD HAVE REPERCUSSIONS ANYWAY.
HM.
WHAT SHALL I—

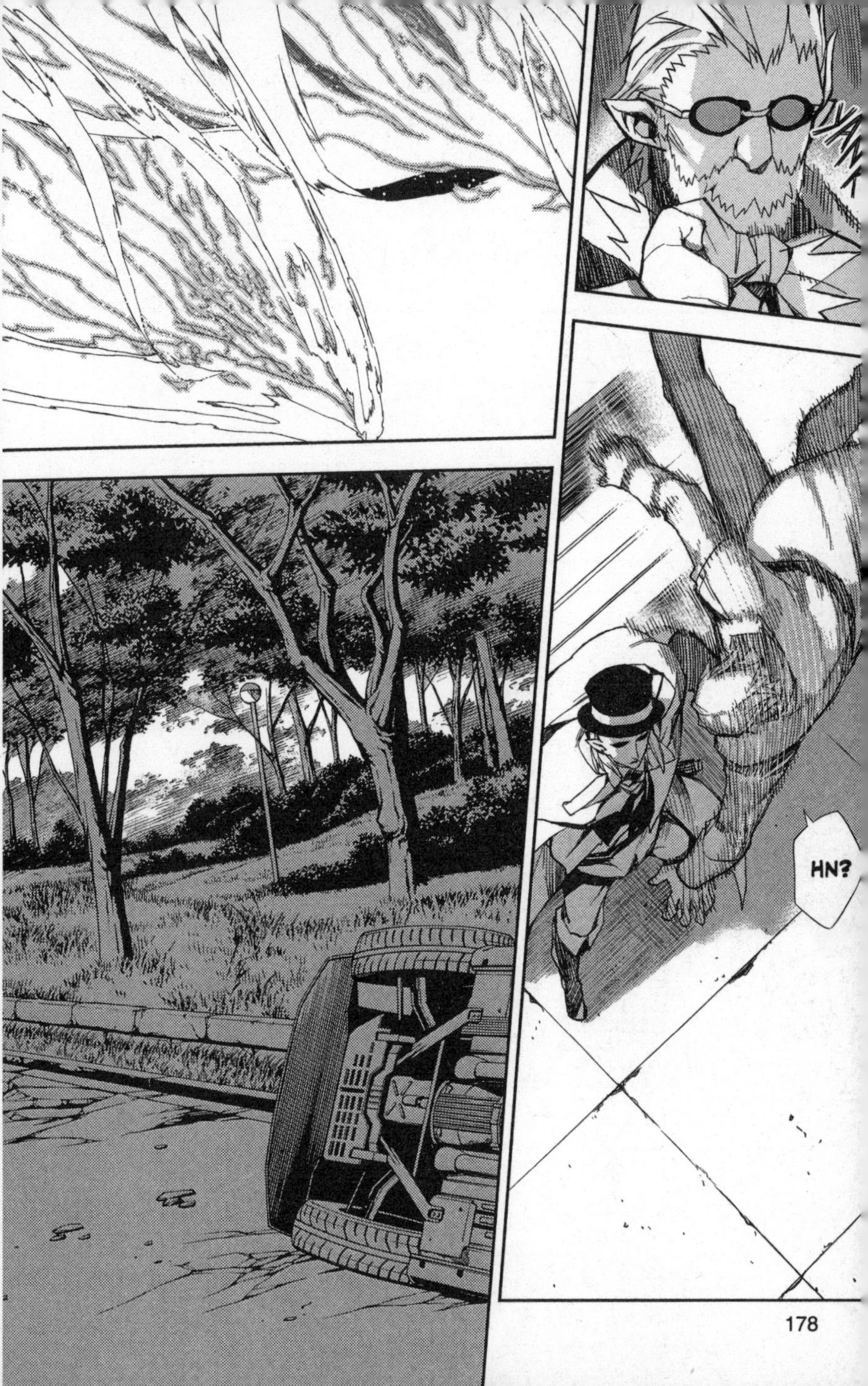
YANK
HN?

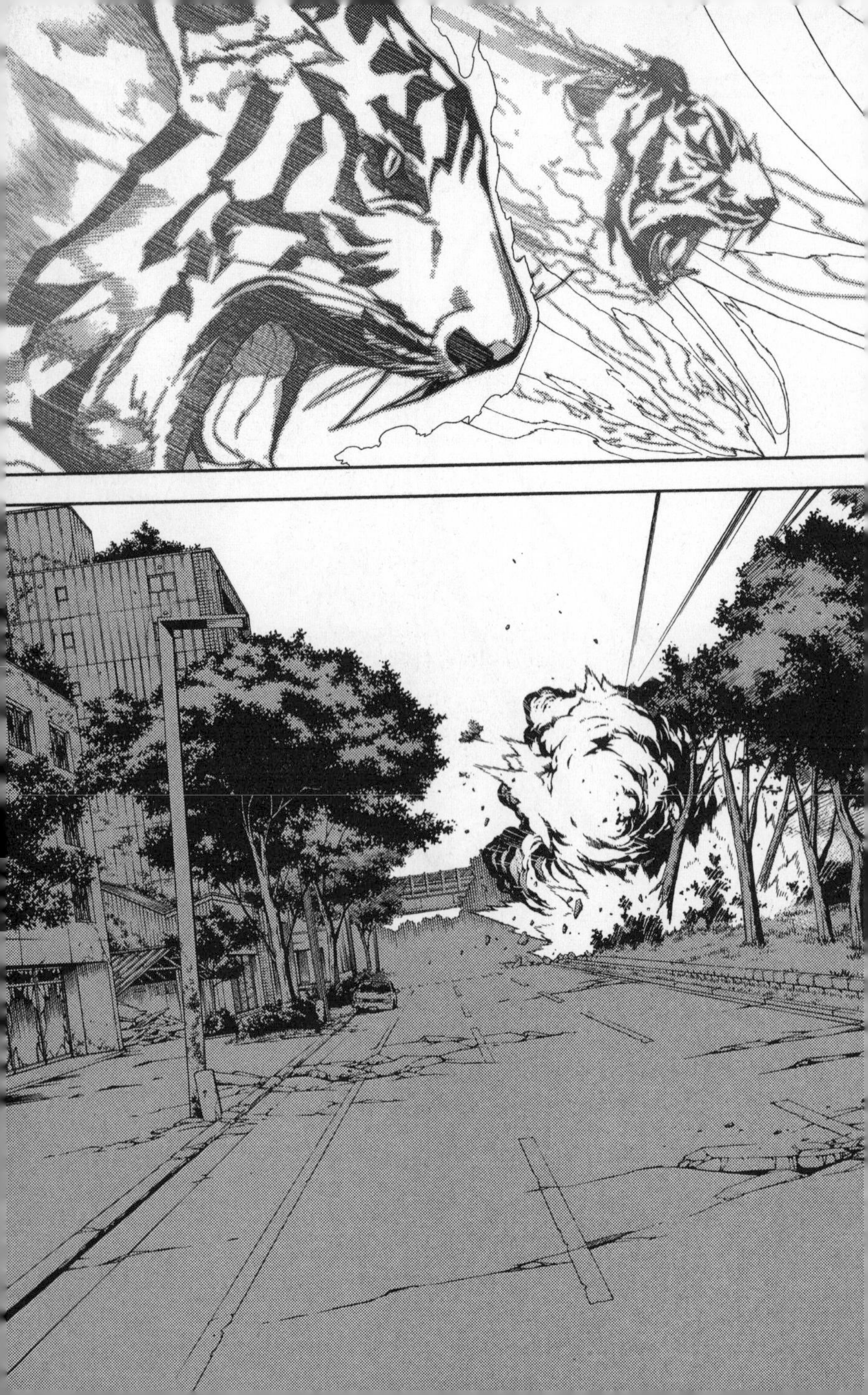

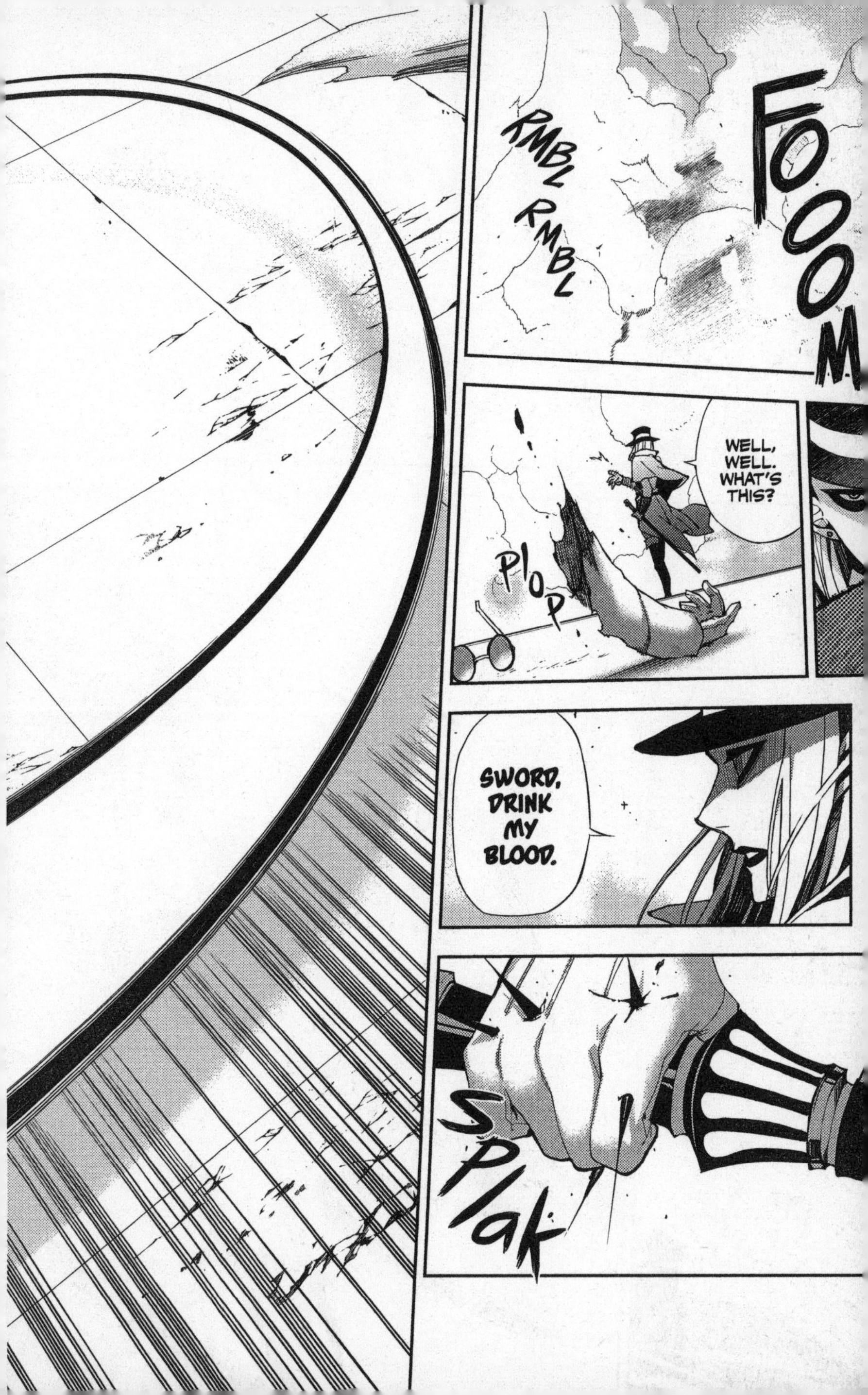
FOOOOM
RMBL RMBL
WELL, WELL. WHAT'S THIS?
PLOP
SWORD. DRINK MY BLOOD.
SPLAK

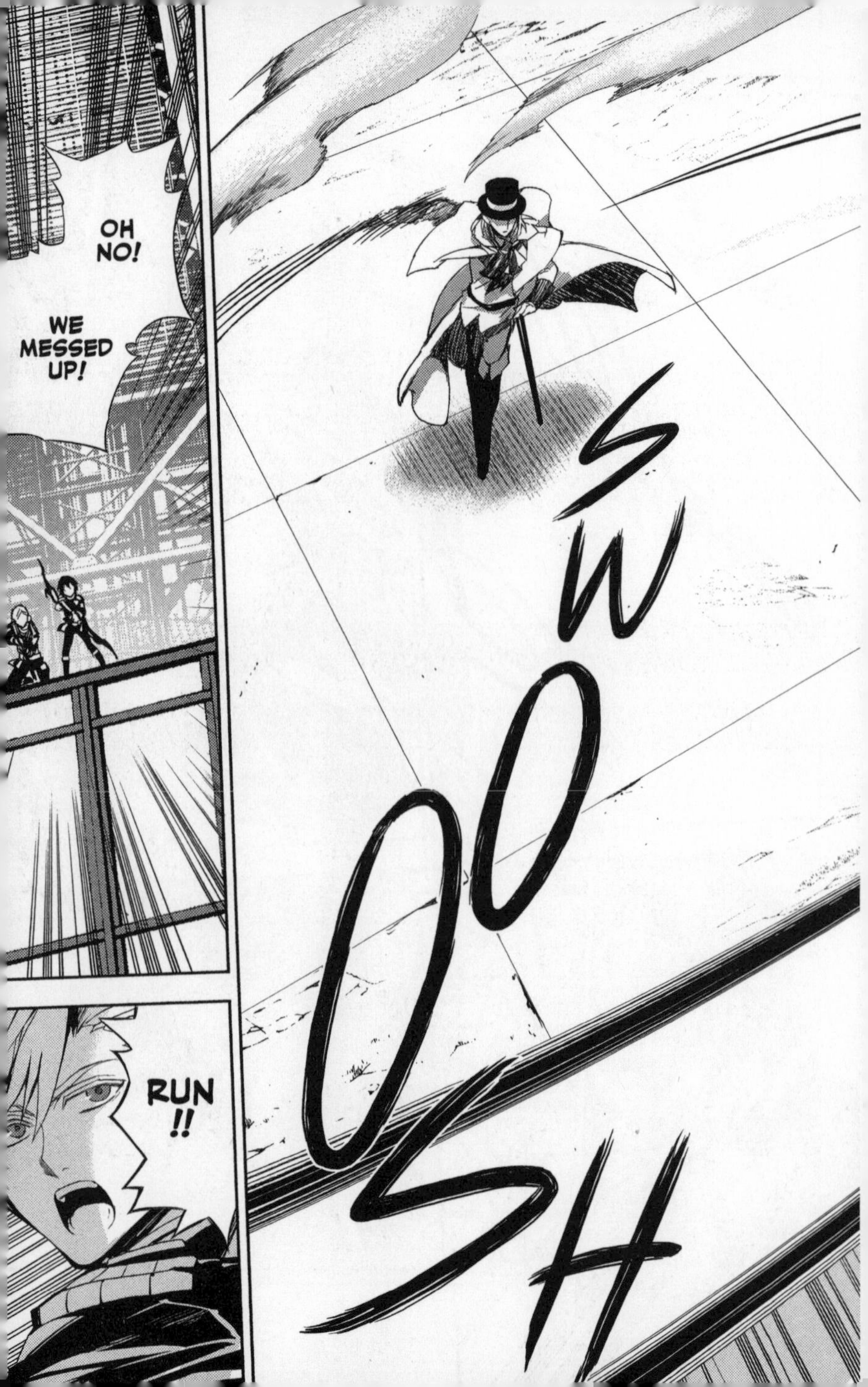
SWOOSH
OH NO!
WE MESSED UP!
RUN!!

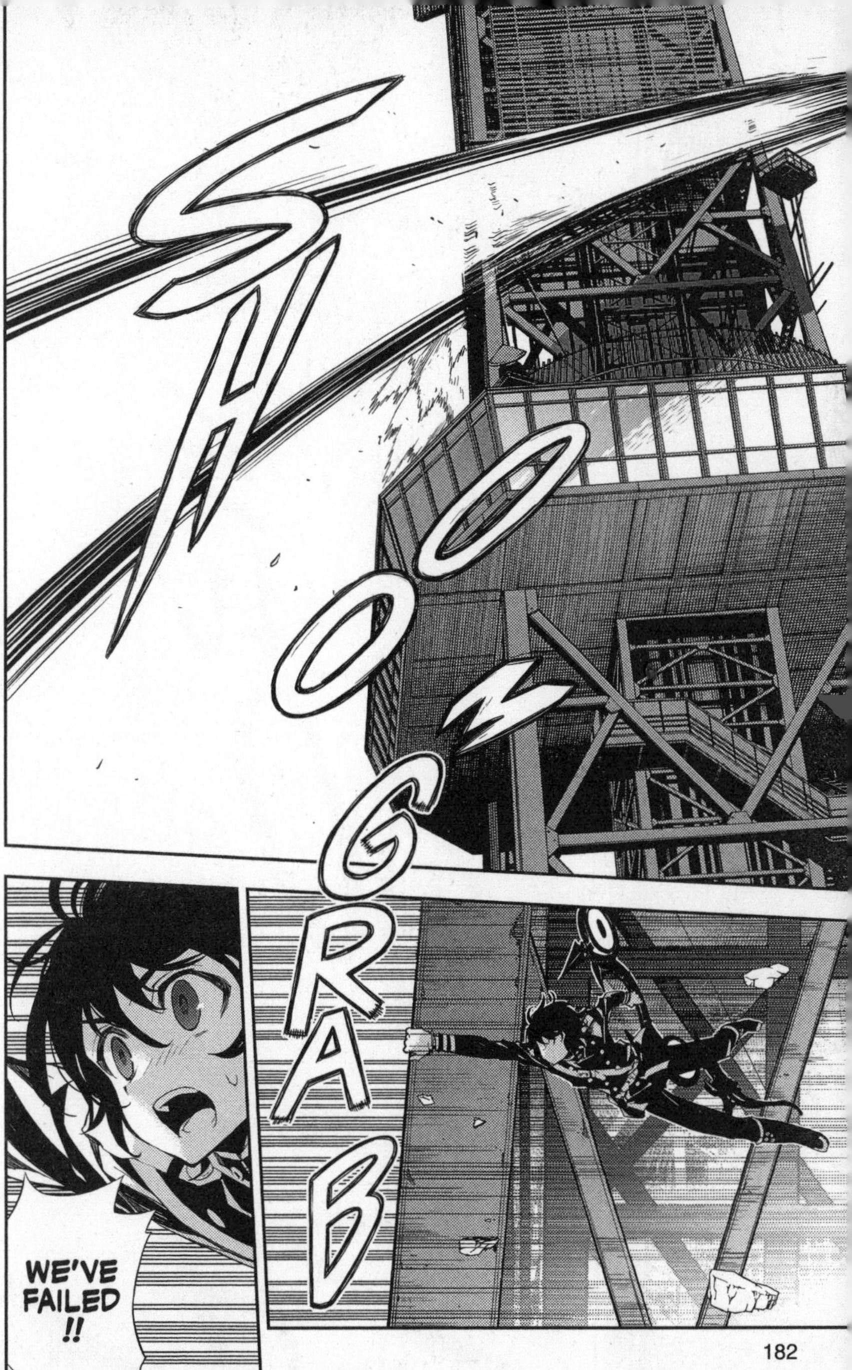
SHOOM
GRAB
WE'VE FAILED !!

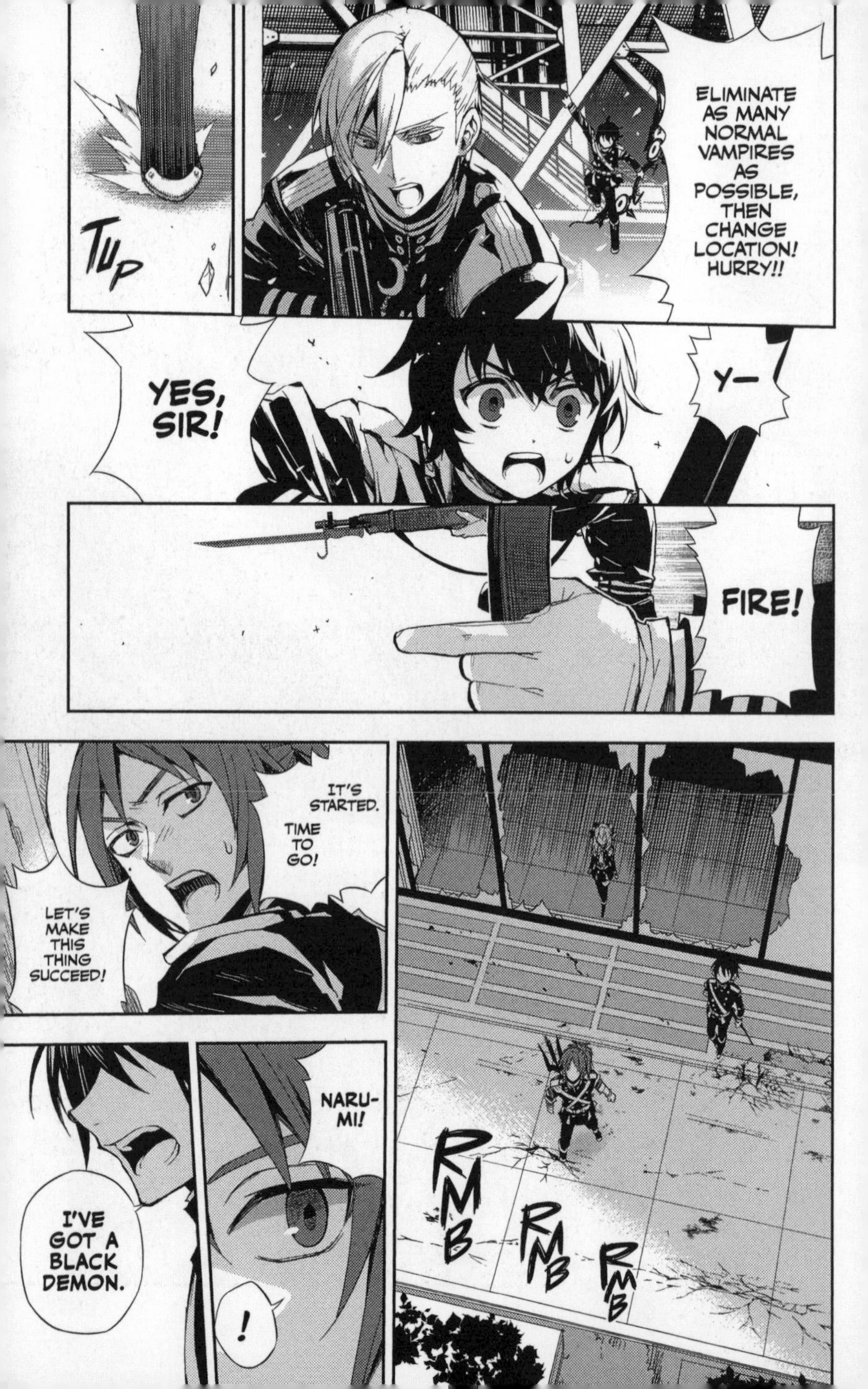
ELIMINATE AS MANY NORMAL VAMPIRES AS POSSIBLE, THEN CHANGE LOCATION! HURRY!!
TUP
Y—
YES, SIR!
FIRE!
RMB
RMB
RMB
IT'S STARTED.
TIME TO GO!
LET'S MAKE THIS THING SUCCEED!
NARUMI!
!
I'VE GOT A BLACK DEMON.

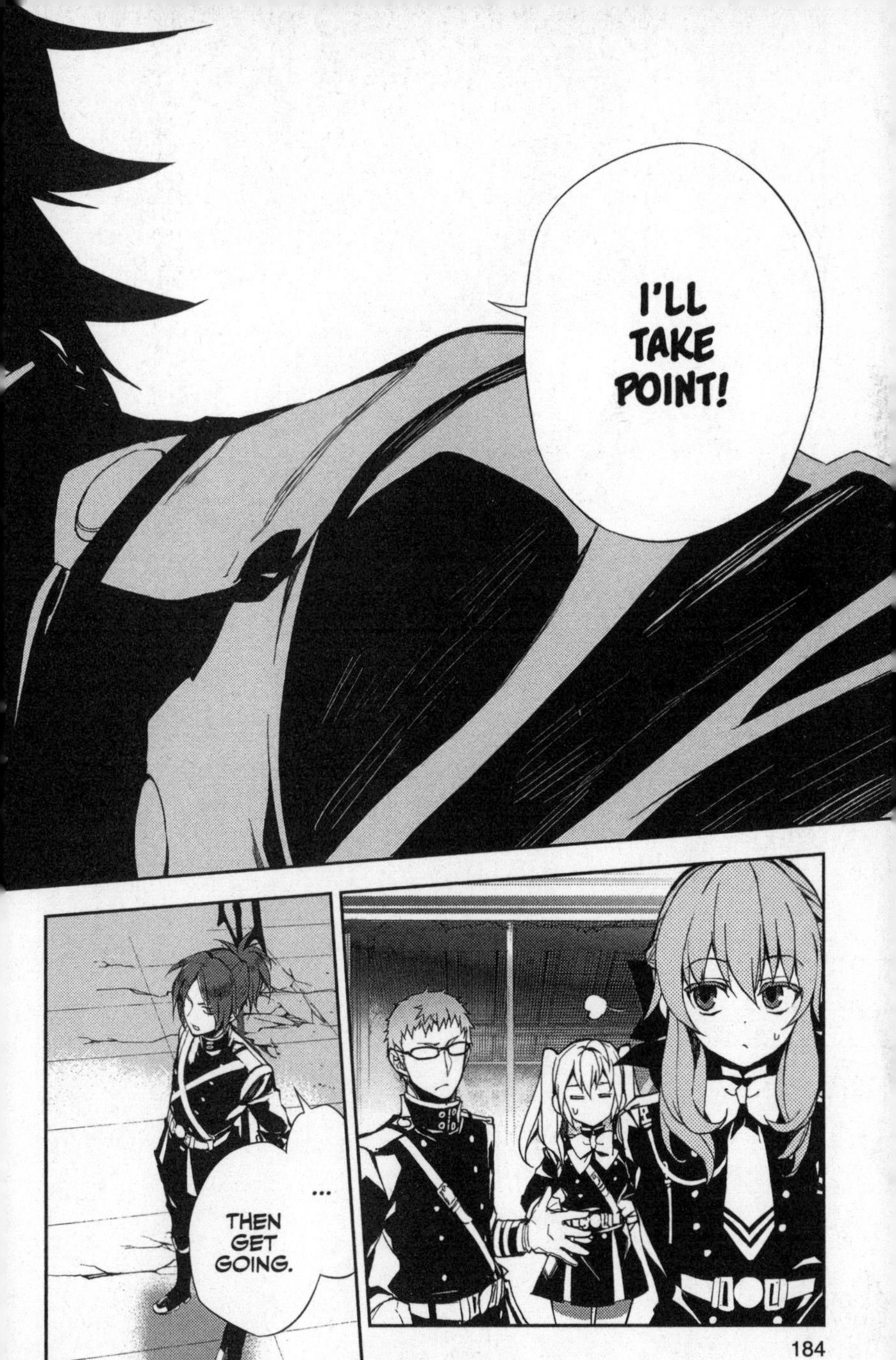
I'LL TAKE POINT!
...
THEN GET GOING.

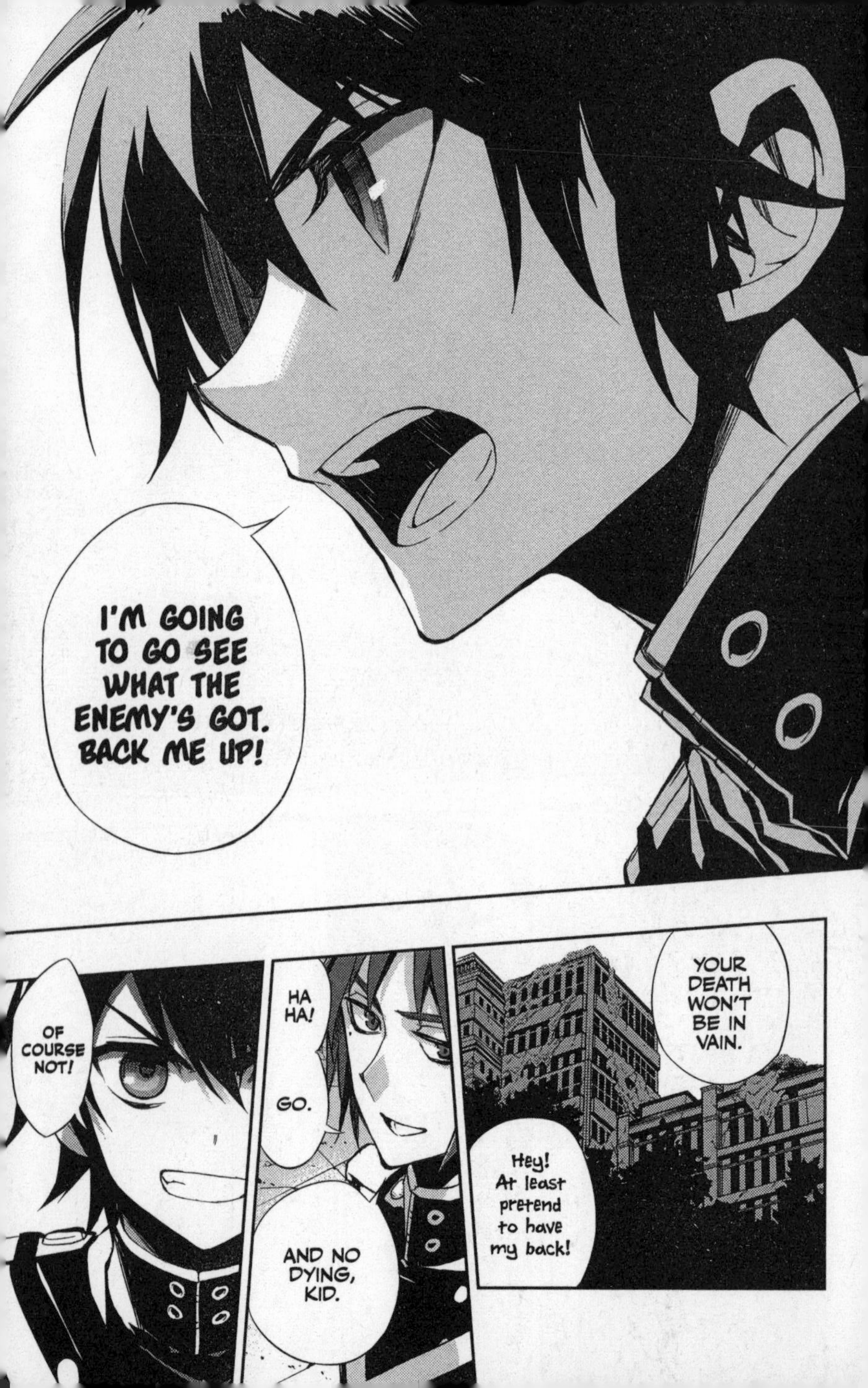
I'M GOING TO GO SEE WHAT THE ENEMY'S GOT. BACK ME UP!
YOUR DEATH WON'T BE IN VAIN.
Hey! At least pretend to have my back!
HA HA!
GO.
AND NO DYING, KID.
OF COURSE NOT!

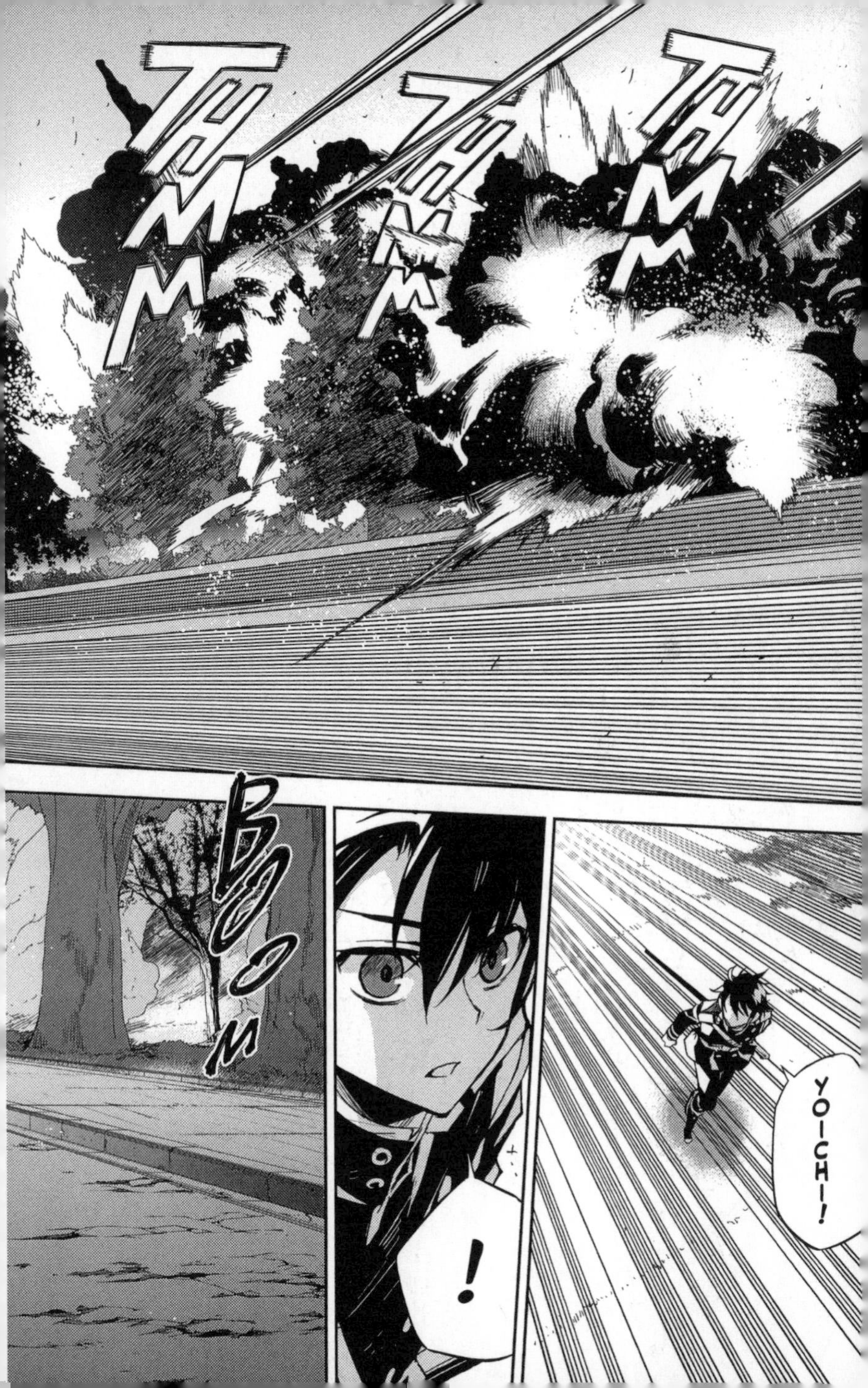
THMM
THMM
THMM
YOICHI!
!
BOOOM

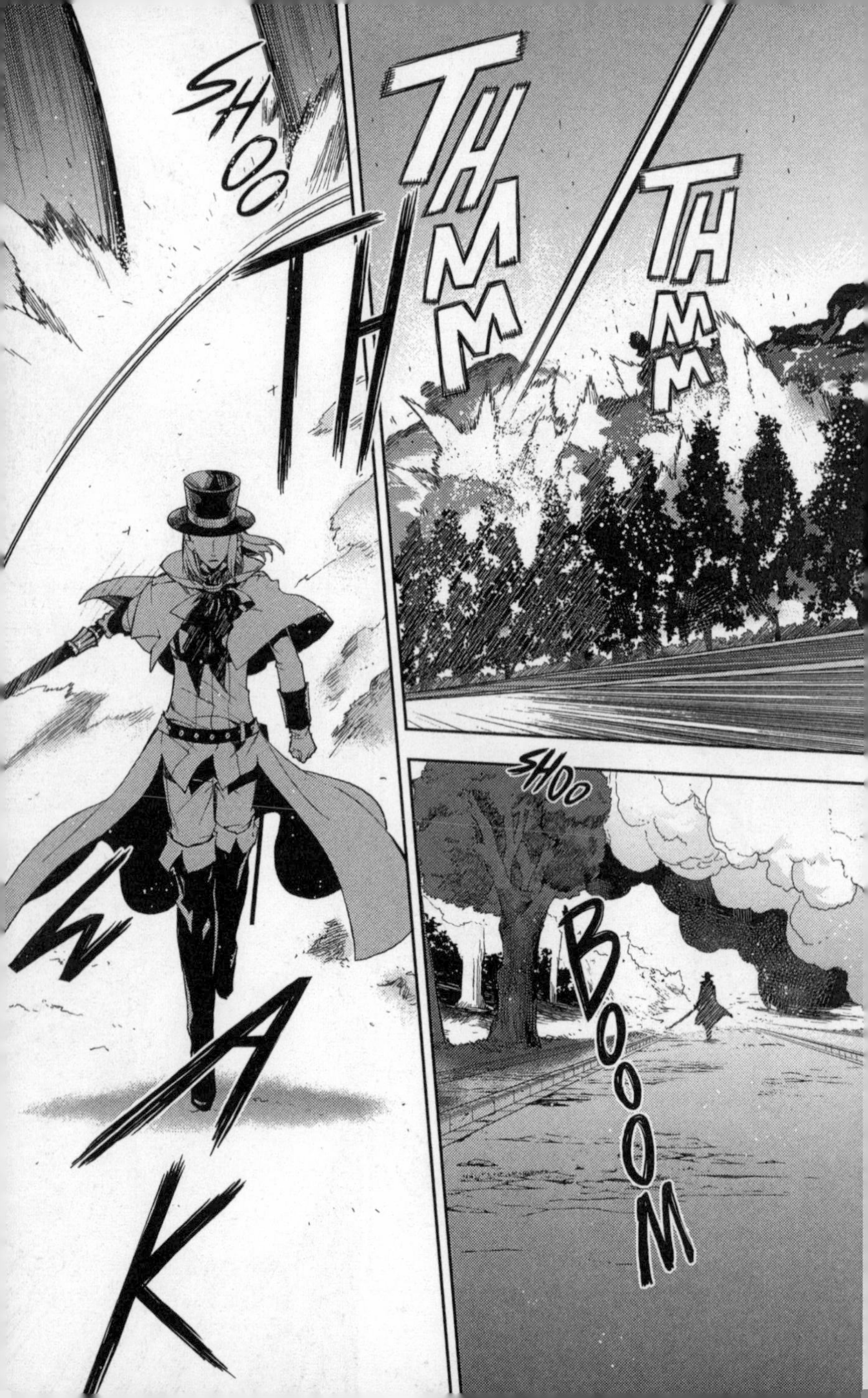
THMM
THMM
SHOO
BOOOOM
SHOO
THWAK

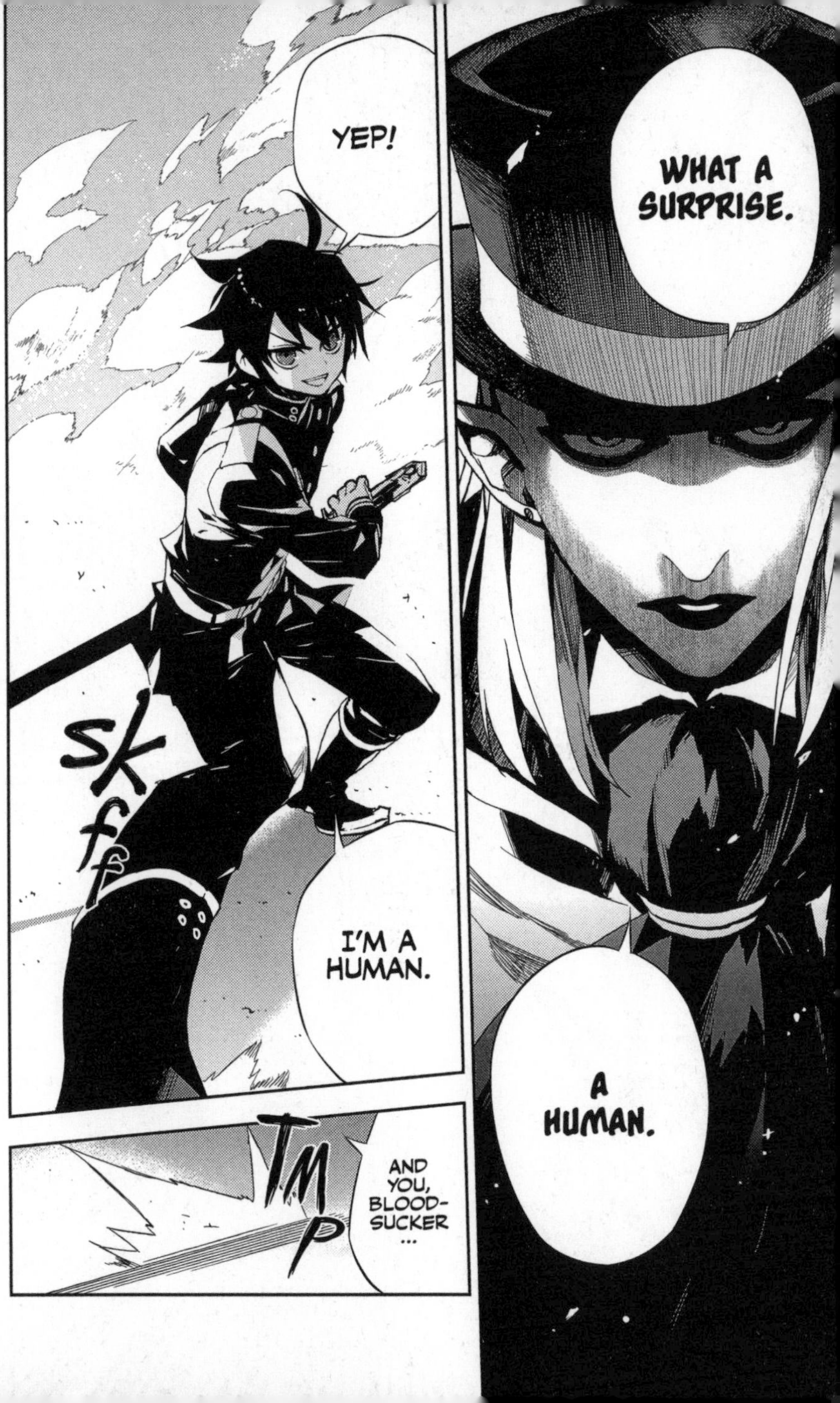
WHAT A SURPRISE.
A HUMAN.
YEP!
SKFFF
I'M A HUMAN.
TMP
AND YOU, BLOOD-SUCKER...

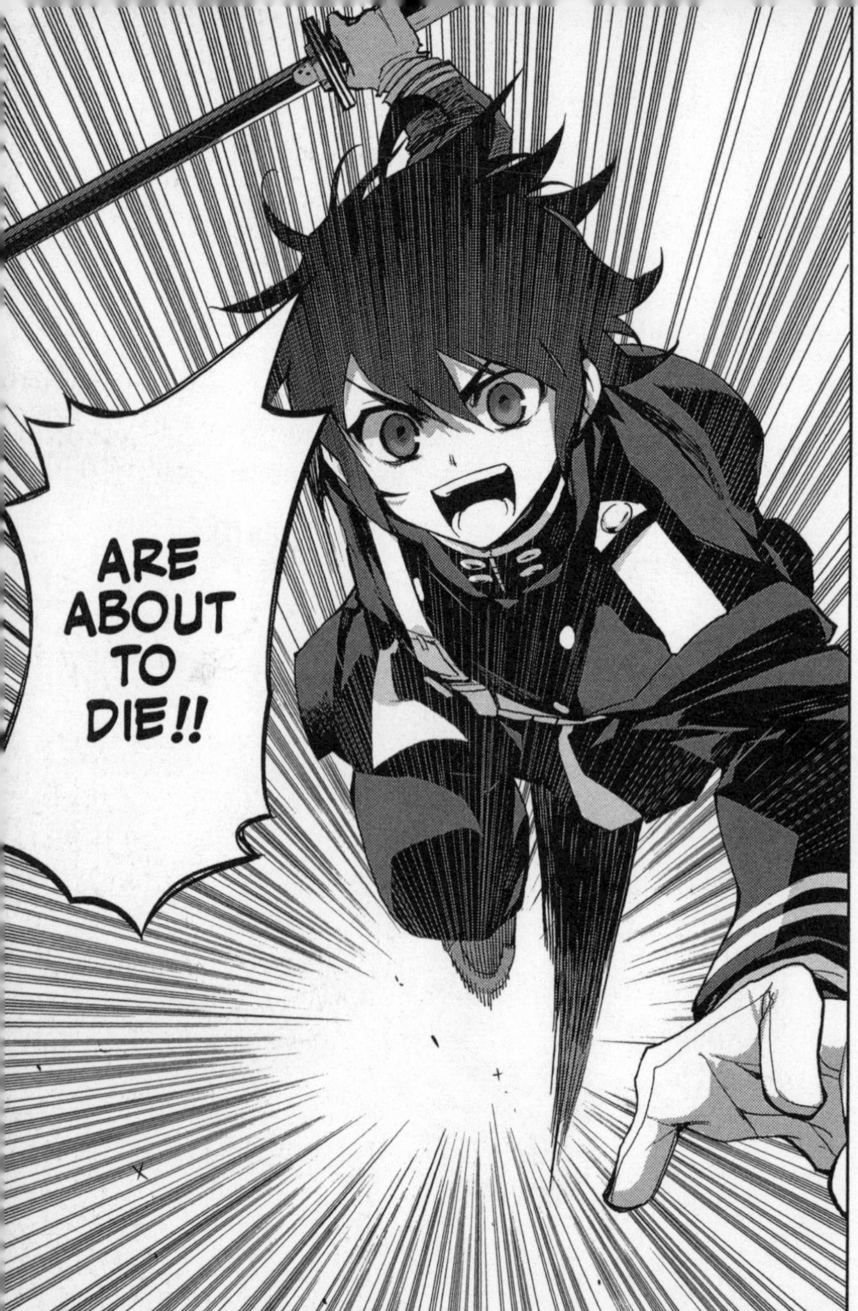
ARE ABOUT TO DIE!!

Seraph of the End: Vampire Reign 7 / END

KURETO HIRAGI

A year older than Guren, he's super bossy and arrogant. Like, he's even more bossy and arrogant than *Guren*.

KURETO: "WHAT IS THAT SUPPOSED TO MEAN?"

GUREN: "SOUNDS LIKE THE TRUTH TO ME."

Kureto is the current heir to the Hiragi family, which controls the Japanese Imperial Demon Army. In the novels he was the student council president at Shibuya High School No. 1. That's also where Guren went to high school.

He's a Lieutenant General in this story.

KURETO: "BASICALLY, DO WHAT I SAY AND NOTHING WILL GO WRONG."

GUREN: "UH-HUH. YEAH, SURE."

KURETO: "HEY! WATCH YOUR ATTITUDE."

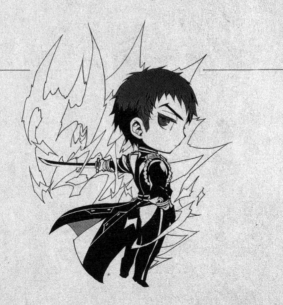

SHINYA HIRAGI

Mr. Third Wheel. He was the fiancé to Guren's former lover.

> SHINYA: "UM, WHAT KIND OF EXPLANATION IS THAT?"

He was adopted into the Hiragi family. He and Guren competed for the attention of the Hiragi protégé and Shinoa's older sister, Mahiru Hiragi. The main reason he was brought into the Hiragi family was to assimilate more talent and intelligence into the bloodline. Unfortunately, Shinya lost his fiancée when Mahiru suddenly died.

> MAHIRU: "WELL? *WELL?* WHO WAS IT? WHO WAS THE ONE WHO ULTIMATELY WON OVER THE PURE MAIDEN HEART OF THE LOVELY MAGICAL PRINCESS, ME?"
>
> SHINYA: "'LOVELY MAGICAL...' WHAT, SISTER?"
>
> MAHIRU: "AHA HA!"
>
> SHINYA: "..."
>
> GUREN: "..."
>
> KURETO: "IF I REMEMBER CORRECTLY... IT WAS GUREN WHO WON IN THE END. RIGHT?"
>
> GUREN: "UHH, WELL... ERM. HEY, UH, SHINYA. YOU WANNA TAKE HER BACK?"
>
> SHINYA: "WHOA, WHOA, WHOA. HOLD ON. WHAT'S DONE IS DONE."
>
> MAHIRU: "EXCUSE ME, WHAT'S WITH THAT ATTITUDE? BOTH OF YOU SHAPE UP OR DIE!"

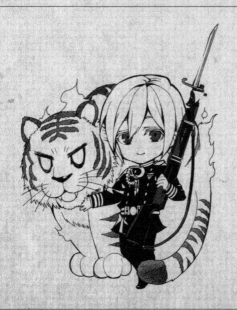

MAHIRU HIRAGI

Shinoa's older sister. Born into the Hiragi family, she was blessed with more talent and intelligence than Shinoa, Shinya, Guren and even Kureto. In fact, she was so smart that her own intelligence was her ultimate undoing when she finally broke.

Mahiru and Guren pledged their love to each other when she was younger.

A little while after, her family had her betrothed to Shinya.

Mahiru and Kureto were the biggest rivals for the position of heir to the Hiragi family.

Before the Catastrophe eight years ago, the lives of those three men, all of whom would eventually play huge roles in the Demon Army, revolved almost entirely around her.

But then she died.

It is said that, despite the large number of sacrifices it required, her continual research into Cursed Gear allowed humanity to barely escape extinction. But what really happened? Check out *Seraph of the End: Guren Ichinose's Catastrophe at 16* for all of the details.

MAHIRU: "YES! THEN YOU CAN READ HOW THE LOVELY MAGICAL PRINCESS THAT I AM BECAME THE BEAUTIFUL, PURE, MAIDENLY LADY THAT ALL YOUNG GIRLS ASPIRE TO BE!"

GUREN: "HOLD ON. I DON'T REMEMBER IT BEING THAT LIGHT AND FLUFFY OF A STORY."

SHINYA: "WORST OF ALL, WHY IS MAHIRU ACTING ALL SUNNY AND CHEERFUL HERE? IT'S STARTING TO SCARE ME."

GUREN: "ME TOO."

KURETO: "YES... IT IS RATHER FRIGHTENING."

YU: "WAIT, I THOUGHT YOU THREE DON'T EVER AGREE ON ANYTHING."

ALL 3: *"WE DON'T."*

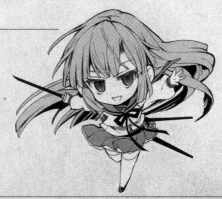

AFTERWORD

HELLO. I'M TAKAYA KAGAMI, AUTHOR AND SCRIPT WRITER FOR THIS SERIES.

VOLUME 7 IS FINALLY ON SALE! IN THE STORY, THE HUMANS HAVE DECIDED TO LEAVE TOKYO AND GO ON A JOURNEY TO THE WEST, TO NAGOYA. SPEEDING ALONG IN THEIR HIP, SUPER-CHARGED SPORTS CARS, THEY RACED THROUGH KANAGAWA PREFECTURE DOWN INTO AICHI PREFECTURE AND EVENTUALLY MADE IT TO NAGOYA! (OKAY, THAT'S NOT EXACTLY WHAT HAPPENED). THIS IS THE BEGINNING OF THEIR VAMPIRE NOBLE EXTERMINATION MISSION.

MEANWHILE, THE VAMPIRES HAVE BEGUN TO MOVE EAST. WHAT WILL HAPPEN NEXT?

IN THIS ARC, YU'S PRESENT DAY TEAM FINALLY MEETS GUREN'S OLD TEAM FROM THE *SERAPH OF THE END: GUREN ICHINOSE'S CATASTROPHE AT 16* LIGHT NOVELS THAT WERE PUBLISHED BY KODANSHA'S LIGHT NOVEL IMPRINT IN JAPAN. SHINYA, SAYURI, SHIGURE, GOSHI AND MITO ARE A VETERAN TEAM TO BE REVERED. EVEN THOUGH THEY WERE ONLY TEENAGERS DURING THE CATASTROPHE, THEY MANAGED TO SURVIVE THE CHAOS AND JOIN FORCES TO EVENTUALLY MEET YU AND HIS FRIENDS. IT'S A TOUCHING STORY REALLY. FOR THOSE INTERESTED IN LEARNING JUST HOW TOUCHING THIS STORY REALLY IS, PLEASE FEEL FREE TO CHECK OUT *SERAPH OF THE END: GUREN ICHINOSE'S CATASTROPHE AT 16*, ON SALE IN THE KODANSHA AREA OF THE LIGHT NOVEL SECTION IN BOOKSTORES (ENOUGH WITH THE ADS ALREADY! HA!).

SERIOUSLY, WRITING THE PRE-CATASTROPHE STORY (WITH GUREN, SHINYA AND KURETO CLASHING ALL THROUGHOUT HIGH SCHOOL) REALLY HELPED ME GIVE THE SCENES IN THE PRESENT-DAY STORY THIS, I DUNNO, GREATER TENSION AND DEPTH THAT I'M NOT SURE I WOULD'VE BEEN ABLE TO CONVEY IF I HAD ONLY WRITTEN THE PRESENT-DAY MANGA STORYLINE.

EVERY DAY I CAN'T HELP BUT THINK ABOUT HOW HAPPY AND
THANKFUL I AM THAT I HAVE GOTTEN TO WORK ON THIS STORY
IN THIS WAY. I'M VERY PLEASED AND GRATEFUL FOR THIS STORY,
BUT NOT SO MUCH FOR THE DEADLINES. ESPECIALLY HOW
TIGHT THEY ARE AND I'M REALLY STARTING TO FEEL LIKE THEY
MIGHT JUST KILL ME SO PLEASE GO EASIER ON ME. (HUH?)

MOVING ON! IT'S NOW THE TIME OF YEAR WHEN THE ANIME IS
JUST ABOUT TO START! THE ANIME HAS BEEN PUT INTO THE
HANDS OF A FAMOUS STUDIO BEHIND A CERTAIN MEGA-HIT
SERIES—WIT STUDIO! YAAAY! CLAP, CLAP, CLAP. THAT'S GREAT!

BY THE TIME THIS VOLUME COMES OUT, I'M SURE EVERYONE
WILL ALREADY HAVE SEEN THESE CHARACTERS MOVE AROUND
ON TV, BUT I'M ALREADY EXCITED FOR IT. IT'S GONNA BE
AWESOME! I MEAN, WIT STUDIO MAKES SOME REALLY GREAT
STUFF WHEN THEY PUT THEIR HEARTS IN IT. I HAD A BLAST
WORKING WITH THEM. I CAN HARDLY WAIT TO WATCH THE SHOW!

AS A SIDE NOTE, AFTER THE ANIME ANNOUNCEMENT I HAD A
CHANCE TO ATTEND A PARTY WITH SEVERAL OTHER CREATORS
AND PUBLISHERS. NO MATTER WHERE I WENT, EVERYBODY WAS
LIKE, "MR. KAGAMI, I HEAR THAT *SERAPH OF THE END* IS BEING
ANIMATED BY WIT STUDIO! THAT'S AMAZING! CONGRATULATIONS!
I'M SO JEALOUS!"

IT HAS REALLY HELPED ME COME TO UNDERSTAND JUST HOW INCREDIBLE AND WELL-REGARDED WIT STUDIO IS. ALL OF THE STAFF MEMBERS I WORKED WITH WERE EXCITED AND PASSIONATE. DURING MEETINGS AND EMAIL EXCHANGES, EVERYTHING THEY SENT BACK TO ME FOR APPROVALS WAS AMAZING. IT WAS AN ALL AROUND GREAT EXPERIENCE.

NOT ONLY IS THE STUDIO AMAZING, BUT WE ALSO GOT AN ALL-STAR LINEUP OF VOICE ACTORS BEING ANNOUNCED ONE AFTER THE OTHER. AT THE MOMENT, HERE ARE THE VOICE ACTORS WE CAN CONFIRM:

YUICHIRO HYAKUYA:	MIYU IRINO
MIKAELA HYAKUYA:	KENSHO ONO
GUREN ICHINOSE:	YUICHI NAKAMURA
FERID BATHORY:	TAKAHIRO SAKURAI
SHINOA HIRAGI:	SAORI HAYAMI
YOICHI SAOTOME:	NOBUHIKO OKAMOTO
SHIHO KIMIZUKI:	KAITO ISHIKAWA
MITSUBA SANGU:	YUKA IGUCHI

THE FIRST SEASON WILL PREMIERE IN JAPAN IN APRIL 2015 AND THE SECOND SEASON WILL PREMIERE IN OCTOBER 2015.

I HOPE YOU WILL READ BOTH THE *SERAPH OF THE END* MANGA AND THE LIGHT NOVELS WHILE YOU'RE WAITING FOR THE ANIME TO PREMIERE. PLEASE LOOK FORWARD TO IT!

TAKAYA KAGAMI

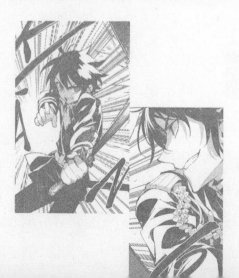

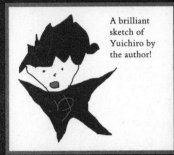

A brilliant sketch of Yuichiro by the author!

TAKAYA KAGAMI is a prolific light novelist whose works include the action and fantasy series *The Legend of the Legendary Heroes*, which has been adapted into manga, anime and a video game. His previous series, *A Dark Rabbit Has Seven Lives*, also spawned a manga and anime series.

66 So this is the volume right before the anime comes out. I've been so buried under work lately that I was thinking that the weight of it all might just kill me. But then I was treated to curry on my way home after a meeting and I felt way better. Curry is awesome. Hope you enjoy volume 7! 99

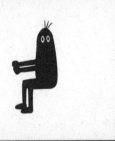

YAMATO YAMAMOTO, born 1983, is an artist and illustrator whose works include the *Kure-nai* manga and the light novels *Kure-nai*, *9S -Nine S-* and *Denpa Teki na Kanojo*. Both *Denpa Teki na Kanojo* and *Kure-nai* have been adapted into anime.

66 Volume 7 is the buildup to Yuichiro and his friends' big confrontation in Nagoya. We will all be working together to try our best. I hope you like it. 99

DAISUKE FURUYA previously assisted Yamato Yamamoto with storyboards for *Kure-nai*.

Seraph of the End

—VAMPIRE REIGN—

VOLUME 7
SHONEN JUMP ADVANCED MANGA EDITION

STORY BY **TAKAYA KAGAMI**

ART BY **YAMATO YAMAMOTO**

STORYBOARDS BY **DAISUKE FURUYA**

TRANSLATION **Adrienne Beck**
TOUCH-UP ART & LETTERING **Sabrina Heep**
DESIGN **Shawn Carrico**
WEEKLY SHONEN JUMP EDITOR **Hope Donovan**
GRAPHIC NOVEL EDITOR **Marlene First**

OWARI NO SERAPH © 2012 by Takaya Kagami,
Yamato Yamamoto, Daisuke Furuya
All rights reserved. First published in Japan in 2012 by SHUEISHA Inc., Tokyo.
English translation rights arranged by SHUEISHA Inc.

Printed in the U.S.A.

Published by VIZ Media, LLC
P.O. Box 77010
San Francisco, CA 94107

10 9 8 7 6 5 4 3 2 1
First printing, December 2015

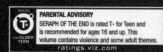

www.viz.com   www.shonenjump.com

PARENTAL ADVISORY
SERAPH OF THE END is rated T+ for Teen and
is recommended for ages 16 and up. This
volume contains violence and some adult themes.
ratings.viz.com

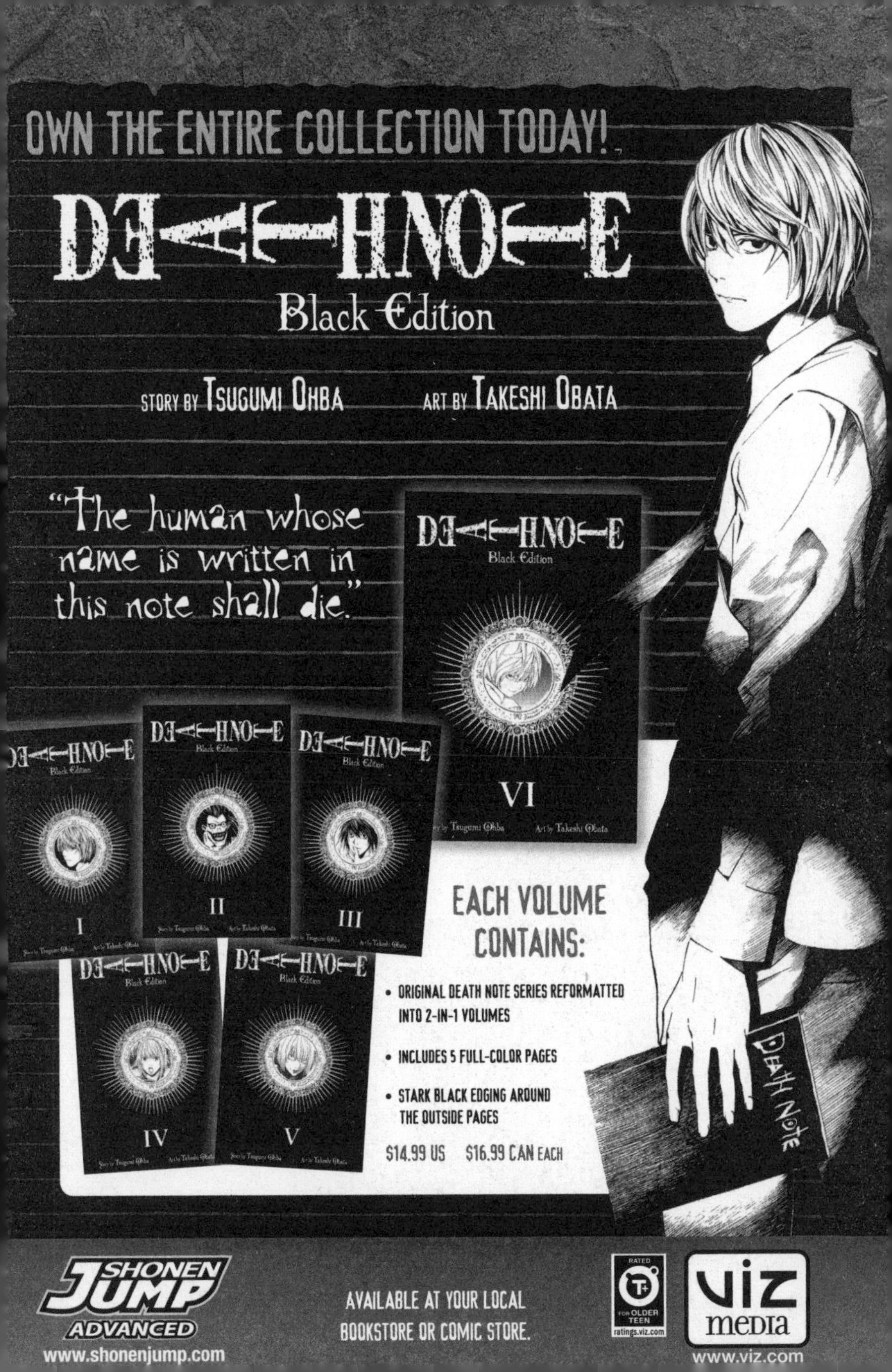
OWN THE ENTIRE COLLECTION TODAY!
DEATH NOTE
Black Edition
STORY BY TSUGUMI OHBA
ART BY TAKESHI OBATA
"The human whose name is written in this note shall die."
EACH VOLUME CONTAINS:
• ORIGINAL DEATH NOTE SERIES REFORMATTED INTO 2-IN-1 VOLUMES
• INCLUDES 5 FULL-COLOR PAGES
• STARK BLACK EDGING AROUND THE OUTSIDE PAGES
$14.99 US $16.99 CAN EACH
DEATH NOTE
SHONEN JUMP ADVANCED
www.shonenjump.com
AVAILABLE AT YOUR LOCAL BOOKSTORE OR COMIC STORE.
RATED T+ FOR OLDER TEEN
ratings.viz.com
VIZ media
www.viz.com

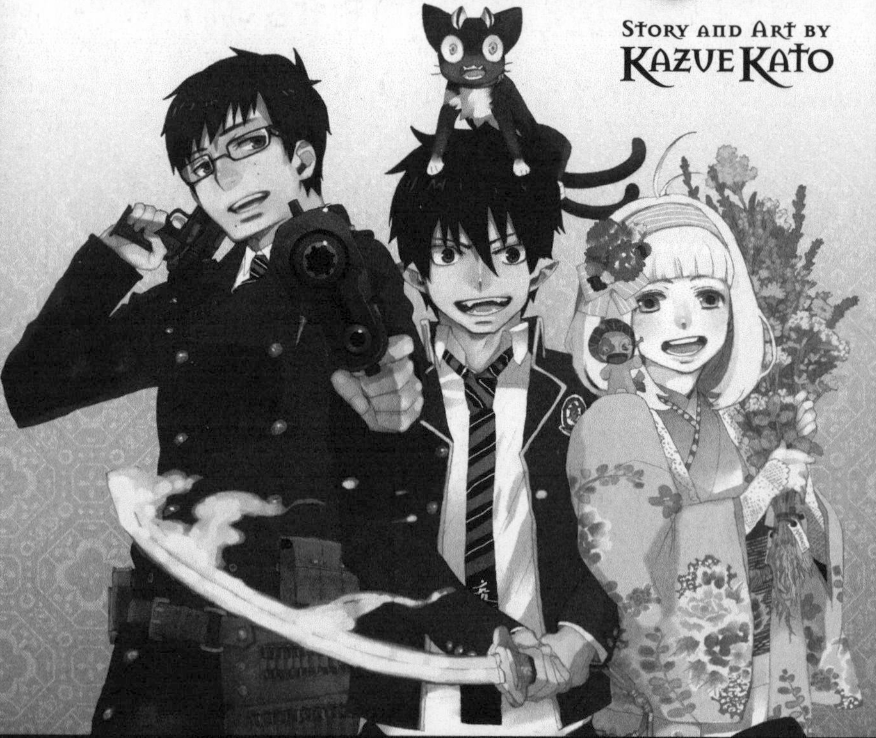

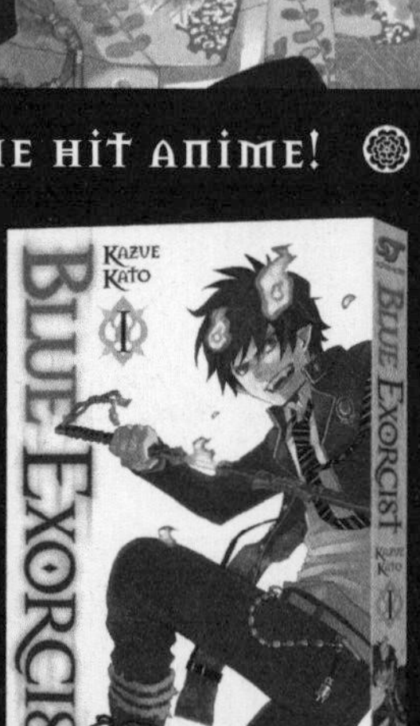
KAZUE KATO
BLUE EXORCIST
1
BLUE EXORCIST

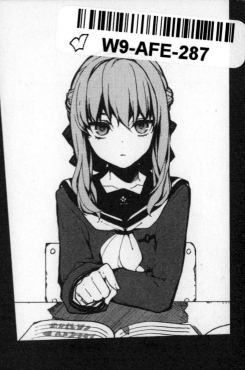

YOU'RE READING THE
WRONG WAY!

SERAPH OF THE END reads from right to left, starting in the upper-right corner. Japanese is read from right to left, meaning that action, sound effects, and word-balloon order are completely reversed from English order.

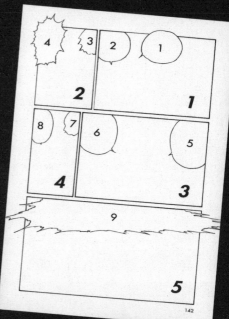

142